ALEX NORTH,
FILM COMPOSER

ALEX NORTH, FILM COMPOSER

A Biography, with Musical Analyses
of *A Streetcar Named Desire*,
Spartacus, *The Misfits*,
Under the Volcano, and *Prizzi's Honor*

SANYA SHOILEVSKA HENDERSON

Foreword by John Williams

McFarland & Company, Inc., Publishers
Jefferson, North Carolina, and London

Frontispiece: Alex North in his forties. Photograph by Marthe Krueger.

LIBRARY OF CONGRESS CATALOGUING-IN-PUBLICATION DATA

Henderson, Sanya Shoilevska.
    Alex North, film composer : a biography, with musical analyses of
A streetcar named desire, Spartacus, The misfits, Under the volcano,
and Prizzi's honor / Sanya Shoilevska Henderson ; foreword by John
Williams.
        p.   cm.
    Includes bibliographical references and index.
    Discography: p.
    Filmography: p.

    ISBN 0-7864-1470-7 (illustrated case binding : 50# alkaline paper)

    1. North, Alex.   2. Composers— United States— Biography.
    I. Williams, John, 1932–.   II. Title.
ML410.N6745   2003
781.5'42'092 — dc21
                                                        2003007867

British Library cataloguing data are available

Cover photograph: North conducting the music for 1960 film *Spartacus*

Manufactured in the United States of America

McFarland & Company, Inc., Publishers
    Box 611, Jefferson, North Carolina 28640
        www.mcfarlandpub.com

To my family and to Dr. Beverly Grigsby

Contents

Foreword by John Williams

For those of us coming of age in the 1950s, and seriously interested in film music, Alex North was an inspiration, a role model and a hero. He was then and remains so today.

His appearance in Hollywood immediately proclaimed the arrival of a major new voice in an art form that heretofore had relied on European antecedents for its inspiration. Alex brought with him an Americanism that combined a sophistication and a cosmopolitanism that had been honed in his studies here and abroad and developed in his work in theatre and ballet. Overnight he became the idol of a whole generation of aspiring young film composers perhaps most prominently represented by Jerry Goldsmith whose own work has been so outstanding.

I first met Alex at the home of lyricists Marilyn and Alan Bergman sometime in the mid–1950s. I remember being very nervous as I was being presented to a famous and great man, but I was astonished and relieved to discover how very approachable he was. His nature was tender, affectionate and somewhat introverted and he made me feel immediately comfortable. We continued to be good friends for the remainder of his life and he was always greatly encouraging to me in my attempts at composing. One always felt that, had he chosen to be, he would have been a brilliant teacher.

There was a romance and an idealism about Alex that perfectly fit his temperament to the era of the 1930s in which he was maturing. The excitement of the social ideas of the time, of modernism and the promise of a future in which things could be "put right" all combined to shape the atmosphere in which he flourished. It's interesting to note that Alex, along with his near contemporaries Gershwin, Bernstein and Copland among others, were all first generation children of Russian-Jewish immigrants, who in a very few short years produced works that were rightly regarded as quintessentially American. This is an astonishing fact that speaks to the rich talent of these families and the nourishing artistic soil that welcomed them here in America. It is a phenomenon of which I think we can all be very proud.

It's often been said that Russians and Americans with their sprawling countries share temperaments that are similar. I remember during the seemingly endless and tragically wasteful cold war, one would often hear people remark out of frustration or sadness that our two peoples shared a commonality that was much more significant than whatever our disputes had been. This may explain the phenomenon of Alex and his contemporaries somewhat, though it's hard to say. I have often felt that if you could perform a magical act of alchemy and combine some of the great Russian-Soviet composers, say Shostakovich or Prokovief with Duke Ellington or Billy Strayhorn, you might produce a wonder such as Alex North. By whatever mysterious process, these influences were conjoined in Alex to create music that is uniquely his own, and for that we can all be grateful.

To present and future generations, Alex North is a treasure to be discovered and enjoyed, and the publication of this book will go a long way toward securing the enduring legacy that this most important artist warrants and deserves. To the ever increasing number of students and devotees of film music around the world, Sanya Henderson has made a singular and invaluable contribution and I want to thank her for offering me the great privilege of saying these few words about one of my greatest heroes.

Acknowledgments

The work on this book was one of the most valuable professional and personal experiences of my life. Over the past seven years many individuals and institutions have helped me in various ways. My thanks go, above all, to Dr. Beverly Grigsby, professor emerita at California State University in Northridge. I cannot find the words to express the depth of my gratitude to Dr. Grigsby for her continuing help and friendship over the last several years. First of all, she arranged my official stay in the United States as a visiting scholar at California State University in Northridge. Then she provided the contacts with important people from the film music industry, various libraries and institutions. The opinions and the advice from this experienced composer, musicologist, and teacher were more than valuable during the entire period of research and the writing of this book. She was also the first one to proofread the manuscript. I am grateful to her, above all, for her enduring trust and confidence in my work.

I am enormously indebted to Annemarie North for sharing with me her memories about Alex North during several interviews, and for letting me stay for days and nights in Alex North's studio in their home in Pacific Palisades where I could analyze the original manuscripts of his film scores and other compositions, and collect all the information about the published articles in various magazines, journals, newspapers and books. There I recorded the entire discography of Alex North (including some tapes from original recording sessions), and taped most of the films that North scored (available on video cassette). Besides that, Mrs. North referred me to the other collections of Alex North's music kept at the University of California in Los Angeles and at the Academy of Motion Picture Arts and Sciences, as well as to the individuals who had to be interviewed. Without her help the bibliography on Alex North would have been no longer than two pages, the musical analyses would have been far from detailed, and the personal data on Alex North would have stayed poor and incomplete. Considering the fact that the primary original sources for this kind of research are very hard to locate and access, I am aware of how fortunate I was to meet this wonderful, extraordinary woman. She was also kind enough to allow me to use a large number of photos from her family photo collection which greatly enhance the documentary value of this book.

Special thanks are due to Jeannie Pool, former executive director of the Film Music Society, who introduced me to Annemarie North, and provided me with an opportunity to present parts of this book at the International Conferences of the society, as well as in the journal *Cue Sheet* in the form of published articles. I appreciate all the suggestions and advice she gave me during my work on this book. Many thanks to the employees at the various libraries and archives, especially to Steven Fry from the Music Library at the University of California in Los Angeles, and Warren Sherk from the Margaret Herrick Library of the Academy of Motion Picture Arts and Sciences, as well as to all the other librarians for their assistance during the endless hours of my research (California State University in Northridge, University of California in Los Angeles, University of Southern California, Central Hollywood Library, American Institute of Film, Academy of Motion Picture, Arts and Sciences).

I would like to express my special thanks to the individuals who devoted a part of their precious time to talk about Alex North, and provided my work with valuable information: Arthur Miller, Michael Fitzgerald, Anna Sokolow, Harry and Esther North, Steven North, Sherle North, David Raksin, Fred Steiner, David Amram, Farley Granger, Robert Calhoun and Milton Key. I am thankful to Tom Di Nardo from the *Philadelphia Inquirer* who helped me find some of the early articles on Alex North, as well as to Fred Steiner for lending me the materials from his personal interview with Alex North. Many thanks to Rosemarie Dittbern and Harry and Esther North who provided the book with several important photos. Thanks also to the Margaret Herrick Library of the Academy of Motion Picture Arts and Sciences for letting me use documents from their special collection, such as the cover photo of the book and selected correspondence. I deeply appreciate the encouragement I received from many colleagues, personally or in letters, among whom are Jon Burlingame, John Williams and Henry Brant.

I am indebted to Robert Townson from Varèse Sarabande who referred me to the right publishing companies and copyright holders of Alex North's music scores. Special thanks to Rosemarie Gawelko from Warner Bros. Publications, Ms. Swearingen from Hal Leonard Corporation, David Sherman and Debra Leonard from American Broadcasting Music. Hence, the permission to use the musical examples in this book was kindly granted by the following copyright owners:

Bernstein & Co., Inc., New York. Copyright Renewed. International Copyright Secured. All Rights Reserved. Used by Permission.

Prizzi's Honor by Alex North ©1985, American Broadcasting Music, Inc. All Rights Reserved. Used by Permission.

Finally, my deepest heartfelt gratitude goes to my family and my husband and best friend Scott Henderson for their permanent encouragement, infinite patience and trust, and for being with me when I needed them most.

Preface

The period of the Fifties brought notable changes in the world of Hollywood film music. The concept of lush romantic film scores was gradually abandoned and replaced with more contemporary musical approaches. The expressionistic musical treatment became convenient for the new type of realistic dramas produced after World War II and in the Fifties. Dissonant, and even atonal music gradually became acceptable within certain film genres. The new generation of American composers brought more contemporary, as well as popular sounds to the film composition. These new tendencies were already initiated during the Forties in the works of several composers, such as George Antheil, Miklós Rózsa, Bernard Herrmann and David Raksin. The American folk music was popularized through the film music of Aaron Copland whose contribution to the world of film includes several musical scores: *Of Mice and Men* (1939), *Our Town* (1940), *The Red Pony* (1949), and *The Heiress* (1949). Although Copland composed music for only a few films, he showed that a film score does not necessarily have to be an ultimate symphonic piece, and that other musical styles, besides European romanticism, can also be convenient and appropriate for film scoring.

While Copland initiated a different approach toward film composition in the Forties, Alex North and Leonard Rosenman continued his efforts in the Fifties. Their film scores enriched the contemporary sound of symphonic Americana and showed that the use of dissonant musical language can increase the dramatic impact of music in films. North was one of the few composers whose different style and approach toward film composition were immediately accepted by Hollywood. His score for *A Streetcar Named Desire* was the first functional, dramatic jazz score ever composed for a film. By that time jazz was used only as source music. North's new approach greatly influenced Hollywood musical trends, indicated the end of the Golden Age era, and marked the beginning of a new wave in the history of film music. His sophisticated use of jazz in film scoring influenced the scores of many other composers, such as Elmer Bernstein's scores for *The Man with the Golden Arm* (1955) and *Some*

1

Alex North (left) and Leonard Rosenman in North's home studio in Pacific Palisades.

Came Running (1958), Franz Waxman's scores for *A Place in the Sun* (1951) and *Crime in the Streets* (1956), John Lewis' score for *Odds Against Tomorrow* (1959), Johnny Mandel's score for *I Want to Live* (1958), Leith Stevens' score for *The Wild One* (1954), Leonard Rosenman's score for *The Chapman Report* (1962), and others. North himself scored several more pictures using jazz idioms, but he also indulged himself to explore different musical styles in the process of writing music for various film genres.

His contemporary musical approach toward film composition included a series of novelties, such as sparse scoring, use of small chamber ensembles instead of big studio orchestras, more individual instrumental treatment, and above all, a careful consideration of the dramatic needs of the films before the decision of what type of music and musical techniques were going to be applied. Working in Hollywood for over four decades, Alex North followed only one ultimate rule in film scoring — to provide a film with an appropriate musical comment.

Rosenman's compositional approach, on the other hand, was characterized by the radical use of expressionistic musical language in films. The wide range of his progressive musical affinities was already evident in his early scores in which he went from the creation of an expressive dissonant "James Dean sound"[1] in *East of Eden* (1955) and *Rebel Without a Cause* (1955) to a completely atonal concept in *The Cobweb* (1955). In their common efforts to include new, progressive musical concepts and styles in film composition, North and Rosenman established two new courses in the development of Hollywood film music and influenced many younger film composers. There is an interesting fact that both composers were brought to Hollywood by the distinguished director Elia Kazan, who persuaded the film studios that these were the right composers for his particular films (*A Streetcar Named Desire* and *East of Eden*). Kazan introduced several talented composers to the Hollywood film world in the Fifties. Besides North and Rosenman, the list includes Leonard Bernstein (*On the Waterfront*, 1954), Kenyon Hopkins (*Baby Doll*, 1956 and *Wild River*, 1960), Tom Glazier (*A Face in the Crowd*, 1958), and David Amram (*Splendor in the Grass*, 1961).

This book is devoted to the musical legacy of Alex North. It is a biographical and an analytic study rather than a historical one. Since life circumstances, education and professional experience greatly affect the musical style, preferences and skills of every composer, the first part of the book contains a biography of Alex North with a concise overview of his work. The analytic part of the book is focused on several films whose music scores offer invaluable information about the essential aesthetic aspects of film scoring, such as the relation between the film subject and musical style, the problem of musical form in film scoring, and the use of appropriate orchestration and compositional techniques to enhance the dramatic undercurrent and unity of the film, to mention just a few. Most of North's scores can be considered distinguished examples of film composition. North collaborated with many leading directors, such as Elia Kazan, Stanley Kubrick, Daniel Mann, Martin Ritt, William Wyler and Mike Nichols. However, considering the fact that the collaboration between North and Huston lasted for a period of over twenty years, longer than with any other director, this book includes musical analyses of three of their films: *The Misfits*, *Under the Volcano*, and *Prizzi's Honor*. These highly innovative films are very diverse and contain a variety of musical techniques used to fulfill the dramatic requirements of the films. The other two analyses are devoted to the music of his landmark films: *A Streetcar Named Desire*, directed by Elia Kazan, and *Spartacus*, directed by Stanley Kubrick. The former is an exceptional example of scoring an intimate drama, while the latter is a valuable source for a research of the function of music in a historical epic spectacle.

The opportunity to access and analyze North's complete original music scores was the most valuable part of the research. The analysis of *A Streetcar Named Desire* is based on a full orchestral score, the music for *The Misfits* is analyzed from a conductor score, while the material for the analysis of *Spartacus* included both, a conductor and a full orchestral score. The sources for the musical analyses of *Under the Volcano* and *Prizzi's Honor* were compiled from original sketches, orchestrated music cues, and conductor excerpts. The musical examples in the book are short, simplified extracts of the main thematic material and the leading melodic lines, used to support and verify the analytical procedure.

Alex North earned a special place among those composers who greatly influenced the development of film music. As one of the most distinguished and prolific film composers in the history of American music, he developed a truly unique and thoughtful musical approach toward film scoring. There have been composers who could not deal with the uncertainty of the musical standards in Hollywood, and decided to compose for film only periodically. Alex North came and stayed in Hollywood, composing "visual" music for forty years and devoting his life to film composition. North's musicianship was highly appreciated and admired by his peers. "Alex is a perfectionist," said Jerry Goldsmith, the prominent film composer. "Of all of us, he's the master."[2] With an artistry of a master, North wrote music for more than sixty motion pictures, creating many unforgettable film scores of the highest musical quality.

PART I

NORTH'S LIFE AND CAREER

1

From West to East:
Search for Knowledge

Give Mr. North a theme, and he goes straight to the heart
of it without any musical pretensions.
                                        — *Brooks Atkinson*[1]

In the interview with David Kraft for the magazine *Soundtrack!* from 1985, Alex
North said that if he ever wrote an autobiography, it would start with the quote from
the review by the critic Brooks Atkinson, which is used as an epigraph for this chapter. Atkinson made this statement in regard to the play *The Innocents*, but also referred
in his critique to the music of Alex's *Death of a Salesman*. Alex appreciated the critic's
recognition of his theatrical scores and admitted that he had tried to adhere to those
words throughout his entire career.[2] And he really did it successfully for many decades
afterwards.

Alex North was born on December 4, 1910, in Chester, Pennsylvania, a small
town near Philadelphia. He was the third son of Russian Jewish immigrant parents,
Jesse and Baila Soifer. His original name was Isadore Soifer. In some reference books
the year of 1909 is listed as the year of his birth. Although his birth certificate is from
1910, it is probably true that he was born one year earlier. His wife Annemarie North
explained that, as far as she could remember discussing this issue with Alex, the confusion about the year of his birth was due to a mistake made in city hall. Despite this
fact, the year of 1910 is officially recognized as the year of birth of Isadore Soifer, alias
Alex North.

Young Isadore grew up in poverty with his two older brothers Joe (Jerome, later
called Joseph) and Abe (Abraham), and his younger brother Harry. Their father,
Jesse, was a blacksmith, and worked very hard to support the family. Their mother,

Bessie Soifer (center) with her sons (clockwise from top left): Abe, Joe, Alex, and Harry, early 1920s.

Bessie Soifer with her sons 40 years later (same positions).

Baila, who was better known as Bessie, ran a grocery store. They both had to go a long way to finally settle down in America. The young couple was one of the millions of Russian Jewish families who wanted to leave tsarist Russia during the big migration wave at the turn of the century, hoping to start a new life in the "promised land," America. Bessie was originally from Odessa, and Jesse was from Biela Crkva, near Kiev.[3] He met Bessie when he moved to Odessa. Around 1906, after his release from the Army, Jesse joined his fellow immigrants on the crowded steamship and came to the United States. Bessie and their first son Jerome followed him later.

Both young parents worked hard to save money for a small house and to provide a normal life for their four boys. Unfortunately, in 1915 Jesse Soifer died on the operating table from appendicitis. He was only thirty years old. Years later the family found out that it was a botched operation. Alex had a hard time accepting the death of his father. He was too scared to attend his father's funeral. In despair, he ran away from home for several days. This aversion toward funerals continued for a long time, and he kept refusing to attend any family funeral in the years to come.

Life was not easy for the young widowed Bessie and her four sons who were three, six, nine and twelve years of age when their father died. The urge to survive forced Bessie to keep her strong spirit and to develop her sense for business. When Jesse died she was left with a tiny little grocery store. She gradually sold out the store in order to buy property which she used as a boarding house. She rented out the rooms of the big four storied house mostly to sailors who were having their boats repaired at the old Sun Shipbuilding Corporation located across from the Soifer's house. Much later, recalling childhood, Alex North said, "I'm grateful for growing up in a working class neighborhood. It has helped me to translate music to human feelings."[4] His mother, Bessie, was a strong, good-hearted woman, known for her hospitality and good cooking. The house was always crowded with people and one could always stay there and feel welcome. But, Alex also described her as a person who believed in culture. For instance, he recalled his mother going to a rabbi across town to study Hebrew.[5] Bessie Soifer was remembered as a woman who "loved to laugh, and there was nothing she loved to laugh at more than hypocrisy and pretension. She was a down-to-earth woman who loved life. She loved company, talk, food, children, music and laughter. She had a natural dignity, but she loved fun. She made a small, overheated, ugly room on Edgemont Avenue into a magic place that people returned to over and over again to be reminded that life is good, that strength and courage exist, that love and loyalty are powerful."[6]

The musical interest of young Alex was awakened and noticed, as it usually happens with artists, during his early age. The earliest musical influence came from his mother singing Russian folk tunes to her four boys.[7] She somehow managed to buy a second hand grand piano (a dollar down, a dollar a week forever) which took up the whole living room of their house. Bessie wanted to provide a musical education for all of her sons. The oldest brother Joe was the first one to have music lessons. In time, Joe became a very good pianist, and at the age of sixteen he even accompanied silent films in Chester's old Washington Theatre. Later, when the family gathered together, he would always be at the piano, playing popular tunes and leading the family into song. He had a big influence on Alex's musical education, as well as the development of his intellectual and social interests. Alex was seven years old when Joe started teaching him piano.

Although Alex grew up surrounded by his brothers and numerous family members, he was a loner, living in his own world. However, almost all the family stories center around Alex, because he had a vivid sense of humor. He was the one who always made fun, invented various jokes and tricked everybody in the family. As a kid Alex loved to play sports: baseball, basketball, and football. But, he also loved playing piano. Alex's first piano instructor was a local mediocre teacher whom he blamed for developing "bad technique."[8] However, with him Alex studied a great deal of Bach and Beethoven and developed his sight-reading skills. From the age of nine until twelve Alex studied piano with William Hatton Green, who was considered the best teacher in Chester. Green used the "Leschetizky method" in his piano instructions which helped Alex improve his piano technique. Alex's interest in music was evident, and he was constantly practicing, playing and creating his own tunes. His brother Harry remembers him often playing until two o'clock in the morning, waking everyone up. Bessie's three sisters and a brother, who used to visit the family every Saturday night, always made Alex play the piano for them. He was advancing very well in his piano studies. At nine, he won five dollars at an amateur night at the 7th Street movie house.[9]

At the age of twelve he felt that he had to continue his musical education on a more serious basis, and at that point he went to study at the Henry Street Settlement Music School in Philadelphia. For the next four years he was traveling from Chester to Philadelphia by trolley car No. 37, which was a distance of approximately one hour in each direction. At the Settlement School he studied essentially piano, theory and sight-singing. His piano teacher was George Boyle, a pupil of Busoni, who taught both at the Settlement School and at the Curtis Institute. At that time Alex had a chance to attend the master class of Leopold Godowsky, which he considered one of the most exciting experiences of that period.[10] Subsequently, Alex became a private student of Boyle's while further attending Chester High School.[11]

One of Alex's friends from early childhood was Samuel Barber. They used to take piano lessons from the same piano teacher in Chester, William Hatton Green. Later, they both went to study in Philadelphia — Alex at the Settlement Music School and Barber at the Curtis Institute. Barber came from a good home. Sometimes they used to give piano recitals in his parents' living room in West Chester.[12] Alex's home was also a good one, but a poor one, in another section of Chester. From an early age Alex had to work at many odd jobs to help his mother make ends meet. He worked as a pin boy in a bowling alley, as a cub reporter for the old *Chester Times* covering Third Street, and in the summers he used to work on the boardwalk at Atlantic City, squeezing oranges. At night he would listen to Ethel Waters, who was from Chester, singing with the bands on the Steel Pier.[13] Around that time, when he was fourteen, Alex was drawn to American jazz. He would specially go to Atlantic City to hear the bands of Coon Sanders and Paul Whiteman.[14] But, he also remembered taking the No. 37 trolley car up through the Essington swamps to stand in line every Friday in order to buy a ticket for the symphonies at the Academy of Music.[15] In general, the teenage years were the time when Alex showed his interest in discovering various

Letter from George Boyle to North, August 22, 1930.

styles and forms of musical expression, and formed his musical taste which influenced and determined the qualities of his future compositions.

Alex decided to study telegraphy in New Jersey and thus to support himself during the years of his music study. He started working for Western Union at night as a telegraph operator while still attending Chester High School. After studies at the Settlement Music School and graduation at Chester High in 1927, Alex aimed for the Curtis Institute in Philadelphia. He attended Curtis part time from 1928 until 1929. But, his piano teacher George Boyle recommended Alex continue his studies at Juilliard School of Music in New York, where Boyle also had a piano class. Therefore, Alex had to move to New York. Looking back to the years spent in Philadelphia, Alex concluded that there are "some cities you want to forget, but Philadelphia has only happy memories for me."[16]

At that time Alex's oldest brother Joseph was already in New York pursuing his career as a reporter and a journalist. He was an intellectual aware of social events around the world. He started to work as a reporter with the *Chester Times*, a paper that he used to call "North of New York."[17] Later, when he moved to New York, he became a founder and one of the editors of the left-oriented weekly paper *New Masses*, which published the articles of some of the best social-protest writers from the late Twenties and early Thirties. Through Joseph, Alex made social contacts with some of the most progressive thinkers of that period. Joseph very much influenced Alex's radical attitude and active curiosity about the social events of the time. Getting involved with the International Labor Defense (ILD), Joseph started to sign his

INSTITUTE OF MUSICAL ART OF THE JUILLIARD SCHOOL OF MUSIC		

February 6th, 1932.

NAME **MR. ALEXIS SOIFER**   COURSE **REGULAR PIANO**

SUBJECT	LESSONS PRESENT	ABSENT	TEACHER'S REPORT
PIANO	hours 15	0	Application excellent; progress very satis-factory. George Boyle
THEORY II	27	1	Term work good; examination very good. Bernard Wagenaar
EAR-TRAINING II S.S.	13	1	Good. Belle J. Soudant
DICT.	13	1	Good. Helen W. Whiley
KEYBOARD HARMONY II	12	2	Good. Louise Havens
LECTURES	13	1	General Musicianship - 85%. Charles L. Seeger
			Frank Damrosch

North's certificate from the Juilliard School of Music, February 6, 1932.

articles with the pseudonym Joe North in order to protect his family from criticism of his activities. In time North became his legal last name. Alex was the next to accept the name North when he came back from Russia and started his professional music career. Afterwards everyone else in the family took the name North, except Abe who kept the name Soifer.

George Boyle arranged an audition for Alex with Frank Damrosh at Juilliard in 1929. One of the pieces that he played for this occasion was Schumann's *Kreisleriana*.

He was accepted at Juilliard and received a four-year scholarship which helped him to pay the school tuition. Alex continued to study piano with George Boyle, but he also started to study theory and composition with Bernard Wagenaar. Somewhere along the way, he realized that he was not a concert pianist and was able to express himself better in original composition.[18] Alex attended courses at Juilliard for three years, until 1932. His certificate from 1932 shows that he attained high marks in his exams of piano, theory, ear-training, keyboard harmony, analyses, and general musicianship. However, the graduating piano recital definitely convinced Alex to forget the idea of being a concert pianist. "My fingers were so wet from fright that they kept slipping off the keys," he said remembering that event. "I finally just got up, walked off and went home."[19]

In early 1932 Alex met Anna Sokolow. She was a pretty, slim, twenty-two-year-old modern dancer. She joined Graham's professional dance company in late 1929, and remained for eight years. In this period she became one of the most distinguished dancers in Martha Graham's group. In the early Thirties she started to perform her own choreographies. Anna was deeply touched by social injustices and her works were very much inspired by actual social issues. Her performances usually took place in the meeting halls of the workers' unions. Anna met Alex during one of these occasions. Remembering those days Anna said, "I think he liked the idea that I was a dancer, and he used to come and watch my work. I was very thrilled to have a pianist, a composer and an artist interested in what I was doing. So, from then on we created works together."[20] Anna and Alex had many things in common. They both came from working-class Russian Jewish families, they were the same age, they both were interested in actual social-protest issues and humanity in general, and they both had endless hunger for the arts and artistic creations. One must give Anna credit for getting Alex seriously involved with composition. "He was a shy pianist when we met," Anna recalled. "The discovery that he could compose came from my asking, 'Why don't you do this?' or my saying, 'I think you can write this.' I took him to the theater for the first time in his life. I think he was aghast. I had been going since I was a child. I'm sure he must have found me naive in many ways."[21] Anna deeply admired Alex's talent and believed in it. "He was born with it," she said. "But he really didn't know it until we started working. Then he realized it."[22]

Alex used to accompany the rehearsals and the performances of Anna's group. He also wrote the music for many of her choreographies. At first, they were invited to perform for many different workers' organizations, such as the Workers Dance League which was founded in 1932. They did that for quite a long while. Anna found in Alex a wonderful collaborator. "We had a very good report about the subjects and the themes that we wanted to express through our art work," she remembered. "The audience was receptive, the atmosphere at the performances was very beautiful and rewarding to both Alex and me. These things kept us together."[23] Remembering about their ideals in those days, Alex said, "All of us felt that we were trying to do our part to improve the domestic situation during the Depression. We wanted to give some hope. By reflecting the period in our work, we were trying to do positive things, lifting the spirit of the so-called 'masses.'"[24]

The first major work for Anna as a choreographer and for Alex as a composer was the *Anti-War Trilogy* (later retitled the *Anti-War Cycle*). The work was performed

at the First Anti-War Congress of the Theatre Union Dance Group, and it was sponsored by the American League Against War and Fascism. The performance took place
at the St. Nicholas Arena on August 29, 1933. The *Anti-War Trilogy* was divided into
three sections: "Depression — Starvation," "Diplomacy — War," and "Protest." The
last movement was later retitled "Defiance."[25] This work received very positive critical acclaim, and it was the beginning of Anna's and Alex's long-term and prolific
collaboration. They also started to live together. The beginning of their relationship
was very romantic, although they lived in poverty. Their first home was like a little
commune — a loft on West 12th Street which they shared with ten other people. Later
they moved into a small apartment on 13th Street between Second and Third avenues,
which looked like a luxurious private space in comparison with their previous place
of living. Although their tempers and characters were different, it seemed that they
complemented each other. Anna was extremely emotional, impulsive, and bursting
with energy, while Alex was more reserved, contemplative, to the point of being shy,
but also witty and charming. In the eyes of Alex, Anna was brave and a rebel, and
in some ways very naive. One of their friends described their relationship as "a serious and, at the same time lighthearted one. The empathy they had for each other was
extraordinary... They were very important to each other in the formulation of their
artistic beings in their early years. One of the great things about the relationship was
that there were two artists in it."[26]

During these years in New York Alex continued to support himself working
most of the time as telegraph operator for Western Union on 60 Hudson Street. They
put him on the Schenectady wire — the General Electric line — which involved a great
deal of coding. In that regard, he thought that apparently his dexterity as a pianist
helped.[27] He also used to say that telegraphy helped him to develop his sense of
rhythm.[28] These early years in New York were not easy for Alex. He had to work
every night from six until two o'clock in the morning at the Western Union, and then
attend the classes at Juilliard during the day, run to the rehearsals with Anna and...
write music. After three and a half years of this exhausting and tough life style his
health was nearly wrecked. But, it also enabled him to save some money and prepare himself for a major change in his life — musical studies in Russia. At that point,
Alex wanted to concentrate entirely on his compositional work and studies without
any concerns about the financial problems of everyday living. At first, this seemed
to be a wild and an adventurous idea, but its realization came much faster than Alex
expected.

The story about Alex's departure for the Soviet Union is not a usual one. Alex
himself used to recall that story on many occasions, adding a comical note to it.
There were two circumstances which helped convince Alex to pursue his idea. The
first one was the complete support and encouragement that he had from his brother
Joe, who used many of his connections in order to provide funds for Alex's studies
and make his stay in the country of their parents easier and valuable. The second
circumstance was more of a practical nature. At that time, the Russian government
needed many skilled professionals from various fields (engineers, doctors, scientists,
architects, technicians etc.) to help the development of their industry. All expenses
were paid. In late 1932 Alex applied to the Soviet agency in New York for a job as a
"telegraphist," which in Russian had a much greater kind of connotation, that of a

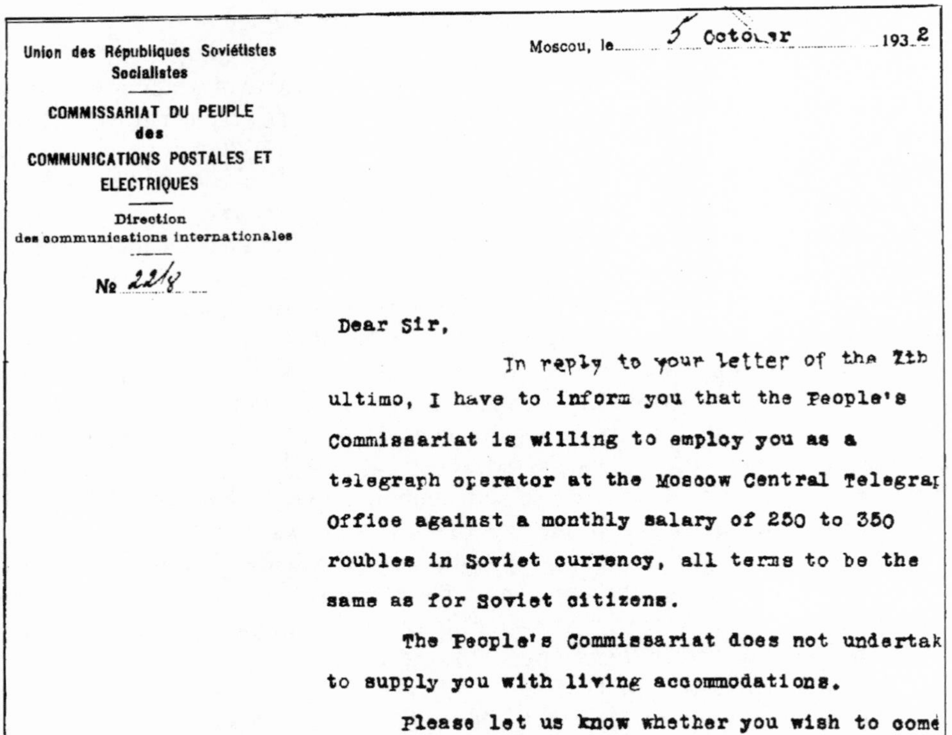

Union des Républiques Soviétistes
Socialistes

COMMISSARIAT DU PEUPLE
des
COMMUNICATIONS POSTALES ET
ELECTRIQUES
Direction
des communications internationales

№ 22/8

Moscou, le ___5 Octobre___ 193 **2**

Dear Sir,

In reply to your letter of the 2th ultimo, I have to inform you that the People's Commissariat is willing to employ you as a telegraph operator at the Moscow Central Telegraph Office against a monthly salary of 250 to 350 roubles in Soviet currency, all terms to be the same as for Soviet citizens.

The People's Commissariat does not undertake to supply you with living accommodations.

Please let us know whether you wish to come and work in the USSR at the terms proposed, in which event we would make the necessary arrangements towards obtaining a visa for you.

Yours truly,

Director

Mr. Alexis Soifer

Care of Joseph North

International Labour Defense

80, East 11th Street

New York, U.S.A.

Letter of invitation from the Russian officials, October 5, 1932.

telegraph engineer. In early 1934, after all the correspondence and arrangements with the Russian Commissariat of the People, Alex was on his way to Moscow. "I wanted to go somewhere where my musical education could be subsidized. I was attracted to the idea of studying in Russia, partly because I idolized Prokofiev," Alex admitted later.[29] After his arrival, the Russians showed him his huge telegraph office. They probably expected him to overhaul and re-work their entire telegraphic system. But, all that Alex knew as a telegraph operator was the Morse Code, and after a couple of weeks they discovered his limitations. They wanted to send him right back. At that point, Alex's very good friend and interpreter, Grisha Schneerson, who was a pianist and concertmaster at a Moscow theater, revealed the fact that Alex was a composer, and that his real motive to come over to Moscow was to study music. For the audition at the Conservatory Alex played all the pieces that he had previously written, and he was admitted on a scholarship. He spent nearly two years at the Moscow Conservatory, studying composition with Anton Weprik and Victor Bielyi.[30]

Several months after his enrollment at the conservatory, Alex invited Anna Sokolow to visit him. In his enthusiastic letter to Anna in March, 1934, he wrote, "When you receive this, April will be here and then, and then, and then! MOSCOW the birthplace of civilization! The kernel of the new Renaissance — where millions are struggling to make for themselves a decent society. And you and I shall witness it together...."[31]

Alex liked the fact that he could finally study music and live normally without working other jobs in order to survive. He was impressed by the benefits and facilities the students in Russia enjoyed. In April 1935, Alex published an article for *Dynamics* in which he wrote, "A student is assured of a job when he finishes his studies and while he is studying he receives a stipend from the Commissariat of Education which enables him to concentrate entirely on his studies. Dormitories are also attached to the conservatory where students live free of charge. The lowest stipend received by a student is 45 rubles and he may eat three meals a day for the month in the dining room of the conservatory for the small amount of 26 rubles. Entrance to concerts are free with the presentation of the school card. Fares on trolleys are reduced for students and other privileges are given them at reduced rates. Students who are unable to buy instruments are supplied by the conservatory. There are regular student meetings where grievances are voiced."[32] Alex was also amazed by the high technical, artistic and professional level required from the students at the conservatory. In his article he continued, "The standard of the conservatory is quite high. A student must finish the 'technicum' before he can enter the conservatory. The technicum covers a course of two to three years and the conservatory, five years. Those students who intend becoming concert performers enter the 'meister school' or master school after graduating from the conservatory. The first year of the conservatory is equivalent to the last year in many schools in America. The technical equipment [ability] is much higher than students here (in the United States) [have] because of the amount of time a student has free to practice and study."[33] However, as much as he exulted with the achievements in various fields of the arts in Russia, he was disappointed with the situation in the field of dance, and the dominance of the old-fashioned classical ballet. After working with progressive modern dancers in the United States, he expected a more revolutionary approach toward dance in Russia. "With all the progressive strides made in the fields of theatre, cinema, music, and painting, the art of the dance in the Soviet Union lags behind. This is most paradoxical since the dance, before the Revolution, when the Diaghilev ballet was at its height, was the most advanced of these arts," he wrote in the article for *Dance Observer* in May 1934.[34]

Contract between the Union of Soviet Composers and Alex North, June 29, 1934.

In June 1934 Anna arrived in Leningrad. Alex was waiting for her there, and they spent two days in Leningrad, going to the theaters and enjoying the city. They saw there a performance of Tchaikovsky's *Swan Lake*, whose production Anna found "old fashioned, elaborate and sentimental, and so banal that it sickened me. The pure ballet I enjoyed tremendously."[35]

In Moscow Alex and Anna lived in an apartment on Karaka Street. It had a large room with a piano where Alex used to practice and compose. On June 29, 1934, he received a commission from the Union of Soviet Composers to write a set of piano variations and two choruses. This was due to the recommendations from his composition teachers, Weprik and Bielyi, who were very satisfied with his work at the conservatory and found him a talented composer. Thus, Alex was the first and only American composer who became a member of the Union of Soviet Composers, which was considered a great honor.

During Anna's stay in Moscow, Alex and she rehearsed two to three hours daily in the facilities of the Foreign Workers' Club. The rest of the time they visited the museums and the theaters in Moscow, attended parties with their Russian and American friends, toured the city, and had midnight suppers at the exclusive club of the Bolshoi Theater. Alex provided the membership for the club and a pass for all the events at the Bolshoi Theater through his friend Grisha Schneerson, who was at the time a secretary of the International Bureau of Music. From the performances that they attended at the Bolshoi Theater, there were two operas which immensely impressed them, and which they remembered a long time afterwards—*Prince Igor* by Borodin and *Katerina Izmailova* by Shostakovich.[36]

While in Moscow, Anna was asked to do a lecture-demonstration of the Graham technique. After this presentation she also gave a dance recital. The response of the audience and the critical comments were controversial, because the concept of the modern dance was strange to the Russian audience. Although some of her dances were considered "a product of bourgeois decadence," she was invited to come back to work with a group of dancers for a year. At the end they added, "We could make an artist of you," at which Anna laughed and returned, "Spasiba bolshoi (thank you very much)."[37] In September 1934 she left Russia and returned to the United States.

Alex stayed in Moscow by himself for one more year. Besides composing, he was also engaged in other musical activities. For a while, he was musical director of the Latvian State Theater, and in the summertime, he was active as musical director of a group of German exiles called "Kolonne Links," who toured the German Autonomous republic with works of other exiled compatriots.[38] Studying at the conservatory until the end of 1935, Alex perfected his compositional technique and musically enriched the solid foundation he received at Juilliard. But, at the same time, he felt that he was writing in a style that was not expressing his originality. "I felt that this was not right for me. I was writing like Ippolitov-Ivanov."[39] The popular and often told tale was that Alex became overwhelmed with melancholy and longing when he heard at a party the recording of the song "Mood Indigo" by Duke Ellington, his all time favorite composer. At that point, he found himself wondering, "What am I doing here? Well, it's time to get back to the roots."[40] Soon, he was on his way back to his homeland, America.

2

Music and Movement:
The Beginning

My music is written to be played, to be functional and to catch the spirit of the American people.
— *Alex North*[1]

Despite his classical training and academic education, Alex North basically formed his compositional style through his experience in the fields of modern dance, theater and film. As a musical collaborator of Anna Sokolow for years, Alex became a well-known and highly appreciated composer in the dance circles in New York. He was known as a sensitive musician with an evident gift to adjust the music to the movement, and a skill to feel and musically match the rhythm and the pace of the dance. Although Alex periodically composed notable and renowned concert compositions throughout his career, the circumstances very naturally led him into deeper involvement with functional music.

When Alex returned from Russia in late 1935, he continued working with Anna, but he also extended his activities to teaching music for dance at some of the most prestigious colleges, and composing music for the most famous dancers and choreographers of the time, such as Martha Graham, Hanya Holm, Agnes De Mille, Marthe Krueger, and Doris Humphrey. Alex's teaching experience covers a short period from 1935 until 1938, during which he was invited to give lectures on functional music at Finch College, Briarcliff College, Sarah Lawrence College, and Bennington College. However, he had no interest in pursuing an academic career, even though he was invited to teach and lecture at many distinctive schools. "He did not like to talk too much about music, especially not in front of a large auditorium," remembered his wife Annemarie.[2]

Despite the busy and demanding schedule, Alex still managed to find time to continue his studies of composition. In the period between 1935 and 1940 he worked with two prominent composers, Aaron Copland and Ernst Toch. Before his studies with Copland in 1936 and 1937, Alex had already developed his lyrical, melodically defined style which became one of the landmarks of his entire compositional work. He later remembered one of his meetings with Copland where, trying to remain faithful to his own style, "I brought him a very romantic piece, and he said, 'Alex, we're living in a different age.' But I stuck to my guns with this lyrical kind of writing, just as Samuel Barber did with his style of writing."[3] Alex stayed in touch with Copland for many years afterwards. Later, when he moved to California, he wrote to Copland in November 1957. "Someday I will tell you why I have worked like mad out here these past five years, writing scores in three weeks, sacrificing my yen to write 'absolute'—I never knew when the axe would fall."[4] Copland's biographer, Vivian Perlis, pointed out that "in 1956, Copland included North, along with Herrmann, Rosenman, and Gail Kubik, on a list of composers he most admired in Hollywood. Copland knew what it took to compose a successful score for a major film. He thought that a composer such as North, who had a special talent for film composition and who could write a score like *Death of a Salesman*, had little reason to be apologetic."[5]

In 1938 North continued his studies with the distinguished German émigré composer Ernst Toch. He actively worked with him for two years. At first he attended group classes at the New School for Social Research, and then he was asked by Toch to continue work with him privately.[6] Their relationship continued even when Toch went to Hollywood. "He was a beautiful man. He would comment on my music, correct things and send them back. It was a great help," Alex later commented.[7] During these years of work with Copland and Toch, North composed most of his little known chamber music, such as the *Woodwind Trio* for flute, clarinet and bassoon (1936), and his *String Quartet* (1939), as well as the symphonic suite *Quest* (1937).

Nevertheless, in the mid–Thirties Alex was professionally preoccupied with writing music for modern dancers. He had always considered this experience the most valuable preparation for his later career as a film composer. In December 1969 he commented, "...in the modern dance, the dancer would work her particular dance out first, and she would give you the counts, and one bar would be a 3/8 bar, and the next would be a 5/8, and the next would be a 2/4. That in a sense was good training in attempting to make a formal piece of music with all these mixed bar meters so that after eight or nine years of that kind of training, I was more or less prepared, plus the documentary experience, to step into the Hollywood scene."[8]

Alex often performed with Anna during these years. One of the most popular places where the modern dancers used to have concerts was the Kaufman Auditorium of the 92nd Street Y.M.H.A., known as the "Y." Alex performed many of his pieces there in the late Thirties and early Forties. On April 5, 1936, at the "Y," Anna had a full evening concert of her own work, which included two of Alex's compositions, *Inquisition '36* and *Ballad in a Popular Style*. The first one did not receive particular attention, and it was never shown again, while the *Ballad in a Popular Style* became "something of a trademark for Anna."[9] Anna's biographer Larry Warren wrote that the *Ballad* was "a wistful, lyrical excursion into jazz.... It was a stunning

dance, at once subtle and exuberant, pure dance with no reason for being other than
its rhythm and beauty of motion."[10] Another very significant dance for Anna from
that period was *Excerpts from a War Poem*, based on the poem *War Is Beautiful* by
the Italian Futurist Marinetti. [11] It was presented at a concert on February 28, 1937.
Later, this work was called just *War Poem* or *War Is Beautiful*, after the title of the
poem. Alex's music "used all the resources of contemporary music to deliver a sav-
age attack on Fascist barbarism."[12]

In 1936 Alex and Anna received a grant to participate in a workshop called "Arts
in the Theater." One of the group projects was the theater play *Dog Beneath the Skin*
by W. H. Auden. The entire faculty of the workshop was included in this project. It
was Alex's first score for a theater play. This was a very useful experience for Alex,
although the play was never produced. In the same year, Alex wrote the music for
his first documentary films, a field to which he made an enormous contribution in
the period between 1936 and 1950. The music for *China Strikes Back* (1936) was characterized as sparse and full of dignity. "The folk portions, sung and played by Chinese, are, for precision's sake, contemporary and Western-influenced," wrote the
critic Martin McCall.[13] The following year Alex wrote music for another film, Herbert Kline's pro–Loyalist documentary *Heart of Spain*, directed by Paul Strand. This
documentary was praised as "one of the finest of documentary films," and "the most
compelling document ever shown of war-torn Spain." The expressive score is based
on Spanish motifs. McCall found the introduction of native bagpipes particularly
effective.[14] Elizabeth Noble, a critic of *New Messes*, commented on the score. "For
the wounded at the front, music with the tearing effect of wounds. For the hospital,
two guitars playing a sad and gentle Spanish folk air. At the end, renewal, new life...,
and over all a woman's throaty voice singing an heroic *fandaguilla*."[15]

Another documentary film from that period was very important for Alex. It was
the 1938 production of *People of the Cumberland*, an essay about the restoration of
economic security in the Appalachian region of Tennessee. The director of the documentary was Elia Kazan, whom Alex met through Anna in 1938.[16] But they met just
casually, as he was not really involved in the scoring of the documentary.[17] Their
close professional and personal relationship began in 1949 with the stage production
of Arthur Miller's *Death of a Salesman*. Elie Siegmeister praised North's score for the
film *People of the Cumberland* and his "uncanny sense of musical timing, derived
from his dance experience." And then he continued, "Two aspects of the composer's
talent found free play: his sense of jazz rhythms and his unusual melodic invention.
He is not specifically a jazz composer. But the tempo and the quality of popular
rhythm and melody are in his bones; they come out naturally in the midst of any
American subject he touches."[18]

During 1937, despite the exhausting schedule, Alex still found time to travel and
accompany Anna on her dance recitals. It was a rewarding experience. During this
year he wrote some of his best ballet compositions, and met many artists with whom
he had future collaboration. For instance, Leonard Bernstein met Alex for the first
time at Anna's debut recital in Boston. "One evening we found ourselves in Jordan
Hall in Boston, attending the out-of-town debut of a dancer called Anna Sokolow,
then 'married' to composer Alex North, who wrote all the music for her dancing and
was playing in the wings," remembered Bernstein. "We became real fans of this girl,

who was then completely unknown."[19] Anna invited Bernstein to her Broadway debut in New York in November 1937, where Bernstein met his favorite composer, Aaron Copland.

In August 1937, Anna and Alex had a performance in the Bennington Festival in Vermont State Armory. The program contained several of Alex's dance compositions, *Ballad in a Popular Style, Speaker* (first performed in 1935), and a new piece *Façade-Exposizione Italiana*. This piece which denounced Fascist Italy has four sections called *Belle Arti, Giovanezza, Prix Femina,* and *Phantasmagoria*. The *New York Times* critic John Martin wrote that this "group work is a piece of extraordinary cleverness and skill." He also added that Anna Sokolow is "very fortunate, incidentally, in having Alex North as composer of her music."[20] For Anna's Broadway debut in the Guild Theater on November 14, 1937, Alex arranged the *Opening Dance* for soloist and group, and composed another notable work, *Slaughter of the Innocents*. This dance was inspired by the documentary film *Heart of Spain*, and it was complemented with footage of the bombing of Barcelona. Siegmeister, who praised the graceful charm, easy lyricism, and clean emotional warmth of Alex's music in general, wrote of this piece that it was "one of the most moving American scores of recent years, even when listened apart from the dance."[21] Alex's contribution was also rewarded by John Martin who described him as "an invaluable collaborator whose music possesses vitality and imagination and that rarest of attributes, a feeling for movement."[22] By the end of 1937 another ballet piece of Alex's was performed at the Guild Theater. It was a dance for soloist and group called *American Lyric*, composed for Martha Graham and her dance group. Its first performance was on December 19, 1937. Although it did not stay on Graham's repertoire, this piece was an important credit for Alex. At that time, Alex became very friendly with Martha Graham and her husband, the choreographer and composer Louis Horst.[23] These concerts in late 1937 were at the same time Anna's last performances with the Graham dance group.

The years of the mid–Thirties were very prolific for Alex. Besides exploring his musical potentials in the fields of documentary film and modern dance, he also joined the Federal Theater Project where he started a career in composing for theater. At that time the Federal Theater Project was a very fertile field which gathered and gave creative opportunities to many talented artists of the period. It was a formal organization, founded at the height of the Depression by the first Roosevelt administration, mostly for political reasons. The arts projects were sponsored and administered by the Work Projects Administration (W.P.A.). Alex wrote scores for several productions sponsored by the Federal Theater Project, including George Sklar's lyric drama *Life and Death of an American* which won him warm commendations, and opened the doors for his further engagements on Broadway in the Forties. The premiere of the play was on May 19, 1939, in Maxine Elliott's Theater in New York. He was also in charge of some musical parts of the 1938 production of the revue called *Sing for Your Supper*. After many troubles and delays the project was completed in 1939. The most popular numbers from this revue were "Ballad for Americans" and "The Last Waltz." Anna was also involved in this project as a choreographer of several dance numbers. While working for the theater Alex discovered that composing music for stage demanded a different approach than composing music for films. The stage timing is variable and changes with every performance, unlike the screen timing which

Alex North with Anna Sokolow, 1936. From the 1991 book *Anna Sokolow: The Rebellious Spirit* by Larry Warren. Used by permission of Annemarie North.

requires split-second timed music to fit the permanent set of pictures. In the theater, every music cue can be condensed or expanded depending on the dramatic situation and the actor's timing. Therefore, the general themes are gradually adjusted to the final demands of each dramatic scene.[24]

In 1939 Anna was offered performances in Mexico City. The offer came from the Mexican painter Carlos Mérida who had been the first director of the Dance Department in Mexico City's School of Fine Arts. He saw one of Anna's performances in New York and was deeply touched by her work. After the performance he went backstage and asked Anna if she would like to come and dance in Mexico. At first Anna thought it was just a joke. But, very soon after this encounter Anna received an official invitation from the Department of Fine Arts of the Mexican government. Thus, in April 1939 Anna and her nine dancers, joined by Alex as a musical director, the singer Mordecai Baumann, and the stage manager, Allen Wayne, left for Mexico. They were to give several concerts over the period of two weeks in the most exclusive theater in Mexico City, the Palace of Fine Arts (Palacio de Bellas Artes). The reception of the audience was wonderful and they became very popular in Mexico City. Therefore, they were asked to increase the number of their performances. By the end of the ballet season Alex had conducted twenty-six concerts with a chamber orchestra. The program of the concerts was based on Anna's standard

```
P R O G R A M                                              (PART TWO)

           (PART ONE)                           A program of music composed by Alex North for
        ANNA SOKOLOW                            Concert, Theatre, Musical Revue and Film.

    Alex North, Musical Director.
                                                CONCERT
1. Ballad in a Popular Style...............Alex North
              ANNA SOKOLOW                        1.  Four Piano Preludes.................... Milton Kaye

2. Case History No. — _____Wallingford Reigger      2.  Two movements from Suite for Piano and Orchestra
   A study of a majority of case histories shows that petty criminals usually                    (arranged for two pianos)
   emerge from a background that begins with unemployment and follows          a.  Blues
   its course from street corner to poolroom, from mischief to crime.          b.  Scherzo
              ANNA SOKOLOW
                                                      MILTON KAYE and ALEX NORTH
3. Slaughter of the Innocents................Alex North
   A Spanish mother protests against the barbaric Fascist air raids.                  *  *  *  *
              ANNA SOKOLOW
                                                THEATRE
4. Songs For Children.............Sylvestre Revueltas      3.  Two songs from "Life and Death of an American"
                  Lyrics by GARCIA LORCA                              By GEORGE SKLAR

   a. The little horse.                                    a.  Lullaby
                                                           b.  Soldiers' Blues
   b. At one o'clock the moon comes out.                        MORDECAI BAUMAN

   c. Song of the foolish child.                        4.  Vuss iz Jazz?
      "mama I want to be of silver"                                MARK FEDER
   d. The alligator's lament
      "the alligator is crying because he lost his wedding ring"          *  *  *  *
   e. Cradle Song.
      "Go to sleep my carnation"                    MUSICAL REVUE
   f. Serenade.                                         5.  Rhumba
   g. The Truth.                                                 ESTELLE PARNAS and ALEX NORTH
      "Ay: it is very hard to love you in the way I love you"    6.  Mooch Motif
              ANNA SOKOLOW                                       DOROTHY BIRD and WILLIAM BALES
5. The Exile (A Dance Poem)...........Traditional Folk Music    7.  Four a.m. ................(Lyrics by John La Touche)
          Arrangement by ALEX NORTH                              SIMON RADY
             Poem by SOL FUNAROFF
                                                       8.  Nocturne
   a. "I had a garden"                                           DOROTHY BIRD and BEATRICE KAY
   b. "The beast is in the garden"
              ANNA SOKOLOW                                       *  *  *  *

ESTELLE PARNAS, Assistant Pianist    ESTELLE HOFFMAN, Soprano    FILM
              ARNO TANNEY, Baritone                     9.  One reel from Frontier's "People of the Cumberland"
                                                                 (courtesy of Garrison Films)
           INTERMISSION
```

Concert program from the recital of Anna Sokolow and Alex North, February 18, 1940.

repertoire works which included the following pieces composed by Alex: *Opening Dance, Ballad in a Popular Style, Slaughter of the Innocents, War Is Beautiful, Façade — Exposizione Italiana*, and *The Exile*, a new work based on traditional Palestinian folk music.[25]

During the period spent in Mexico, Alex became a very close friend of the composer Silvestre Revueltas. Alex enormously respected Revueltas' work and considered him the top composer in Mexico. Therefore, he eagerly attended Revueltas' composition classes at school. They also spent much time together beyond the classes, discussing music over a glass of beer in the Mexican bistros.[26] Unfortunately, Revueltas died a short time afterwards, in October 1940, of a lung infection. In Mexico, Alex started to compose his *Rhapsody for Piano and Orchestra*, but he completed it later, when he returned to New York. Alex loved Mexican folk music, and he tried to absorb it in his memory as much as he could. This experience was very helpful for his future work as he was asked to compose music for several films dealing with Mexican themes.

For Anna and Alex this was a very important period, both professionally and personally. Preoccupied with their own activities and interests, their personal relationship started to wane and very soon came to its end. Anna, at age 85, remembered of her youthful experience, "It was Alex who wanted to separate, not me. I don't know exactly what the reason was. I think that, after all that he had done for me, he

Thursday, Jan. 28, 1982

Dear Alex,

Larry Warren gave me your address, and so, I am happy to write. I always remember you, and all wonderful relationship we had – it was truly creative –

I am always involved with work, in the U.S. and many countries abroad – I got work in Israel every summer and also Mexico – They both are my second home. A few months ago, I worked in Dublin, with a Ballet Company and then in December, I worked in Austria.

Now, I am in New York until my summer schedule – I may be in California in early May – I hope I will see you – I would love to hear from – and I hope you still keep creative.

Love, Anna

Letter from Anna Sokolow to Alex North, in which Anna reestablished a contact with Alex after several decades, January 28, 1982.

felt he should be alone, doing creative things on his own. He began to feel that he had to do something else in his life, apart from me and the dancers, and he left. I wasn't upset or offended by that. Not at all."[27] After seven years of a personal and professional relationship (they had never been officially married), Anna and Alex probably felt a necessity to explore different sides of their own personalities. Larry Warren was right when he pointed out that the relationship between Anna and Alex had been primarily one of loving comrades.[28]

After the ballet season was over, Anna was asked to stay in Mexico and form a dance group there. She accepted this offer, and prepared a group of young professional dancers for several performances. Anna started at that time many long-term relationships in Mexico. She used to visit her friends and perform in Mexico City almost every year for a long time afterwards. Alex, on the other hand, decided to return earlier to the United States, especially when he heard that Russia and Germany had signed their nonaggression pact. Thus, they returned separately to the United States, and continued their lives and their careers individually.

Nevertheless, upon their return from Mexico, Alex and Anna still collaborated. Anna included Alex's compositions in her standard repertoire and for many years afterwards danced to his music. In the Forties they often shared the programs of concerts and gave joint recitals in which Alex performed his own music. For instance, very soon after they came back from Mexico, on February 18, 1940, they organized a concert at the Kaufman Auditorium at the 92nd Street Y.M.H.A. In the first part of the concert Anna presented several dances (including three dance pieces by Alex), while the second part was devoted to the music composed by Alex. The program contained two concert pieces (*Four Piano Preludes* and two movements from his *Rhapsody for Piano and Orchestra* in arrangement for two pianos), songs from the theater play *Life and Death of an American*, four numbers from different musical revues (*Rhumba, Mooch Motif, Four a.m.,* and *Nocturne*), and one reel from the documentary film *People of the Cumberland*. In the review by Martin McCall, North's music was praised as "...concise, eloquent and vivid. The clean craftsmanship is similar to that which identifies the successful music he has written for films." Commenting on Alex's concert and theater music, McCall wrote, "A gift for melodic creation, such as North possesses, is uncommon."[29] However, as time went by, Anna and Alex performed less and less together. Warren described their professional relationship at that time as "... stormy and frequently punctuated with intense arguments. It was difficult for these two strong personalities, now living separate lives, to arrive at [any] kind of healthy compromises that had been possible when they were romantically involved."[30] One of the last pieces that Alex composed for Anna was *Mama Beautiful,* based on the poem by Mike Quinn, and first performed on December 13, 1942. After that, Alex and Anna periodically collaborated until Alex moved to Hollywood, but not with such intensity as before.

The relationship with Anna greatly affected the beginnings and the further development of Alex's career. His involvement with modern dance had a big influence on forming and developing his compositional style and principles. In a way, his work with Anna determined the path of his further career. In the interview with Larry Warren in 1982, Alex acknowledged the importance of his relationship with Anna with the following words: "She was very instrumental in my putting notes down on paper. I really have to give her a lot of credit for where I am today. I had the opportunity — the privilege of working with her and it was invaluable to me later when I was writing film scores. The dancer does the dance first. The film is shot first. You have to tailor the music to the dance as music is tailored to a film. This skill I first learned working with Anna. Through her I met people connected with the theater and this led to my work in films."[31]

After the separation from Anna, Alex was ready to close one chapter of his life and career, and to move on toward new challenges and achievements.

3

New York, New York: The Forties

I find it practically impossible to score anything which
does not move me emotionally...

— *Alex North*[1]

By the end of the Thirties Alex had completely finished his musical training and felt ready to explore various musical fields and genres. After the work he had done in the field of modern dance, Alex had become a well-known figure in New York dance circles, respected as a widely educated and talented composer with a special sense to musically complement the movement. But, after that experience Alex wanted to try different forms of musical expression. He wanted to write concert music and hoped to compose for Broadway theater plays.

In the early Forties Alex was often involved in productions of various musical shows, revues, and theater projects. In this period musical revues were an especially popular genre among the young artists. They were usually semi-professional productions prepared by young talented musicians, actors, singers, and dancers. Many of these productions were part of the activities within so-called summer camps, often organized by various Workers Unions. Alex loved to participate in these activities of the summer camps, because for him it meant writing music for stage, meeting many talented artists, and having a good time and fun in general. In the summer of 1939, immediately after his return from Mexico, Alex became involved in the preparation of the musical revue *'Tis of Thee*. The production took place in the Camp Unity of the International Ladies' Garment Workers Union (ILGWU) in Bushkill, Pennsylvania, where the members of the union spent their vacations. They usually invited there a large staff of musicians, actors, and entertainers in order to have them arrange various entertainment programs and shows. The revue *'Tis of Thee* was conceived and directed by Nat Lichtman. It was a miniature intimate revue organized in two

'Tis of Thee, musical rehearsal, 1941 (from left to right): Vivian Block, Alex North, Virginia Burke.

acts (twenty four scenes) with musical numbers composed by Alex North, Alfred Hayes and Al Moss. The cast included twenty-six entertainers—actors, comedians, dancers, and singers. Among them was a gifted comedienne and entertainer Sherle Hartt with whom Alex became very friendly and soon started a romantic relationship. Sherle Hartt, who was to become the first Mrs. Alex North, remembered those days. "Alex was then thirty, very soft spoken, extremely talented, and humorous. He was an absolutely charming man. We worked there for three months. We became very good friends and lovers during that period. I was a comedienne, dancer, singer, actress. I did it all. We performed every night. It was very hard work, but we had a wonderful summer."[2]

The production of *'Tis of Thee* at the summer camp was seen by members of the Schubert Theater Organization. The head of the organization, Lee Schubert, who also was the owner of the Maxine Elliott Theatre on Broadway, offered the artists a presentation of their show in New York. Thus, the company, full of enthusiasm, prepared the premiere for the following season on Broadway. Unfortunately, they did not know that Schubert had ulterior motives when he engaged the show for performance.

He had to open the theater for at least one night and engage it for a show in order to lower his fire insurance. Therefore, the revue had only one performance on October 26, 1940, and it was never shown again.[3] Although some of the critics considered the revue "amateurish" (Brooks Atkinson), they all pointed out the contribution of Alex North, praising especially his song 'Tis of Thee as a rousing first-act finale.

In 1941 Alex worked on two other revues organized by American Youth Theatre. You Can't Sleep Here was a group project staged by David Pressman and musically directed by Lou Cooper. The musical numbers were composed by Alex and eight other composers, among whom were Earl Robinson, Lou Cooper, Al Moss, George Kleinsinger and Lewis Allan. Anna Sokolow was in charge of the choreography. The revue was first presented at the Barbizon-Plaza Concert Hall on April 26, 1941, and was followed by several other performances in April and May 1941. Several months later, on October 25, 1941, at the Malin Studios, the same theater group presented another musical revue entitled Of V We Sing. It consisted of about twenty numbers—skits, songs and dances. Alex provided four numbers for this revue, Rhumba, Tom, Dick and Harry, Five Gallon Hat, and Juke Box. The most successful was Juke Box, a song composed with lyrics by Alfred Hayes. In general, these revues were entertainment shows which contained many different numbers of variable quality. However, for Alex they presented a possibility to gain more experience as a stage composer, as well as to meet many young artists with whom he could share his love for collective arts.

Alex continued to compose dance music in the Forties. In 1941 he wrote a dance piece for Hanya Holm and her dance company. The piece was entitled The Golden Fleece, and it was first performed at the Mansfield Theatre, on March 17, 1941. Hanya Holm imagined this dance as "an alchemistic fantasy" in a surrealistic manner. While John Martin wrote that the music Alex had written "takes the work at its face value and though it contains some effective passages, especially in the closing section, it provides no such fillip for the interest as the desecration of some mossy masterpiece might have done,"[4] Louis Biancolli described Alex's music as "an accolade for snug appropriateness."[5]

In 1942 Alex collaborated with two other dancers, Marthe Krueger and Truda Kaschmann. He composed three dance pieces (Prelude, Will-O'-Wisp, and Trineke) for the joint recital of Marthe Krueger and Atty Van Den Berg which took place at the Barbizon-Plaza Concert Hall on January 26, 1942. Krueger also invited Alex to teach at her newly opened School of Dance in Ridgefield, Connecticut.[6] Alex's next dance project was more demanding. In May 1942 he was asked to compose music for the ballet Clay Ritual by Truda Kaschmann as a part of the program "Elements of Magic" presented by the Friends of the Arts in Wartime at the Avery Memorial in Hartford. Reviewing this event, Marian Murray wrote that Alex's music "is exciting and admirably suited to the theme, building up dramatic climaxes emphasized by effective use of percussion."[7]

In the early Forties, besides writing music for various stage productions, Alex explored different genres of vocal music. In 1940 he wrote a cantata, Negro Mother, with text by Langston Hughes. Elie Siegmeister wrote the following of this cantata: "He [Alex] evolved a style in which popular and serious elements are so completely fused that there is no longer any question of 'how to bring jazz and classical music together.' Here they are in one single American music. In the slow, easy melody with which *Mother* opens, there is syncopation and the Charleston rhythm; but also a serious beauty and dignity never known to Tin Pin Alley. *Mother*, with its direct, effortless melodic and its structural simplicity — a simplicity enriched by all the resources of modern harmony when needed — is definitely music of the American people…"[8] Despite these qualities, the cantata was performed only once — at the American-Soviet Music Society choral and folk music concert.

One of the most successful works by Alex from this period was the musical for children*The Hither and Thither of Danny Dither*. The production of this musical comedy was described as a new type of musical play, a form toward which both Broadway and Hollywood had been heading more and more at that time. Unlike the average play, music and dance were used almost throughout the entire work. *Danny Dither*, based on the book and lyrics by Jeremy Gury, in its first version was organized into three acts consisting of three to four scenes. Composed in 1941, the musical had its premiere at the Avery in Hartford on June 4, 1943. This first performance was directed by Ann Randal with choreography by Anna Sokolow. The musical was again presented in 1949 by the Young People Theatre at the Master Institute of United Arts in New York, and later in Los Angeles in 1953. The musical, with its blend of fantasy and social satire, gained plaudits from the critics. "Its warm lyricism, its atmosphere of human sympathy, the love and joy that exudes from this music … stamp Alex North as one of the inevitable composers of tomorrow," wrote Elie Siegmeister.[9]

In 1941 and 1942, Alex collaborated with the poet Alfred Kreymborg on several choral patriotic ballads. Among them, the choral songs *There's a Nation* and *The Ballad of Valley Forge* became widely popular during the war years. They were produced and broadcast on the Treasury Star Parade programs. In 1943, *The Ballad of Valley Forge* had its first public performance in a concert in Town Hall in New York. Later, it was also performed on a CBS coast-to-coast broadcast.

Sherle and Alex got married in December 1941, hoping that by this Alex would avoid being drafted in the Army. They moved into a small, two and a half room apartment on Riverside Drive. Sherle North described their new home, "The apartment house was facing the river, but I took the cheapest apartment on the first floor in the back of the house. The back side of the house was facing 99th Street which started to go up a very steep hill, so that our apartment was like in a basement. It was very nice, but a dark apartment."[10] One month after they got married Sherle found out she was pregnant. Soon after the birth of his first son Steven, Alex was drafted into the Army.

Alex spent the first two years in the Army as a private, generally stationed at Camp Robinson and Camp White. He was a music director of the Army's 23rd Regiment Chorus with which he prepared musical programs performed at the service clubs or at the camps' outposts. Before he left for the Army, Alex expressed in patriotic spirit some of his ideas about songs and music generally for the *Hartford Times*. "We, song-writers, should make use of our own culture, particularly folk music and jazz. We must lose our highbrow attitude toward jazz, take what is good in it and put it to work writing American music as vital, democratic and dynamic as our land."[11] However, Alex did not compose much during the first three years in the

ANN RANDALL

presents

"DANNY DITHER"

A NEW MUSICAL COMEDY

Music by Alex North   *Book & Lyrics by Jeremy Gury*
Directed by Ann Randall   *Choreography by Anna Sokolow*

ACT I.   Scene 1. IN HEAVEN
          Scene 2. THE BIG CITY
          Scene 3. THE SAME, NEXT MORNING

INTERMISSION

ACT II.   Scene 1. IMMIGRATION OFFICE
          Scene 2. THE RADIO STATION
          Scene 3. INSTITUTION FOR RESTITUTION
                 OF DESTITUTION

INTERMISSION

ACT III. Scene 1. DANNY'S DREAM
          Scene 2. THE WATERFRONT
          Scene 3. IN LIMBO
          Scene 4. THE WATERFRONT

THE CAST
In Order of Appearance:

Danny Dither   Arnold Goldman
Miss Charity   Julia Farley
Miss Faith   Ebba Melrose
Miss Hope   Elmina Brooks
Mr. Judkins   Murray Gitlin
Lucifer L. Lucas   John McNulty
Shoppers, Pedestrians, etc.:
    Rose Lischner, Ethel LeVan, Olga
    Dzurich, Sue Sage, Edith Whitman,
    Ruth Grauert, Harriet Schuman,
    Muriel Horwitz, Elaine Benewitz,
    Lorna Drago, Arline Momm, Mona
    Richman, Sandra Cohen, Analie
    Gelman, Deena Farber.
Droopy   Carl Roberts
The Duke   Francis Healy
The Prosperous Woman   Rose Lischner
Daisy   Dorothy Alden
O'Shaughnessey   Dick Iacino
Organ Grinder   Harry Gold
Two Little Girls
    Gail Andersen and Toni Sussman
Josey   Betty Levine
Shoeshine Boy   Bobby Schwartz
Toby   Tovia Mancoll
City Brats
    Isadora Mancoll, Naomi Goldman,
    Jacqueline Graff, Ann Marie Shan-
    non, Irma Goldman, Ann Frances
    Dunbar

Immigration Chief   George Malcolm Smith
His Secretary   Elaine Benewitz
Baseball Announcer   Dick McCarthy
Reporters
    Nora Breshnan, Dick McCarthy
Sponsors
    Arnold Goldstein, Harry Gold
Announcer   Bob Steele
Sound Man   Wilbur Randall
Penpushers
    Sandra Cohen, Olga Dzurich,
    Mona Richman, Muriel Horwitz,
    Lorna Drago, Deena Farber.
Stevedores
    Buzz Ralston, Bud West, George
    Blumenthal.
The Fish   Dick McCarthy
A Little Devil   Stephen Randall

· · · · · ·

ASS'T TO THE DIRECTOR   Nora Breshnan
MUSIC Beatrice MacLaughlin Smith, assisted
    by Helen Waterman. *Trumpeter,*
    Billy Nemeroff.
SCENERY Designed by Irving Katzenstein,
    constructed by Arthur J. Gross.
COSTUMES   Dorothy Segal
LIGHTING   Maurice Jaffer
PRODUCTION STAFF..Teddy Sussman, Arline
    Baum, Doris Gelman, Michael
    Adrian, Clifford Purinton, Althea
    Greenwald, Esther Troub, Arnie
    Kupper, Forest Norton.

AT THE AVERY, HARTFORD, JUNE 4 and 5, 1943

Concert program from the premiere of *The Hither and Thither of Danny Dither*, June 4, 1943.

Army. He would occasionally put together a musical show, as he did for the Army Air Base in Charleston in 1944. The show was called *Blow Your Top* and engaged a large cast of about sixty people. There were dancers, singers, actors who performed accompanied by the orchestra of the Army. The show was very successful and brought popularity to Alex among his fellows in the Army.

Alex was very surprised when he was offered officer training at the Ft. Washington School in Maryland. He accepted the offer and by the end of his service in the Army he had been promoted to the rank of captain. After becoming an officer, Alex was in charge of self-entertainment programs in general hospitals throughout the country. He had to devise certain programs that would activate those soldiers who were sent back from the battle with traumatic experiences or psychotic illness. The programs usually included sketches, puppet shows, music and theater activities. Alex managed a group of people who were writing specific sketches for these individuals to help them recover from their particular self-centered traumatic experiences.[12] During this period Alex worked closely with the psychiatrist Dr. Karl Menninger on the development of these therapeutic activities, so called "psycho-dramas." They were later accepted and used as common techniques in group therapies for the mentally ill in general. Although this job was not an easy one, especially because it dealt with psychologically unstable individuals, Alex was happy knowing that he would help many patients to overcome their mental problems. Sometimes it was hard to deal with the patients. Alex was once attacked by a patient who had a phobia against the military brass. He confused Alex with an officer who had given him a rough time.[13]

Alex was musically engaged more seriously in 1945, when he was offered to score documentaries for

North in the Army, May 1943.

the Office of War Information (OWI). His credits already included music for several documentaries, such as *Heart of Spain*, *China Strikes Back*, and the *People of the Cumberland*. He had collaborated with the Department of Agriculture on two documentary films, *Venezuela* and *Recreation* (1939), and with Willard Pictures on the documentary *Rural Nurse* (1940). He had also composed music for the State

Department documentary film *City Pastorale*. Some sources indicate that Alex was assigned by the Office of War Information to compose scores for over twenty-five documentary films. This number of films might not be factually reliable as there is not a complete list of the films' titles. What is known for a fact is that two of these films generated much interest at that time. Both films were produced in 1945, and directed by Alexander Hackenschmied. The first one, *The Library of Congress*, dealt with the extent and purpose of this institution, while the second one, *A Better Tomorrow*, reviewed the public school system in New York. The latter was even a runner-up for the Academy Award.

In May 1946 Alex took a leave of absence from the Army in order to compose music for a historical pageant entitled *Song of Our City — a Saga of Detroit*. It was a spectacular musical and dramatic tribute to Detroit's 150 years under the American flag commemorated during the Golden Jubilee of the automobile industry. The musical was based on a story by Karl Hoffenberg, and produced and directed by Jess Kimmel. This musical brought another collaboration between Alex and Anna Sokolow, who was in charge of the choreography. Shortly after this engagement, in August 1946, Alex was discharged from the Army.

The last months of 1946 were very prolific for Alex. He was commissioned to write two compositions which were important for the further development of his career. On the recommendation of Virgil Thomson, Alex was commissioned by the *New York Herald Tribune* to compose a cantata based on a poem by Millard Lampell for the annual Herald Tribune Forum. The Forum theme was "The Struggle for Justice as a World Force." The cantata, called *Morning Star*, was based on the Nuremberg trials. The first performance was given by the Lyn Murray Singers and Robert Montgomery as a narrator at the opening of the forum on October 28, 1946. This work, as well as the other cantata, *Negro Mother*, which was performed in March the following year, reflect Alex's commitment to subjects dealing with social justice — an important issue in which Alex was interested throughout his entire life. *Morning Star* was performed again in May 1947 by the C. I. O Chorus at Town Hall. In the review of this concert, the critic of the *New York Herald Tribune* described North's cantata as an official American style for works of patriotic sentiment or social content. He wrote that "North's own grasp of the idiom is respectable and workman-like enough...," but at the end of the review he added that "*Morning Star* suffers from episodic conception...," and that "it is like so many works that are adequate to a given occasion and to communicate a given message, but have not the inner spark to survive beyond this occasion."[14]

The other commission for Alex came from the clarinetist Benny Goodman, who wanted to include new works on his program for a concert with Leonard Bernstein and the New York City Symphony Orchestra, planned for November 1946. There is a story which tells that when Benny Goodman asked Alex to write a clarinet concerto for him and Lennie Bernstein, Alex requested a fee of twelve hundred dollars. Goodman responded, "I gave Bartók two hundred dollars to write *Contrasts* and you ask for twelve hundred dollars!" Finally Alex was paid a check of only two hundred dollars, which he saved for good luck.[15] The *Revue for Clarinet and Orchestra* received an outstanding response and a standing ovation on its premiere on November 18, 1946, at the City Center. The critical acclaim was also remarkable. The *Revue* has three short movements: *Colloquy*, a Gershwinesque lively dialogue between clarinet and orchestra, *Lyric*, a quiet, atmospheric blues-flavored slow movement, and *Specialty*, a virtuoso jazz-oriented rhythmic finale. The critic of the *New York Times* wrote, "While he uses jazz idiom, he has assimilated it in a style that is flexible and quietly assured. His writing for the instrument is felicitous, with orchestral color neatly emphasizing and contrasting solo clarinet."[16] Another reviewer added, "Ably exploiting the mechanical and expressive possibilities of the clarinet, it provides its sponsor with a happy vehicle for his extraordinary virtuosity and interpretive skill."[17] After this success it was very strange that this piece was never performed again. According to Sherle North, Alex claimed that the entire music scene at that time was controlled by homosexual composers, who helped each other get performances. Alex blamed them for it. On the other hand, Sherle noticed that Alex never pushed himself to become a part of that scene.[18] But, Alex just did not have that kind of self-assertive and aggressive personality. The only thing he really wanted was to compose music.

By the end of the Forties Alex had completed several more concert pieces. In 1945 he worked on a piece for chamber orchestra, called *Holiday Set*, which was marked by "easy, unself-conscious use of Gershwinesque jazz idiom."[19] Although never performed in public, this work was recorded for S. P. A. Records in 1954 by the Vienna Philharmonic Orchestra under the direction of Charles Adler. The record was entitled *American Life*, and included several other works by George Antheil, Frederic Jacobi, Henry Cowell and Elie Siegmeister. Another intriguing composition from that period was *Three Pieces for Chamber Orchestra*, which was performed on January 23, 1950, at Times Hall by the New York Chamber Orchestra conducted by Hershey Kay. This piece, rich in orchestral colors, and rhythmic, melodic and textural sensations, gained the attention of several New York critics. Clyde praised North as a deft creator of orchestral effects, but described the piece as merely atmospheric rather than fully communicative.

Although a pianist, Alex devoted only one cycle of short preludes to piano, composed over a period of several years. The complete cycle includes twelve preludes. Seven of these preludes, entitled *Little Dance Preludes*, were performed on September 21, 1947, in Town Hall in New York by pianist Joan Slessinger. Upon this occasion the reviewer of the *New York Sun* wrote, " Despite the title, the spirit of the dance — as exemplified by a folk quality at least — did not play much of a part. The composer's treatment is intellectual, which does not preclude interesting and effective writing for the instrument. Most of the sketches had a moody, somewhat dissonant, intense flow, and the final one had a very brilliant build-up that should make it popular among subsequent recitalists."[20]

Alex found the writing of compositions for children very rewarding, especially after the success of *The Hither and Thither of Danny Dither*. After he completed and recorded the fantasy *Yank and Christopher Columbus* in 1943, he wrote another orchestral work for children entitled *Little Indian Drum*. Its premiere was on October 18, 1947 at the Town Hall concert for children under nine. Commenting on this concert, the critic of the *New York Herald Tribune* described North's composition as "a quaint pictorial work, replete with all sorts of virtuoso orchestral effects, yet constructed along the simplest rhythmic and melodic lines."[21]

Alex and Sherle established a very artistic and creative atmosphere in their small

PM, WEDNESDAY, NOVEMBER 20, 1946

BENNY GOODMAN (left) will be soloist with the New York City Symphony on Monday and Tuesday evenings at City Center when Leonard Bernstein (center) conducts the world-premiere of Revue for Clarinet and Orchestra by Alex North (right). North's piece will be one of three by veterans to be introduced on the program. The others are *Ode to the Milky Way* by Vladimir Dukelsky and *Box Hill* Overture by John Lessard.

(Left to right) Benny Goodman, Leonard Bernstein and Alex North, 1946.

New York apartment. Steven remembered that there were always musicians, artists, people that would come and stay around until odd hours of the night, as well as through the night. They worked on show tunes, or sang and amused themselves. One of Alex's closest friends was the composer Henry Brant, who would later become one of the best orchestrators of some of Alex's Hollywood film scores. Steven also remembered his father writing music and composing tunes late at night, a habit that Alex kept throughout his entire life.[22] The period of the late Forties was career-wise very difficult for Alex. Working on so many different projects, Alex felt torn between writing concert music that would bring him the status of a "serious" composer, and creating functional music

BENNY GOODMAN
654 MADISON AVENUE
NEW YORK 21, N.Y.

RHinelander 4-1715

September 24th, 1946

Mr. Alex North
265 Riverside Drive
New York City, New York

Dear Alex:

I received both copies of the "REVUE". I'm hard at work.

I do think that Harry would like to publish the score, so let me know if this can wait until I return, about the latter part of October.

Everything is going along well here, and I am looking forward to seeing you.

Best regards,

Benny

BG:bb

Letter from Benny Goodman to Alex North, September 24, 1946.

which was bringing more commercial and financial success. This dilemma bothered Alex for many years.

However, despite the effective presentation of the concert pieces in the late Forties, Alex achieved the *real* success as a Broadway theater composer. In the early months of 1947, he composed scores for two plays produced by the Experimental Theatre of the American National Theatre and Academy. The first one was the postwar story *O'Daniel* by Glendon Swarthout and John Savacool, presented on February 23, and the second one was the musical play *The Great Campaign* by Arnold Sundgaard, performed on March 30, both at the Princess Theatre. The latter received much better reviews. *The Great Campaign* was a political satiric play with surrealistic elements, and contained several musical and dance numbers. Here Alex collaborated once more with Anna Sokolow, and their contribution was noticed and

Programs from the plays *The Great Campaign* and *O'Daniel*, 1947.

emphasized by all of the critics. Brooks Atkinson praised Alex's "lively prairie music" as being "jubilant,"[23] Louis Kronenberger described it as "agreeable enough music,"[24] and Otis Guernsey wrote that "the show was embellished with music by Alex North."[25]

In 1947 Alex's hard work was rewarded. He received a Guggenheim Fellowship and decided to write his first symphony. The fellowship was twenty-five hundred dollars, which he thought was a large sum of money. Exhausted from the tense life style in New York, Alex wanted to compose peacefully somewhere else. Since he had never been to the West Coast, he chose to visit California. Thus, Sherle drove him, Steven and their French poodle Bonnie to California, where they rented a little house in the San Fernando Valley. During his stay in California Alex was offered the chance to write music for a C film for Eagle Lion, which he turned down as he felt happy in New York, doing his documentaries and serious music, and working with ballet and theater.[26] The peaceful period in California, however, was not meant to last long. After three months, in the middle of his work, Alex got a call from the Broadway producer Kermit Bloomgarden, who asked Alex to come back and work with Elia Kazan's wife, Molly Day Thatcher, on a musical, titled *Queen of Sheba*. Alex could not refuse such an opportunity, so he immediately flew back to New York, leaving Sherle and Steven to drive back by themselves. The symphony had to be finished later.

Alex started to work with Molly and spent much time in Kazan's house in the country, in Sandy Hook, Connecticut. Elia and Alex met just casually when they worked on the documentary *People of the Cumberland*, so this was the first time that they really spent some time together. Kazan became more familiar with Alex's music, and he liked it. They actually became very close friends. Sherle pointed out that Elia was Alex's first real friend — Alex and he spent much time together socially, going fishing, and picnicking with their families.[27]

Alex finished the music for *Queen of Sheba*, but for some reason the show never opened. Nevertheless, this experience was very important for Alex. In the summer of 1948 Elia Kazan was preparing with Arthur Miller the production of *Death of a Salesman*. He wanted Alex to compose the incidental music for the play. Thus Alex was introduced to Miller. Arthur Miller remembered the beginning of their collaboration. "It was Kazan's idea to put Alex on *Death of a Salesman* project. It was a brilliant idea," said Miller. "I met Alex in Kazan's house in Manhattan where we were preparing the production of the play. At our first meeting he played some music of *Death of a Salesman* on the piano. I was very touched by that. It was very moving music. It was the first time in my experience that I heard of a symphonic approach to the theater. In other words, each of the main characters had a theme as they would in a symphony. And those themes were combined, they were fugal, all kinds of forms created around those themes. I don't think we changed very much of what he first initiated."[28] Miller found in Alex a wonderful collaborator. "There were times when we didn't want any music, and of course Alex overwrote the music, he wrote too much," remembered Miller. "He understood that probably some of that music wouldn't be used. He was enormously receptive to both the play and to what I thought it required."[29]

North's score was inventive in many ways. He believed that theater music should reveal phases of a character not present in the literal words and situations on stage. He also used music as emotional counterpoint to the action. "I was anxious to write a music for Willy emphasizing the human values which lay beneath his surface behavior," pointed out Alex.[30] In the written version of the play Miller considered the use of a flute to stress certain emotional states. In the stage version, Alex decided to use four instruments — alto flute, cello, trumpet, and clarinet with occasional change to alto clarinet. The instrumental ensemble and the duration of the score were partially determined by the regulations of the Musicians Union. The theater productions could not use more than four musicians or have music for more than twenty-four minutes, without their expenses greatly increasing. The music was not taped, but played live for every performance. North applied a new stage sound technique. He required the musicians to perform from an off-stage room of the theater, so called "padded cell," located way up at the top of the stage. Since they could not see the scene, the musicians had a red flash light in the room, which the assistant manager would turn on when they were supposed to start playing, and turn off when they had to stop. The music was transmitted through a microphone to the speakers in the theater with the volume controlled behind the stage. The musicians unfortunately never had a chance to see the play. However, they had the advantage of coming casually dressed, talking during the show, and even playing cards between their musical performances.

The play was first performed on February 10, 1949, at Morosco Theater. It had enormous success. Alex's music received national critical acclaim. The critics praised his beautiful score, the novel instrumentation, and his stage technique. The reviewer Barbara Strong wrote, "The collaboration of these three men [Kazan, Miller and North], resulting in so perfect an achievement, is perhaps the actual beginning of a new era in the theatre."[31] She also wrote that "this is the music written, not as the primary aspect of drama, as in opera, nor as an accompaniment, as is movie sound-track music, but as an integral part of the drama itself."[32] Arthur Miller had the same opinion. "You can't separate the music from the play, or the play from that music," he said.[33] Appreciating Alex's contribution, Miller wrote on his copy of the *Salesman* the following words: "To Alex North and all his blessed flutes and clarinets that turned our Willy's dream into music. My Thanks, Arthur Miller."

After this great success, the doors of Alex's international career were suddenly widely opened. His collaboration with Kazan continued with *A Streetcar Named Desire*, which brought Alex into the film world of Hollywood, he arranged the *Salesman* symphonic suite for concert performance by the Philadelphia Symphony Orchestra, Miller used Alex's music in the Chinese and the Swedish productions of the *Salesman*, and later Alex adapted the score for the film and the television versions of the play. Alex kept in touch with Arthur Miller throughout the coming years. "I always felt warmly toward Alex," commented Miller. "He was music, he was only a musician. It was all that really, truly interested him all the time."[34]

Before Alex started his Hollywood career, he composed incidental music for the play *The Innocents*, based on Henry James' story *The Turn of the Screw*. The premiere was at the Playhouse on February 1, 1950. For this occasion Alex also employed a very interesting instrumental ensemble consisting of a Novachord, English horn, oboe, flute, bassoon, and various percussion instruments (vibraphone, temple blocks, xylophone, and timpani). Alex's approach toward the scoring of this play was described in the article by Barbara Strong. "Mr. North feels that in *The Innocents* it is advisable to reflect, not the mood or tension of the actor at a particular moment. He wants, instead, to portray their basic traits of character. Thus the theme of the governess, the major character in the play, is a simple musical study of the line between normal and abnormal and an endeavor to show the only slight margin between the two."[35] The critic Brooks Atkinson praised North's compositional skills. *The Innocents* in a way concluded Alex's New York career. Soon afterwards, Alex was offered a new challenge — to compose music for films. He was ready to enter into a whole new world of Hollywood's moving illusions.

4

Welcome to Hollywood: The Fifties

I feel that whatever gifts I possess have to do with the
function of theater. Adding that other dimension to the
film or to a play or to a dance that isn't there visually, in a
sense, just enhances the drama of a film, establishes the
character or goes beneath the character, and that's not
easy to do. The audience may not grasp it, but you, as the
creator or as the composer, you know yourself what
you're saying.

— *Alex North*[1]

While working on the play *Death of a Salesman,* North did not have an idea that
his collaboration and friendship with its director, Elia Kazan, would drastically determine the direction of his career and change his life forever. In the early Fifties Kazan
was a renowned and respected name in the Hollywood film world. He was known as
a self-assured director with a strong will to have things done his own way. In the
Fifties he introduced several musical talents to the Hollywood film industry.[2] North
was one of them. Pleased with North's innovative score for *Death of a Salesman,* and
assured of the quality of the compositional work of his new friend, Kazan offered
North two projects, the scoring of *A Streetcar Named Desire* and *Viva Zapata.* According to North, *Zapata* was the film he was contracted to do first, but *Streetcar* preceded it.[3] Thus, in 1950, North was on his way to California, where he started the
work on his first big film for Warner Brothers, *A Streetcar Named Desire.*

However, despite a promising career as a film composer, Alex could not decide
immediately to move permanently to California. He was a genuine New Yorker who
loved the spirit of the East Coast. He had already established his connections with

the artistic world in New York, his career was set and his name well known. He dreamed of being a Broadway theater composer and of writing serious concert pieces, and New York was the right place for his plans. Furthermore, he had a family that needed a home. His son Steven was just nine at that time, and in 1951 his daughter Elissa came into the world. They moved into a bigger, more spacious apartment on West End Avenue in New York, where he finally had a separate room in which he could work and compose. After the small, dark apartment on Riverside Drive where they had lived all those years, this seemed "a palace."[4] They also bought a house in Ridgefield, Connecticut, where they spent their weekends. On the other hand, North found Hollywood to be "a closed shop" in terms of new composers, or composers coming from the East.[5] The film studios wanted to include known and proved film composers in their projects, and they were rarely or almost never willing to give a newcomer a chance. In the beginning, North had a difficult time being accepted in Hollywood. "Kazan had quite a problem to persuade those in power to have me do the score for *Streetcar*," he recalled.[6] North was aware that if it had not been for Kazan who insisted on having him as the composer for *Streetcar*, he would probably not have been in Hollywood.[7] North was often regarded as a "groundbreaker" in the film music of Hollywood. But North himself thought that his film scoring came as a natural continuation of his previous work. "I started in New York scoring many documentary films, had done a lot of ballet and theatre plus was in the Army for four years working myself up to a captain, so I never came out to Hollywood to be a 'groundbreaker,'" he pointed out. "I only did what I became accustomed to doing all those years."[8] Thus, when North was asked to send out to Hollywood the scores that he had previously composed for the documentary films, he had an impressive amount of work to submit. The scores were evaluated by Alfred Newman and Ray Heindorf who were heads of the music departments at 20th Century-Fox and Warner Brothers.[9] After North had been given his first big assignment in Hollywood, to score *A Streetcar Named Desire*, his life became constant traveling from the East Cost to the West Cost and back. "I ran back and forth to New York for five years in the Fifties," he recalled. "In those days I especially missed the stimulus of the East Coast, the people. In New York I'd go to Broadway late at night to take a walk. In Beverly Hills I got stopped twice by cops when I was out buying a paper."[10] Whenever Alex and his family came to Los Angeles they rented a house. Alex would do the film, and afterwards they would return to New York.

Alex was very happy to first work with Ray Heindorf at Warner Brothers, who conducted the score for *A Streetcar Named Desire*. "He was a marvelous, innate musician," remembered Alex. "He made me feel very much at home in Hollywood, as opposed to other composers and studio music heads who felt I was some guy coming from some attic in New York suddenly doing major films. I did feel very much out of place. The only one besides Heindorf who befriended me was Hugo Fried-hofer."[11] He used to say, "Thank God, Alex, that you've come out, 'cause now we can do perhaps some of the things we've been wanting to do for a long time."[12] When North started doing films for 20th Century–Fox, Alfred Newman also made him feel welcome. He reviewed the scores with Alex, supported his ideas, gave him suggestions and advice about film scoring, conducted some of his scores, and helped Alex in terms of being accepted into the mainstream of Hollywood film music.

The music for *A Streetcar Named Desire* had a big impact on the film music in Hollywood, and brought Alex North an immediate success and recognition. The musical score for *Streetcar* was revolutionary in many ways, especially with its musical style, thematic treatment, and orchestration (the score is analyzed in detail in Chapter Seven). Besides the prevailing jazz idiom, North did not fear to apply striking dissonances which usually resulted from the linear, contrapuntal orchestral movement. "I believe strongly in tension and relaxation in functional music," North explained. "Because of this you may find strident string chords over an innocent melody to punctuate an emotional response—or brass figures interspersing a melodic line to convey the ambivalent nature of human behavior."[13]

Although the score for *Streetcar* was North's first big introduction to the Hollywood film world, it was immediately nominated for an Academy Award. He did not win, but that was not as important as the fact

Letter from Elia Kazan to Alex North, 1951.

that he was accepted as a peer, and his nominated work was found "in company" with the scores composed by Newman, Waxman and Rózsa. After the film score was finished, North used the music from *Streetcar* for a symphonic suite in ten sections. In this revised form, the score was ready for concert presentation and for soundtrack recording. Later, he reworked the score and used it for a ballet whose premiere was at Her Majesty's Theatre in Montreal, Canada, on October 9, 1952. The New York premiere was shown at the Century Theatre on December 8, 1952. The ballet score was orchestrated by Rayburn Wright, the choreography was by Valerie Bettis, and it was staged by the Mia Slavenska and Frederic Franklin ballet company.

The film premiere of *A Streetcar Named Desire* was delayed until the fall of 1951. In the meantime North was already engaged to score his first film for 20th Century–Fox. It was *The Thirteenth Letter*, a mystery drama produced and directed by

Otto Preminger. It happened that this film was released before *Streetcar*, in January 1951. For Alex this was a chance to meet and to work closely with Alfred Newman. Newman was probably the most powerful music director in the history of the Hollywood studio system. As the head of the music department at 20th Century–Fox for twenty years (1940–1960) he helped and promoted many young composers. It seems that North developed a closer relationship with Newman than with Preminger whom he encountered only once.[14] Filmed in Quebec, Canada, *The Thirteenth Letter* deals with the difficulties and the fear engendered in a provincial town by a series of poison-pen letters. Among the threatened members of the community is the lovely young Denise (Linda Darnell) whose musical characterization is probably the most successful part of North's score for this film. In many of his future film scores North provided the female main characters with distinguished musical themes. North often discussed with Newman the problems in the scoring process. For instance, in *The Thirteenth Letter* there was a scene where a demagogic mayor gives an anxious speech at a funeral, which North underscored with a piece of a rather satiric character. He remembered Newman saying, "You cannot score a funeral scene in this style. I don't care what you think about the mayor. The mayor is a … a fool, but this is a funeral."[15] It was the only time, as far as North could remember, that he had to rewrite something. "I realized that in the context of the whole score, the mayor meant nothing, he was just a subsidiary character in the whole story, so why expose this character," commented North. "It was not important [or] in keeping with the whole story. And that is a part of film scoring, getting to the roots of the story, the basic conflict that is in the picture, and not scoring a scene because it happened to appeal to *me* to do it in that manner."[16]

That year, 1951, was a very prolific one for North. Besides *Streetcar* and *The Thirteenth Letter* he composed two more film scores in this year, *Viva Zapata* and *Death of a Salesman*. The score for *Viva Zapata* was completed in October 1951, and the *Salesman* score was finished one month later. However, *Death of a Salesman* was released in December 1951, while *Viva Zapata* was premiered later, in February 1952. Kazan had thought of North as a composer for *Viva Zapata* even before *Streetcar* appeared as a possible project. In fact, Kazan included North's name in every contract that he signed with the Hollywood studios in the early Fifties.[17] Kazan wrote to North in 1951, "Don't take yourself too cheaply. You are in the first rank of composers for films now, and everybody *good* will want you to do their pictures. Everybody crumby will too—but you shouldn't ever." Unfortunately, *Viva Zapata* was the last project that Kazan and North worked on together.

Viva Zapata was an appropriate and a fortunate project for North. Produced by 20th Century-Fox, the film was based on the script by John Steinbeck. It was a story about the Mexican revolutionary hero Emiliano Zapata, starring Marlon Brando. There was probably not any composer who would approach a period of Mexican history better and more authentically than Alex North. His extensive knowledge and understanding of Mexican music, due to his stay in Mexico and study with Silvestre Revueltas in 1939, proved here more than useful. During the year spent in Mexico North had an opportunity to get a good feel of this country and its people whom he loved. He was also very fortunate to be hired by Kazan from the very beginning of the production. "He [Kazan] and I often wandered around our Mexican locations together, going from village to village," remembered North. "I would jot down little tunes I heard peasants humming or singing. This really was a luxury, this is ideal for a composer because you can work directly with the director and get to know exactly how he feels about the story. It doesn't happen very often."[18] In the book about *Viva Zapata*, Steinbeck wrote, "Alex North's score is integral; instead of drenching the film with the usual overblown symphonic score of the 1950s, North had much of his music function as a natural part of the action — as religious chants, mariachi bands, serenades, military parades — all in indigenous Mexican modes."[19]

However, besides the presence of authentic Mexican flavor, North's score possessed a notable personal approach in its musical concept. This was

Alex North in his early forties, portrait. Photograph by Marthe Krueger.

the first time that North had to deal in his film scoring with a subject matter echoing the universal theme about a reluctant hero who responds to injustice in the name of the people. Therefore, the score is characterized by a more objective type of writing. It utilizes an extended orchestra with liberal use of percussions that provide the "epic" qualities of the music. However, as Lan Adomian pointed out, this was an ideal blending of the individual or subjective and epic or objective approaches. "North's sensitivity to individual drama did not make this another 'epic' score. The composer found many opportunities to let the music complete a dramatic situation."[20] Thus, there are simple harmonized folk tunes used to create a more personal ambience. Such scenes are, for instance, the one between Zapata and his wife, Josefa, where oboe d'amore brings a folk melody in Mexican style over strumming sounds of guitars, mandolins and marimbas, or the scene where a flute solo, introducing an Indian death chant in Aolian mode, accompanies the death of a peasant in the nearby cornfield. These musical moments act opposite to the collective scenes and are often accompanied by frantic orchestral sequences which skillfully integrate indigenous instruments, highly rhythmic movements with displaced accents, and modal musical language.

An especially effective scene in terms of musical conception is the one entitled "The Gathering of the Forces" (also known as "Peasants' Telegraph" sequence), which North often mentioned as one of his favorite scenes that he scored for films. As he explained in the interview with David Raksin, this is a scene in which the "rurales," the government forces, are about to hang Zapata. The peasants are very concerned. The whole musical sequence is inspired by the physical action when one of the peasants starts a signal by knocking little stones against each other, passing the word (like a primitive telegraph) that Zapata has been captured. The peasants gather slowly and join the clapping sound. As the clapping rises in volume it is accented by a measured beat of timbales and bongos. The orchestra gradually joins the beat with flutes, guitars, plucked strings, and thematically develops a piece in a style of a Mexican bolero. The music rises in volume, "demanding" the liberation of Zapata. The "rurales" are surrounded and intimidated by the peasants, and compelled to free Zapata, who joins his people. North found it unique that Kazan insisted on having music carry this scene instead of sound effects.[21] North's original musical concept gained much recognition, and his score was nominated for an Academy Award for 1952, but it lost to Dimitri Tiomkin's for *High Noon*.

The collaboration with Arthur Miller and Elia Kazan on the play *Death of a Salesman* was a unique experience for North. He felt very fortunate to be included in the project from the very beginning which allowed him to profoundly discuss the contribution of the music with the writer and the director. This type of extended collaboration is very rare in films. When Stanley Kramer decided to produce the film version of the play for Columbia Pictures, Alex North was hired to do the music for it. Since North's music for the play had had such an enormous success, it seemed logical that he was assigned to extend this score for the screen. For North this was a special opportunity to learn how to balance the different musical requirements in the play and in the film. A composer seldom has a chance to write music for both, the stage play and its film version. The chamber score for the play, initially written for four instruments (flute, clarinet, trumpet, and cello) had to be extended into a full orchestral score enriched with strings and other instruments. Unlike the score for the play which had to be adjusted to the live performance of the actors in the theater (what North used to call an "expandable" or "collapsible" score), the film score had to be strict and precise in terms of timing and placement.[22] North was thoroughly familiar with the play and the tragic character of its main hero, Willy Loman, who was a victim of the delusion of the American Dream. "This particular play had a very personal appeal to myself as opposed to *A Streetcar Named Desire*," said North. "It was much easier to identify with the characters in *Death of a Salesman* than in *Streetcar*."[23] North decided to use the opening alto flute solo from the theater score as the opening music theme for the film as well, because it perfectly portrayed the tragic character of Willy Loman. This type of musical opening was without precedent in Hollywood film scoring which favored bombastic symphonic main titles. The score was generally influenced by jazz and blues with orchestrally developed musical sequences for the film version, as for instance the final suicidal "Death Ride" of Willy

Loman. The film version, directed by Laslo Benedek and starring Fredric March, unfortunately did not appeal at all to the creator of the play, Arthur Miller. "I disliked the film so much. The problem with the film was very simple. The director and the screen writer, and probably the producing company, they had no sensitivity to what the material really was," remembered Miller.[24] "It was the hermetic concept of Willy that defeated it [the film], I think; it made him simply a mental case, and I felt at the time — the early 1950s — that this convenient distortion grew out of a political fear of indicting American society, something that would have been dangerous in those years."[25] Nevertheless, the film score for *Death of a Salesman* brought Alex North the second nomination for the Academy Award for 1951, an incredible success for the composer who had "just arrived" in Hollywood.

The first year in Hollywood was a very successful one for North. He finished four film scores, and three of them were nominated for an Academy Award. North was recognized as a talented composer who had new ideas regarding film composition, and who was daring enough to apply them whenever there was an opportunity for it. In the period between 1952 and 1955 he was hired to do five more films, mostly dramatic adaptations. In 1952, 20th Century–Fox engaged Alex to score two films, *Les Misérables*, a historical drama based upon the novel by Victor Hugo, and *Pony Soldier*, a western based on the original story by Garnett Weston. 20th Century–Fox often produced films which dealt with different periods in the history of various foreign countries. In the case of *Les Misérables* it was the French Revolution in Paris. North approached this film with a musical concept based on French music of the 18th century. The first characteristic lyrical motif in the score appears when the voice of the narrator recites, "sometimes a dog is born in a pack of wolves, and the mother destroys it right away." This lyrical motif is further developed into a theme of Cosette. There is also a very subtle musical characterization of the main protagonist, Jean Valjean. The stages in the life of Jean Valjean are separated with dramatic musical sequences.[26] In 1954, 20th Century–Fox offered North another film to score based on a subject from French history. This time it was a historical romance *Desirée*, which illustrated the love story between Napoleon (Marlon Brando) and his mistress Desirée (Jean Simmons). The film score was melodically rich, and it was musically more focused on the intimate, "domestic" scenes, than on the scenes of action. North worked closely on this project with Alfred Newman who had written the love theme for the score. North was naturally expected to vary this theme whenever Napoleon and Desirée had a confrontation. But, according to North, the romance was not as important to him as the defeat of Napoleon as a man. Therefore, at the end of the picture, for the scene when Napoleon is exiled to Elba and he is all alone, North decided to write a piece for two muted trumpets and percussion. Refusing to comply with the principles of the old fashioned, conventional film scoring, North commented, "I just couldn't conceive of doing a lush, thematic variation of a theme which was again a romantic theme. That was not the key to the conflict. It was the inner man, the man himself."[27]

Among the films from this period, *The Member of the Wedding* (1952) was personally the most appealing project for North. Directed by Fred Zinnemann and produced by Stanley Kramer for Columbia, this film was based on the novel and the play by Carson McCullers and dealt with the emotional and mental turmoils of a twelve-year-old girl, Frankie (Julie Harris), entering a troubled adolescence. As with most of the stories by Carson McCullers, this one is located in the South, which enabled North to use his "jazzy-bluesy" musical approach. "This film was a lovely, wonderful change and get away from the epic style of writing for *Zapata*," remembered North. "It was a joy to get onto something as light, and fragmentary, and delicate as this story was."[28] Although the film did not have much impact at the time, North found the work on this film a delightful experience. The musical sequence "Jody's Lament," which accompanies the scene when the Negro cook (Ethel Waters) speaks about her dead lover, was one of North's favorite musical pieces that he composed for films.[29] North came up again with a new jazz score in 1954. It was composed for a sports drama *Go, Man, Go,* released by United Artists. The film was about the famous basketball team the Harlem Globetrotters. The reviewers praised North's score as "topnotch, emphasizing a rhythmic jazz mood that fits the Globetrotter personality. This is particularly noticeable in his treatment of 'Sweat Georgia Brown' whenever the stars are clowning."[30]

Upon his arrival in Hollywood, North had his first experience in the television medium. He pioneered "live" TV music performance on the *Billy Rose Show*. Television music performed "live" was in its birth stage at that time. As composer-conductor North had an unusual and not an easy task. He had to watch the score to cue the musicians and the screen of a monitor set to watch the action; he had to listen to the dialogue through one earphone and the director's camera directions through a second earphone; he had a stopwatch for timing. In 1953, North conducted "live" the music for Medallion Theater's TV presentation of *Time for Heroes*. After this type of experience North found that scoring a Broadway play could be the easiest of the three mediums (film, TV, and theater) to work in for a musician, because "you usually get a script well in advance of rehearsals and you work right along with all parties involved as the creation is prepared for the public."[31]

Even though North wrote some memorable musical pieces for the films in the period between 1952 and 1955, neither the films nor their music reached the popularity of *Streetcar* or *Zapata*. In this period North continued to travel from New York to Los Angeles whenever he had to work on a certain film project. It was interesting that despite the numerous engagements to compose scores for films produced by various film studios, he never signed a long-term contract with any of these studios. He preferred to keep his creative independence and freedom, and to stay a free-lance composer. He always thought that if he stayed independent he would have more chances to work in different fields—theater, ballet, and concert music. His son Steven commented later upon this matter. "He was asked various times in his life to join 20th Century–Fox, to join CBS at one time. He wasn't a joiner. I don't think he was member of a club, or a political party in his entire life. I think he voted republican, democratic or Communist depending on who the candidate was. He never signed a contract with a studio, nor with anybody else. He kept his independence."[32] According to Steven, Alex always wanted to be based in New York; he never really wanted to come to California or to move to California. He felt much more at home in New York, and he was always looking forward to getting back.[33] Arthur Miller also remembered North being very conflicted about going to California, especially because of the dominating tendency in Hollywood to make a composer anonymous. North knew that. He also feared the commercialization of his work. "He just wanted to compose music; he didn't want to compose music for any particular story," commented Miller. "He would rather feel free. Or so he thought. Maybe his real talent was doing just what he did. But, I know that he kept saying, 'I am sick and tired of it out here. I just want to write music, or I want to work in a theater.' Of course, there was no theater anymore for him to work in. After the Fifties plays didn't need any music. The main plays were by Becket, Ionesco etc., and these had no place for music."[34] In fact, North wrote his last musical scores for theater in the early Fifties. It was for the plays *Richard III* directed by Margaret Webster, premiered at New York City Center on December 9, 1953, and *Coriolanus*, directed by John Houseman, and first performed in Phoenix on January 19, 1954.

However, as much as North wanted to compose concert music, his experiences with the performances of his concert works were disappointing. "I sent my first symphony to various conductors and learned you get one performance if you get any," remembered North.[35] From his point of view, securing performances was the greatest problem for the contemporary composer. Even if the composition had a first performance by a major symphony, it might never get the even more important second, and third performances. This is probably one of the reasons that North decided to get more and more involved with functional music. He was aware that in most cases the music in films had a subsidiary role, but on the other hand, he also knew that his music was going to be performed by competent musicians and heard by millions. Composing for films also offered great opportunities to experiment with all kinds of orchestral colors and unusual and rare instruments, which is evident in many of North's film scores. Therefore, it was very hard for North to decide to settle down in California for good. Torn between his dreams and the reality he kept traveling back and forth for a whole five years.

One should not forget that the early Fifties were also politically very difficult for those working in the performing arts. These were the years of the Cold War, and of Senator Joseph McCarthy. The House Committee on Un-American Activities guided a thorough investigation of the infiltration of Communist ideas and propaganda in American artistic and intellectual circles. This was one of the darkest periods for progressive minds in American history. Artistic and intellectual freedom was threatened, and people were called to testify and "name" friends and colleagues who had been connected with the Communistic movement or showed sympathies for the Communistic ideas through their work. The fear was escalating as more names of artists and intellectuals were added to the "blacklist." North had reasons to be afraid that he could be called to testify. He had sympathies for the socialist movement, he studied in the Soviet Union, he performed in his youth for various working organizations, he was a member of the American-Soviet Music Society, and he was even a member of the Union of Soviet Composers! According to Sherle North, early in his life Alex was for a while a member of the Communist Party, and his political ideas were greatly influenced by his brother Joseph, whom Alex idolized.[36] However, Alex was never politically active, and his primary connection with the socialist ideas was through Joseph North, who was the editor of the Communist magazine *New Masses*. Although left-oriented, Alex was, above all, a humanist. Thus, one of the reasons that North kept traveling was to avoid the possibility of being called before HUAC.

"He would go to Hollywood to do a movie, and then come back to his house in Connecticut. He really avoided the committee," remembered his brother Harry.[37] Even though North was never blacklisted, at one point there was a rumor that the committee had issued a subpoena for him to testify. This was a hard period for the Norths. Sherle and Alex decided to move temporarily with the children to their house in Connecticut. Their property was in the woods, and they could see if anybody unwanted was coming. "I kept looking out the window," remembered Sherle North, "and if anybody strange appeared, I'd put Alex in the basement of the house to hide him. They never got him, but we were afraid."[38]

Like many other artists and intellectuals, North was very unhappy with the political situation in the country. But the biggest disappointment for him came in 1952, when he learned that his friend Elia Kazan had testified in front of the committee. North was shocked. Sherle North said that Kazan never let them know he was going to do that, never gave them any feeling that he was. It was very strange because they were very close, like family. One day they bought the *Sunday Times*, and that is how they found out that Kazan had testified before the committee as a "friendly witness."[39] Being a member of the Communist Party in the early Thirties, Kazan was accused of alleged Communist leanings himself, so he named the people who were involved with the Communist Party, some of them his best friends. Even though he never named North, this was the end of their relationship. "We were like brothers until he went to the committee, and got a lot of my dear friends into trouble. That's my stand, right or wrong. It was a tough period politically, and I don't know how close we are to going back to it."[40] North never spoke to Kazan after this incident.

In the mid Fifties, after years of constant moving and traveling, North's family was exhausted. They needed a permanent home. It was especially hard for the children to keep moving. Steven changed nine schools within a couple of years. North became a sought-after figure in Hollywood, and it was obvious that he was going to continue his career as a film composer. Therefore, they decided to move to California. Sherle North took the responsibility of finding a good house for them. She was lucky to make an incredible deal for a spacious, beautiful house in Bel Air, located at the corner of Beverly Glen and St. Pierre Drive. The house was built by Al Jolson, and it was an unbelievable buy. In September 1955, the Norths moved into their new home.

Soon after they moved in, Sherle and Alex developed a vivacious social life. The parties and the evenings at the Norths' home were always fun to attend. Alex enjoyed life as much as he did working. He enjoyed his friends, and he felt at his best when he was surrounded by a few of them. He would play his music on the piano, and talk about past times in Russia and New York, about politics, and about life in general. He was a terrific tennis player, and a wonderful cook. Alex was remembered as a unique, lovable, dear, caring, and a charming man. Although Alex was never seen in a rage in public, the dark side of his character would sometimes come out in the late hours of the night, usually after much drinking. Then, he would call producers, directors, and critics with whom he disagreed about certain issues, and become belligerent. Sherle North commented that with these incidents Alex made enemies of many people who had been very fond of him and his work. However, in most cases Alex succeeded in getting over these incidents. Many people who knew Alex pointed out that he actually never "went Hollywood." As much as his house was open to his friends, he did not want to go out to parties and socialize with the Hollywood crowd.[41] Composer David Amram said, "He was stronger than Hollywood. It was really a joy knowing someone who could spend his life working in that environment and never lose the beautifulness (*sic*) as a person and the gift as an artist. He transcended the decadence, narcissism, greed and bad taste of Hollywood, and left us with something beautiful and artistic that will endure."[42]

The year 1955 started with the music for the prison drama *Unchained*. The song from this film, "Unchained Melody," with the lyrics by Hy Zaret, became one of the most popular hits of the day. In the film, Todd Duncan sang the song with a cigar in his mouth. But, when the film itself was long for-

Sherle North (1917–2002).

gotten, this song continued its life, on its own, and to this day it has been one of the top twenty songs in four different decades. It has been recorded in numerous times by many singers, including Elvis Presley, Roy Hamilton, Al Hibbler, Dionne Warwick, Willie Nelson, the Righteous Brothers and others. Most recently, Maurice Jarre used the song in the film *Ghost*. After this great success North commented, "It's ironic. After years of study, you write one twenty-four bar tune that hits and suddenly the money starts rolling in."[43]

Unchained was followed by a film about European automobile racing, entitled *The Racers*. This film, starring Kirk Douglas and Bella Darvi, was produced by 20th Century–Fox and directed by Henry Hathaway. Besides a couple of interesting musical sequences ("Montecarlo" and "Black Jack"), North came up with another attractive song, "I Belong to You," in the film sung by Peggy Lee. The score was orchestrated by Edward Powell, with whom North already had collaborated on the score for *Pony Soldier*.

After *The Racers* North worked on another project for 20th Century–Fox. It was the musical *Daddy Long Legs*, released in May 1955, for which North provided ballet music. The dancing sequences were performed by Fred Astaire and Leslie Caron. This was one of North's favorite projects from this period because he was able to write the music in advance without the restrictions that conventional film scoring usually imposed.[44] Also, ballet music was one of his preferred fields of musical expression. The ballet sequences were conceived as a three-part fantasy dance, entitled *Paris—*

LISA WEINSTEIN

July 2, 1990

Mr. Alex North
630 Paseo Miramar
Pacific Palisades, CA

Dear Alex,

First, let me reintroduce myself, I am Hannah's middle daughter. Secondly and guiltily I live up the road and have been for a couple of years. I've been a little shy about just knocking on your door which is why you haven't heard from me before.

About a year ago, I was driving in my car listening to an oldies station on the radio when I heard the Righteous Brothers recording of "Unchained Melody". I was in pre-production on a film called GHOST for Paramount and I thought your song would be perfect for the film. The film is now completed and "Unchained Melody" is the most sublime music we have.

I am having a screening of GHOST on Monday, July 9th at 7:30 p.m. in the Gower Theater at Paramount. I would be thrilled if you could come. If not, the movie opens on July 13th.

Warm regards,

Lise

(left) Alex North with Lisa Weinstein, the producer of *Ghost*. (right) Letter from Lisa Weinstein, July 2, 1990.

Hong Kong — Rio. These dances were staged by the famous French choreographer Roland Petit, and performed solo by Leslie Caron. North's ballet music won international critical acclaim and the Downbeat Magazine Music Award.

Some of the films that North scored in this period were of passing interest, as for instance the western *Man with the Gun* (1955) with Robert Mitchum and Angie Dickinson. But, once in a while, North would be offered a project which would allow him to express his best qualities and potentials as a composer. Such was the case with *The Rose Tattoo*, a film adaptation of Tennessee Williams' play, directed by Daniel Mann for Columbia Pictures. Alex North seemed to be the most appropriate composer for this sensual drama, because he was already known for his superb scores for literary adaptations and his special capacity of scoring intimate stories. This film brought an Academy Award to Anna Magnani for her magnificent performance of a Sicilian-American widow, torn between the feelings and memories of her late husband who was killed in a tragic accident, and a new romance with her clownish neighbor — a truck driver who eventually becomes her suitor (Burt Lancaster). In the role of Serafina, Magnani showed a wide range of emotions which allowed North to approach the score with humor, lightness and pathos, and musically to say what he had to say.[45] The film score was greatly influenced by Italian folk music, but since the story was set in the South, North composed several musical sequences in jazz

The director Daniel Mann (left) with Alex North.

style. North explained his musical approach in the article published in 1955 in the magazine *Film Music.* "In general the score is divided into three categories: folk, jazz and abstract (or absolute) music. I discovered after extensive research that the Sicilian folk music is far richer and more varied than the Neapolitan folk tunes because of its Moorish, North African influence, and I found a tune which I treat in various scenes in accordance with the dramatic values of the scene. In the "Main Title" it is started in its pure form, more or less, with use of contralto solo voice and children's choir so that it has directness and purity like the love Magnani has for her husband. As the story develops it is stated now and then within the texture of the abstract score to point up the disillusionment and torment of Magnani regarding her husband's fidelity, etc."[46] The "Main Title" song is an original folk tune, "Song of the Wagoners," in which Marilyn Horne, then a gifted teenager, hummed the main theme. North further explained in his notes that he used four mandolins and four guitars extensively because of the Sicilian characters involved. "The first part of the score is stated mostly in the folk idiom, more or less as a prologue," continued North. "I established jazz in the scene *Clown* in which the two prostitutes come to Magnani's home.

At the musical rehearsal of MGM's *I'll Cry Tomorrow*, 1955. (left to right): Johnny Green, Alex North and Harry Lujewski.

This jazz motif is also indicated in various scenes where there is some implication of sex."[47] The chamber treatment of the musical score with combinations of small instrumental groups enhanced the intimate atmosphere of the entire picture. Besides a couple of original folk songs, the remaining material in the score was a "simulation of the Italian music,"[48] or purely abstract music which mostly served to "highlight the two main musical streams"[49] — Sicilian folk music and American jazz. This score was one of North's most evocative and delightful works from this period. *The Rose Tattoo* was nominated for eight Academy Awards, including its musical score, but it won Oscars only for the best actress and the black-and-white cinematography.

The Rose Tattoo was the beginning of North's prolific collaboration with the director Daniel Mann. They worked together on six projects. Their second film followed immediately after *The Rose Tattoo*. It was the film *I'll Cry Tomorrow* (1955), based upon the biography of the actress Lillian Roth, starring Susan Hayward. The truthful story about the actress who indulged herself into alcoholism was based on her own bestselling book. Dealing with the dark side of the character of this passionate, successful actress, this film allowed North to sweep again into the field of jazz. It seemed that for North jazz was always an appropriate and a convenient way to musically express passionate emotions, self-destructive tendencies, sexual undercurrents, smoky night ambiences, and the melancholy of melodramatic situations.

In 1956 North had a chance to experiment with various types of film scoring because he was hired to work on four pictures, very different in their genres and musical requirements. His first experience with the genre of horror drama was through the score for *The Bad Seed*, based on the novel by William March and the play by Maxwell Anderson. This suspenseful and dramatic film is a tragic story about the eight-year-old girl whose psychopathic need to commit murders is disguised by her sweet, innocent look of an adorable little child. For North, it meant a possibility to apply the principles of variation technique to a French children's tune "Au Clair de la Lune." Heard as a simple and innocent melody while the girl practices her piano, this tune is transformed through a wide range of orchestral variations, from a lullaby enriched with the sounds of a children's choir ("My Baby Sleep Well"), to tense, ghastly orchestral sequences with harsh dissonant string and brass figures ("At It Again" on the soundtrack). Several sequences feature the motifs of the main tune "running" through different instrumental groups.

The next picture, *The Rainmaker*, was quite a different project for North. Unlike the previous film, this one is a light-hearted, romantic tale about a simple, quite ordinary spinster, Lizzie (Katharine Hepburn), who is seduced by the amusing con-man Starbuck (Burt Lancaster). He comes to a small town in the Southwest claiming that he can bring rain for the "thirsty" land. During his stay Sturbuck develops a romantic relationship with Lizzie, convincing her that she is a gorgeous, loving woman. With this new self-confidence, Lizzie's behavior alters and her view on life changes forever. The film is an adaptation of a play by Robert Nash. North approached the scoring of this film as a musical explaining that "the over-all film score was to suggest and develop thematic ideas that could apply to a stage production."[50] There are many musical moments in the film that have the "feel" of a song form, or could be developed into such a form. In the journal *Film and TV Music* North wrote, "Because of the robustness of the characterizations, I tried to evolve music with a definitive American flavor, without being hillbilly as such. Also the texture of the instrumentation had to be transparent and not thick and overpowering, except for rare moments of high emotional tension."[51] North achieved the contrast between the realistic world and the world of fantasy created by Starbuck with the deviation from a diatonic to a chromatic type of writing. An example of such is the sequence entitled "Golden Fleece." It uses a slow chromatic waltz theme to accompany the scene in which Starbuck gives Lizzie the name Melisande and transports her into the imaginative, romantic world of the queen who sailed over the ocean to bring back the Golden Fleece. North and Hepburn were nominated for Academy Awards for their achievements in *The Rainmaker*, but none of them won. North's approach was proven right and valuable when *The Rainmaker* was reworked later as a Broadway musical under the title *101 in the Shade*, but with the music by another composer (Harvey Schmidt).

The scoring of the following film, *Four Girls in Town*, was an unusual project for North. He was asked to compose the music before the film was finished which was an exception from the usual routine in film scoring. Thus, North decided to compose a piece for piano, trumpet and orchestra entitled *Rhapsody for Four Girls in Town*. It was a contemporary, jazz-oriented composition in three movements, written for an extended orchestra. Mark Evans described this work as "a stunning jazz piece ... with a breezy jazz opening for piano and snapping, dissonant brass chords, a lyrical middle section in ballad style, and a recapitulation."[52] After its recording (with André Previn playing piano and Ray Linn playing solo trumpet), the rhapsody was adapted to match the needs of the film dramaturgy. It seems, however, that the quality of the film score was above the quality of the film itself, whose story about the talent hunt for a new movie set was seen as "an excuse to showcase the talents of some of Universal's contracted talent."[53]

From 1956 to 1958 North did not get much work done in Hollywood. The reason for that might have been the lack of offers for attractive film projects, but it could also have been a consequence of the political turmoil after the peak of the McCarthy era. After the scoring of the western *A King and Four Queens* (1956) with "the king" of the film business, Clark Gable, North worked on one more film — *The Bachelor Party* (1957). It was based on the screenplay by Paddy Chayevsky, originally written for television, and it was "a little picture about little people,"[54] a group of bookkeepers in New York who decide to toss a bachelor party for their colleague. North tried to provide the film with realistic musical expression, utilizing modern rhythms and harmonies derived from jazz.

After this quiet period, in 1958 North was "back in business" when he was offered the chance to write music for several new film projects. The most tempting proposal came from 20th Century–Fox. It was a film adaptation of William Faulkner's novel *The Hamlet* which contained four principal sections (books). Although the film title, *The Long Hot Summer*, was borrowed from the third book of the novel, the material for the film was drown mostly from the other three sections of the novel. The film adaptation, which brought some changes in the relationships among the characters in Faulkner's work, was concentrated on the main protagonist, Ben Quick (Paul Newman), and his relationships with the members of the Varner family. Ben Quick is an appealing character, an outsider who quickly makes himself a part of the powerful and rich family of Will Varner (Orson Welles), and develops an intense relationship with his sensible and intelligent daughter Clara (Joanne Woodward). Facing again a film subject associated with the passionate American South, North wrote a jazz-oriented score which alternated between luscious lyricism and tense, dissonant jazz figures. The score for *The Long Hot Summer* was the only one of North's Southern scores that had a title song in the beginning of the film. The lyrics for this song were written by Sammy Cahn, and it was sung by Jimmie Rodgers. Commenting on the title song Ross Care wrote, "With its sophisticated, jazz-tinged harmonies and innovative structure (extended and freely treated *a a b a* form, e.g.), this title tune seems closer to Broadway than Hollywood, and suggests North could have been a wonderful songwriter had his inclinations led him in that direction."[55] Most of the lyrical sequences in the film score, especially those that underscore the relation between Ben Quick and Clara Varner, derived from the title song. This type of musical approach resulted in a delicate and subtle film score, though not as dramatically extended as, for instance, the score for *A Streetcar Named Desire*. After this experience North had an opportunity to score two more film adaptations of Faulkner's literary works, *The Sound and the Fury* (1959) and *Sanctuary* (1961). During the work on *The Long Hot Summer* North developed a warm relationship with Tony Franciosa (Varner's son Jody in the picture), which grew into a close and long-term friendship during the following years.

North was always delighted when he had an opportunity to write music independently, without the stress imposed by time restrictions, deadlines, and specific musical requirements. Therefore, he was thrilled when he was asked to write ballet for the 1958 World Fair in Brussels, Belgium. The ballet was entitled *Le Mal du Siècle* (*Souvenirs for Another Generation*, its English title), and it was performed by the International Ballet De Marquis De Cuevas. North conducted the premiere himself. The successful performance of this ballet brought international acclaim to North, who later commented, "For me success is not necessarily achievement. It's a certain need to fulfill myself. I felt like a new person — no deadlines, and I was writing solely for my own satisfaction."[56]

After several months spent in France with his family, North returned to the United States and continued his work on various film projects. He worked again with the director Daniel Mann on the film *Hot Spell* which was "a heavy, deep South drama that feels as though it was conceived by Tennessee Williams but written by someone else."[57] Since the story was set in New Orleans and dealt with the problematic relationships of a dysfunctional family, it was not strange that North turned again toward jazz as source of his musical expression. However, the film did not have much success at the time. Another film released in 1958 was *Stage Struck*, directed by Sidney Lumet. It was a story about a young girl from a small town (Susan Strasberg) who becomes a famous Broadway actress with the help of a successful producer (Henry Fonda). This film was a remake of an older movie, *Morning Glory*, based on a play by Zoe Akins. North approached this old story about the dreams and struggle for fame in a light Broadway style, using a full orchestra with the strings as a leading instrumental group.

One of the most demanding projects for North in 1958 was the scoring of Cinerama's wide-screen travelogue *South Seas Adventure*. This travel documentary, which hardly had any plot, included visits of a young, just married couple to the Hawaiian Islands, Polynesian Islands, New Zealand, and Australia. The rather descriptive nature of the film required an extensive musical accompaniment, ranging from source music with authentic folk elements and "mood music" of the Fifties to highly imaginative music cues for a large chorus and a ninety-seven-piece orchestra enriched with exotic ethnic percussions. In the review of the reissued soundtrack, Ross Care wrote that *South Seas Adventure* "might even be seen as the lush scherzo of the great quartet of big symphonic scores—*Spartacus*, *Cleopatra*, and *Cheyenne Autumn*... that North produced during this period."[58] North returned once more to this type of film scoring in 1967 when he composed an extended symphonic score for the television documentary *Africa*—"a crown" of North's work in the field of documentary films.

By the end of the decade North had scored two more films—*The Sound and the Fury* and *The Wonderful Country*, both released in 1959. *The Sound and the Fury* was for North the second excursion into the Southern world of Faulkner's novels, as it was for the director Martin Ritt who had also directed *The Long Hot Summer*. However, despite the previous experience with the adaptation of Faulkner's work, Ritt

North at the recording session of *South Seas Adventure* (Cinerama, 1958). Behind North stands Norman Luboff who was in charge of choral works.

felt that *The Sound and the Fury* was not as successful artistically as *The Long Hot Summer* which he thought was "a good entertaining commercial film."[59] Truly, the individual episodes from Faulkner's novel *The Hamlet* were well brought together in the film *The Long Hot Summer*, resulting in an interesting comedy-drama. On the other hand, the idea of *The Sound and the Fury*, one of Faulkner's darkest novels, was essentially changed by providing the film with a happy ending. The novel is a tragedy of two women, Caddy, an alcoholic nymphomaniac ruined by a sinful life, and her illegitimate, abandoned daughter Quentin. In the film, Caddy (Margaret Leighton) is granted a redemption by returning home to her family, while Quentin (Joanne Woodward) and her step-uncle, Jason (Yul Brynner), eventually get into an obsessive love relationship, thus adding a romantic dimension to the story. In the analysis of the film adaptation, Gene Phillips pointed out that Faulkner "must have judged the picture to be a dilution of one of his darkest, most uncompromising works."[60] Nevertheless, North composed a very effective and an extensive film score which distinctively complemented the film story. His music here was much more dramatically involved in the film dramaturgy than it was in *The Long Hot Summer*. This score summarizes the qualities of North's previous Southern jazz scores characterized by sparse orchestration, dissonant accents in the intense, forceful jazz passages, and warm lyricism of widely developed, sensible melodies.

The "Main Title" theme is described by Darby and Du Bois as "genuinely lyrical and tender ... and one of North's most appealing melodies."[61] The theme that characterized the main heroine, Quentin, became one of the big hit songs of the Fifties, and it was performed by many jazz orchestras of the time. The score for *The Sound and the Fury*, with its emphasized lyricism and jazz punctuations, presented in many ways a logical progression of the musical principles that North introduced in the score for *Streetcar*.

The last film score of the decade for North was *The Wonderful Country*, called by the reviewers "a Mexican western." The plot of this excellent western was set below the Mexican border which for North meant one more opportunity to use Mexican music as a main source of musical inspiration. This film, directed by Robert Parrish and starring Robert Mitchum, received excellent reviews that praised North's "excellent and atmospheric score." Such reviews were not a surprise, given North's affection for Mexico and his extensive knowledge of Mexican music.

The decade of the Fifties was an enormously prolific period for North. Over these ten years he composed music for twenty-five Hollywood movies, and he was six times nominated for an Academy Award. He became an expert at scoring films which were adaptations of literary works, plays and novels, including those by Tennessee Williams, Arthur Miller, Carson McCullers, Victor Hugo, Lillian Roth, William March, and William Faulkner. But, North also developed his versatility as a film composer by writing music for different film genres, ranging from mystery (*The Thirteenth Letter*) and western (*Pony Soldier, The Man with the Gun, A King and Four Queens, The Wonderful Country*), history (*Viva Zapata!, Desirée*), to horror drama (*The Bad Seed*), comedy (*The Rainmaker*), musical (*Daddy Long Legs*), and travelogue (*South Seas Adventure*). However, coming from a theater background, North always preferred to compose film scores for intimate dramas based on intense relationships and deep emotional conflicts between the characters. Among these works there is a special place for his "Southern" film scores in which he used jazz as an appropriate type of musical expression (*A Streetcar Named Desire, The Member of the Wedding, The Rose Tattoo, The Long Hot Summer, The Sound and the Fury* among others). North not only pioneered the use of jazz in Hollywood film scoring, but he also applied it consistently whenever the subject and the atmosphere of the films needed or allowed such an approach. North's jazz scores, whose stylistic roots may be found in New Orleans jazz and the style of Duke Ellington, featured jazz not just as a "rhythmic" and an "atmospheric" component of the films' actions, but as a vital element of the film dramaturgy in the characterization and the emotional realization of the protagonists. Besides the use of jazz, North's scores of the Fifties featured a variety of compositional approaches depending on the film genre and subject. He became accustomed to evoke the folk music of different countries (Mexico in *Viva Zapata* and *The Wonderful Country*, Italy in *The Rose Tattoo*, France in *Les Misérables*, etc.), and to absorb their musical idioms to the point of producing original scores in the required style.

Most of North's basic principles of film scoring were already formed by the end of the Fifties. It is evident that in this period North preferred composing chamber scores versus extended scores for huge orchestras. The orchestration was rather sparse with an apprehensive and careful underscoring of dialogs. It favored the wind instruments over the strings and there was a notable move toward the individualization of the instruments. North always related to the film script as a source of musical ideas and a guide for good musical pacing. He learned how to balance tension versus relaxation, and dramatic versus lyric in film scoring. North deeply cared about the musical unity of the film score. Therefore, he always tried to apply themes that would be recognized throughout the film, whether he used versions of the leitmotif technique or principles of variation. His musical language was basically tonal, but he did not hesitate to incorporate tense and harsh dissonances in his regular musical expression, as opposed to his wide lyrical melodies, which were often marked by an "innocent" triadic profile. His lyrical talent was recognized and further developed in many of his unforgettable, introspective and heartbreaking love themes.

5

The Decade of the
Big Epics: The Sixties

Movie music, like stage music, has to be functional. People argue that the only good screen music is music the audience is not conscious of hearing. I don't agree. Music has a powerful emotional influence and should be part of the whole film. After all, music is to be listened to, not ignored.

— Alex North[1]

After ten years of experience in Hollywood, North accepted the fact that his career was ultimately developing in the direction of film composition. He still had dreams of composing symphonies and concert music, but once he became accustomed to the principles and the benefits of the film business, he realized that it was a "one way street" without a way out. In the field of film music, his artistic skills were recognized and his work was highly praised, he was offered work on many good and interesting film projects, he had an opportunity to experiment with all imaginable sounds and sizes of orchestra, his music was heard all over the world as film soundtracks, and ... he was well paid for what he was doing. Of course, there were frustrating moments with which North often had to deal, such as disagreements with the ideas of various directors and producers, the adjustment and "tailoring" of his musical ideas to the films' requirements, composing under time pressure and inflexible deadlines, just to mention a few. However, after years of such experience, North had become deeply involved with film composition, and he could not simply change course and start working in a different field of music. In time, North became so used to working under deadline that he would not compose unless he had an assignment. Working long hours in the night, and sleeping late in the day became an everyday routine for Alex North. Steven North remembered that his father was "a man who was very much into his music, but also, particularly later in his life, he wasn't inspired to write music on his own. He talked a lot about it, as most writers and artists do, but he worked much better under a deadline, and if he had an assignment he was much happier. Long periods of time would go by when he would work only on a suite from one of his scores, or he would work on small things. But, he wasn't a man who was dreaming to sit at his piano when he didn't have an assignment. He enjoyed life as much as he did working."[2] Thus, by the Sixties, composing for films had become North's ultimate field of creative expression.

North's career as a film composer greatly changed when he accepted the offer from Universal to compose music for *Spartacus*, the twelve million dollar gladiator epic. This gigantic project took two years to finish, and after its release in October 1960 it achieved an enormous success. The film was based on historical fact and dealt with a slave rebellion that threatened the domination of the Roman Empire for more than two years. The screenplay was written by Dalton Trumbo, for whom this was the first project after his blacklisting. It was based on a novel by Howard Fast, who had also been blacklisted. This picture brought North back from France, where he had been staying after the Brussels World Fair in 1958, because, in a way, it broke the blacklist in America. Steven North remembered that, together with Fast's and Trumbo's names, this picture was very important for North, both politically and artistically.[3] Kirk Douglas, who was also the executive producer of the film project, gave North thirteen months to prepare the film score, which was probably the longest time that any composer was given to create music for a film. Usually film composers are expected to complete a film score in ten weeks, with three weeks to compose the music, and seven weeks to do the orchestration and make eventual changes. For *Spartacus*, North had the kind of luxury to spend several months just researching the sources of ancient Roman music and studying the script before he composed the music for the film.

The result of North's compositional efforts was an extensive and complex score, which provided music for over two hours of the film. Since Romans mostly used music in such occasions as battles and parades, North consciously insisted on barbaric, brassy and percussive music, with an extensive use of the march form and brass fanfares. The rhythmic element is strongly emphasized. However, despite the overall brassy, heavy musical effect of the score, the music of certain intimate scenes possesses chamber-like qualities. For instance, the scene where Crassus tries to seduce Varinia features musical accompaniment by solo violin, strings, and ondioline. Who can forget the sensuous, expressive love theme of Varinia and Spartacus introduced by the solo oboe? Or the sparse, exotic orchestration of the sequence "Oysters and Snails" when Crassus attempts to seduce his slave, Antoninus? The music of certain scenes has balletic qualities and supports the dynamic of the motion, as, for instance, in the scenes of the gladiators' training. The score is basically united through an elaborated utilization of the leitmotif technique which enhances the sense of the dramatic continuity (see a detailed musical analysis in Chapter Eight).

After the success of the Oscar-nominated score for *Spartacus*, North's wide artistic span and versatility as a film composer was fully proven. He was not any-more regarded only as a master composer of intimate dramas, but also as an excel-lent composer of grandiose epic spectacles. The period of the Sixties was, in general, a decade of the big spectacles in North's career. But, North's credits in the Sixties also included scores composed for several smaller pictures, which brought him further recognition as a composer for intimate dramas, and opened new opportunities for collaboration with various directors. Thus, in the period between *Spartacus* (1960) and *Cleopatra* (1963) North wrote music for four dramas, all dealing with rather depressing subject matters and conflicting, troublesome relationships. In 1961, upon the recommendation of Arthur Miller, North started his collaboration with John Huston on *The Misfits* (see Chapter Nine for a detailed analysis). Being the last film of Clark Gable and Marilyn Monroe, this film has a special place in the history of film. North's score for *The Misfits* is developed as a series of nostalgic, jazzy varia-tions, concluding with a four-movement symphonic cycle for the famous "Roundup" scene. This prolific collaboration continued during the Seventies and the Eighties, in which period North and Huston worked together on four projects: *Wise Blood*, *Under the Volcano*, *Prizzi's Honor*, and *The Dead*.

North composed another jazz-oriented score for a third film adaptation of Faulkner's work. This time it was the tragic film *Sanctuary*, a depressing South-ern story about the tragedy of decadent, sex-driven characters. The film was adapted from two Faulkner books, *Sanctuary* and *Requiem for a Nun*. The other two movies from this period dealt with obscure and problematic relationships between the main protagonists. In *All Fall Down* (1962), it was the heavy rela-tionship between two brothers (Warren Beatty and Brandon de Wilde), and in *The Children's Hour* (1961) it was the relationship between two school teachers (Audrey Hepburn and Shirley MacLaine) who were accused of lesbianism. *The Children's Hour* was based on the play by Lillian Hellman, and directed by William Wyler. For this film North composed a serious, contemporary symphonic score featur-ing some dissonant and pointillistic dramatic passages, as well as lyrical sequences with romantic melodies, usually played by the strings.[4] In general, the composi-tional approach was similar to that in *The Bad Seed*, in that North incorporated a simple American children's song, "Skip to My Lou," as a musical "motto" for the dramatic sections of the score.

Despite North's personal taste for the genre of intimate dramas, he composed music for some of Hollywood's most spectacular epics of all time—*Spartacus*, *Cleopa-tra*, *The Agony and the Ecstasy*, and *The Shoes of the Fisherman*. He found the scor-ing of the big epic picture far more difficult, because he liked to identify with the film's subject and empathize with its characters. In this regard, he always tried to personalize the films as much as possible and to concentrate on the personal rela-tionships between the characters. While he could identify with the subject matters and the characters in such films as *Viva Zapata* and *Spartacus*, it was not nearly as easy for him to identify with the subjects of the other epics that he was assigned to score. Therefore, he developed an "objective" type of writing whenever the films implied such an approach. It meant supplying the dramatic situations with the most authentic and objectively most appropriate musical background without deep per-sonal and emotional involvement. "Spectacles call for writing that is objective in

character. I prefer to be subjective. I like to say something that has something to do with myself personally and mould it, so it fits the content of the film. I write best when I can empathize. When you can't do that, then you have to fall back on technique and write programmatic music. Each picture calls for its own solution."[5]

North had an opportunity to continue his research of the Roman music and instruments while preparing the score for the enormous, forty million dollar historical spectacle *Cleopatra*, produced by 20th Century–Fox. The love duet, Elizabeth Taylor and Richard Burton, starred as Cleopatra and Antony, and Rex Harrison played the role of Julius Caesar. The final version of the film was four hours long, and North provided almost three and a half hours of music for it

North working on the score for *Viva Zapata*, 1951.

("almost enough for a Bruckner symphony" as David Raksin said of this score).[6] The film was completed in 1963 after more than two years of preparation and shooting. North was fortunate, again, to be hired early on in the project. He spent some time in Rome for preliminary research and consultations with the director Joseph Mankiewicz. For this film North also prepared temporary tracks to be used for the timing of this huge spectacle and its dancing scenes.

Trying to approach the scoring of this picture in an objective manner, North composed an innovative score which emphasized the experiments with various orchestral colors and instrumental sounds rather than the emotional side of the story and the characters. The lyrical nucleus of the score is presented by the "Caesar and Cleopatra" love theme which is used as the main romantic theme throughout the picture.[7] However, the love themes in *Cleopatra* do not possess the lyrical power of the love theme in *Spartacus*, for instance. Although the main love theme appears in the principal romantic situations within the film, it is not extensively developed as a dramatic factor throughout the score. Greg Rose found the love music of *Cleopatra* beautiful, but "in the best sense decorative,"[8] and Page Cook, regarding the love themes, noted the lack of "moving and stimulating variations throughout his score."[9] But, one should bear in mind that North wanted to musically emphasize Cleopatra's unrestrained ambition rather than her romantic and emotional concerns. Therefore, one of the most musically powerful sequences in the film is "Cleopatra's Entrance into Rome." "Love, joy, and fear are easy emotions to write music for," North commented. "Ambition is not so easy to interpret musically. I wanted an unromantic, driving theme, so I used pure brass, woodwinds, percussion, no strings at all."[10]

In the score for *Cleopatra* North went even further with the instrumental experiments than in *Spartacus*. He enriched the orchestra with an enormous number of various percussions including sistrum, crotales and small dinner-bells, gamelan, tuned cowbells, five suspended

The saxophone section in *Cleopatra* (20th Century–Fox, 1963). The contrabass soxphone (far right) was used for the first time in a film score.

cymbals (different pitches), five suspended triangles (also different pitches), and five small gongs. In the score there are sequences composed for the whole family of saxophones (sopranino, soprano, alto, tenor, baritone, bass, and contrabass), or four alto flutes. With this rich and exotic instrumentation, the music in *Cleopatra* effectively captures the mystique of ancient Egypt and the power of ancient Rome. Thus, one could say that North's score for *Cleopatra* is more ambient and experimental than dramatic. North was especially satisfied with his collaboration with the director Joseph Mankiewicz, whom he described as "a musically sensitive man."[11] Mankiewicz deemed that North's music contributed enormously to the film. Regarding the scene of Caesar's assassination, which was one of North's personal favorites, Mankiewicz said, "If it has succeeded, much of the credit must go to the vividness and the understanding of Mr. North's musical collaboration. Utilizing the three basic themes of Caesar, Cleopatra and Caesar-Cleopatra he brings all three to a finish as fateful and as terrifying as that of Caesar himself."[12] The director was particularly touched by the musical sequence in the scene of Antony's death, entitled "Grant Me

North after a recording session for Fox's *Cleopatra*, 1963.

an Honorable Way to Die." "I don't think I have ever written or directed a dramatic episode which was so fully realized, enhanced and made more meaningful by musical collaboration," remembered Mankiewicz. "As the muted trumpets scream, in Antony's name for honorable death — they scream an anguish which cannot be written, in a voice no actor can project."[13] In 1963, North's innovative score for *Cleopatra* was rewarded with the first Annual Composers and Lyricists Guild Award, and it was also nominated for an Academy Award.

North spent a whole year working on the score for *Cleopatra*. Writing music for epics required much time from the composer, because it included composing hours of music, as well as extensive research of authentic musical sources. After the two Roman spectacles, North was offered the opportunity to work on a different type of epic project, *Cheyenne Autumn* (1964), the last of John Ford's big westerns. The great director created a powerful and touching chronicle about the exodus of the Indian nation. It was a tragic saga about the migration of three hundred Cheyenne Indians to their old homeland in Wyoming. North found himself emotionally very much touched by this subject. "That's one of the joys of writing functional music, if you can identify with your subject," North explained. "This was especially interesting because it allowed me to study Indian music. It's not a case of using the music *per se*, it's a matter of letting itseep into the recesses of your mind so that when you sit down to write, the subconscious is permeated with the sound and the style of that music."[14] Indeed, North's contribution to the film resulted in a very personal, bitter musical score with a "thick" orchestral texture. There is, in fact, very little simulation of Indian music. The score is mostly developed on the basis of two principal themes — the dramatic, forceful and ominous theme from the "Overture" and the "Main Title" related to the Indians, and the gentle love theme for the Quaker school teacher Debborah (Carroll Baker) and Captain Archer (Richard Widmark). Typical American traditional songs, like "Camptown Races" and "The Yellow Rose of Texas," are used only in the Dodge City sequence which has comical connotations and captures the ambience of the West.[15] However, despite the noble intentions, *Cheyenne Autumn* was not as successful as the two Roman epics. North's score, although interesting and serious, never reached the popularity of *Spartacus* or *Cleopatra*.

Before getting involved with the next big epic project, North wrote a film score for a smaller western picture, *The Outrage* (1964). It was a version of Kurosawa's film *Rashomon*, but not nearly as successful as the latter, despite the direction of Martin Ritt and the acting of Paul Newman in the role of the Mexican bandit Carrasco. The story was set in the 1870s in the Southwest and gave North a chance to compose another score inspired by the folk music of Mexico.

The Agony and the Ecstasy (1965) was North's next big epic project from this period. The score for this film represented the ultimate reflection of North's objective musical approach toward grand, spectacular film subjects, and it was rewarded with an Academy Award nomination. The plot of *The Agony and the Ecstasy*, based upon the novel by Irving Stone, was focused on Michelangelo's (Charlton Heston's) most painful and most glorious artistic experience — the painting of the ceiling of the Sistine Chapel. The film portrayed Michelangelo's personal anguish and inner conflicts in the process of fulfilling this artistic task given by Pope Julius II (Rex Harrison). Although there are some historical moments associated with the Pope leading the Roman troops in battles against the invaders, much of the story is based on the relationship between Michelangelo and the Pope who constantly persuades him to accomplish his work. North approached again the compositional process as a scholar, this time doing research of Renaissance music. The president of Fox studios, Daryl F. Zanuck, invited North to come to Rome and to join him and the director, Carol Reed, in the preliminary discussion about the film concept. North used this opportunity for serious research. In Tony Thomas' book *Film Score: The Art & Craft of Movie Music*, North explained his principal concerns regarding this film. "It was pictorially vast. How can you musically illustrate anything so magnificently illustrative as the ceiling of the Sistine Chapel? I did a lot of research into music of the Renaissance period, particularly Gabrieli. I listened and listened and I arrived at a concept. I decided to stay close to that style and interject my own manner of writing."[16]

North's understanding and absorption of the Renaissance style is particularly evident in the scenes of Michelangelo's intimate communication with Contessina de Medici (Diane Cilento), the most important woman in his life. The musical sequence "Contessina" presents a pair of characteristic period dances, pavanne and galliard, composed for a solo lute, which was the most popular instrument of the Renaissance. Another sequence, "The Medici," is written in a typical Renaissance style for a chamber ensemble featuring flutes, recorder, harp and replicas of authentic string instruments. North's knowledge of Renaissance music and his ability to reproduce it is especially evident in the sequence entitled "Festivity in St. Peter's Square" which is a type of a wind sinfonia with all the characteristic features of the Renaissance instrumental style, such as an alternation of smaller instrumental groups with a *tutti* and contrasts in dynamic and motif-like texture. In the *Tavern* sequence North used a popular secular song, "L'Homme Armé," as ambient music of the period. This song originated in the Middle Ages, but it was one of the most popular *cantus firmi* for the church music of the Renaissance composers, and thus was appropriate for this occasion.[17] North's musical approach is, however, most original and personal in the sequences which deal with Michelangelo's anguish and with the glory of his work, such as "Genesis" and "The Sistine Chapel." In these sequences he used a large orchestra and contemporary orchestral techniques in combination with quasi-Renaissance musical motifs, and thus created masterful and glorious orchestral comment. In this achievement North was assisted by the orchestrator Alexander Courage and Franco Potenza who composed the choral parts of the score.

After the series of grand, epic pictures that North scored in the Sixties, in 1966 he became involved with the entirely different film genre. It was a film adaptation of the famous play by Edward Albee, *Who's Afraid of Virginia Woolf?*, which explored the values and the problems of marriage and the traditional family in modern society. This project was the film directing debut of Mike Nichols, and it brought memorable performances from Elizabeth Taylor (Martha) and Richard Burton (George). In the radio interview with David Raksin, North confessed that, despite his previous rich experience of writing music for film adaptations of theater plays, this was one of the most difficult assignments in his whole career.[18] North's initial problem emanated from the character of the play which was entirely based on intense, brilliant dialog. In theater, such a play with "wall to wall" dialogue would not need any musical accompaniment, whereas the picture, with its interludes, moments of reflection and sections when the actors step outdoors, allows the composer to make some sort of a musical comment.[19] In general, North was always very careful in underscoring dialogues; nonetheless, this assignment was still a challenging one for him. "Because of the amount of dialogue and because I had to write behind the dialogue for most of it, I took a purely subliminal approach," North explained. "That is to say, to try to describe in music the thoughts and motivation of the actors rather than the action."[20] North had certain disagreements with the director, Mike Nichols, in regard to what kind of musical approach would be the best for this film. While Nichols thought that an application of musical themes from Beethoven's String Quartet Op. 132 would be appropriate, North had several completely different ideas.[21] After the consultation with the head of Warner's music department, Ray Heindorf, North even received a personal call from Jack L. Warner who approved any musical approach that North thought was right. "Mike cried over the phone to me when he heard the "Main Title" later, and apologized profusely," North remembered. "When I came back to New York, he invited me to dinner, and to his penthouse."[22] At the end, Nichols was very happy with the score.

At first, North was not sure what kind of compositional approach would be the best for this bitter personal drama of a married couple who verbally torment each other. First, he tried a jazz approach, but soon he abandoned that idea because he was afraid that the jazz accents might interfere with the dialogue and make it unclear. Next, he attempted a serial, twelve-tone approach, but then he felt that it was too abstract for such a personal story. Finally, he decided to compose music which would act as a counterpoint to the action. "The solution came from my own rather romantic concept of the man-woman relationship, and I decided on a quasi-Baroque feeling, one that would play against the picture and suggest that these people basically had something going for them despite the fact that they were haggling and fighting — a common problem in society today," North explained. "The obvious thing to have done was to write 'schrecklich' music (cruel, fierce) to go along with the hysteria and the violent situations, but I thought something rather pure would work. I wanted to get to the soul of these people and suggest they were really meant for each other. Frantic music would have tipped the scales too much in one direction. You have to let the scenes play themselves."[23] Thus, North established an introspective, melancholic and sympathetic musical statement which counterbalanced the tension and agony exposed by the characters on the screen.

The basic theme of the score, written for a solo guitar and a harp accompanied by muted strings, is introduced in the "Prelude" (main title).[24] The beginning three-note mordent is the principal motif, consistently used throughout the score. Darby and Du Bois compared the role of this initial motif to that of an *idée fixe*. The score is actually conceived as a series of character variations, interspersed with several remarkable, independent music cues (such as "Bergin," "Party's Over"). Despite the domination of warm lyricism, the music is occasionally colored with dark and sometimes dissonant sonorities as a comment on the bitter tone of the film (for instance the music cue "Total War"). The score is, in general, one of the finest examples of the use of variation technique in film scoring.[25] The chamber-like orchestration, with its solo guitar, harpsichord, two harps, celesta, strings and a variety of woodwinds, provided a universal dimension to the contemporary subject of the film. Or, as Mark Evans pointed out, "North's baroque style, with its chamber-music delicacy, succeeded in making Albee's characters seem more human and more sympathetic. In a very real sense, his music relaxed the pace of *Who's Afraid of Virginia Woolf?*"[26] The picture received excellent reviews and followed the success of the original theater play. It won five Academy Awards, among others for best actress. North earned again a nomination for best original score. For this score he also received the National Academy of Recording Arts and Science Award nominations for best original score and best instrumental theme.

Ironically, at the time when North worked on *Who's Afraid of Virginia Woolf?* his own marriage was falling apart. The separation did not come suddenly. The problems between Alex and Sherle were building up throughout the years. Their son, Steven, explained his parents relationship from his own point of view. "In terms of the early years they were a very good couple. My mother had been an entertainer, a comedienne, a dancer, and she was very much involved in the theatrical world of New York City. They both were quite bohemian in their own ways, and their early years together were very creative. But, my father was not someone who was driven either for financial success or for fame. He was a very modest man, and he was very happy to live very simply. My mother liked to live less simply, and I think she was very concerned in designing his career. When they did break up, she was very hurt. The split that they had was a very uncomfortable one. It led to much more pain on my mother's side than it did on my father's, since he was the one who wanted out of that marriage. They went through a terribly long lawsuit which continued for a number of years. I don't think they talked to each other from the moment of their divorce until the end of my father's life, which is a long time to be angry. The anger was on both sides."[27]

Sherle's and Alex's life priorities were developing in different directions. When they moved to their house in Bel Air, Sherle used to joke that it was the house of divorces. Al Jolson divorced from Ruby Keeler, William Wyler divorced from Margaret Sullavan...[28] In time, Alex became very busy. He traveled very often, and spent less and less time at home. Especially in the Sixties their relationship became very tense, when they separated and reunited a couple of times. Then, in 1967, Alex went to Munich to work on the ABC television documentary *Africa*, where he met Annemarie Hoellger. She worked for the Symphony Orchestra Graunke in Munich, doing secretarial work, translations, setting up concerts and film recordings. Soon, Alex and Annemarie developed a romantic relationship, which included numerous trips from the United States to Germany and traveling through Europe, until Annemarie finally came to the United States. Alex and Sherle finally divorced in 1970. More than two decades later, remembering those times, Sherle North said, "It was a long time ago. I have not had a life that was not interesting, and I'm grateful for that. The divorce came too late, but it actually was a blessing."[29] That same year, 1970, Annemarie gave birth to Alex's son, Dylan Jesse.

Despite the turmoil in his private life, North continued to work with an immense intensity. By the end of the Sixties he had composed several remarkable works, among them scores for *Africa*, *The Shoes of the Fisherman*, and the unused score for Kubrick's *2001: A Space Odyssey*. One of North's most ambitious achievements from this period was his score for the ABC four-hour TV documentary on Africa. "My unique commission was to write a four-movement symphony and then the producers would lay in the music after the show had been properly put together. In other words, I was able to sit down and write a four-movement work without the crutch of scenes and 'footage' to catch and support," North explained in the interview with Christopher Palmer.[30] He went to New York to look at thousands of feet of the material as they assembled it, and then he spent some time in research of authentic African music in the New York public library. "Finally, after all the study and assimilating of rhythms and instrumental sounds, I decided to write music that would reflect the birth of a new continent with all its turmoil, joys and dramatic upheaval," North said.[31] For this project North had ABC ship over to Munich, where the score was recorded, seventeen thousand dollars worth of traditional percussion instruments. For the recording North used an enormous orchestra of a hundred and eight musicians. The final result of North's compositional efforts was a four-part *Africa Suite* ("Man in Africa"— "The Joyful Days"—"Kilimanjaro"—"Main Title") and a thirty minute long, four-movement symphony, which was actually his second symphony, entitled *Symphony to a New Continent*. The music was very contemporary, unconventional and innovative, and raised to higher level all the trademarks of North's epic orchestral style. Because of the complexity of the project, North had his long-term friend and collaborator Henry Brant help him conduct the score during its recording in Munich. Splitting their time between the recording stage and the control room, North conducted the suite and sections of the symphony, while Brant was responsible for the final recording of the symphony.

North remembered the year of 1968 as one of the most disappointing and frustrating years of his career. The disappointment concerned the score that Stanley Kubrick asked him to compose for the legendary film *2001: A Space Odyssey*. North was very excited about the possibility of working again with Kubrick, whom he respected as one of the most talented and musically sensitive directors. During the work on *Spartacus* they experienced a deep, mutual understanding, and the new project was supposed to be the next step in their further collaboration. After *Who's Afraid of Virginia Woolf?* which was completely based on dialogue, North was looking forward to writing music for a film that contained about twenty-five minutes of dialogue. The music was on its own, without sound effects, which was an ideal situation for the composer. The complex circumstances that surrounded the creation of this film score were best explained by North himself. He commented upon this event on many occasions, but the most detailed "confession" is included in the book *The Making of Kubrick's 2001*, edited by Jerome Agel. Here are the main parts of it:

"I was living in the Chelsea Hotel in New York (where Arthur Clarke was living) and got a phone call from Kubrick from London asking me of my availability to come over and do a score for *2001* ... I flew over to London for two days in early December to discuss music with Kubrick. He was direct and

Alex and Annemarie North, 1986.

honest with me concerning his desire to retain some of the 'temporary' music tracks which he had been using for the past years. I realized that he liked these tracks, but I couldn't accept the idea of composing part of the score interpolated with other composers. I felt I could compose music that had the ingredients and essence of what Kubrick wanted and gave it consistency and homogeneity and [a] contemporary feel. In any case, I returned to London December 24th [1967] to start work for recording on January 1, after having seen and discussed the first hour of film for scoring.

"Kubrick arranged a magnificent apartment for me on the Chelsea Embankment, and furnished me with all the things to make me happy: record player, tape machine, good records etc. I worked day and night to meet the first recording date, but with the stress and strain, I came down with muscle spasms and back trouble. I had to go to the recording in an ambulance, and the man who helped me with the orchestration, Henry Brant, conducted while I was in the control room.

"Kubrick was present, in and out; he was pressured for time as well. He made very good suggestions, musically. I had written two sequences for the opening, and he was definitely favourable to one, which was my favorite as well. So I assumed all was going well.... But somehow I had the hunch that whatever I wrote to supplant

Henry Brant (left) and Alex North in a recording studio.

Strauss' *Zarathustra* would not satisfy Kubrick, even though I used the same structure but brought it up to date in idiom and dramatic punch. Also, how could I compete with Mendelssohn's Scherzo from *Midsummer Night's Dream?* Well, I thought I did pretty damned well in that respect.

"In any case, after having composed and recorded over forty minutes of music in those two weeks, I waited around for the opportunity to look at the balance of the film, spot the music, etc. During that period I was rewriting some of the stuff that I was not completely satisfied with, and Kubrick even suggested over the phone some changes that I could make in the subsequent recording. After eleven tense days of waiting to see more film in order to record in early February, I received word from Kubrick that no more score was necessary, that he was going to use breathing effects for the remainder of the film. It was all very strange, and I thought perhaps I would still be called upon to compose more music; I even suggested to Kubrick that I could do whatever was necessary back in LA at the MGM studios. Nothing happened. I went to a screening in New York, and there were most of the 'temporary' tracks.

"Well, what can I say? It was a great, frustrating experience, and despite the mixed reaction to the music, I think the Victorian approach with mid-European overtones was just not in keeping with the brilliant concept of Clarke and Kubrick."[32]

Despite this unpleasant surprise, Kubrick never apologized to North. Even though North was disappointed and unhappy with such an outcome, he did not bear ill will toward Kubrick. He understood that Kubrick, after having worked for three and a half years on his film, had become convinced that the temporary tracks, which included music by Richard Strauss, Johann Strauss Jr., Ligeti and Khachaturian, could best fulfill his ideas. "He just did in good conscience what he thought was the right move artistically," North said.[33] North's good friend and colleague Jerry Goldsmith, who in 1993 recorded the symphonic *2001* score (unfortunately two years after North's death), thought that this score was never really intended to be in the picture. "It was only there as the backstop in case the rights couldn't be gotten for the classical music recordings. There was never an issue whether the music was appropriate or inappropriate for the film. It was not an aesthetic decision. It was a business decision, a political decision. That doesn't make it any easier to swallow," Goldsmith pointed out.[34]

In any case, North reworked the score for *2001* into a symphonic suite of twelve movements (the suite was later arranged for the recording by Christopher Palmer). After it had been recorded for *Varèse Sarabande*, it drew the attention of many critics and reviewers who highly praised North's outstanding score, and even considered it far superior to the original soundtrack.[35] This great orchestral work, written for a one hundred and five-piece orchestra, brought together the best qualities of North's original musical language. For an imagined film score it possessed very contemporary overall sound, with freely treated dissonances and, for that time, advanced compositional solutions.

The score was generally divided into two large sections. The "Dawn of Man" matches the first, primal part of the film, while the second musical part is devoted to the film's space sequences. The score dramatically develops from primitive, aggressively barbaric music in the first six movements toward heavenly serene, peaceful and calming music in the final six movements. The dominating, wild percussions from the first half are replaced by strings in the second half. Kubrick's conceptual influence is most evident in the opening "Main Title," formally patterned after Richard Strauss' *Zarathustra*, and in the "Space Station Docking" sequence, which is in the film accompanied by Johann Strauss's waltz *The Blue Danube*. For the latter North wrote a fast-moving, "ethereal" scherzo for alternating woodwinds and floating strings. From the "space" sequences the most memorable are the colorful instrumental piece "Trip to the Moon," and especially the sequence "Moon Rocket Bus" which features a celestial soprano vocalize. Although it is very hard, from today's point of view, to imagine Kubrick's film without the opening motif from *Zarathustra*, *The Blue Danube* waltz and Khachaturian's *Adagio*, there is no doubt that North's score would have greatly enhanced the dramatic structure of this legendary film.

North's only excursion into the field of war drama was his score for *The Devil's Brigade* (1968), an average film dealing with the training of an American-Canadian brigade to fight the Nazis in the Second World War. The brigade successfully accomplishes the military goal and defeats the Nazis in a battle, thus earning the sobriquet the "devil's brigade." Most of the music has march-like character, with occasional Scottish timbre. The principal theme of the score is a typical military march with the soldiers singing the tune "I Want a Woman," which is used as a basis for several variations during the film. The score also features a few popular songs from the period, such as "I'll Never Smile Again" and "You Always Hurt the One You Love," as well as "jazzy" adaptations of two carols, "Good King Wenceslas" and "Joy to the World."

Among North's last epic scores of the decade was the one composed for *The Shoes of the Fisherman* (1968), a story about a Russian (Catholic) priest who becomes Pope Kiril I (Anthony Quinn), and tries to appease the growing tension between East and West. North's music was one of the best and the most effective attributes of this vast and expensive, but not very successful movie. Therefore, the score earned a nomination for an Academy Award and a Golden Globe Award. Page Cook, the critic of *Films in Review*, described the score as a "pastiche of mundane travelogue music, folk melodies, and Roman Catholic church music."[36] This type of diverse musical compilation is particularly evident in the random exposition of the principal themes in the "Overture" for the film, which is stylistically and compositionally very heterogeneous. North's biggest problem was the creation of the main theme for Kiril, because the producers exclusively requested a Russian theme for the musical characterization of the Pope. "I resisted this," North commented. "The dramatic theme of the picture seemed to me to be much broader — it had to do with a possible clash between Russia and China, the possible devastation of the world. But the composer is an employee and I decided to write a Russian theme for the Pope. I thought it was wrong and I still do. I don't think it means much dramatically when you see the Pope, when he is alone and troubled and you hear a simple Russian theme. However, your ideas don't always prevail. You must compromise."[37] Nevertheless, many critics thought that the theme of Kiril was a potent musical statement when reoccurring during the film in its original or varied form. This theme is particularly effective as a musical reflection of Kiril's solitude and meditation, when it is introduced by solo balalaika (a type of Russian plucked instrument). However, the Russian origin of the theme might not be dramatically justified considering the fact that the film dealt with the Roman Catholic Church in modern times. The overall tone of the score is much more lyrical and sentimental in comparison with the other epic scores by North. Joan Padrol pointed out that, compared to the score for *The Agony and the Ecstasy*, the music for *The Shoes of the Fisherman* is like "the other side of the coin."[38] The best lyrical moments appear in the music cues related to Dr. Faber (Barbara Jefford) and her confession of the intimate problems with her husband. For these scenes North wrote a tender, sensible melody in the violins, developed and supported by the counterpoint in the cellos and violas. North's skillful approach toward polyphonic arrangements of religious songs is evident in the use of the chant "Veni Creator Spiritus" as the cardinals enter the Sistine Chapel to proclaim the new Pope. This chant, borrowed from the Roman liturgical sourcebook of chants *Liber Usualis*, is first presented in its authentic form *in unison*, and then it is polyphonically arranged for a mixed choir, in the style of the Renaissance.[39] For the final coronation scene, which shows the magnificent procession of the Pope to the Sistine Chapel, North wrote a powerful finale which incorporated the singing of the chant "Tu Es Petrus" followed by a massive orchestral conclusion.

In 1969, after an enormously tense period of creating music for big epic pictures, North was happy to work on two less demanding projects. One of them was *Hard Contract*, an action crime drama with James Coburn in the role of a cold-blooded assassin who goes through an ethical and emotional revitalization. The second project was another collaboration with the director Daniel Mann, on the film *A Dream of Kings*. It is a story about a Chicago Greek, Matsoukas (Anthony Quinn), whose main obsession is to find money in order to get his ill son back to their sunny homeland. North's sensuous and warm music greatly capture the authentic atmosphere of Greek America.

In general, North's musical style drastically changed in the Sixties. That was due primarily to the new musical demands imposed by the vast, epic spectacles — a completely different film genre from that of an intimate drama which was North's specialty in the Fifties. From the sixteen film scores that North composed in the Sixties,

North surrounded by the members of the Greek ensemble during the work on *A Dream of Kings* (National General, 1969).

eight were for big, spectacular films. This was, without doubt, a very challenging period for North. To meet the requirements of the new film genre, North developed his "objective" compositional approach, which meant writing music that dramatically supported the collective, massive scenes in the spectacles, and enhanced the authenticity of certain periods or historical events. This type of compositional approach usually included an extensive scholarly research of authentic musical materials and instruments. The experience of writing for the epic spectacles was not only beneficial for his versatility as a film composer, but it was also valuable for the development of his orchestral compositional technique. North was very much challenged by the opportunities of writing for huge orchestras of over a hundred players, which allowed him to experiment with the enormous orchestral possibilities and very exotic, rare instruments. Nevertheless, the "subjective" approach in North's film scoring was not neglected. On the contrary, his ability to musically empathize with the emotions of the individual characters is more then evident in many of his film scores from the Sixties, such as those for *The Misfits* and *Who's Afraid of Virginia Woolf?* North's memorable achievements from this period, many of them considered classics of the world of the cinema, assure him a place among the first rank of American film composers.

6

The Final Stage: The Seventies and the Eighties

Fear is a problem with film music and films... If you're not daring in your art, you're bankrupt.

— *Alex North*[1]

In the Seventies, Hollywood film music was dominated by a new wave of commercialism. The increasing number of independent productions had an enormous impact on the entire film industry, but the changes were the most evident in the field of film music. The understanding of the music as a dramatic factor within the film dramaturgy, which was gradually established during the previous decades, was not anymore of primary interest. Instead, the producers began to regard the music as a powerful commercial device which could act as a financial "boomerang." The film music was primarily expected to please large audiences in order to sell the picture soundtrack, thus helping the return on the financial investment. Therefore, the majority of filmmakers aimed for music that was oriented toward pop, rock or R&B (rhythm and blues) idioms. Since the entire musical industry was influenced by Beatlemania, a popular title song became an essential, if not the sole, requirement of the film composers. Hence, the songwriters became the major providers of film scores in the early Seventies. The orchestral scores were considered old-fashioned, and the hiring of a full orchestra presented an unnecessary expense for the low-budget productions.

These musical conditions were not favorable to North and the other traditional composers from his generation. In 1970, Bernard Herrmann said, "If I were starting now I'd have no career in films."[2] The work of many film composers was affected by the Hollywood new age of commercialism. North was one of them. He had no interest

76

in scoring films on the basis of one popular title song and its numerous repetitions and variations. For North, the subtle, dramatic approach was an essential feature of good film scoring. If the use of theme and variations was dramatically justified and appropriate for the film, he would not hesitate to apply such an approach. But, if it was the only given possibility to score the film, he would rather refuse such an assignment. North found the situation in the film business of this period very unfortunate for the film composers, and he hoped that it would change and improve. It *did* improve, but not until the late Seventies and early Eighties. Thus, in this period North had less work than ever in his career. Asked by Irwin Bazelon about his opinion on the title-song mania and the current influx of record companies into the film scene, North responded, "It's a commercial field, let's face it. And the producer's interested in a song, whether it's about rats or whatever, that becomes a hit; it may have nothing to do with the content of the film, but it's there, and it enables the producer to promote the film and accumulate some extra money advertising the film in that sense."[3] Such an opinion, however, did not mean that North was not interested in the new musical currents and achievements. On the contrary, he was very open and eager to know what was happening in popular music. His friend Farley Granger remembered that "every time a new Beatles record came out, Alex would be the first one to have it, and get even an advance copy of it."[4] Arthur Miller also pointed out that, regardless of the style, "one thing Alex respected was the talent."[5]

It seems that in the Seventies the production of major, epic movies suddenly decreased. After the Sixties, North did not work on any epic film projects of the type of *Spartacus, Cleopatra,* or *The Agony and the Ecstasy* (with the exception of *Dragonslayer* which belonged to the genre of "epic fantasy"). Most of the scores that he wrote in the Seventies were for smaller film productions. But, not all of these films inspired North's creative spark. For instance, in 1971 North was offered the chance to write music for the horror film *Willard,* another film project directed by Daniel Mann, which dealt with rats that were trained by a psychotic teenager (Bruce Davison) to attack and kill humans. Regarding this project, North said, "There are very few films that I have been involved in where I had that so-called inspiration. I mean, *Willard* was about rats. So where does my inspiration come from? There was a scene where the rats were chewing up a man, so you try to write a piece of music that lends something to the scene that isn't there..."[6] However, as the author Joan Padrol noticed, North's music was "one of the most powerful elements to provoke the sensation of hidden fear that was brought out by the story."[7] Despite the unpleasant subject, the film drew wide public attention and brought large audiences into the theaters.

North enjoyed his newly found happiness in the relationship with Annemarie Hoellger. In 1970, they settled down in a beautiful new home in Pacific Palisades with their son, Dylan. Alex married Annemarie in March 1972, and they stayed together until the end of Alex's life, sharing all the good and bad times for over twenty years. North's friends were glad to see him happy in the new relationship. The actor Farley Granger, who was one of their close friends, commented upon their relationship. "Alex adored Anna. More than anyone else she fulfilled him the way one person can fulfill another. She understood his strengths and his weaknesses, and she complemented him beautifully."[8] Unfortunately, in this period North began to suffer from severe back pain, a serious condition with which he lived for the rest of his life. In

1972 he had a spinal operation, but it proved to be just a temporary relief from the persisting affliction.

Despite the unfavorable situation in the film music industry and personal health problems, North wrote music for several films during these early years of the Seventies. In 1972 he completed the scores for *Rebel Jesus*, a smaller independent film, and *Pocket Money*, a modern western with Paul Newman and Lee Marvin. The latter was based on characteristic country and folk music of the American West, and besides North's music it featured a title song written and sung by Carol King. The following film, *Once Upon a Scoundrel* (1973), was a love story with a comical plot, set in a Mexican milieu. For North it meant one more opportunity to compose a score flavored with the sentiments and the folk idioms of Mexican music.

The prolific, long-term collaboration between North and the director Daniel Mann encompassed two film projects from this period, *Lost in the Stars* (1973) and *Journey into Fear* (1974). Huston and Mann were two directors with whom North established the longest professional relationships. They were also the directors who provided the most work for North during the last decades of his career. *Lost in the Stars* was a film version of an earlier Broadway musical play by Kurt Weill and Maxwell Anderson, based on Alan Paton's novel of South Africa, *Cry, the Beloved Country*. North was in charge of the musical direction and the dramatic adaptation of Weill's incidental music which was inspired by the American Negro music. The other film project directed by Daniel Mann, *Journey into Fear*, was a remake of Eric Ambler's spy novel, previously also adapted by Orson Welles. For this mysterious, spy drama North created a very intense orchestral score which musically enhanced the tension of suspense and dramatically complemented the action of the international intrigue. North explained his general approach, as follows: "I was intrigued with the assignment, since my longtime friend and talented director Daniel Mann was involved — as well as an outstanding cast (Sam Waterston, Zero Mostel and Yvette Mimieux). In my musical approach, including the obligatory 'Love Theme,' I sought to unify thematic material as it related to the various characters, plot and situations while focusing on the suspenseful pacing and action. Intentionally, there is no psychological delving beneath the surface, as there was in my scores for *Virginia Woolf*, *Children's Hour*, *The Misfits*, etc. The aggressivness inherent in this propulsive story did not, I felt, call for that kind of reflective mood or subtlety."[9]

One of the most exciting and demanding projects for North from this period was the film *Shanks* (1974), produced by his son Steven North. Steven pursued his education in Europe, and he spent some time directing for the theater. But, he ended up as a producer, as he said, "quite by accident." He had great pleasure working with his father on two projects, *Shanks* and *The Last Butterfly* (1990). "To work with my father was a learning process for me," remembered Steven. "He was the master. I have learned so much, and I still utilize what I've learned from him about film music when I work with other composers."[10] *Shanks* was the last film for the director William Castle, and it was devoted to the celebrated mime artist Marcel Marceau. He appeared in a double role, playing Shanks, a deaf-mute puppeteer, and Old Walker, an aging scientist who discovered how to resuscitate the dead animals. Working for the scientist, Shanks learns how to move the dead by remote control, and he widely uses this knowledge after the death of the scientist. Since this film was generally based on

North with his family (clockwise from top left): Alex and Annemarie, ca. 1985; Annemarie, Alex and Dylan, ca. 1977; Alex, Dylan, and Alex's brother Harry, ca. 1974.

North conducting a mixed chorus of sixty singers (not seen) from the platform, *Lost in the Stars,* **1973 (Ely Landay/American Film Theater)**

mimicry, North had to compose over an hour of music. The fascinating, bizarre story inspired North to write a very innovative and touching score which was a capital element of the film. Steven North noted that the score had certain similarities with the unused score for *2001,* because his father reworked some parts and used them in *Shanks.* According to Steven, the film profited a great deal from that. The resemblance is probably most evident in the music for the opening credits which is characterized by a gleaming melody played by the floating high strings with the backing sounds of a celesta and a "celestial" solo female contralto voice. North skillfully integrated parts for solo instruments within the orchestral texture, and achieved a very colorful and rich orchestral expression (in this regard, the orchestrator Henry Brant also deserves a credit). The critic Page Cook wrote in his article for *Films in Review* that the scoring of the film was never routine music. "North takes *Shanks* seriously," commented Cook. "North's dramatic planes and juxtapositions, his virtuosic writing for divided strings, his imaginative play of color and line, suggest a sense of humor and delicacy that reveal the fanciful side of the composer's mind (North's mastery of creating atmosphere has never been in question)."[11] George Burt, the author of the book *The Art of Film Music,* pointed out that "the musical sound was a metaphor, combining, in a sense, the living with the mechanical."[12] Without doubt, North's profound and creative insight enormously enhanced the quality of the entire picture, adding a dimension that raised this achievement above the ordinary. His musical contribution was rewarded with a nomination for an Academy Award.

North earned another Oscar nomination the following year, 1975, for the score that he composed for Richard Brooks' western *Bite the Bullet.* During his career, North had several occasions to deal with the genre of the western (he had previously scored six western pictures), but *Bite the Bullet* was certainly one of his best and most

(left to right) Steven North, David Wolper and Alex North, 1960s.

typical western scores. It was an extensive work (the LP record contains fifteen music cues), characterized by driving, rhythmic musical sequences which occasionally alternated with typical "cowboy" plaintive melodies for a harmonica or a guitar. Some of the sequences were variations of popular American folk songs, as for instance the impressive orchestral adaptation of the song "Camptown Races" (the film itself was about horse racing). In a few sequences the influence of Mexican folk music is evident. Working with Brooks, who was known as a maverick director, was an exciting experience for North. "Brooks won't allow a composer to attend the final dubbing, and the musicians couldn't look at the film during playback, " remembered North. "He didn't want anyone to get an idea of what he was doing."[13]

In 1976, North received a challenging commission to compose music for the twelve-hour television series *Rich Man, Poor Man,* based on a novel by Irwin Shaw. Challenged by the dramatic potentials of the project North accepted the assignment, even though he had health problems at the time (he was successfully treated for cancer in Stanford). "They'd send me the script, I hired a Fender Rhodes keyboard and worked on it after radiation treatments," remembered North.[14] As a unifying musical principle North used the leitmotif technique, and created principal themes for all the characters (Axel, Julie, Tom, Rudy and the others). The themes' variations or

January 10, 1980

Dear member of the Academy:

I write on behalf of Mr. John Huston and myself to make you aware of Mr. Alex North's musical score for Mr. Huston's recently completed picture <u>Wise Blood</u>.

Mr. Huston and I feel that Alex North's adapted musical score has contributed immesurably to the pictures' moods of bizarre humor and to the haunting nature of its subjectmatter. Alex North's quiet musical counterpoints to the action, the balletic quality of his orchestrations and the explosive zest that his music injects into the blackest humor are an essential ingredient of the pictures' effectiveness and success.

Therefore Mr. Huston and I would urge you to consider Mr. Alex North for an Academy Award Nomination.

Thank you for your attention,

Sincerely

Michael Fitzgerald
Michael Fitzgerald
Producer

Letter from the producer Michael Fitzgerald to the Academy of Motion Picture Arts and Sciences, recommending the *Wise Blood* score for an Academy Award nomination, January 10, 1980.

transformations depended upon the dramatic conflicts and relationships between the characters. "Roughly equivalent in length to six two-hours feature films, the treatment of the score called for a virtual musical anthology spanning twenty years in the lives of the Jordache family," North commented.[15] The complex score included some very dramatic, passionate, and romantic sequences, with the melodic principle as a leading creative device. The series was well received, and North's score won an Emmy Award. North's other credits in the field of television music include the title themes for *Playhouse 90* and *77 Sunset Strip*, music for a series of twenty-seven documentary episodes, *F. D. Roosvelt* (1961), the Anthony Quinn thirteen-part series *The Man and the City* (1972), *The Word* (1978), and the television movie *Sister-Sister* (1982).

By the end of the Seventies North had written music for just three more films. After *The Passover Plot* (1976), a Biblical film on Christ which did not draw much attention, in 1978 North scored *Somebody Killed Her Husband*, a crime comedy with Farrah Fawcett and Jeff Bridges. The latter was an original, modern score based on sequences written in pop manner and musical pastiches of classical motifs, skillfully arranged to emphasize the humorous and the parodic aspects of the film. North's last achievement in the Seventies was *Wise Blood* (1979) which presented a reunion of the composer with the director John Huston. *Wise Blood* is an adaptation of a novel by Flannery O'Connor. The bizzare story deals with a religious fanatic, Hazel Motes, and his rebellion against Christ. North decided to score this picture in the style of folk, country music, using the popular tune "Tennessee Waltz" as a main theme for numerous variations.

The beginning of the fourth decade of North's career as a film composer was marked by an inspired and dramatically effective score for *Carny* (1980). On this project he joined forces with Robbie Robertson, a former rock musician and founder of the rock music group *The Band*, whose farewell concert was documented in Martin Scorsese's film *The Last Waltz* (1978). Being in the movie business for many years, Robertson decided not only to produce *Carny*, but also to co-write the script, star in the movie, and compose a part of the film score. He wrote several songs in blues and rock style which were recorded on the *Carny* soundtrack under the name "Midway Music." North was in charge of the dramatic part of the score. "The experience of meeting and discussing musical dramatic approach with Robbie Robertson was refreshing and we hit it off in rare fashion, compared to the many phony producers and directors who know everything about everything," commented North. "I was amazed at his instincts involving all the aspects of good film making. Needless to say, he gave me free rein to do my own thing!"[16] *Carny* was a little, atmospheric picture about the colorful world of the carnival. The plot focused on the relationship between the carny Bozo (Gary Busey) and Patch (Robbie Robertson), whose friendship was disturbed by the appearance of a teenage girl Donna (Jodie Foster) who joined the carnival show and became involved in the private lives of Bozo and Patch. "Working on *Carny* was a real gratifying and unusually unique experience, " North remembered. "Although I had reservations about the basic thin story line, I was fascinated (as I was in *Wise Blood*) with a particularly off-beat slice of American 'culture.'"[17] The score for *Carny* was not an extensive one, but each of the sequences possessed a distinctive and special quality. All of the seven pieces from the soundtrack are breathtaking—from the sarcastic, dissonant "Carnival Bozo" and the romantic theme from "Remember to Forget," through the seductive jazz sequence "Lust" and the polyphonically developed melancholic piece "I'm a Bad Girl," to the whirling scherzo "Rednecks Rumble," the linear growing "Fear and Revelation," and, at the end, the circus waltz theme for *Carny*. All of these sequences could musically stand as excellent, independent, short musical pieces, yet they were all closely and skilfully tied to the dramatic situations and the characters of the film. Some of the sequences, as for instance "I'm a Bad Girl," "Redneck Rumble," and "Fear and Revelation," rank among the finest examples of contemporary orchestral scoring (the credit must be given also to the orchestrator Henry Brant). The critic Page Cook was quite right when he wrote that the music for *Carny* drew the listener "back again and again with ever-deepening affection."[18] He added that the score was "a work of the composer's full awareness, touched with the freshness of filmic inspiration and not yet spoiled by overfamiliarity with the composer's style. Risk-taking, it is a ferociously physical exploration of a territory bounded by blues, jazz, honky-tonk *and* the composer's individual and moving poignancy."[19] Despite his unique musical contribution to several films from the Seventies, such as *Shanks, Bite the Bullet*, and *Wise Blood*, North was especially proud of his score for *Carny*. "I think *Carny* is the best work I've done since *Virginia Woolf* and only wish the film were better received. Every time I hope to retire from this business and devote all my time to 'serious' music, I find myself constantly intrigued with functional music and the variety of challenges it offers."[20] Robbie Robertson, who was greatly influenced by North's work, concluded, "For my money, he is one of the masters of film music."[21]

North's mastery reached its peak during the last decade of his career. Most of his scores from the Eighties glimmer with dazzling beauty, maturity, simplicity, and dramatic potency. It seemed that after the frustrating and disappointing experiences with the unused score for *2001* and two other film scores, for *Sounder* and *Cattle Annie and Little Britches*, North always came back with even more powerful musical achievements. Ken Sutak, the author of an extensive article on the film music for *Dragonslayer*, properly noted that "for the junked *Sounder* we get the brilliant *Shanks*.

From the *Cattle Annie and Little Britches* scrapheap rises the resolve that produces a *Dragonslayer*... Here's a guy who turns around and gives you his blood every time he takes a wound."[22] *Dragonslayer* was the next important film project that North was offered, in the summer of 1980. There is an anecdote saying that Hal Barwood and Matthew Robbins, the producer and the director of *Dragonslayer*, came to the office of Steven Spielberg, with whom they were friends, to ask him for advice as to what composer they should engage for their film. Spielberg let them listen to three different records, without identifying who composed the music. The music in question was from *A Streetcar Named Desire*, *Viva Zapata* and *Who's Afraid of Virginia Woolf*. Apparently, Barwood really liked one, Robbins liked another, and Spielberg said he was partial to the third, but that still did not help them solve their problem. "You don't have a problem anymore," said Spilberg; "they were all written by the same composer — Alex North."[23] In September 1980, North flew to London to look at some rough footage of the film, and to discuss the general concept with the producers and the director. But, it was not until February 1981 that he began to compose the music, after he had seen and discussed the entire film with Robbins. North had only six weeks to complete the extensive score of almost ninety minutes for the recording sessions. No wonder that the score occasionally echoed motifs from his previous works, as the Church motif from *The Shoes of the Fisherman*, brief quotations from *2001*, or brass figures from *Cleopatra* and *Spartacus*.

Dragonslayer is an epic fantasy based on a medieval legend about a dragon, called Vermithrax Pejorative, who terrorizes the land of king Tyrian (John Hallam). The king can keep the peace only by sacrificing the virgins from his kingdom to the evil, monstrous dragon. After much trouble, the old wizard Ulrich (Ralph Richardson) and his apprentice Galen (Peter MacNicol) succeed in defeating the dragon and save the kingdom. Because of certain scenes of terror and violence this film was more fantasy for adults than for children. *Dragonslayer* was North's last work in his remarkable opus of epic scores. It was not only a resumption of all the best qualities of his previous epic scoring, but it was also a powerful expression of his most contemporary musical tendencies. The linear conception was developed through transparently layered, polyphonic orchestral texture dominated by modal harmony, which suggested the medieval origins of the story. The instrumentation was inventive (the orchestrator was again Henry Brant), and the symphonic orchestra was enriched with such instruments as clavitimbre, tack piano, organ, harpsichord, two pianos, wind machine, bell tree, thunder sheet and others. In the notes on *Dragonslayer*, John Fitzpatrick wrote, "The gloom-and-doom heavings emitted by North's Wagnerian complement of low strings and brasses are here seasoned with enough sharp modernism to give the picture a tang often lacking from script and direction."[24]

The score for *Dragonslayer* is unified through a developed system of principal motifs, but it also features musical sequences which are treated as independent orchestral miniatures. John Lasher, who wrote the notes for the released soundtrack of *Dragonslayer* (SCSE CD-3), pointed out that North's score was largely based on five major thematic concepts: 1) A plaintive motif for the Urlanders, capturing their suffering and anguish; 2) a motif suggesting "magic"; 3) a motif initially associated with Ulrich's amulet, for Galen; 4) a motif for the maiden's sacrifices; 5) Galen and Valerian's romance. North explained his basic musical approach as follows: "In the case of *Dragonslayer* I saw several opportunities from a purely dramatic standpoint—Vermithrax, the dragon, and his relationship to the events which unfold throughout the film. Except for the relationship between Galen and Valerian everything was impersonal. This allowed me complete freedom to compose set pieces (i.e. scherzo, rondo, et al.), such as I might do when composing for the concert hall. *Dragonslayer* also posed the challenge of maintaining musical continuity during cross-cutting between bits of action, location, and characters."[25] From the dramatic standpoint, North was very disappointed that his musical concept related to the dragon was not entirely used in the final version of the film. Some of the musical sequences were cut, and some were replaced with the music from other parts of the score. "I wrote a very lovely waltz for when the dragon first appears, with just a slight indication that this may not be a bad dragon," North commented. "I didn't want to tip the audience off that this might not be an ogre. That waltz would get more and more distorted as the dragon kept appearing. Well, they cut out the whole waltz concept. They substituted other music I had written for another scene for when the dragon first appears. They chopped up a four-minute cue to thirty seconds, a three-minute cue became twenty seconds..."[26] Without doubt, this musical concept would have greatly enhanced the dramatic gradation in the film. North was very proud of his score, and he considered it one of the most inspired works that he had done. However, he was musically much more satisfied with the soundtrack than with the music in the film. Many critics praised North's musical contribution. For instance, Pauline Kael wrote for the *New Yorker*, "Alex North's score is a beauty. At times, the music and the fiery dragon seem one; the elusive imagery and the music gradually enfold you." Royal S. Brown in the magazine *Fanfare* noticed, "Not only is *Dragonslayer* one of the best scores of 1981, its disc realization makes this one of the most attractive albums ever put together."[27] Even though the film did not achieve the expected success, North's music attracted much interest and admiration, and received a more than merited nomination for an Academy Award.

The period between 1984 and 1987 was when Alex North and John Huston collaborated the most. This collaboration of the two masters in the concluding stages of their careers resulted in three very different film achievements—the obscure drama *Under the Volcano* (1984), the black comedy *Prizzi's Honor* (1985), and Huston's poetic farewell *The Dead* (1987). All of these films are film adaptations of literary works. *Under the Volcano* is based on a novel by Malcolm Lowry, *Prizzi's Honor* is an adaptation of Richard Condon's novel, while *The Dead* is Huston's artistic vision of a short story from James Joyce's collection *The Dubliners*. For *Under the Volcano* North composed a remarkable dramatic score which earned him an Academy Award nomination (the music for *Under the Volcano* and *Prizzi's Honor* is analyzed in Chapter Ten and Chapter Eleven). North's score for *Prizzi's Honor* is a witty adaptation of Italian opera sources, while the music for *The Dead* evolves from an old Irish ballad entitled "The Lass of Aughrim." *The Dead* also features a great many Irish tunes and dances originating from the nineteenth century, heard in the film as source music for solo piano, or arranged for chamber ensemble. Discussing the film scores of 1987, the music critic Page Cook wrote the following about *The Dead*: "Low key and never intrusive, the ever-brilliant master fixed the whispered tremors of Huston's adaptation of the Joyce work with the same sureness of touch he has always possessed...

Mr. North brings unerring sensitivity with delicacy and depth and the lightness of a keen eye and ear for film."[28] North's scores for *Prizzi's Honor* and *The Dead* had similar destinies in regard to the Academy Award nominations. They were both considered by the Academy "an adaptation of other composers' music" and thus ineligible for nomination.[29] North felt that such characterization of his scores was not proper. He and many of his colleagues publicly expressed their concern that the academy had not provided a category for musical adaptations in films.

Among North's last projects in the Eighties was the television version of Arthur Miller's *Death of a Salesman*. It seems that this work was destined to mark each important stage in North's career — the height of his theater experience, the rise in the world of film music, and, in 1985, the concluding part of his prolific career. This work is also an excellent example of dramatic adaptations of one score to different artistic fields — theater, film, and television. According to Arthur Miller, the director of the television film, Volker Schlondorff, thought, at first, to have different music. He wanted to create a very contemporary sound. "He engaged a very good composer and the music was extremely interesting," Miller said. "But, it didn't compare to Alex's music. It was cold, basically very unemotional. It didn't really express Willy. Finally, I insisted that we get Alex to come back."[30] Thus, North reworked his original score for the *Salesman*. He basically used the same thematic material, but he dramatically adjusted it for the new, television medium.

The offer to compose music for the film *Good Morning, Vietnam* (1987) came as a big surprise to North. In this film the Vietnam war is shown from a different angle than usually — through the activity of the disc jockey Cronauer (Robin Williams) who adds a new dimension in the lives of the soldiers with his provocative entertaining radio program. Considering this fact, it was expected that the film would use pop music of the period as a

---

THE GORFAINE/SCHWARTZ AGENCY

January 18, 1988

Mr. Arthur Hamilton
Academy of Motion Picture Arts and Sciences
8949 Wilshire Blvd.
Beverly Hills, CA 90211

Re: Alex North/"The Dead"

Dear Arthur:

I am deeply concerned that the Academy has provided no category for the consideration of Alex North's score for the motion picture, "The Dead." It is debatable whether it should qualify as an original score, but it most certainly should be eligible in the category of adaptation.

That his contribution to such a memorable film should be eliminated from contention for want of an appropriate category is grossly unfair to the composer and to the Academy members who deserve the right to evaluate the work of a composer of Alex' calibre. Is there no recourse simply because, in a given year, the number of adaptation scores is insufficient to warrant a separate category?

The Academy has, wisely, maintained flexibility in its award structure so that justice can prevail in most circumstances. Surely it will be unacceptible if a composer of the highest quality such as Alex North can go unrecognized while some, of much less quality, are nominated for consideration.

I am appealing to you in the hope that you will want to remedy this inequity. I know the Academy has the power to do so.

Thank you for your attention.

Sincerely,

Michael Gorfaine

Letter from North's agent Michael Gorfaine to the Academy of Motion Picture Arts and Sciences, regarding the score for *The Dead*, January 18, 1988.

Top left: Arthur Miller (left) and Alex North (center) and unidentified man during the Chinese production of *Death of a Salesman* in Beijing, 1983. Top right: Composer David Raskin (right) is presenting North with the Career Achievement Award by the Society for the Preservation of film Music, 1986. Bottom (clockwise from top left): Robert Colesberry, Rosemarie Dittbern (Annemarie's twin sister), Annemarie North, Fred Steiner, Alex North, and Dustin Hoffman during the TV production of *Death of a Salesman* (Roxbury & Punch Production, 1985).

North's 80th birthday organized by ASCAP. (clockwise from top left): Todd Brabek, Nancy Knudsen, Lyn Benjamin, Steven North, Martin Ritt, Alex North and Karl Malden, 1990. Photograph by Lester Cohen.

basic source for musical accompaniment. Truly, the first part of the picture uses songs by Martha Reeves, the Beach Boys, James Brown, and Louis Armstrong, mostly as source music played on the radio. But, with the scene of the bombing of the bar visited by the soldiers, the mood of the film drastically changes. Therefore, the director Barry Levinson asked North to provide this part of the film with dramatic music. North composed about twenty minutes of music, avoiding any descent into unnecessary lyricism, even for the relationship between the disc jockey and the young Vietnamese girl (Chintara Sukapatana). "The stronger relationship in the film is between Williams and the girl's brother. I avoided a standard romantic theme, instead opting for a more universal theme," North explained. "I wrote with less of a subjective viewpoint. It wasn't chromatic, just simple diatonic chords." Knowing that Levinson had become attached to Morricone's theme from the film *The Mission*, which the director used as a temp track in the film, North consciously tried to achieve that effect in his score by the use of quarter tones, little frills and figurations in the woodwinds. "I used no violins; they weren't right for this picture," North said. "Instead I employed eight violas, eight cellos and four basses. This gave a deep feeling in the strings. I used a harpsichord instead of piano. Most of the 'effects' were in the percussion and the woodwinds." North worked on the orchestration of this score with his longtime friend and colleague Henry Brant.

In 1988 North wrote music for *The Penitent*, a little known, somber drama with religious context. The producer of the film, Michael Fitzgerald, said that "North's music was much better than the film itself."[31] North's final musical score followed in 1990. It was written for the film *The Last Butterfly*, an international co-production between France, Great Britain and Czechoslovakia. On this project North joined forces again with his son Steven, who produced the film. At the time of the preparation of this film North was already very ill, and he collaborated closely with the orchestrator Alexander Courage. According to Steven North, his father started to work on some themes used in this film as early as 1987 or 1988. For the last time North composed dramatically poignant music which complemented the psychological aspects of intimate relationships in an economical and unobtrusive manner. The score incorporated several traditional Yiddish songs and additional ballet music and cabaret songs composed by the Czech composer

North receiving the Academy Award for Lifetime achievement, 1986.

Milan Svoboda. In the notes for the compact disc release of the soundtrack, Robert Townson wrote, "North does not need to write a great quantity of music or to incorporate the forces of a large hundred plus piece orchestra for a score to be successful, less is unquestionably more. His touching bittersweet melodies orchestrated for a carefully assembled ensemble make *The Last Butterfly* a wonderful vehicle to usher Alex North's music into the 1990s."[32]

Unfortunately, North did not live long enough to enrich the films of the Nineties with his powerful musical imagination. After a long and exhausting period of illness, he died from pancreatic cancer on September 8, 1991. His sea burial was attended by his closest family, friends and colleagues.

North's legacy enriched the heritage of American film music with unforgettable, enduring, and vigorous musical achievements. His music enhanced numerous very important, and less important films. For North, music was the best device of communication with the world around him. A composer with inexhaustible melodic inspiration and enormous dramatic talent, North had supplied films over the period of four decades with music characterized by innovation, simplicity, unobtrusiveness, and, above all, profound human and artistic honesty. In March 1986, North became the first composer to receive an honorary Oscar for Lifetime Achievement from the Academy of Motion Picture Arts and Sciences. After fifteen Oscar nominations, he deserved this award more than any other composer. In his acceptance speech North exposed his basic concept of film scoring. "In composing music for films I attempt to achieve the following goals: to meet the demands and needs of the story conflict and the interrelationship of the characters involved and also, hopefully, contributing my own personal comment. I would like to make a humble plea to all of us involved in the movies and that is to encourage and convey hope, humor, compassion, adventure and love as opposed to despair, synthetic theatrics and blatant, bloody violence." At the end, he concluded, "And sex, sex, sex, by all means, indeed, but with a bit of mystery, a touch of charm and elegance, and lots of imagination."[33] In recognition of North's musical oeuvre for films, John Huston said, "Alex is a past master at speaking to the unconscious. It is his genius to convey an emotion to the audience with its hardly being aware of the existence of a score."[34] Indeed, North expressed his creativity in a very subtle and personal way. Therefore, his best works live as a genuine, warm, glorious, and humane reflection of his own inner personality.

PART II

MUSICAL ANALYSES

7

A Streetcar Named Desire (1951)

I don't want realism. I want magic! Yes, yes, magic! I try
to give that to people. I misrepresent things to them. I
don't tell truth, I tell what ought to be truth. And if that
is sinful, then let me be damned for it!
> — *Blanche in* A Streetcar Named Desire,
> *Scene 9 (Tennessee Williams)*

Illusions versus Reality: A Tragedy of Misunderstandings

Three years after the huge success of the 1947 stage production of *A Streetcar Named Desire*, playwright Tennessee Williams asked Elia Kazan to direct the film adaptation of the play. "Oh, God, Tenn," Kazan responded, "it would be like marrying the same woman twice. I don't think I can get it up for *Streetcar* again."[1] Kazan preferred new challenges. He thought that working on the same project might diminish his creative inspiration. But, Williams was persistent and the director ultimately agreed to do the film version of *Streetcar* for Warner Brothers.

Initially, Kazan wanted to "open up" *Streetcar* and "extend" the screenplay by adding outdoor scenes that would precede the play's action. However, he realized soon that such a treatment might impair the coherent structure of the play and he decided to film the play as it was initially written. He collaborated closely with Williams on the film script. Hence the screen version is a very close reconception of the original theater play. Besides several considerable changes required by the censors, including the ending of the film, there are only a few minor alterations in the film dialogue and setting. Despite the long monologues and expressive poetic language the screen adaptation preserved the initial fluency of the play. That was achieved, according to Kazan, by filming the play in a manner of heightened, stylized realism which justified

93

the theatrical speech and dialogue.[2] In general, Williams' plays possess an extraordinary sense of continuity and smooth flow of action. This is greatly due to the replacement of the conventional act structure with a series of scenes which provided his plays with a loose and flexible form. These qualities made his plays highly appealing for screen adaptation. Many renowned directors found Williams' work a rewarding and inspiring source for filmmaking, including, among others, John Huston, Richard Brooks, Sidney Lumet, Daniel Mann, and Elia Kazan.

Williams began to work on *Streetcar* in the winter of 1944–45. There were many revisions of the play before it was presented to the public in the legendary New York production on December 3, 1947. It was the first American play that won three prestigious drama awards: the Pulitzer Prize, the New York Drama Critics Award, and the Donaldson Award. *Streetcar* became a classic play and one of Williams' most outstanding and best-known works. During the course of writing Williams had several possible titles for his play on his mind: *Blanche's Chair in the Moon*, *The Moth*, *The Poker Night*. It was not until 1946 that he finally decided to call his play *A Streetcar Named Desire*. In a way this play epitomizes the main aspects of Williams' style, such as a loosely constructed plot developed through eleven scenes, a sentimental story based on ambivalent feelings and moral values, and principal characters who go through an emotional upheaval with which audiences can easily empathize.

The relativity of the reality and its different perception by each of the characters is one of the basic subjects with which Williams deals in this play. All of the major conflicts, misunderstandings, and troubled relationships are caused by the inability or refusal of the characters to acknowledge and accept each other as individuals with their own values, needs, ethics and philosophies of life; in other words, to grant the right to each other to be different. *Streetcar* is a tragedy of subjectivity and obsession in as much as the characters fail to recognize that their own comprehension of reality is neither perfect nor the ultimate perspective of life. In a letter to Kazan, Williams clearly described his intentions in the play: "…I think its best quality is its authenticity or its fidelity to life. There are no 'good' people or 'bad' people. Some are a little better or a little worse but all are activated more by misunderstanding than malice. A blindness to what is going on in each other's hearts. Stanley sees Blanche not as a desperate, driven creature backed into a last corner to make a last desperate stand — but as a calculating bitch with 'round heels.' …Nobody sees anybody truly but all through the flaws of their own egos. That is the way we all see each other in life. Vanity, fear, desire, competition — all such distortions within our own egos—condition our vision of those in relation to us. Add to those distortions in our *own* egos, the corresponding distortions in the egos of *others*, and you see how cloudy the glass must become through which we look at each other. That's how it is in all living relationships except when there is that rare case of two people who love intensely enough to burn through all those layers of opacity and see each other's naked hearts. Such cases seem purely theoretical to me."[3]

The ambivalent nature of *Streetcar* is defined by the confrontation between the romantic illusions of Blanche DuBois and the physical, even vulgar, realism of her brother-in-law, Stanley Kowalski. Blanche tries really hard to maintain the illusions of her romantic ideals and youthful innocence, protecting them with all of her heart from harsh and brutal reality. She was once a school teacher married to a young man who committed suicide after she discovered his homosexuality and reproached him for it. This painful experience torments her mind and gradually leads her into a mental decline. Afraid to face the truth of her lost ideals, she chooses to live them in her imagination.

The illusion of who she wants to be becomes her subjective reality of who she is, justified with her claim that she has never lied in her heart. Since the incident with her husband she has subconsciously tried to revive their innocent relationship by seducing other young men, hoping to give them the understanding and protection she denied her husband. Thus, she has been fired from the school for seducing a student and consequently compelled to leave her home town. With no place to go, she seeks harbor with her younger sister Stella who lives in New Orleans. There she is forced to face the brutal, physical reality embodied in the character of Stella's husband, Stanley. He is the complete opposite of Blanche, her "negative" on every level of physical, psychological, and emotional existence.

As different as they are, they both pose a threat to each other. The sophisticated and intelligent Blanche is a threat to Stanley's simple comprehension of life limited to physical and hedonistic enjoyment. He is also afraid that she might destroy his home nest by turning Stella against him. On the other hand, Stanley poses an even more dangerous threat to Blanche. He destroys her last hope for a fulfilling emotional relationship with his friend Mitch by tracking down and uncovering her disgraceful past. At the end he enforces his physical reality upon Blanche by raping her and thus ultimately driving her into insanity.

The ambivalence of the play was underlined by the fact that Williams did not want the audience to favor any of the characters. Even though Blanche ends up in the mental institution while Stanley succeeds in keeping his home and his wife (a change in the film version of *Streetcar* due to the censorship demands), Williams pointed out that he doesn't want to focus guilt or blame on any one character but to have it a tragedy of misunderstandings and insensitivity to others.[4] According to the playwright, the audience should be able to make its own choice between the characters. "Blanche is not an angel without a flaw, and Stanley's not evil.... This play should not be loaded one way or the other. Don't try to simplify things.... Don't take sides or try to present a moral," Williams directed Kazan. However, he suggested that at the end the viewer should certainly feel for Blanche. "It is a tragedy with the classic aim of producing a catharsis of pity and terror and in order to do that, Blanche must finally have the understanding and compassion of the audience," Williams wrote to Kazan. "This without creating a black-dyed villain in Stanley. It is a thing (Misunderstanding) not a person (Stanley) that destroys her at the end. In the end you should feel — 'If only they had known about each other.'"[5]

Some sources indicate that the character of Blanche originated in an image of Williams' sister Rose, whereas others point out that his Aunt Belle was the main overall prototype for his heroine.[6] The truth is that Blanche bears features from both of them. The love affair of Williams' sister with a young man might have triggered the playwright's imagination as to inventing the character of Blanche. They were seeing each other every other night, but suddenly he just stopped calling her. "That was when Rose first began to go into a mental decline. From that vision *Streetcar* evolved," claims Williams. Aunt Belle, on the other hand, was a school teacher in the South.

Like Blanche, she was intelligent, eloquent and beautiful, strongly opinionated and somewhat rigid, but also tender and fragile. Blanche's controversial personality bears a close resemblance to Aunt Belle's. Furthermore, as Kazan pointed out, many aspects of *Streetcar* are autobiographical. The playwright himself in many ways parallels

A Streetcar Named Desire, still (Warner Bros., 1951). From left to right: Blanche (Vivien Leigh), Stanley (Marlon Brando), Stella (Kim Hunter), Mitch (Karl Malden).

Blanche. "Tennessee Williams equals Blanche," Kazan explained. "He is Blanche. And Blanche is torn between a desire to preserve her tradition, which is her entity, her being, and her attraction to what is going to destroy her tradition. She is attracted to a murderer, Stanley.... He [Williams] was attracted to things that were replacing him. That's the source of the ambivalence in the play. Blanche wants the very thing that's going to crush her."[7]

Kazan admired Williams because he had found his story in his own life's struggles. From him Kazan learned that the true artist must have the courage to reveal what the rest of mankind conceals. After the experience with *Streetcar* Kazan saw every play and film that he worked on as a confession and self-revelation. "Truth was the best basis for fiction," Kazan concluded.[8]

During the making of the film version of *Streetcar* the main concern of its creators was how to satisfy the strict censorship demands, and at the same time to preserve the artistic entity and unity of the work. The industry censor, Joseph Breen, indicated that what was permitted on the stage could be inappropriate for film presentation. Indeed, there were a number of scenes in *Streetcar* that the censors required changed or simply omitted. Among the others, there is the issue of the homosexuality of Blanche's husband, the scene of Blanche's rape, and the ending of the film in which Stella doesn't stay with Stanley after Blanche is taken to the asylum. The censors insisted that Stanley should be punished for what he did to Blanche, and therefore Stella must leave him forever. For the first two demands Williams and Kazan found a way to entwine clear assumptions within the film story that indicated the issues of homosexuality and Blanche's rape, but the change of the last scene eventually weakened the ending of the film. Nevertheless, after its premiere in September 1951 the film was critically acclaimed and achieved the same success as the stage production. It truly launched the career of Marlon Brando (Stanley), and it brought Oscars to Vivien Leigh (Blanche), Kim Hunter (Stella), Karl Malden (Mitch), Richard Day for art decoration, and George James Hopkins for set decoration.[9] The New York Film Critics chose *Streetcar* as Best Picture, and awarded Leigh's acting and Kazan's direction. Leigh also won an award as best actress at the Venice Film Festival. *Streetcar* is as intriguing and captivating a film today as it was half a century ago. It is rightfully considered a movie classic and one of the most successful adaptations of a theater play.

General Perspectives of the Musical Score

North's Breakthrough in Hollywood

Kazan and North first worked together in 1937 on the documentary *People of the Cumberland*. Even though they became close friends as early as 1947, the real professional bond was not established until the 1949 stage production of Miller's *Death of a Salesman*. When Kazan was signed on to film *Streetcar* in Hollywood, he insisted that North should be brought out to write the music. Despite the initial resistance from the film producers, Kazan stayed firm in his decision to have North as the composer for *Streetcar*. His instinct proved to be right because North's music significantly intensified the dramatic impact of *Streetcar* and it was commensurate with the quality of the play, film direction, and acting. However, nobody could foresee the immense influence that North's first major film assignment would have on the art of film scoring.[10]

North had never regarded the offer to compose the music for *Streetcar* as merely a job. "It was a creative challenge," he said, " an opportunity to make music talk, and talk very much in the American musical idiom of jazz, rather then to imitate the frequently overrated gods of music in Europe, whose influence too frequently tends to dominate and stultify American composers."[11] Indeed, the score for *Streetcar* is historically acclaimed and mostly known for its pioneering use of jazz for dramatic purposes in a film. Such a stylistic approach was enabled, and even imposed, by the fact that the film story was set in New Orleans, considered the home of jazz. Moreover, the slummy two-story building where the action took place was located, as Williams described, "just around a corner, or a few doors down the street from a tinny piano being played with the infatuated fluency of brown fingers," referring to a jazz club called "Four Deuces."[12] North was delighted by the opportunity to incorporate jazz, blues and ragtime in his score. "*Streetcar* is high art in motion picture entertainment, high art in writing, directing and acting, but emotionally it is lowdown basin street blues— sad, glad, mad New Orleans jazz in terms of human beings. And that's the kind of music that drummed in my head," North concluded. " It had to be American music. No other music would do. Anything else, I felt, would be pretentious and unreal, unworthy of the integrity of *Streetcar* as a motion picture. Elia Kazan gave me *carte blanche* to compose, and I loved him for it."[13]

Kazan even sent North to New Orleans to feel the atmosphere of the city, walk around, and go to jazz clubs. This experience was very beneficial for North, who had always had a special affection for jazz. In many of his earlier statements he stressed that jazz was by far a more authentic indigenous ingredient of American music than the folk music which is expressed in mountain ballads and cowboy songs which are, for the most part, of English and Scottish derivation. He thought that an attempt should be made to extract the essence and spirit of jazz and to project it with all the resources of craftsmanship at one's command to produce a product which would have an artistic integrity as well as an emotional impact.[14] In *Streetcar* North had a chance to adhere to these words and to fulfill his ideas about the use of jazz in the course of his own composition.

Commenting on the musical style of his score, North modestly noticed: "I'm sure jazz had been used before, but I just felt that it was the right approach in keeping with the style of Tennessee Williams— the South. I couldn't conceive of it in any other way."[15] Before *Streetcar* jazz was mainly used as a background music. The most challenging task for North was to adjust the improvisational nature of the jazz style to the strict timing of the music cues in the film. This is where North had to apply his compositional skills in a witty and inventive manner. He found a way to maintain the swinging mood of jazz throughout the score within precisely structured musical sequences. North pointed out that he tried to simulate jazz, to get its essence rhythmically and harmonically, and apply it to drama.[16] Such a treatment of jazz was not new to North. He used a similar approach in his *Revue for Clarinet and Orchestra* where he also simulated jazz within a classical compositional structure. In *Streetcar* this approach proved most beneficial in the transitions between the music coming from the neighboring jazz club and the dramatic underscoring.[17] These transitions are very smooth and at times one would not even notice the alternations between the source music and North's ingenious musical comment. In this regard North commented, "It may be interesting to note that in the first five reels there is more stylized jazz than in the remaining reels because these take place mostly at night when the 'Four Deuces' dive is in operation. (One sees flickering lights throughout.) I tried to make the transitions from the source music (popular tunes) to the underscoring as imperceptible as possible so that one was not completely aware of the transition. I don't say this was entirely successful, but it was worth trying."[18]

Besides its fame as the first composed jazz score for a film, *Streetcar* cannot and should not be entirely labeled and defined as a jazz composition. As North mentioned, jazz influence is mostly evident in the first five reels of the film. The composer tried to correlate the source music coming from the club Four Deuces with the sensuous, sexual undercurrent among the film's protagonists, and felt that jazz could best reflect those particular moments. However, the music covers fourteen reels of the film with forty-five music cues altogether, and as the drama develops so does the music. The score is progressive in its compositional development, and the cues become musically more elaborate as the emotional issues between the characters grow more and more complicated. From chamber sounding jazz sequences with an emphasis on the solo parts, the score expands toward the end into an impressive symphonic composition with complex polyphonic texture, modern dissonant harmonies, and massive orchestral accents. The score is interspersed with occasional nostalgic romantic sequences as well as with numerous restatements of a dance tune "Varsouviana," the latter having a role of an *idée fixe* throughout the score. North did not hesitate to apply diverse musical techniques in order to musically evoke a wide gamut of human emotions on the screen — from sensuality, longing, and nostalgia to lust, madness, pain, and remorse.

The Evolution of the Music: from Williams' Dualism toward North's Musical Drama

In the play Williams gave clear indications as to what type of musical comment he had envisioned in certain scenes. There are thirty-five musical directions in the play that define the basic musical concept of *Streetcar*. The music coming from the club Four Deuces is recurrent in the play as an indicator of location, ambiance, and general mood, but it also underlines the crucial dramatic moments. Williams' "blue piano," clarinet, trumpet and drums clearly imply jazz music as an essential part of the realistic world in *Streetcar*. On the other hand, the "Varsouviana" polka tune is associated with Blanche's haunting memory of her husband's suicide. This tune reappears as a subconscious reminder of her sordid past and acts as an explicit symbol of her unstable state of mind. Williams always considered music a vital element in his plays. For instance, in *The Glass Menagerie* a touching sentimental melody reoccurs throughout the play to emphasize particular points of the story. However, the music does not reflect the inner lives of the characters in the way the music in *Streetcar* does. In *The Glass Menagerie* Williams rather uses the musical statements to express his own sarcastic perception of the characters, whereas in *Streetcar* he musically underlines the characters' emotional states at every stage of the drama.

Although very general, the musical directions in *Streetcar* reveal Williams' intention to musically support and match the ambivalent nature of the play. Thus, the "blue piano," trumpet, and drums heard from the jazz club generally represent Stanley's brutish reality, while the "Varsouviana" polka tune represents Blanche's illusory world. This basic contrast motivates the further treatment of the music as objective versus subjective, realistic versus commentative, and source versus dramatic music. The latter should be taken figuratively since in some instances the source music bears dramatic significance. The dualistic musical concept of the play has been thoroughly discussed by many scholars.[19] Basically, there are nineteen cues in the play indicating source music coming from the club. They are different in their mood, tempo, volume, and dramatic significance. Twelve of them are for the "blue piano" solo, one for piano, trumpet, and drums, one for clarinet, two for trumpet and drums, one only for drums, one indicates the song "Paper Doll," and one does not identify any particular instruments. There is source music coming from the radio on two occasions, and in two other scenes Blanche is heard singing from the bathroom. On the other hand, Williams had the polka tune appear twelve times during the play, almost at every mentioning of Blanche's marriage. When Kazan directed the play he used a four-piece orchestra that played ferocious jazz tunes which defined the location setting and the present reality. He reduced the use of the "blue piano," replaced it in several scenes with the orchestra, and did certain adjustments in the use of the songs that Williams indicated in his script. Kazan also made very consistent use of the polka tune in terms of linking it not only to Blanche's memory of the painful incident from the past, but also to her declining mental condition.[20] All of these directorial adjustments were used and further developed by North in the film version of *Streetcar*.

North's rich theater experience greatly influenced his approach toward film scoring. While working in the theater North developed a habit of reading and profoundly analyzing the original text of the play prior to composing music for it. This routine proved very helpful in the process of film scoring because in the plays of certain playwrights, such as Tennessee Williams or Arthur Miller, the role of the music is determined quite precisely. "I get a lot out of a phrase," said North, "especially an Arthur Miller phrase, which kicks off a musical idea. And I use them quite often. Certainly in *Streetcar*, the titles, Belle Reve, Della Robia Blue, and certain very poetic phrases gave me an 'inspirational' feel about how to approach the scene..."[21] Unlike many film composers who prefer to start composing after they have seen the finished film, North kept the habit first reading the script and making the initial notes about the music in consultation with the director. He would often come up with the basic musical concept and several thematic ideas after reading the script.

In the case of *Streetcar* North tailored the music both to the action and to the dialogue. "I try to write a phrase of music that fits the phrase of dialogue," explained North.[22] His sensitive approach to the dialogue led him toward sparse and minimal scoring. Throughout the score he often used chamber-like instrumental sound rather than full orchestral, lush sounding wall-to-wall musical accompaniment. North insisted on using small instrumental groups whenever it was necessary to make a smooth transition between the source music coming from the club Four Deuces and the original musical commentary. Similar to Kazan's concept in the stage production,

North substituted the "blue piano" with an extended jazz band, thus enabling a subtle and unobtrusive transition toward the dramatic parts of the score, featuring a chamber ensemble of strings with many combinations of brass and woodwind solos (trumpet, trombone, saxophone, clarinet, etc.). This chamber type of orchestration that North initiated in *Streetcar* became one of the landmarks in his film scoring, especially when dealing with the genre of intimate film dramas which emphasized personal conflicts and relationships. Remembering his first Hollywood scores North commented, "They asked me why are you using only eight or ten musicians or a chamber style when we have fifty musicians under contract? I said I only need two guitars, or a flute, or whatever. Wall-to-wall music doesn't pinpoint the contribution music can make. I try to avoid using music under dialogue, for example, if the performance comes off in its own right."[23] North had approximately eight weeks to compose the score for *Streetcar*. He used to orchestrate his own compositions and he had five or six reels of *Streetcar* personally orchestrated. However, being under pressure to finish the score by a certain deadline, North was obliged to use an orchestrator. He started to work with Maurice de Packh, an experienced and well-known orchestrator. Their collaboration continued in the following fifteen years.[24]

As Kazan succeeded with his film direction to highten the characters' dramatic expressions and their feeling of detainment within the physical and mental boundaries of their existence, thus North succeeded in transforming Williams' initial musical directions into highly developed dramatic composition that highlights the mental and emotional state of each of the principal characters, adds deeper meaning to their personal relationships, and creates meaningful dramatic comment. The inner logic of the score, its complex but coherant structure, the entwinement and development of the musical themes, the symbolic musical connotations, all of these elements make the music an important factor in the creation of the drama. North developed Williams' directions, such as "the distant piano goes into hectic breakdown," or "the distant piano is slow and blue," into music with its own identity. He transformed the general musical remarks into strong personal statements which made the dramatic impact of *Streetcar* even more profound and powerful. North enhanced the basic dualistic musical concept by creating additional thematic material which intensified the complexity of the ambivalent relationships. Furthermore, the music in the film successfully underlines not only the two types of antagonism in *Streetcar* — the strong confrontation between the two different worlds of Stanley's realism and Blanche's illusions — but also the emotional contradictions that characterize Blanche's deranged psyche: she is disgusted by Stanley, but she is also attracted to him; her desires directly oppose the tradition and ideals of her own world. Even though jazz represents Stanley's world of reality, North intentionally associated several jazz sequences with the character of Blanche, thus indicating her inner unbalanced emotions. Writers Darby and Du Bois criticize North's association of jazz with all of the main characters claiming that "jazz seems limited in its response to dramatic nuances and emotional change of pace."[25] One could easily disagree with this statement because North, first of all, associates jazz rather with provocative situations than characters (with the exception of Stanley). And when he uses the same type of musical themes for different characters or in different situations there is always a profound dramatic reason for it. To be truthful, North's jazz creates an intense sensual and emotional rapport between the characters, rarely seen on the screen. Further, besides successfully using and developing the jazz themes throughout the film, he combines them or confronts them, depending on the dramatic needs, with the musical material of other stylistic origins. North composed a score that not only satisfies the dynamics of the drama, but also creates emotional statements that are only implied or even contradicted by the visual action. Therefore, one could rather agree with Ken Sutak's commentary from his article on *Streetcar*: "Building to a subjective act in itself from a base of purely objective musical implications, North's score tore at an audience — it seared the heart and begged compassion of the intellect simultaneously."[26]

Musical Themes as Mental Statements and Their Interaction

Another novelty in the score for *Streetcar* was the treatment of the thematic material which introduced new and more subtle ways to use the principles of the leitmotif technique. Instead of having a separate theme for each character, which was a widely accepted trend in film scoring, North used the themes as so called "mental statements" to underline the inner tensions and the conflicts between the characters. That is, however, not to say that the principal characters were left without any particular musical characterization. The first appearance of Stanley on the screen is accompanied by an explicit jazz number (cue #6) that links his character to the other major jazz themes used to pinpoint the passionate and sexual undercurrents in the film. His musical characterization also defines jazz as a style that represents the physical world of reality throughout the film. The major jazz theme that is used and developed as "mental statements" is the lust theme, first introduced in cue #8 when Stanley meets Blanche.

Blanche, on the other hand, is musically characterized by several themes that are not strictly related to the jazz idiom. One of them, the "Varsouviana" polka, is a simple dance tune associated with Blanche's memory of the sudden suicide of her young husband and eventually with her declining mental health. As previously stated, it appears consistently throughout the score in a manner of an *idée fixe*, representing Blanche's subjective world of illusions. The other theme is a lyrical musical vision of the romantic ideals that Blanche projects in her relationship with Mitch. Both of these themes act as "mental statements" and undergo various transformations, especially Blanche's lyrical theme. They appear as separate music cues or in interaction with other musical themes. The group of Blanche's themes includes additional musical ideas, like the second theme from the "Main Title," and the angst theme, which is introduced later on in cue #32 and is entitled "Birthday Dinner." The music from the scene "Flores para los muertos" ("Flowers for the Dead") is also closely related to Blanche. It underlines the symbolism of death, metaphorically seen as the death of her ideals and illusions.

The other two principal characters, Stella and Mitch, are caught in the middle of the endless conflict between Stanley's and Blanche's worlds. As they try to find their peace with Stanley and Blanche, they end up disappointed in both of their worlds. Therefore, North does not use new musical themes for their characterization but rather reflects their ambivalent feelings toward Stanley and Blanche in the context of already existing contrasting material. There is only one theme specially composed for Stanley and Stella which had to replace the original music from the famous scene of their reunion considered "carnal" by the Catholic Legion of Decency.

North had the music sometimes running against the scene, trying to express the inner feelings of the characters regardless of the outgoing visual action. An excellent example of such musical treatment is the ending scene of the film in which Stella, upon the demands of the censors, leaves Stanley in order to punish him for his deeds. Since this was the ending by Hollywood standards and not as Williams originally intended, North accompanied this scene with the sweet sounding love theme of Stanley and Stella that was in sharp contrast with Stella actually abandoning Stanley. The music thus clearly suggested that she would eventually return to Stanley.

North's comment on his treatment of the thematic material in *Streetcar* is one of his most popular quotes, cited in almost every book and article dealing with this film: "I attempted to convey the internal, rather than external aspects of the film. By this I mean the music was related to the characters at all times and not the action. Instead of 'themes' for the specific characters, there were mental statements, so to speak, for Stanley vs. Blanche, Mitch vs. Blanche and Stanley vs. Stella.... I think you will find some of the scoring running counter to the scene because of the attempt to reflect the inner feeling of the personalities rather than the situation."[27]

Musical Analysis of the Score

The Main Title and Sisters' Reunion

The title music for *Streetcar* defines the essential qualities of the film and the score in many aspects. It is an impressive piece of symphonic jazz heard over the visuals of Kowalski's two-story apartment house and the opening credits. Its "slow blues" tempo, indicated by North, evokes the locale of the French Quarter in New Orleans where the story takes place. The rich symphonic orchestration of the basic jazz motifs slightly remind one of Gershwin's symphonic approach; however, North's musical conduct is more determined by the basic antagonism and cinematic background of *Streetcar* which is implied by the strong clash between the strings and the brass, and the concise exposition of two opposing thematic ideas. In other words, North goes straight to the core in his definition of a style that establishes the steamy urban ambience, the sensuous, profane background of the story, and thereby implicates a heavy drama. This type of musical opening was without precedent in the Hollywood film tradition. The "Main Title" music, however, not only anticipates jazz as a crucial musical element in the score, but also implies North's classical symphonic approach in the treatment of the musical material. This fusion of both, jazz and classical composition, defines the diversity and the dynamics of the musical commentary in *Streetcar*.

The main motif of the score is introduced strongly by the brass section (trumpets and trombones) in the two opening measures of the "Main Title." Its two beginning notes in a downward half step movement announce like fanfares the principal motif later connected with Stanley and his physical world of sexuality. The vamp figure that follows establishes the swinging blues *ostinato* movement throughout the first part of the "Main Title." It leads directly into the exposition of the first major, soaring musical theme in the film, played by the violins in a high register:

A Streetcar Named Desire (Warner Bros., 1951). The first page from the "Main Title" Orchestral score.

Ex. 1

This eight measure phrase is performed against the continuous vamp movement in the brass and saxophones' sections. A new piano figure joins the orchestral *ostinato* movement:

Ex. 2

The violins' theme is continued by a trumpet's four measure vibrant solo, after which the clarinet *glissando* leads toward the violins' conclusion of the first theme (Ex. 3). In this thematic section the accompanying piano figure is joined by the orchestra, thus rising in volume and intensity toward the ending of the first part of the "Main Title."

Ex. 3

After the opening credits there is a cut to a train arriving in New Orleans. At that moment the second important theme of the "Main Title" is introduced. While the first principal theme is primarily related to jazz, the second theme is rather its nostalgic, melodramatic counterpart, based on wide melodic movement. It is a short, three measure violin theme which fades out under the noise of the traffic and the crowd at the train station:

Ex. 4

    Amidst the crowd at the station and the steam from the train appears the fragile figure of Blanche DuBois. This first scene introduces several elements that symbolize Blanche's suffering throughout the film. The author Maurice Yacowar elaborates on these elements in his scholar analysis of *Streetcar*.[28] The engine steam and the crowds at the station represent the heat motif that indicates her discomfort with her own sensuality, the contact with others, as well as the pressure of people intruding into her life. The other element is noise, which appears as a product of her real environment (street noise, people shouting, passing trains) or as a haunting dance tune in her mind. Another element that bothers Blanche is light. Throughout the film she tries to cover the light and thus her age and her fading beauty. At the station Blanche approaches a young sailor who is whistling the tune "Somebody Loves Me" and asks him for directions to her sister's apartment. Her very first line comprises meaningful symbolic connotations: "They told me to take a streetcar named Desire, and then transfer to one called Cemeteries and ride six blocks and get off at Elysian Fields." Even though the streetcars Desire and Cemetery really existed in the old streetcar system in New Orleans they did not run as far as Elysian Fields which was located outside the French Quarter. Hence, their combination has poetic and symbolic significance. Desire and death, symbolically linked to Blanche's sordid past, bring her to her last destination, ironically called Elysian Fields, where she unfortunatelly does not find her paradise.[29]

    Blanche's arrival in New Orleans, her journey through the French Quarter to Stella's apartment, and the ensuing sequence in the bowling alley where she meets her sister, these are the scenes where Kazan decided to "open up" the play and vividly establish the atmosphere of the area where the Kowalskis live. Heading toward Stella's place, Blanche is surrounded by wild music tunes coming from the night clubs. These beginning scenes are underscored with source music (cues #2 and 3) in an exuberant Dixieland style which creates a sharp contrast between the loose atmosphere of the dirty neighborhood and Blanche's lady-like appearance. For these opening scenes North initially composed a rhythmic jazz piece entitled "New Orleans Street," but it was later cut out of the film and replaced with source music. The source music continues softly during the dialog between Blanche and Eunice, the landlady of the two-story building where Stella and Stanley live. She confirms that Blanche has arrived at the right place, and tells her where to find her sister. The music stops with the shot of the bowling alley where Stella watches Stanley bowling. Stella is excited to see Blanche and runs to greet her. Their meeting is not underscored with any music.

Upon their arrival at the apartment, Stella prepares a hot tub for Blanche, one of the many during the film. Some authors suggest that the hot tubs represent a retreat from the outside world for Blanche, but they also imply her efforts to "wash off" her past.[30] During this scene, the transition from the source music to the dramatic underscoring occurs. The conversation between Stella and Blanche is first accompanied by a rag time *Japanese Sandman* (cue #4), heard as background source music coming from the neighboring club, Four Deuces. The piece is played by a piano solo, and afterwards joined by a jazz band. Blanche looks over the place where she will be living, while Stella talks about Stanley and her love for him. The music fades out for a moment and returns after Blanche's ironic comment on Stella's emotional fondness for Stanley: "I guess that's what's meant by being in love." The new cue that follows is entitled "Belle Reve Reflections" (#5, R2 P2 [Reel 2 Part 2]) and it is North's first musical comment in the film after the "Main Title." It is basically a new arrangement of the title music for a jazz band, extended by a new section after the exposition of the second theme. With its new orchestration, slower tempo, and additional theme this cue enhances the feeling of Blanche's solitude during her agitated monologue about the loss of Belle Reve, the estate of the family DuBois in Laurel, Mississippi. Blanche, in a way, blames Stella for leaving her to deal all on her own with their family problems, deaths and financial issues.

Since the music is dramatically linked to Blanche's confession about the loss of their home property, the principal theme from the "Main Title" is often identified as a Belle Reve theme. It is exposed by different solo instruments which change every two measures. This was to become one of North's favorite ways of thematic exposition. Whereas in the "Main Title" the tempo indication was "slow blues" in "Belle Reve Reflections" it was marked as "tender, reflective." Unlike the "Main Title," this sequence is arranged for an extended jazz ensemble which allows smooth transition from the source rag-time music heard from the club Four Deuces. Similarly, the thematic material in the "Belle Reve Reflections" is given to solo instruments (English horn, bassoon, alto sax), while in the "Main Title" violins are the dominant orchestral group for the introduction of the principal themes. All of these elements provide the sequence "Belle Reve Reflections" with more intimate, personal, and chamber character.

The principal musical idea (Ex. 1 and Ex. 3) is expressed by a solo bassoon and English horn which alternate in the continuous exposition of the theme. The second theme (Ex. 4) is given to a solo piano. The music is for a moment covered by the sound of the passing train which emphasizes Blanche's agitated reaction to Stella's questioning. The monologue that Blanche delivers in a tense, nervous manner is accompanied by the new musical section which brings an expressive alto sax solo in counterpoint with a piano figure originating from the previous, second theme:

Ex. 5

This theme is used only on this occasion and it is not further dramatically developed. The cue is expressed by a short coda based on the beginning phrase from the principal theme, played by a solo bassoon. The music ends as men's loud voices indicate Stanley's return home. In general, "Belle Reve Reflections" does not have a symmetric musical form, but it is composed more as an elegy following the rhythm and dynamics of the spoken dialog.

The themes from the "Main Title" are used in several other cues in the score. The first principal theme reappears, however, only in two more occasions in combination with other thematic material (Blanche's birthday dinner, cues #33 and 34), and it also concludes the film as "End Title" music. The second theme (Ex. 4), on the other hand, is used more consistently throughout the film either as principal thematic material or as musical counterpoint. It reoccurs in seven other music cues. This theme is reminiscent of Blanche's arrival in the city (it accompanies the train entering the New Orleans station), and as such it could be included into the group of Blanche's themes.

Stanley and Blanche

Stanley's initial appearance and his first meeting with Blanche are underscored with a jazz piece entitled "Stan" (#6, R2 P3). His visual sex appeal is evidently overwhelming for Blanche. The music enhances the feeling of his elemental sex drive that dominates the screen. In an interview entitled "Brando is a sexy sax," Alex North comments on his use of saxophone for Brando's role of Stanley Kowalski: "A saxophone has such sex appeal. It can wail, be mournful and can arouse the physical and the sexual." [31]

The basic mood is established with a bouncing piano jazz vamp that continues throughout the sequence. The cue consists of two phrases brought out by an alto sax solo and a clarinet solo. The first phrase, combined with the visual effect of Stanley's sensual appearance, sounds sexy, insinuating, and somewhat mocking. It is a swinging melody with a "lazy" moving dotted rhythm and a repeated half-step motif which forms the actual theme:

Ex. 6

The musical movement continues with a short bouncy phrase, interspersed with eighth rests. This creates an interesting "hiccup" effect. The first half of the phrase is played in by an alto sax solo, then followed by the clarinet :

Ex. 7

These two phrases repeat in a slightly varied version. The first phrase is short-ened, and the second is extended and played an octave lower. The same music cue, somewhat varied and extended with an introductory clarinet solo, was later used to accompany the famous "carnal" scene of Stella's and Stanley's reunion. But after the alto sax solo, the music was cut and replaced with a new music sequence (cue #17).

The scene between Blanche and Stanley ends with the first statement of the polka tune "Varsouviana," initiated by Stanley asking Blanche if she was married before. The music begins as Stanley's question echoes in Blanche's mind; and after she confirms the fact that she was once married, she covers her ears with her hands which clearly shows that the tune is a product of her imagination. The music is cut by a gun shot, as happens most of the time when Blanche hears the melody in her mind.

Ex. 8

The following scene in the film is the equivalent of the second scene in the play. The music begins as Blanche comes out of the bathroom, after one of her hot tubs. This cue is entitled "Stan Meets Blanche" (#8, R3 P1) and it brings out a new major theme in the score, identified as the lust theme. It underlines the sexual undercur-rent during the long conversation between Blanche and Stanley. It emphasizes their different appearances, and it also reveals the flirty, seductive side of Blanche's char-acter which is typical of her behavior with men. This jazz piece is one of the several "mental statements" used to define the essence of the fundamental relationships in the film. The lust theme appears often throughout the film, whenever there is evi-dence of sexual tension between the principal protagonists. The piece is built over a slow walking piano figure supported by a bass *pizzicato* movement. Both provide the composition with a steady rhythmic flow. The piano figure resembles the one from the "Main Title" (Ex. 2) which might have served as its source of origin:

A Streetcar Named Desire, still (Warner Bros., 1951). Blanche (Vivien Leigh) and Stanley (Marlon Brando).

Ex. 9

The lust theme is an eight measure phrase introduced by a muted trumpet solo. It is based on a half step motif associated with Stanley's basic musical motto:

Ex. 10

Ex. 10 *cont.*

The piece further develops through five consecutive solos of different instruments (alto sax, trumpet, trombone, clarinet, and tenor sax), each introducing a new melodic line. In spite of its rhapsodic structure and several different melodic phrases, this long musical sequence is defined by its basic lust motif which is easily recognized in its later appearances.

As the scene continues Stanley asks Blanche to show him the papers of the sold estate. He wants to be sure that Blanche is telling the truth about the lost property. When Blanche takes out of the trunk a box in which she keeps the documents, Stanley sees another sheaf of papers and asks what they are. Blanche responds that these are love letters. At this moment the "Varsouviana" is heard. The viewer knows immediately that the letters are from Blanche's dead husband. Stanley grabs the letters from Blanche and she struggles to get them back. The letters fall on the floor and Blanche kneels down and starts gathering them up. She is really upset for a moment, but then she quickly recovers control of herself. This scene is underscored with an extended version of the polka tune consisting of two repeated phrases (the form is *a b a b*).

As the conversation comes to its conclusion Stanley mentions to Blanche that Stella is pregnant. This revelation is followed by a short music cue entitled "Reaction to Birth" (#10, R4 P1a). North used the second theme from the "Main Title" to express Blanche's surprised reaction. It is just a concise reminiscence of the theme with the flute playing the beginning motif, after which the trumpet carries on the melody. This brief musical statement is encircled by a bass clarinet playing a melodic conclusion in a dotted rhythmic movement which resembles Stanley's motif. During this musical sequence Stella returns to the apartment, and the sisters are ready to go out for dinner. As they leave, Stanley's friends, Steve and Pablo, enter the house carrying a case of beer.

The Poker Night

The scene that includes the events of the poker night matches the third scene of the play. The beginning of the scene demanded use of source music as a part of the action. Eunice, the landlady who lives in the upper apartment, wakes up to the sounds of the source music coming from the club Four Deuces, where a jazz band (sax, trumpet, piano, bass, drums) plays the tune "I Got a Right to Sing a Blues." This song is heard as background music during the opening part of the scene. The sisters return home and Blanche meets Mitch for the first time. She comments that he looks "superior to the others," and asks Stella if he is married. The music fades out as the sisters chat and laugh.

Stella goes to the bathroom and Blanche turns on the radio while waiting for her turn to take a bath. The sounds of the song "The Girl with the Spanish Shawl" fill the room. The dancing rhumba music disturbs Stanley. Ignoring the comments from his pals who do not mind a little entertainment, he jumps up, turns off the radio, and returns to the poker table.

Mitch is getting ready to leave the game, and on his way to the bathroom encounters Blanche. Their conversation is accompanied by the first statement of Blanche's theme (#14, R4 P1B). After the lust theme, this is the second major theme used throughout the film as a "mental statement." It is linked to the relationship between Blanche and Mitch. This theme is introduced by a clarinet solo accompanied by piano, guitar, bass, and drums. The music is very soft, and it can be hardly heard under the dialog which diminishes its overall impact as a musical commentary. Blanche's theme is a dreamy, nostalgic, lyrical tune which indicates her romantic ideals and hopes for a fulfilling relationship with a man. It is a lyrical antithesis to the lust theme and it provides the intense score with moments of relaxation and serenity. The music expresses Blanche's true, inner desire to establish a successful relationship with Mitch whom she considers her last chance for survival in a world full of cruelty and suffering. The musical sequence is built out of two phrases:

Ex. 11

Ex. 12

The subsequent music cue, entitled "Blanche and Mitch," is a short version of Blanche's theme which emerges during their conversation. As they chat, Blanche asks Mitch to cover the light bulb with a paper lantern, which is one of her many attempts to avoid the direct light and hide her age and fading beauty. Her aversion to light is expressed in her statement, "I can't stand a naked light bulb, any more than I can a rude remark or a vulgar action."[32] She wants to transform her little space into a replica of Belle Reve and, moreover, turn the reality into magic. The music starts at the moment he disagrees with Blanche who claims to be an "old maid schoolteacher." He says: "You may teach school, but you're certainly not an old maid."[33] This is a cue for a new rendition of Blanche's theme in a different, more "emotional" arrangement, indicating the growing compassion between the two characters. Regarding the musical structure, this cue resembles the previous one, only in this version the first phrase is omitted. The main melody is given to a violin solo with a transparent and unobtrusive accompaniment of harp, piano, flutes, vibraphone, and strings joining toward the end of the sequence. The music is timed to end exactly when Stella enters the room.

Blanche turns on the radio to celebrate with music the hanging of the paper lantern over the light bulb. The waltz "Wien, Wien, nur du allein" begins to play, and Blanche starts dancing to the music (as is indicated in Williams' play). Mitch joins her with clumsy movements and gestures. The optimistic atmosphere does not last for long because Stanley, already drunk, fiercely storms into Blanche's little cubicle, grabs the radio and throws it out the window. His action upsets Stella who rushes into the poker room and chases Stanley's pals out of the apartment. Stanley becomes furious and violent, he takes Stella out and smacks her. This causes a commotion, the men try to subdue Stanley, and Blanche takes Stella to Eunice's apartment.

The ensuing musical sequence accompanies the legendary scene of Stanley's and Stella's reunion that the Legion of Decency and the Breen office considered too sexual and carnal and required certain changes to. These included the substitution of a series of close shots with one long, distant shot, as well as the replacement of the music which was labeled too "suggestive" of Stella's sexual behavior. "Now that incident is in law books dealing with the First Amendment of the U. S. Constitution of right to free speech and expression," North recalled. "…I had already written a sensuous piece … for a small jazz combination of cup-muted trombones, saxophone solo, and drums … what Herb Spencer called 'early Ellington style' … I had to re-do it with a French horn and strings, and a mournful quality…. In a sense it worked, but the other was more consistent with the character of Stanley." That was true because for this scene North basically used the music from cue #6 which suggested Stanley's irresistible sexual superiority (Ex. 6). In this case, North added an extended clarinet solo as an introduction to the music cue. The truth is that the beginning section of the original music cue is kept in the film (cue #17, R5 P3). The clarinet solo develops through eight measures while Stanley takes a shower and slowly regains his senses:

Ex. 13

He recalls the past event and remorsefully looks for Stella. During this part of the scene the alto sax solo plays the varied melody from Ex. 6. Stanley calls Stella by phone, but Eunice refuses to let him talk to her. He goes out, comes to the bottom of the stairs leading to Eunice's apartment, and begins yelling his famous Stell-lah-hhhh! After thirteen measures of the alto sax solo the music is cut, and Stanley's final scream for Stella is left without musical accompaniment, which is actually a nice effect before Stella's decision to come down the stairs. The new music cue (R5 P3a) begins as she seductively approaches Stanley while he kneels down with an apologetic gesture. Their reunion is sensual and intense. The music cue that replaced the original one is composed in a more traditional Hollywood manner which is not compatible with the usual jazzy tone of the musical comments for such sensual behavior throughout the film. The sequence is opened by a two note horn motif followed by gentle harp and flute arpeggios. The beginning motif develops into the main theme of this sequence, introduced by a bass clarinet with violins' counterpoint:

Ex. 14

After the initial exposition of this theme the lower strings take over the melody and carry it on until the end of the music sequence, while the high violins continue their counterpoint. Even though the musical style of this sequence might be slightly digressive from the general course of the score, it is a very lyrical, beautifully arranged piece of music.

Stanley lifts Stella and carries her into their dark apartment and the music stops abruptly at that moment. Blanche comes out of Eunice's apartment and with a concerned look on her face runs down the stairs. She stops in front of the closed door of Kowalski's home. As she steps back in confusion, Mitch appears from around the corner. They have a short conversation which is accompanied by a music cue entitled "Mitch and Blanche on Staircase" (#18, R5 P4). It has only twelve measures, and starts with a single piano chord as an opening signal. This musical interlude is a varied version of Blanche's theme written for clarinet solo. The tempo marked in the score is "slow/freely in blues style." The melody and the rhythm of the theme are freely altered. The melodic line is much more developed, and the dotted rhythm emphasizes the swing movement and its jazzy effect:

Ex. 15

However, the harmony under the clarinet solo clearly preserves the contours of Blanche's theme. Blanche thanks Mitch for being so kind to her, especially because "there's so much confusion in the world…" Their conversation concludes the events of the poker night.

The Aftermath of the Poker Night

The following morning Blanche returns to the apartment. She is astonished when she sees that Stella is calm and happy after the events of the previous night. Blanche can explain Stella's lack of resistance only as a result of brutal desire, even though Stella keeps persuading her that she actually loves Stanley. During their conversation there is a shot showing Stanley approaching the house. He hears Blanche criticizing him, and one can notice the devilish look on his face. Blanche's ambivalent behavior, her flirty gestures and remarks when they are alone, as well as her criticism that is directed against him, all of these elements cause Stanley's revolt and escalating rage that sharpen the tension between him and Blanche.

The music starts when Stanley enters the apartment. Blanche is terrified of the encounter with Stanley. The music cue is entitled "Stan" (#19, R6 P1) and has two contrasting sections. The ominous dark mood is established with the repetitions of a rising short chromatic figure under the solo of the muted trumpet. The melody is made of motifs from the lust theme (Ex. 10) and Stanley's theme (Ex. 6), indicating his crude instincts and rough nature:

Ex. 16

The trumpet solo lasts while Stanley is entering the apartment, and it is continued by a new repeated motif played in the low violins' register as Stanley looks around for Stella:

Ex. 17

Stella cannot resist Stanley's charm, runs toward him, and to Blanche's astonishment she falls into his embrace. Stanley is holding Stella, gazing over her shoulder at Blanche with a look full of victory and revenge. The music sharply changes its mood, bringing a new section characterized by a harmonic upward movement in the strings:

Ex. 18

This new musical section evokes a romantic, sweet, and optimistic mood. In this regard it reminds one of the music from the previous scene of Stella's and Stanley's reunion. North achieved an excellent emotional contrast and a skillful transition between the grim first section and the light, cheerful second section of the sequence.

Blanche and Stella

The next musical sequence appears in the ensuing scene (the fifth one in the play), after Stanley's threatening implications that he learned something about Blanche's past in Laurel. He leaves the apartment and Blanche, frightened of his insinuations, starts questioning Stella as to if she heard any gossip about her. This is basically Blanche's soliloquy about her deepest fears of aging, losing her beauty, and thus the power over men. Her concern of losing her chances for a survival in the world of reality is easily understood since she is deeply affected by the Southern tradition according to which a woman is self-realized only through a male protector. The music cue that underscores this scene is entitled "Belle Reve" (#20, R7 P1). The music portrays Blanche's anguish as she recalls her last years at Belle Reve, while its bitonal harmonic quality underlines her more and more evident mental instability. The sequence has a strong emotional impact and it is not composed in a jazz manner. It shows North's compositional skills in combining and varying the important motifs from the score and adjusting them to the dramatic situation. The music develops through three sections in which new thematic material is entwined in a very subtle way with the various motifs from the "Main Title," "Varsouviana," Blanche's theme, and Stanley's theme.

The first part of the cue brings a plaintive theme for solo violin (Ex. 19), interspersed with celesta motifs from the second theme of the "Main Title." The theme is accompanied by the clarinet vamp figure from the "Main Title."

Ex. 19

The strings are the dominant orchestral group and they bring out the main melodic lines in this cue. In the second section they are divided to create a rich harmonic texture with the viola and violoncello playing a bitonal melodic phrase while violins perform wailing parallel triads. There are slight indications of Stanley's motif in the viola's part (measure 15). The violins' triads gradually develop the beginning motif from the polka theme which Ross Care appropriately calls "an impressionistic statement of the 'Varsouviana.'"[34] The vamp figure from the "Main Title" returns and prepares the third section of the cue which is based on an extended exposition of the second theme of the "Main Title" in the violins' part. It includes vague reference to Blanche's motif (measure 31), and gradually rises in volume and intensity and culminates with Blanche's hysterical scream when Stella by accident spills some coke on her dress.

Blanche calms down and the conversation continues. She begins to talk about Mitch and how she deceived him about her age just "enough to make him want her." Her revelation that she would really like to have a stable relationship with him is accompanied by a sentimental, nostalgic statement of Blanche's theme for high violins (#21, R7 P1a). This cue contains only the first phrase of the theme joined by a chromatically developed clarinet counterpoint. The music enhances the feeling of hope as Stella kisses Blanche and expresses her belief that Mitch and Blanche will be together. Blanche's fantasizing is abruptly interrupted by the laugh of the noisy neighbors which replaces the fading music and brings Blanche from her dream world into reality. Stanley calls Stella and she leaves Blanche to join him in the club Four Deuces.

The Newspaper Collector

Blanche is alone in the apartment waiting for Mitch who is coming to take her out on a date. A young man who appears to be a newspaper collector rings the bell and enters the apartment. This scene is underscored by a long and complex music cue entitled "Collector" (#22, R7 P2). Again, this piece is a wonderful example of North's modernistic, concert style composition, deeply related to the dramatic events on the screen. Blanche is taken by the youth of the handsome paper boy and tries to seduce him, but in a different way than she does with other men — without any manipulation. The whole scene looks as if it is a product of her imagination. Brenda Murphy suggests that this incident with the newspaper collector reenacts what happened with the seventeen-year-old student in Laurel.[35] The earlier incident was the reason Blanche lost her job in the school. In general, young men evoke the memory of her dead husband. Hence, her need to give them protection is as strong as her desire to find somebody to protect her.

The music cue uses the "Varsouviana" as a main musical commentary for this scene. There are two sections in this sequence. The first one is characterized by an alternation of melodic phrases for strings and short statements of the "Varsouviana" for celesta, while the second section brings a full exposition of the polka tune. The first part of this piece is developed over a steady piano beat which implies the character of a funeral march. The strings are divided, and the first viola and violin form a musical dialog. Each of the string phrases ends with a dissonant harmonized chord, followed by the first phrase from the "Varsouviana" played by celesta. The steady piano beat which remains under the polka tune is in sharp contrast with the "music-box" childish effect of the melody. The dialog between the viola and the violin continues in the second phrase. The dissonant effect is even sharper than in the first phrase. The "Varsouviana" tune follows after the second phrase. The third and the fourth string phrases are built in similar manner, including the statements the "Varsouviana" which are superimposed over the string motifs and the steady piano beat.

The second section starts as Blanche compares the boy to "a young prince out of Arabian Nights." The first phrase of the "Varsouviana" is heard in the violas' high register in a slow, augmented movement without the usual dotted rhythm. The "music box" effect is maintained with the celesta and harp counterpoint. The second phrase is played in the violas' low register. This chamber, melancholic piece has a dissonant and somewhat bitonal quality and supports the element of fantasy in this scene. It almost sounds as if it were a musical conviction of Blanche's preoccupation with youth and beauty confronted by her fear of the aging process.

Blanche and Mitch

The newspaper collector leaves after Blanche kisses him tenderly on his mouth. A moment later Mitch appears with a bouquet of roses, ready to take Blanche out to a dance. The next scene, equivalent to the sixth one in the play, is another example of Kazan's attempt to "open up" the play. Blanche and Mitch are seen in a dance casino for a moment, then they go out on the pier where they have a long conversation which ends with Blanche's story about her husband's suicide.

This scene is underscored with a series of music cues (#23 to #28). There is a jazz band in the casino (trumpet, saxophone, clarinet, piano, bass, and drums) that plays two songs in a row. The symbolic reoccurrence of "Somebody Loves Me," the tune that the sailor whistled at the beginning of the film, suggests Blanche's hope for a happy future with Mitch. As Blanche and Mitch go out on the pier, the source music continues under their dialog as background music. Their causal chatting reveals Mitch as both a naive and a strong man, who perfectly suits Blanche's needs to dominate and to be protected at the same time. On the other hand, Blanche awakens his instincts and needs to be a man, thus giving him a chance to break free from his mother. Hence, they are both in need of each other. North's music begins after Mitch asks Blanche about her age. The subsequent music cues use Blanche's theme and the "Varsouviana" as basic thematic material to accompany Blanche's extended monologue.

The music sequence entitled "Medley" (#25, R8 P2) begins with a slower, very emotional version of Blanche's theme (Ex. 11), played softly by a trumpet solo over syncopated strings. The first phrase is repeated by the violins. During this part of the sequence Mitch says that he talked to his sick mother about Blanche, and that she wants to see him settled down because she will not live forever. The second phrase of the theme (Ex. 12) is heard when Blanche starts telling the story of her lost youthful love. While the violins play this phrase, the "Varsouviana" is superimposed on the celesta. The clash between the original key, F minor, and the exposition of "Varsouviana" in E flat major creates an eerie effect. The contrast is intensified by the combination of different metric flows— 4/4 for Blanche's theme and 3/4 for the polka tune. These elements, in addition to the conflict between the instrumental timbres of the violins and the celeste, clearly indicate Blanche's neurotic state of mind. The two phrases from the "Varsouviana" and Blanche's theme end at the same time, but the music continues with the middle section from the "Varsouviana" in E flat major, heard for the first time in the film:

Ex. 20

This musical section evokes a light-hearted, optimistic feeling and it is an excellent example of music running against the action. The first phrase of the polka reappears in the violoncellos' low register in the key of G major, and it is extended by the phrase from the previous section (Ex. 20), this time played by violas. This concludes the musical sequence #25.

As Blanche continues her excited description of the night when her husband committed suicide, the violins repeat in a faster tempo the two beginning phrases from the "Varsouviana" in the key of G major, interrupted by a gun shot. The cue is entitled "Consummation" (#26, R9 P1), and it is followed by another repetition of the entire "Varsouviana" dance for celesta while Blanche concludes her story in Mitch's embrace. The scene between Blanche and Mitch ends with them kissing each other and Blanche whispering, "Sometimes there's God so quickly!" The musical conclusion brings the beginning phrase from Blanche's theme, played by the violins in the key of G major, the same key as the "Varsouviana," maybe as a sign of Blanche making peace with herself after the confession, as well as an indication of hope for a possible future with Mitch. The series of music cues underscoring this scene create an amazing contrast to the dramatic monologue that Blanche delivers in an intense theatrical style. The optimistic, dance-like music reflects Blanche's memory of the night she danced with her husband in a similar casino where he committed suicide. The music sounds ghostly, almost unreal, and in the context of Blanche's confession it perfectly portrays the deep disturbance of her mind caused by the unhappy events of the past. The music was a precious dramatic device in this scene, especially because the censors banned the subject of homosexuality from the script, thus leaving the cause for the suicide of Blanche's husband just vaguely indicated.

The Birthday Party

Stanley's investigation of Blanche's past has disastrous consequences for Blanche. By telling Mitch and Stella about Blanche's bad reputation and her flighty life style in Laurel, Stanley ruins the last hopes for her happy future. Therefore, Williams' indication of Blanche singing the song "Paper Moon" from the bathroom while preparing for her birthday party strongly emphasizes the sharp contrast between her fragile illusions and harsh reality. Her singing is heard in the background while Stanley reveals to Stella what he has learned about Blanche. The words of the song symbolically refer to Blanche's character: "It's only a paper moon, Just as phony as it can be — But it wouldn't be make-believe/If you believed in me." Stella is visibly distressed by Stanley's revelation, but tries to hide her feelings when Blanche comes out from the bathroom. Blanche, however, sees the change in Stella's behavior and senses that something bad has happened, although Stella refuses to talk about it.

The musical sequence that follows is a modern piece for chamber ensemble, entitled "Birthday Dinner" (#32, R9 P2). It links the previous scene to the next one (the eighth scene in the play) which shows the three characters — Blanche, Stella, and Stanley — at the dinner table. There is a great deal of tension in the atmosphere, and Blanche is obviously puzzled by the fact that Mitch has not showed up for her birthday. She tries to cover up her disappointment with a second-rate joke that nobody finds amusing but herself. As the emotional tension in the film grows, the jazzy tone of the music is gradually replaced by a more dissonant orchestral treatment of the thematic material. In fact, this musical sequence introduces a new theme known as Blanche's angst theme. The melody of the theme does not have a firm tonal center, thus appropriately reflecting Blanche's growing mental and emotional instability. In its first appearance it is played by the violas in a smooth rhythmic movement:

Ex. 21

The motifs from the angst theme are used later in several other music cues indicating Blanche's mental decline. After the initial exposition of the theme, the melodic movement of the violas and violoncellos continues as a counterpart to a new melodic line for the violins. This sounds like a freely treated variation of the angst theme and further intensifies the dissonant contrapuntal effect:

Ex. 22

The melodic flow is interrupted by a telephone ring and for three measures there is only an ominous steady drum beat indicating Blanche's heavy heart beat as she wonders if that might be Mitch calling. She can hardly hide her disappointment when she realizes that the telephone ringing comes from the apartment upstairs. The beginning motif from the angst theme appears in the violas' part when Blanch makes an unsuccessful attempt to continue the joke. The melody is interrupted and the same motif is repeated in the violoncello part leading toward the end of this sequence as Stella raises her voice and insults Stanley. The music also rises in its intensity and ends when Stanley, angry and violent, hurls his dinner plate to the floor.

The next music cue (#33, R10 P1a) starts a few moments later when Stanley leaves the dinner and goes out on the porch. Blanche's anxiety is growing because she feels that Stanley has told Mitch bad things about her. She questions her sister, but Stella stays reticent and does not want to hurt Blanche by telling her the truth. The music introduces the beginning of the angst theme for the strings in an accelerating upward movement, after which follows a dialog of two new motifs for divided violins:

Ex. 23

Blanche, determined to discover the truth, calls Mitch and leaves a message for him. In the meantime, Stella joins Stanley out on the porch and expresses her feelings of sorrow for Blanche. At this moment the mood of the music changes as Stanley tries to convince Stella that things will change for the better when her sister leaves. The smooth transition to a tender romantic theme for violins reminds one of the similar effect in cues #17 and #19, where violin themes were also used to underline the affectionate moments between Stella and Stanley.

In the course of this scene Stanley presents Blanche with his birthday gift — a bus ticket to Laurel. The music cue that follows is one of the most complex music pieces in the score which combines all of the basic thematic ideas. It contains two different parts: "Birthday Party" (R10 P2) and "Blanche's Solitude" (R10 P3). The first part begins with the reminiscence of Blanche's angst theme, carried on by different string groups: violoncellos, violas, and violins. It is encircled by the second theme from the "Main Title" on the piano and celesta as Blanche leaves the scene, running to her room. The following musical section accompanies Stella's and Stanley's argument in which Stella defends Blanche while Stanley tries to remind her how happy they were before Blanche came to live with them. The bassoons play the beginning motif from the angst theme, while the violoncellos repeat a short three note motif from the same theme in diminished note values. Over this melodic movement violins play a soaring melody which contains an augmented motif from the second theme of the "Main Title." This orchestral texture is enriched with the clarinets' vamp figure from the "Main Title" and the beginning motif from the lust theme. The musical conclusion of the cue is built on the sentimental major version of the principal theme from the "Main Title" for a violin solo. The first part ends as Stella starts feeling labor pains and asks Stanley to take her to the hospital. This music cue is an exceptional example of the combination of motifs from the main themes using various compositional techniques. Such techniques include: dividing the motifs into smaller units and treating them further as counterpoint, involving different instruments for exposition of a continuous phrase, alterations in the rhythm and the melody of the motifs, changing minor motifs into major and *vice versa*, etc.

The second part of the cue #34, "Blanche's Solitude," follows without pause. The scene (the ninth one in the play) opens with Blanche sitting in her dark room, drinking alcohol in desperation. The bells play the half-step motif from the lust theme, clearly indicating Blanche's psychotic state of mind:

Ex. 24

The music suddenly changes its mood when the door bell rings. Blanche is startled when she hears it is Mitch pounding at the door. Preoccupied with her looks even in the most hopeless situations, Blanche runs toward the mirror to daub powder on her face and comb her hair before she opens the door. Blanche's very last hope for a miracle is underlined with the second theme from the "Main Title" played by the violins. The cue is appropriately concluded with a melodic movement based on the angst theme and the beginning figure from Blanche's theme as Mitch breaks into the apartment.

Blanche's Final Breakdown

The scene between Blanche and Mitch brings the *Streetcar* drama to its culmination. Mitch is drunk, unshaven, feeling miserable and betrayed. He confronts Blanche with the facts that he has learned about her past in Laurel. Despite the hopeless circumstances, Blanche makes her last effort to win him back, but Mitch is relentless. In the middle of his offensive tirade Blanche hears the sounds of the "Varsouviana" in her mind, which is usually interrupted by the gun shot. But this time the music goes on after the shot, and Mitch for the first time becomes aware of her unstable mental state. After being disclosed, physically and mentally, Blanche has her famous monologue about death and desire where she reveals her true self, her ideals, her past, and the reasons of being the way she is. The music that accompanies her speech is one of the most powerful sequences in terms of its dramatic, cinematic, and pure musical impact. The sequence is entitled "Revelation" (#36, R11 P1), but it is better known as "Flores para los muertos" ("Flowers for the Dead"). This complex and extended musical piece has three sections. The first section is built on several motifs from the principal themes. It opens with the varied beginning motif from Blanche's theme for flutes, which is followed by a half-step oscillating figure, reminiscent of the lust theme. The oboe plays a descending chromatic counterpoint which will become an important motif in the building of the emotional intensity toward the end of this scene:

Ex. 25

This melodic movement, repeated by different groups of woodwinds, leads toward an exposition of Blanche's theme at the moment when Blanche confesses that meeting Mitch gave her hope for a brighter future. The melody alternates between the high and the low register of the divided violins, and it is played against the chromatic counterpoint of the lower strings. After the exposition of Blanche's theme, the violins continue to play a variation of the second theme from the "Main Title" on top of dense piano chords which establish the rhythm and atmosphere similar to that of a funeral match.

Blanche's exclamation "I didn't lie in my heart..." is a cue for the second musical section that introduces a new musical theme as a woman's ghostly voice is heard calling: "Flores. Flores. Flores para los muertos." Blanche is terrified by the Mexican woman whom she sees as a symbolic messenger of death. The dissonant sonority of this musical section intensifies the macabre atmosphere of the scene. The flores theme is introduced in the violas and violoncellos, and it is further carried on and developed by the violins:

Ex. 26

The third musical section leads toward the final emotional climax as Blanche's monologue grows more and more frantic. The music is built over a wailing descending chromatic movement of the strings, a motif introduced in the first section of the cue (Ex. 25). This movement is intensified with the short upward and downward *glissandi* in the violoncellos while the violins build the melody on the interval of the fifth, deriving from Blanche's theme. The violins, supported by woodwinds and trumpets, bring the cue to its powerful conclusion with the ascending movement of the half-step motifs against the *ostinato* chromatic movement:

Ex. 27

The cue ends with a long dissonant chord as Blanche starts screaming after Mitch's attempt to assault her. Mitch runs away from the apartment while people start gathering around Blanche asking her if she feels all right. She locks herself in the apartment, closes the windows, and turns off the lights, trying to hide from the outside world. Her hysterical behavior is a final proof of her breakdown. This interlude between the scenes is musically underlined with an ingenious scherzo entitled "Mania" (#37, R11 P2 / R12 P1). At this place in the play Williams' musical direction indicates slow and blue music of a distant piano, but North had a different musical vision. The entire sequence is based on a sharp *staccato* version of motifs from Blanche's main theme, first played by a muted trumpet and consequently imitated through different brass and woodwind instruments. Massive *pizzicato* strings form a strong counterpart that creates bitonal harmony and dominates the overall movement of this piece.

The beginning of the next scene shows Blanche's withdrawal into her world of fantasy. Her lonely speech is accompanied by an orchestral version of "Good Night Ladies" which is interrupted by Stanley's return from the hospital. The entire scene is based on an intense and long dialog between Blanche and Stanley that gradually grows into a fight and culminates with Blanche's rape. This scene is underscored with several music cues. The music begins shortly after Stanley's return with cue #39 entitled "Medley." It consists of two parts. The first one is reminiscent of cue #8 and the lust theme, while the second one (R12 P6) is slightly more developed. It starts with a repeated half-step motif from the lust theme resembling the beginning movement from the cue "Revelation" (Ex. 25). It is played by the violas over descending transparent *arpeggio* triads in the parts of harp and celeste. The violas and flutes introduce a new melodic line in a contrapuntal movement with the second theme from the "Main Title." The second half of this cue brings in a violin melody that could be interpreted as a freely treated variation of Blanche's theme. The cue is encircled with the half-step motif from the beginning of this musical number.

The musical sequence that anticipates Blanche's rape is entitled "Lust" (#40, R13 P1). In some sources it can be found under the title "Seduction." A new clarinet motif is introduced in the very beginning of the cue:

Ex. 28

This motif leads toward a reminiscence of the theme "Flores para los muertos." The melodic line is played by brass instruments and afterwards repeated by a bass clarinet as Blanche sees the silhouette of the Mexican woman who sells flowers for the dead approaching her. The harmonic background grows more and more dissonant, and the linear movement of the instruments often creates bitonal musical effects.

The muted trumpet brings out the lust theme when Stanley comes back in his silk pajamas. The trumpet and trombone lust motifs alternate with the new clarinet motif (Ex. 28). There follows an elaborated section based on the new motif, developed in a scherzo manner similar to the cue "Mania." The *pizzicato* strings are opposed to accented fluttering trumpets. The trumpets play a figure consisting of repeated notes and an ascending fifth which reminds one of Blanche's main motif. Blanche tries to protect herself from Stanley with a broken bottle, but Stanley's attack leaves her completely helpless. The increasing volume and intensity of the piano tremolo is supported by a dissonant chord of the entire orchestra, screaming brass and horn *glissandi*. Since the rape is only implied with Blanche's reflection in the broken mirror, the horror of her defeat is strongly indicated with the powerful orchestral effect. In regard to this scene North said: "...I tried to evoke from the orchestra what sounded like the wail of all women suffering, the women of the world; and I think I achieved it."[36]

Blanche's Departure

The last scene of the film begins with a water hose cleaning the garbage off the street. The shot has multiple symbolic meanings.[37] "It was certainly a forceful cut," Kazan commented, "and enabled me to underline the rape implicitly..."[38] But life goes on, there is a newborn in the Kowalski family, and the dreadful event becomes a thing of the past. Except for Blanche, of course. She retreats to her world of fantasy, the only place where she feels safe. In her mind she already has a new beau, the millionaire Shep Huntleigh, who will come to take her away and marry her. Stella and Stanley make arrangements for putting Blanche in a mental hospital because they believe she can no longer function normally in the world of reality. Blanche is left alone, deserted by everyone, even by her own sister who refuses to believe her story. This last scene is underscored with a series of four music cues (#41to #44). The first one is entitled "Della Robia Blue" (R13 P2). It is a tender interlude for solo oboe, woodwinds, and strings which underscores Blanche's preparation for departure. The opening measures with repeated notes and ascending fifths recall Blanche's main motif and prepare for the exposition of a new melodic line:

Ex. 29

After this section in which the new melody is carried on and developed by different woodwind instruments, the original music cue contains a conclusion similar to the beginning of the cue "Revelation" (Ex. 25) with the strings playing the half-step lust motif against the descending chromatic movement in the celesta. Unfortunately, this musical conclusion is cut from the film by the sound of cathedral bells.

When the doctor and the matron arrive, Blanche is told that a "gentleman" is waiting for her. She makes a quick pass through the room where Stanley, Mitch and the two other men play poker. She is completely confused when she sees that the doctor is not Shep Huntleigh and runs back in the house with an excuse that she forgot something. The music cue is entitled "Doctor" (#42, R14 P2). It is composed for a chamber ensemble and evokes a compassionate mood with its solos for French horn, English horn and bassoon. The strings also have a continuous melodic counterpart. The mood is abruptly changed when Blanche encounters the doctor. The music becomes agitated and dark with repeated note figures for brass which lead toward the ending with a brisk upward passage for violins. Blanche quickly returns to her room while the echoes from different voices spin in her mind. There is a long dissonant chord (#43) as Stanley tears up the paper lantern, asking her if that is what she forgot. With her last symbol of illusion destroyed, Blanche's final hysterical outburst is inevitable.

The last music number of the score starts when the doctor comes into the room and asks the matron to release Blanche. The cue is a melancholic lament entitled "Affirmation" (#44, R14 P2). In general, it is based on the second theme from the "Main Title," heard in counterpoint with descending half-step motifs, derived from the principal theme of the "Main Title." The musical conclusion, however, brings a change in the mood. It follows Blanche's famous line "Whoever you are—I have always depended on the kindness of strangers." Blanche leaves with the doctor and the matron in a car, while Stella takes the baby, swears that she will never come back, and apparently leaves Stanley forever. As it was earlier mentioned, the ending was changed in order to satisfy the demands of the Production Code. The musical conclusion can be discussed from two different aspects. Complying with the uniform Hollywood standard of pompous musical endings, North's conclusion sounds too triumphant in comparison with the given dramatic circumstances. However, taking into consideration that the final violoncello theme is the musical reminiscence of Stella's and Stanley's reunion (Ex. 14), the entire musical ending engenders different connotations. The music actually implies that Stella, despite her firm decision, might go back to Stanley which was the original ending in Williams' play. Nevertheless, North himself was not completely satisfied with the ending of the film. He thought that dramatically it did not belong there. "I've had problems in that area since. I didn't want to go out big," North commented. "But in those days ... they insisted I make a big statement for the end.... And there's always the question of retribution. Stanley had to be blamed at the end...."

After the final musical statement the film ends with "End Title" which uses the principal theme from the "Main Title" for a brief and condensed musical conclusion.

Comments

Many scholars have discussed North's musical contribution to the film *A Streetcar Named Desire*.[39] His score is usually praised as a revolutionary work in the way it connects music and drama. The critics and the audience understood the significance of his new approach that made music a powerful device in the expression of the dramatic undercurrents not always visible on the screen. Furthermore, North showed that the music could suggest the characters' emotions and mental states, and even run against the action, indicating the true nature of the characters and the dramatic situations. The music was able to make the audience feel what was going on before anything was said or seen on the screen. North proved that music could be one of the most effective elements for direct communication with the viewer's subconscious, as opposed to the word and the image which are primarily perceived by the conscious, and often cautious, mind.

The score for *Streetcar* is a complex musical work, abundant in thematic material and musical ideas. Some of the themes are used and developed throughout the score as "mental statements," but some of them appear just once or twice in particular scenes that need a new musical comment. Melody was an important element of North's musical expression, and his melodic invention was never exhausted. North used the advantages of his theater experience by having a variety of chamber ensembles emphasize the intimate character of the film. But he also used the advantage of having a full symphonic orchestra at his disposal to create amazing orchestral effects, something that he never could have done in a theater play. The thematic treatment of the score, its orchestration and musical style, the modern compositional approach and minimal scoring, all of these novelties opened a new era in the history of film music and influenced many film composers. Ken Sutak considers the score for *Streetcar* "film music of the very highest order,"[40] while Tony Thomas called the score "a landmark in the history of Hollywood music."[41]

With the score for *Streetcar* North earned his first Academy Award nomination, but lost the Oscar to Franz Waxman for *A Place in the Sun*. There were comments that his score was too revolutionary to win an Academy Award. Nevertheless, from being a "newcomer" North became a respected and promising composer of film music. Considering that this was his first major film score, the success was unexpected and overwhelming. Arthur Miller remembered a scene when he came to meet Alex in the studio in Los Angeles where he was recording the score for *Streetcar*, "They were just finishing recording. Alex was conducting that day, and at the end of this section of music the big orchestra of thirty or forty people, they all stood up and applauded. For these bitter players in Hollywood it was not usual. But they understood what he had done. Musicians loved him. They really respected him."[42]

North's score was successfully used in a ballet production of *A Streetcar Named Desire*. The best and the most complete recording of the score was made by Jerry Goldsmith and the National Philharmonic Orchestra. This recording includes fifteen important cues from the score as well as some music that was cut from the film, such as the cue "New Orleans Streets" and the entire original cue from the "carnal" scene between Stanley and Stella. There is also a piano score that includes nine pieces based on the main musical material from various music cues. It is published by Witmark & Sons.

The score for the *Streetcar* is one of the rare film scores that has been thoroughly analyzed by many authors. This is not a surprise because the film and the music are appealing and as fascinating today as they were a half a century ago. *Streetcar* is an everlasting classic in every aspect of its cinematic expression, including North's extraordinary score. After the success of *Streetcar*, it was often said that Hollywood opened the doors to North, but from today's perspective one could rather conclude that it was North who opened the doors to Hollywood.

8

Spartacus (1960)

He wasn't a god. He was a simple man. He was a plain man. He was a slave.

— *Varinia in* Spartacus *(Howard Fast)*

The Story of Spartacus

After long-term preparations, the filming of *Spartacus* started in 1959. This was one of the most ambitious epic productions in Hollywood and it took its creators two years to complete it. The project was conceived by Kirk Douglas who was an executive producer and a star of *Spartacus*. He persuaded Universal to invest millions of dollars in the film. The superb cast included some of the most prestigious actors of the time: Kirk Douglas (Spartacus), Laurence Olivier (Marcus Licinius Crassus, the general of the Roman army), Tony Curtis (Antoninus, slave poet), Jean Simmons (Varinia, slave-girl and Spartacus' wife), Charles Laughton (Gracchus, the liberal Roman senator), Peter Ustinov (Lentulus Batiatus, the owner of the gladiators' school in Capua), John Gavin (the young Julius Caesar), and John Dall (Glabrus, the feeble Roman commander).

The movie was filmed almost entirely in Los Angeles. It took a year just to plan and build the massive sets for this historical spectacle. The scene in the Libyan salt mines was shot in California's Death Valley, while the big battle scenes were filmed in Spain, outside Madrid. The total number of people who worked on *Spartacus* was 10,500, including about 8,000 Spanish soldiers used in the re-creation of the spectacular battle scenes.

The script was written by Dalton Trumbo and it was based on the historical novel by Howard Fast. Dalton Trumbo was a left-wing writer and one of the "Hollywood Ten," blacklisted artists. This was his first screen credit since he had been blacklisted some ten years before. In fact, *Spartacus* was the first film to break the infamous Hollywood blacklist. Despite some protest from the film studio, the producers, Kirk Douglas and Edward Lewis, made the decision to use Trumbo's real name in the credits.[1]

Stanley Kubrick was brought in to direct this vast spectacle, after Douglas fired the first director, Anthony Mann. Kubrick, although in his early thirties, had already earned a respectable reputation with his 1957 production of *Paths of Glory*. He was not completely satisfied with *Spartacus*, mainly because he had limited control over the production of the film and because he was not involved in the writing of the film script. "Although I was the director, mine was only one of many voices to which Kirk listened. I am disappointed in the film. It had everything but a good story," stated Kubrick.[2] However, despite this statement, Kubrick rewrote many scenes of the script during the shooting, and the film inevitably shows his imprint in many ways. He felt comfortable with the new wide-screen color medium, Super Technirama-70, and created stunning moving compositions which culminated in the final battle scene. Kubrick's objective was to make *Spartacus* as realistic an epic as possible. This was not an easy task because few historic facts about Spartacus' rebellion were known, and therefore the story was occasionally enriched with invented intrigues.

Trumbo's adaptation deals with Spartacus' ideals for freedom, focusing on the fight of the slaves against the cruel repression of Imperial Rome. The story is set in the year 73 B.C. Spartacus, born in the Greek province of Thrace, was sold into the Libyan mines when he was just thirteen. Years later he is brought to Italy and trained to be a gladiator. While in the gladiators' school of Capua he falls in love with the slave girl Varinia who later becomes his wife and gives birth to his son. Spartacus becomes the leader of the slaves' revolt in the gladiators' school. After their victory, the slaves loot the country and then retreat to Mount Vesuvius. In time, the gladiators are joined by ninety thousand slaves. Spartacus and his gladiators train them to fight and thus form an army of slaves. On their way to the sea they defeat many Roman legions.

Their plan is to buy ships from the pirates, leave Italy, and start their new lives in freedom. But the pirates are bribed by the Romans, and Spartacus with his army is forced to turn back and fight against the entire Roman army led by general Crassus. In the final battle Spartacus' army is defeated. Only six thousand slaves survive the battle, Spartacus among them. They are crucified along the Appian Way between Capua and Rome. Varinia and her baby succeed in escaping from Rome with the help of the senator Gracchus. On her way out of Rome she sees crucified Spartacus, shows him his son, and then leaves forever. Some critics thought that the ending was a weak conclusion after the powerful battle scene and the bloody slaughter of the slaves.[3] However, despite some flaws in the story and a fictional interpretation of certain historical facts, *Spartacus* was an outstanding achievement and plea to humanity, and is remembered for its remarkable directing, superb acting, inventive editing, and strong visual and musical impact.

"It took us two years and twelve million dollars to make this movie," Douglas concluded. "We think it was worth every minute and every penny."[4]

Spartacus, still (Universal, 1960). Varinia (Jean Simmons) and Spartacus (Kirk Douglas).

An Epic Score for an Epic Movie

After ten years of composing mostly jazz-oriented scores for Williams-Faulkner types of dramas, writing a score for such a big epic spectacle as *Spartacus* was a real challenge for North. Although North always preferred to write chamber scores for little intimate pictures, *Spartacus* attracted him for two main reasons. North saw Spartacus as a type of universal hero, in many ways similar to Emiliano Zapata. He could identify with the character of Spartacus because of his personal feelings about the social events of the world. The universal theme about a fight for freedom was in many ways very contemporary. "The story itself makes a comment," North said in an interview. "It has something to say about the world which existed then and which still exists."[5] Therefore, the composer tried to capture the feeling of ancient Rome using contemporary musical techniques. "I decided here to conjure up the atmosphere of pre-Christian Rome not by resorting to archaisms and clichés, but in terms of my own contemporary, modern style — simply because the theme of *Spartacus*, the struggle for freedom and human dignity, is every bit as relevant in today's world as it was then," commented North. "I wanted to write music that would interpret the past in terms of the present."[6]

The second reason that attracted North to score *Spartacus* was the possibility to experiment with all kinds of exotic ethnic instruments, and various unusual combinations of instrumental groups within a large symphonic orchestra. "You have an opportunity to get whatever you want," North said. "With an eighty-seven piece symphony at my disposal for *Spartacus*, I wrote one sequence for pairs of reeds, another all for flutes. I used lots of percussion, guitars and mandolins."[7] In a way, North's "overture" to this type of rich instrumentation was the score for *South Seas Adventure*. As much as he preferred chamber orchestration, composing for such a large orchestra was a professional challenge. "In *Spartacus* I tried for a deliberately cold and barbaric quality, avoiding strings until the thirteenth reel, when the love story begins to blossom between Kirk Douglas and Jean Simmons," further commented North. "I relied on combinations of brass, woodwinds and some quite unusual and exotic percussion—for instance, I underscored a party scene with Nova-chord, vibes, marimba, boo-bams, crotales, fixed piano, harp, lute, guitar, sleigh bells (various pitches) and Chinese tree bell."[8] North's long-term collaborator Maurice de Packh was entrusted with the final orchestration of this epic score.

In the research of ancient Roman music North faced similar problems as Miklós Rózsa while preparing the score for *Ben-Hur*. The authentic musical sources available for research were not numerous. There were just a few authentic hymns from that period, but the material for study of Roman music included extensive information about the instruments used in ancient Rome. "We don't know what they sounded like for the most part," commented North, "so, you sort of absorb all the material that you personally can and then if you're making a personal contribution to the film, you can use contemporary instrumentation and thematic material."[9] In the recreation of the Roman war music North relied on the extensive use of brass instruments and fanfares throughout the score. "The Roman music of that time was generally of a military nature, with tremendous brazen effects," North explained.[10] However, this type of instrumental quality was used by the composer for the creation of very contemporary and personal musical commentary. In this regard, the battle music and the musical sequences underscoring the rebellion of the slaves are the best examples of "interpreting the past in terms of the present."

On the other hand, North simulated the social music of the period by creating modal instead of tonal music, experimenting with peculiar rhythms, and combining the timbres of various instruments in order to achieve an "exotic" effect, as for instance, Novachord, fixed piano, harp, guitar, lute, mandolin, sistrum, bongos, boo-bams, bells, and other ethnic woodwinds and percussions. Another novelty was the use of an ondioline, a French instrument that North brought from Paris. Ondioline is an electronic instrument resembling a small piano and producing sounds reminiscent of woodwinds, mandolin and percussion. It was the first time that this instrument was used in America. However, North was, in general, very modest in using electronic instruments, because he always found it more challenging to write for orchestra and, if necessary, to simulate the sound effects that one would achieve with electronic instruments. The ondioline was used in four musical sequences in the second half of the film: "Festival," "Luceria Camp," "Varinia and Crassus," "The Last Fight."

Given more than a year to compose the score North was able to spend several months in diligent research of the period music. Before writing the score, North studied the script and saw the completed film eighteen times. A real rarity was the fact that he was actually asked to compose temporary tracks prior to the editing of the training scenes and the final battle scene. These tracks served as an idea how to cut the film's scenes to the pulse and the accents of the music. The temporary tracks were composed for two pianos and two percussions. Afterwards they were arranged for full orchestra and included in the final film score. North very much appreciated the delicate musical sense of the director Stanley Kubrick and the editor Irving Lerner. "The temp music was done to a click-track — metronomic tempo — so that when it was rewritten to the final cut it was mathematically accurate," North stated.[11] This type of editing proved very powerful in Sergei Eisenstein's 1938 production of *Alexander Nevsky* in which many scenes were cut to previously recorded music by Prokofiev. Kubrick was aware of the effect of this

Note and telegram from Kirk Douglas to Alex North regarding the scoring of *Spartacus*, 1959.

kind of film montage, especially in the massive battle scenes. Therefore he deliberately coaxed North into studying Prokofiev's *Alexander Nevsky*.[12]

The tremendous epic scope of *Spartacus* required quite a different compositional approach from North than did the intimate film dramas. This was the film in which North developed his "objective" type of composition embodied in the musical sequences that underline the heroic nature of the slaves' rebellion, and accompany the long scenes of their journey toward the sea. The "objective" music was a necessary support of the collective movement where no dialog or other extensive sound effects were present.

In a similar way, North used this type of "objective" approach when illustrating musically the activity of the Roman army, as well as to emphasize the dynamics of the battle scenes. In general, the "objective" compositional approach was applied to support the rhythm of the collective action and demonstrate the general feeling of victory, triumph, heroism, hardship or defeat. This approach is characterized by a series of musical solutions, such as the use of the entire symphonic orchestra dominated by an extended brass section; driving rhythm; strident accents; themes plated by horns, trumpets, and trombones; dissonant harmony; dense orchestral texture; and rhythmic-melodic patterns treated as *ostinato* figures.

North also used his "subliminal" or "subjective" approach whenever the story dealt with the personal relationships between the characters. Both Kubrick and North had a common preference in their professional fields— to go beyond the obvious and reflect what lies behind it. As always, in the intimate scenes North tried to imply and underline with music the thoughts and motivation of the protagonists rather than support solely the action itself. "It is a story of tremendous scope, but, after all, when you have characters portrayed by Douglas, Olivier, Laughton, Ustinov, Jean Simmons and Tony Curtis, the personal conflict must be predominant," North commented.[13] In these scenes North aimed for a chamber sound quality using small instrumental groups and chamber ensembles. The musical themes are often given to various solo instruments, mainly woodwinds and strings, the rhythm is smooth and easy flowing, and the music is frequently filled with exotic sounds and lyric passages.

North's musical score makes an impressive musical statement in the film. Providing the film with both grandiose and intimate musical comment, it is also an extraordinary compositional achievement in its own right.

The General Overview of the Score

The score for *Spartacus* is a very complex and elaborate work not only in regard to its musical structure and compositional quality, but also in regard to its extensive duration and amount of composed music. The low word count of *Spartacus*, probably the lowest among Kubrick's films after *2001: A Space Odyssey*, required an extensive musical comment. The duration of the film is three hours and five minutes, of which two hours and fifteen minutes are filled with North's music. North used to compare the length of his score with that of two full-length symphonies.[14] The cue sheet for *Spartacus* contains seventy-four music cues organized in two acts with a total of twenty-six reels. "More sweat and blood went into this score, and more pages were thrown away than any score I've done," North declared.[15]

The musical dynamics and contrasts in *Spartacus* are imposed by the intense dramatic conflict. As in many of his previous film scores, North tried to balance the score by using the principle of tension and release. Such a treatment defined the basic flow of the music in *Spartacus*, which employs musically sharp and utterly evident contrasts. For instance, there are contrasts between the objective and subjective compositional approach, martial battle music vs. lyrical romantic music, symphonic vs. chamber orchestration, brass vs. strings (or woodwinds), homophony (or monody) vs. polyphony, tonal vs. modal musical treatment, strict symmetric vs. free rhapsodic formal contours, harsh chordal dissonances vs. "sweet" minor-major melodies, regular vs. irregular rhythms, just to mention a few.

Most of the music is devoted to the euphoric slave rebellion. It is triumphant, jubilant music with a symphonic quality which is, however, different from the heavy, militant symphonic approach used to depict the power and harshness of the Roman leaders and their army. Much of the martial music opens with shrill fanfares which indicate the combative character of the film. The harmony, as well as the melodies, is often defined by the intervals of fourths that emphasize the hollow, militant, and dissonant musical effect. The dissonant harmony is sharpened in the scenes of the battles and gladiators' combats by adding intervals of seconds and sevenths to the chord structures. Also, dense orchestral structures of a cluster type are found throughout the score. The occasional polyphonic treatment of the thematic material (most notably the theme of Spartacus) creates a nice counter-effect to the richly harmonized orchestral sequences.

Laurence Olivier (left) and Alex North at the premiere of *Spartacus*, 1960.

The musical ideas that are most consistently used as leitmotifs throughout the score are the main theme of Spartacus, the slave theme, and the two Gladiators' army motifs. Using the principles of the leitmotif technique North provides the epic film with systematic musical comment and sense of unity. The leitmotifs are developed and transformed to fit the dramatic needs of the film. They also interact with each other, thus creating a sophisticated dramatic undercurrent. The group of slaves motifs also contains two combat motifs used in the scenes of the training and fight of the gladiators. Others are the death motif, introduced during the first fight to the death between the gladiators, the camp theme accompanying the slaves' activities in their encampments, and two triumph motifs. The Romans on the other hand are represented by fanfare-like brass music with only one distinguishing theme accompanying general Crassus and his final attack on Spartacus.

The only lyrical theme in the score is Varinia's theme which also represents the main love theme in the film. Therefore, it is used extensively in virtually every scene that depicts the love between Varinia and Spartacus. It also appears when they think or remember each other. In the final scene between Crassus and Varinia the theme is presented by ondioline within a dissonant orchestral texture indicating Crassus' madness and his defeat by Varinia whose love for Spartacus is eternal.

The cues in which North simulates the ancient Roman chamber music also bring moments of release to the film. These musical sequences are written in different modes and follow the ancient principle of monody, except one cue ("Source Music #1") whose melody is treated in the manner of early medieval polyphony. The musical idea of this cue is used to indicate Crassus' love for Varinia. There is only one sequence with source music of secular origin. The festive celebration of the slaves' arrival to the beach is accompanied by a lively dance tune — tarantella.

The rhythmic element is strongly emphasized in the score for *Spartacus*. There are many sequences characterized by driving *ostinato* rhythmic movement (for instance, the scenes of the gladiators' training, the duel between Spartacus and Draba, the slaves' revolt and breakout, etc.). The repetitive orchestral figures are sometimes confronted by strong random accents ("The Breakout"). The "barbaric" quality of the score is greatly emphasized by the repetitive rhythmic patterns and frequent metric changes. For instance, the metric flow alternates between 4/4 and 5/4 in the cue "First Pair," between 2/4 and 3/8 in the "Forest Meeting," between 5/8 and 3/4 in the cue "Vesuvius Camp," etc. The asymetric feel of the ancient Roman music is revived by the use of interesting irregular metric flows as, for example, 7/8 ("Source Music #2"), and 3/4 in alternation with 4/4 ("Source Music #1").

North's mastery of dramatic scoring is evident in his work with the main thematic material which undergoes various transformations in order to underline a certain dramatic situation, feeling or mood. The heroic theme of Spartacus, for instance, is transformed into a lament which accompanies the last conversation between Spartacus and Antoninus preceding their final fight to the death.

Not all of the music that North composed for *Spartacus* is included in the final score. Some music sequences were not used because the scenes for which they were composed were cut from the film, such as the death of a baby during the exhausting march of the slaves, and the scene in which Varinia looks for Spartacus' dead body (this powerful musical piece is known under the title "Desolation/Elegy"). The cue "Source Music #3" was not used in the film, and the one entitled "Source Music #4" was originally used to accompany the scene in which Crassus tries to seduce the slave Antoninus. The latter was replaced with the cue entitled "Snails and Oysters." The original overture, intermission, and exit music were also substituted and some sequences were shortened in the final editing of the film ("Glabrus Disgraced," "Fear of Death").

Overall, the score for *Spartacus* is a serious and significant musical achievement. The orchestra is frequently asked to perform in an intense dramatic manner which requires a high level of virtuosity from all the musicians in the orchestra. Such virtuosic sequences are "Training #1" and "Training #2," "Draba Fight," "Breakout," "Glabrus Defeat" and "The Battle," just to mention a few. The percussions are given an important role throughout the entire score (the timpani even introduce Spartacus' theme in the "Main Title"). The brass instruments prevail in many martial, jubilant, and battle sequences, while the strings and woodwinds are used extensively in the scenes of intimate character, although they are also an important factor in the building of the orchestral intensity and contrasts.

North conducting the music for *Spartacus*, 1960.

The Musical Analysis

The Overture and the Main Title

The historic spectacles of the time usually included musical overtures which preceded the viewing of the film. North originally composed a grandiose, four minute overture for Spartacus which was replaced in the final cut of the film with an overture made up of two music sequences that appear later on in the score: "On to the Sea" (#39, 16A) and "Metapontum Triumph" (#44, 17B). The opening fanfares of the "Metapontum Triumph" are followed by the cue "On to the Sea" which is built on elements from the main theme of Spartacus. The "Overture" is concluded with the cue "Metapontum Triumph," followed by a segue into the "Main Title." Besides the Spartacus theme, the opening music introduces several other important motifs which are often used throughout the score (Ex. 1a–d). In general, the "Overture" is a very pompous piece with heroic character which anticipates the epic dimensions of the film as well as the main tone of the film score. The triumphant, march-like battle music was composed for a symphonic orchestra with an extended brass section which is meant to dominate in the exposition of the main thematic material.

Music-1

Date __November 11, 1960__

Prod. No. __#1888__

MUSIC COPYRIGHT DEPARTMENT

UNIVERSAL PICTURES COMPANY, INC.

New York

Music Compositions Recorded in

A Production entitled: _____ "SPARTACUS" _____ | Feature XXXXXXXXX }
                                                      | XXXXXXXX

Recorded by: __Universal Pictures Company, Inc.__ at __Goldwyn Studios, Hollywood, Calif__

UNIVERSAL PICTURES COMPANY, INC.

By: __Joseph Gershenson__

Title of Composition	Composer	Publisher	Extent	How Used	Time
REEL I					
OVERTURE					
1. (Metapontum (Triumph	Alex North	Northern Music Corp.	Partial	Inst.b.g.	:09
2. (On To The Sea (Revised	"	"	"	"	2:22
3. (Metapontum (Triumph	"	"	"	"	1:27
4. MAIN TITLE	"	"	Entire	"	3:40
REEL II					
5. THE MINES	Alex North	Northern Music Corp.	Entire	Inst.b.g.	2:57
6. CARAVAN	"	"	"	"	1:12
REEL III					
7. VARINIA'S THEME	Alex North	Northern Music Corp.	Entire	Inst.b.g.	3:27
REEL IV					
8. TRAINING THE GLADIATORS	Alex North	Northern Music Corp.	Entire	Inst.b.g.	1:29
9. PAINTING	"	"	"	"	1:24
10. SPARTACUS' CELL	"	"	"	"	1:36

The first page of the revised cue sheet for *Spartacus*, 1960.

Ex. 1a-e
a)

On to the Sea: Spartacus theme

Vlas./Cls./Hrns.

b)

On to the Sea: Gladiator Army motif 1

Woodwinds/Vlns./Pno./Xylo.   Flts./Obs./Eb Cl. ⌞—5—⌟

c)

On to the Sea: Gladiator Army motif 2

Woodwinds/Vlns./Xylo.

d)

Metapontum Triumph:
Triumph motif 1

Woodwinds

e)

Metapontum Triumph:
Triumph motif 2

Trpts.

The "Overture" that North originally planned for the opening of the film is recorded as a part of the complete soundtrack release by SVC Records. Similar to the

"Overture" used in the film, this piece is also a compilation of several music sequences from the score. It begins in the same way as the "Overture" from the final film, with the fanfares from the "Metapontum Triumph" (#44, 17B), and comprises sections from the following sequences: "Dusty March" (#43, 17A), "Vesuvius Camp" (#30, 12B), "Forest Meeting" (#29, 11A), and "Vesuvius Montage" (#33, 13 C).

The "Main Title" continues in the same mood established by the music from the "Overture." It was composed for a full symphonic orchestra with a rich percussion section which had to keep the steady march beat throughout most of the "Main Title." After the opening fanfares, similar to those from the "Overture," the Spartacus theme is fully introduced by two timpani soli:

Ex. 2

The beginning motif, built on two intervals of fourths, resembles the fanfares' calling signal, and it is the basic motif of the entire score. The character of this main theme is essentially determined by the overall fanfare-like, martial quality of the "Main Title" music, and indicates the heroic tone of the film. The theme in its first full appearance is presented as an extended phrase consisting of two distinctive half-phrases. The first one is often used alone as an indication of Spartacus' theme. After its initial exposition, this theme usually reoccurs in a rhythmically more condensed form.

The first section of the "Main Title" employs the entire orchestra. The brass's accented figures and the melodic exposure of the main theme by the full body of strings are in sharp contrast to the following section which brings a polyphonic development of the main theme. The theme is adjusted to fit the linear musical progression based on its canon-like imitations by different orchestral groups:

Ex. 3

The polyphonic musical texture gradually involves more and more orchestral instruments and grows in intensity and volume, bringing the "Main Title" to a powerful ending. The dissonant harmonies and contemporary musical treatment indicate that the pursuit of freedom and humanity is as relevant in the modern world as it was for Spartacus and the ancient slaves. The "Main Title" design consultant, Saul Bass, did a great job in adjusting the opening credits and the visuals of Roman sculptures' and reliefs' details to the rhythm of the music. At the end of the "Main Title," a Roman bust is shown cracking and gradually disintegrating as the forceful rhythmic music grows stronger toward its conclusion. Bass also designed the set for the gladiators' school, and helped in the choreography of the final battle.

Spartacus' Slavery

The music continues by segue from the "Main Title" into the cue "Mines" (#5, 2A), heard under the voice of a narrator who tells the prologue of the story. Spartacus is seen working hard in the mines of Libya. His compassionate and rebellious character is indicated from the very beginning in the scene where he helps the young man who has fallen with a heavy load. The guards whip him for it, and Spartacus in return hamstrings one of them. The music cue stops as Batiatus, head of the gladiator school, comes to the labor mines to recruit new gladiators. The music illustrates very vividly the sounds of the work in the mines with great orchestral effects. The main theme of the cue, known also as the slave theme, is introduced by the violas and two English horns:

Ex. 4

The minor theme suggests the hardship of the slavery, whereas its major version is used later in the score to indicate the newfound freedom of the slaves.

The piece has contours of a ternary form with a middle part that brings triplet movement alternating between the trumpets on the one hand, and the violas and horns, on the other. The cue is concluded with a new phrase that anticipates the melodic line from the ensuing cue.

Spartacus is chosen, among other slaves, to be trained as a gladiator. Their trip to the gladiator school at Capua in Italy is accompanied by the music from the cue entitled "Caravan" (#6, 2B). The modal quality of the music is emphasized with a melodic phrase in Aolian mode, based on leaps of a fourth and a fifth like many of the themes in *Spartacus*.

In the School of Gladiators

The gladiators are introduced to their trainer, Marcellus, and their purpose, duties, and privileges are explained. Occasionally they are even given a woman for their pleasure. A beautiful slave girl Varinia is assigned to Spartacus. Their first encounter in Spartacus' cell is accompanied by a tender lyrical melody, entitled "Varinia's Theme" (#7, 3A). Composed for oboe solo, it is one of the simplest and most touching melodies that North wrote:

Ex. 5

Its basic motif is a simple broken triad which changes the mood between minor and major during the course of the music cue. Oboe d'amore is also a leading instrument in this piece and it alternates with the oboe, or it acts as its counterpoint.

The following, fourth reel of the film consists of a series of sequences which alternate between scenes of the gladiators training and scenes of Spartacus' and Varinia's growing affection for each other. Three music cues are heard in continuous movement. The first scene of the training of the gladiators to fight is accompanied by a virtuoso piece for orchestra (#8, 4A). This composition is recognized by its strings movement in the style of *perpetuum mobile*, confronted by short, accented triads in up beat rhythms for an enormous body of brass and woodwinds. The second music cue, entitled "Painting" (#9, 4B), is reminiscent of the slave theme from Ex. 4 for hecklephone and bass clarinet. It serves as background music as Marcellus marks out the vulnerable areas of a man's body using Spartacus as an example. But Spartacus' attention is taken by Varinia; his eyes follow her while she works. She also looks at him. Thus, the slave theme also becomes a musical source for their love theme. The cue entitled "Spartacus' Cell" (#10, 4C) follows by segue from the previous scene as Marcellus teases Spartacus by bringing Varinia to his cell only to laughingly draw her away, and give her to somebody else. The music is reminiscent of Varinia's theme in major.

The scene continues in the kitchen where the gladiators have their meal. Varinia is serving them water, and Spartacus succeeds in exchanging a few words with her. The music cue, entitled "Kitchen #1" (#11, 4D), is a short variation of Varinia's theme, and is followed by another scene of training. The hard preparation of the gladiators for combat is accompanied by a remarkable cue for orchestra, entitled "Training the Gladiators #2" (#12, 4E). Its musical concept resembles the cue composed for the first scene of gladiators training. However, the strings movement in this cue is rhythmically more diverse and is organized in rhythmic patterns, and the texture of the brass

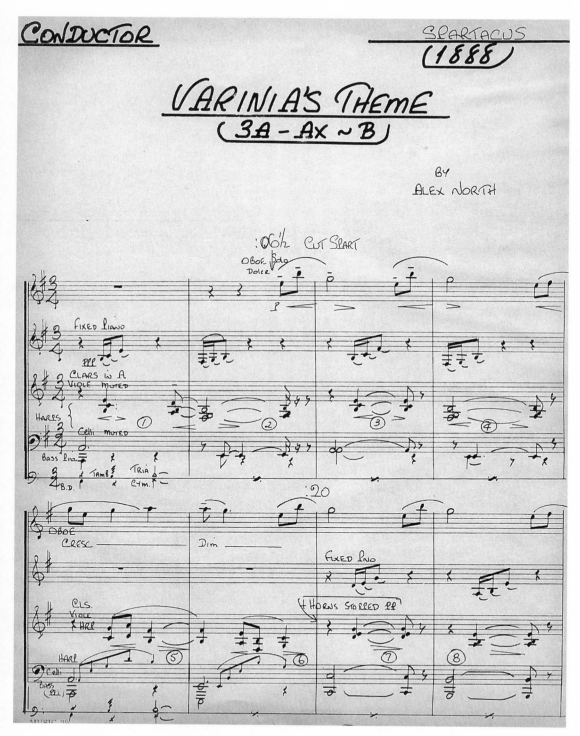

Spartacus (Universal, 1960). Excerpt from "Varinia's Theme" Conductor score.

accents is not as dense as in the earlier cue. This cue introduces two motifs that are later used as basic thematic ideas during the fight of Spartacus and Draba:

Ex. 6a

Ex. 6b

The music for the training episodes possesses ballet qualities, and it was composed prior to the shooting. Thus, the choreography of the gladiators' practice movements are synchronized with the rhythm of the music. This long scene is concluded by one more shot in the kitchen (#13/14, 4F/5A) where Spartacus and Varinia exchange signs of affection to yet another reminiscence of Varinia's theme played by violas and violoncellos.

The Arrival of Crassus and the Fights to the Death

The arrival of Crassus' party at Batiatus' villa is announced by a pompous piece for brass and percussions. The first general of the Roman army and his friends pay a visit to the school of gladiators in Capua, looking for amusement — the gladiators' fight to the death. North's music, entitled "Crassus" (#15, 5B), suits the rank of a general with its dialog between the trumpets on one hand, and the brass section of horns, trombones, and tubas, on the other The mood of a procession is underlined by the ceremonial rhythms of the percussions in 6/8, and the high accents of the woodwinds, bells, gamelan, and harps.

As they enter the home of Batiatus, the music continues by segue to a new cue entitled "Source Music #2" (#16). It serves as background music while the guests make arrangements for the fights. Batiatus tries to avoid the fight of the gladiators to the death saying that it could spread ill feeling to the entire school. During the conversation Crassus notices Varinia who is serving them. North's composition successfully simulates the effect of an ancient chamber ensemble providing the music that was presumably used at such occasions in the homes of the noble Romans. The music is composed in 7/8 (in the flow of 3/8 and 4/8) in the Mixolydian mode for an ensemble that includes, among the other instruments, Novachord, harp, alto flute, oboe, crotales, marimba, vibes, lute, guitar, bongos, sistrum, cymbals, tambourine, and triangle. This music also echoes in the palace music in *Cleopatra* (the conclusion of the cue "Epilepsy" includes the minor version of the same melody). The general tone and melodic structure vaguely remind one of Varinia's theme:

Ex. 7

The next musical number accompanies the scene in which Crassus shows his interest in Varinia and decides to buy her. He orders Batiatus to have Varinia sent to his home in Rome. The music has a chamber quality similar to that of the previous musical sequence, and it is simply entitled "Source Music #1." It is heard once more during the film, in the final scene between Crassus and Varinia. This piece develops from an eight measure phrase in the Dorian mode for oboe solo whose metric flow alternates between 3/4 and 4/4:

Ex. 8

The music gradually grows into a woodwind quintet, using the oboe theme as a repeating *cantus firmus*. The piece is a type of round in which each entering voice is a paraphrase of the original melody. With its linear uniformity and the parallel movement of the voices in intervals of fourths and fifths, this piece reminds one of an instrumental version of early medieval, vocal organum. The oboe melody is repeated four times, every time enriched with a new, lower contrapuntal melodic line played by the English horn, hecklephone, bassoon, and contra bassoon. The linear movement gradually creates very interesting modal harmonic structures. The exotic feeling is enhanced with percussions, such as sistrum, tuned bongos, fine cymbal, tambourine, and triangle.

The ladies who came with Crassus and Glabrus choose two pairs of gladiators to fight to the death. Spartacus is among them. The music starts as the gladiators enter the arena and continues through the first combat. Spartacus and his rival, the big Ethiopian Draba, wait for their turn in a little anteroom to the arena. Spartacus sees parts of a fight through slats in the door, and witness the killing of one of the gladiators. The music, entitled "First Pair" (#18, 6B), is conceived in a tempo of *marche funèbre* as the gladiators walk toward the arena. The Slave theme is brought out in a very low register by the horns, bass clarinet, and tuba. In the second section of the music cue, a muted trumpet solo introduces a new thematic idea in 5/4:

Ex. 9

This section is developed in a polyphonic manner and it gradually grows in intensity with every imitation of the theme. A new melodic figure is introduced as a counterpart to the theme. This new musical idea represents the death motif, used in two other musical sequences ("Brooding" and "Fear of Death/Alternate") to intensify the macabre moments in the story:

Ex. 10

The killing of the gladiator is underlined with an orchestral accent, emphasized by a sudden change of tonality (from B flat minor into A minor).

The music cue that accompanies the fight between Spartacus and Draba (cue #19/20, 6C/7A, entitled "Draba Fight") is one of the most complex orchestral numbers in the score. It is basically a reminiscence of the music for the cue "Training the Gladiators #2," but its main motifs are developed more consistently bringing the music to an orchestral culmination. After an introductory passage for percussions (timpani, snare drums, cymbal, piatti) the two principal combat motifs from "Training the Gladiators #2" (Ex. 6a and Ex. 6b) are developed into a furious, virtuoso orchestral scherzo that culminates with a choral-like, chord presentation of the Slave theme for trombones, contra bass trombone, and tuba. Draba wins the fight but hesitates to kill Spartacus. The music continues by segue to the cue "Kill" (#21, 7AA) as one of the women, Helena, gives the signal to Draba to kill Spartacus. Draba at first does not react, then suddenly turns and attacks the guests, but one of the guards kills him with a spear as he climbs the balcony wall. The music encircles this dynamic and dramatic scene with fast, agitated woodwind and string passages based on the second combat motif (Ex. 6b).

After the fights, the atmosphere in the slave quarters is mournful and gruesome. The dead Ethiopian is hung by his feet in the corridor so the gladiators can see him when they walk toward their cells. The music cue, entitled "Brooding" (#22, 7B), is a plaintive music piece that utilizes the melodic counterpart of the death theme (Ex. 10) as the main theme imitated through different orchestral groups.

The Revolt in the School of Gladiators

The following morning Spartacus sees Varinia leaving the quarters, and he is told by Marcellus that she has been sold. As Spartacus echoes his words, Marcellus lashes him across the face for talking. Spartacus' anger is overwhelming; he attacks Marcellus and kills him. The other gladiators join Spartacus in his rebellion. After a fierce fight they overrun the school, and fly to freedom toward the mountains. This long scene is underscored with three music cues that subsequently follow one after another: "Revolt" (#23), "Breakout" (#24, 8AA), and "Slaves Escape" (#25, 8A).

The first one, "Revolt," is an inventive contemporary piece for string orchestra, built entirely from one short melodic motif:

Ex. 11

The intense motif repetitions are combined with strong string accents in a Stravinsky-like manner. The following cue, "Breakout," is a long and powerful symphonic piece in which the "Revolt" motif (Ex. 11), played by strings and woodwinds, is confronted by massive chords and accents for brass. It could be considered a free-developed variation of the previous cue for a full orchestra. North's orchestral treatment is truly remarkable in this cue, including breathtaking orchestral effects combined with striking rhythm and dynamic intensity. The ensuing cue, "Slaves Escape," emphasizes the slaves' victory with the triumphant rendition of the Spartacus theme which is performed in counterpoint to the motif heard in the "Overture" (Ex. 1b from the cue "On to the Sea"). This long scene of the rebellion is underscored with music that bears notable symphonic qualities and defines North as a first ranking symphonic composer in Hollywood.

The Slaves' Rebellion and the Reunion of Spartacus and Varinia

The music overlaps the scene change and ends with the panoramic view of the Roman senate. Spartacus is the subject of the discussion in the senate. Gracchus, the ruler of the senate, proposes Glabrus to handle the situation with his army, and he appoints Caesar temporary commander of the garrison while Glabrus is away. All of this takes place during Crassus' absence.

Crassus' return to his villa is accompanied by a short music cue entitled "Crassus' Home" (#26, 9A) written for a heavy brass section and percussions. The fanfare-like music is similar to the music from the cue "Crassus," heard earlier during Crassus' arrival at the school of the gladiators. This musical sequence accompanies the first encounter between Crassus and the new young slave Antoninus, the singer of poems. Glabrus is waiting for Crassus with news about his assignment. But instead of being pleased, Crassus is furious because he recognizes Gracchus' intentions as a part of his conspiracy plan.

In the meantime, the rebels loot the countryside, burning and pillaging everything on their way. Then they ride to the deserted school with their loads of supplies. The victorious musical sequence, entitled "Deserted School" (#27/28, 10A), brings in Spartacus' theme played by timpani, exposed in similar manner as in the *Main Title*. The second section of the cue begins as Spartacus enters the deserted school, walks through the corridors where he walked as a slave, and goes inside his old cell. His memories of the past are musically underlined with the reminiscence of Varinia's theme by oboe d'amore.

Spartacus returns among his fellow gladiators who have fun watching the duel between two middle-aged patricians fighting "to the death." Spartacus interrupts the fight with an exclamation: "I promised I'd never see two men fight each other to the death." Then, he goes on with his speech that they should free other slaves, train them, and make an army of gladiators. He suggests that the best way to get out of the country is by sea, and that they should hire the pirates to help them. The men agree with his plan, and as they leave, they burn the former gladiators' school to the ground. This is the cue for the beginning of a long musical sequence entitled "Forest Meeting" (#29, 11A) which comprises several important musical ideas. The music is organized in two big sections. The first section is built from two motifs heard in the "Overture" and the Spartacus theme. In this regard, the music of the first section is similar to the cue "On to the Sea," only in the latter thematic material is exposed in a reversed order. The two motifs from the beginning of the sequence (Ex. 1b and Ex. 1c) are regularly connected to the victorious raids of the gladiators' army. In the context of this scene these motifs accompany Spartacus and his group of gladiators as they ride through a glen, inviting other slaves to join them. The exposition of the motifs by the woodwinds is interspersed with the fanfare-like trumpet motifs based on the interval of fourths, thus anticipating the appearance of Spartacus' theme. The alternation between the woodwinds and brass is emphasized with the alternation of the time signature from 2/4 to 3/8. The timpani announce the triumphant theme of Spartacus with its beginning motif of rising fourths. Subsequently, the entire theme is played by the horns, supported partly by the trombones, and then by the violas. Among the refuges in the forest Spartacus sees Varinia who escaped during her ride to Rome. Looking in disbelief, Spartacus approaches her. The bridge toward the second section of the music sequence accompanies their happy reunion with an alternation between the first gladiator army motif (Ex. 1b) for woodwinds and the beginning motif from Varinia's theme for violins. The ensuing love scene brings an elaborated version of Varinia's love theme in a simple ternary form. The cue is encircled with a major version of the main melody in accordance with the happy, romantic, and sentimental mood of the scene.

Snails and Oysters

Back to Rome, the bisexual general Crassus tries to seduce the poet-slave Antoninus with a metaphoric monologue about the magnificence and terror of Rome before which one must bow. Having his back turned toward Antoninus during his speech, he does not notice the slave's escape. The music cue, entitled "Snails and Oysters" (12A), appears in the restored version of the film and it is not listed in the original cue sheet. This is an inventive musical piece which simulates the sound of an ancient ensemble. The melody is in the Phrygian mode and keeps the same rhythm of long note values throughout. It is played by vibraphone, marimba, crotales, tuned bongos, and Novachord. The melodic movement is supported by a repeated figure of fixed piano, harp tremolo, lute and guitar counter beats, and *glissandi* of Chinese bells.

Ex. 12

Life in the Rebels' Encampment

The music continues by segue with a series of musical sequences which accompany the training and preparation of the slaves for combat. The first music cue from this series is entitled "Vesuvius Camp" (#13, 12B). It is characterized by an optimistic, uplifting mood and driving, pulsating rhythm. Spartacus rides through the camp, supervising the training and the life among the rebels. He is satisfied with their progress. The music is martial, built from a melodic figure with a specific rhythmic movement alternating between 5/8 and 3/4:

Ex. 13

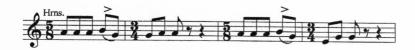

This continuous melodic and rhythmic movement alternates between the horns, on the one hand, and the oboe, English horn, violas, and ondioline, on the other. The sound rises in intensity with the gradual addition of new instrumental lines that support the basic movement. First enter the trumpets, then trombones, then violoncellos, basses, and tuba, and finally the entire orchestra in full intensity bounces in the given rhythm. The second section of the cue reflects the simplicity of a folk dance and brings in the woodwinds. It preserves the metrical flow in 5/8 which provides the music with an archaic quality.

The arrival of the new recruits is underscored with a polyphonic canon based on the Spartacus theme as it is exposed in the second section of the "Main Title" music (Ex. 3). The title of the cue is "New Recruits" (#31, 12C/13A). The theme is first exposed by the basses in *spiccato* (detached) articulation, and then it is repeated in canonic imitation with the violoncellos. In its further development the canon is expanded with a third voice which brings an imitation of the theme in the part of violas and clarinets in a smooth, *legato* movement.

The ensuing piece from the series of continuous music cues sharply contrasts the previous delicate, polyphonic sequence. It is a short, but rhythmically intense interlude, entitled "Glabrus March #2" (#32, 14A). The Roman legions are on their way to destroy the rebels' nest. Glabrus and one of his men stand at the side of the road drinking and laughing while the Roman soldiers march by. The music cue is written in a march manner for brass and percussions, with a dominance of forceful, repetitive figures for trumpets.

In the meantime, different activities take place in the Vesuvius camp. Everyone is involved in the preparation for battle with the Roman legions. The rebels gallop on horses slashing gourds in half with their knives. They are ready for the fight. The series of subsequent music cues is continued with "Vesuvius Montage" (#33, 13C), a cue that resembles "Vesuvius Camp" in its general mood, but it is much more diversified in terms of melodic and rhythmic development. The main theme of this cue is derived from the second gladiator army motif, heard in the "Overture" (Ex. 1c):

Ex. 14

This theme is brought out by horns, violas, and two trumpets over a distinctive walking bass made of ascending fourths. In the middle section of the cue the entire orchestra joins together in a powerful repetitive rhythmic pattern. Even though the meter indicates 2/4, the chord accents suggest a rhythmic flow of 12/8 (3 + 3 + 2 + 2 + 2).

Ex. 15

The cue ends with an augmented version of the main theme which anticipates the change of ambience. The rebels sit around the campfire while Antoninus entertains them with magic tricks. The music is heard softly in the background. The last cue from the long series of music sequences is called "Poem" (#34/35, 13D). It is repeated louder as Antoninus recites a poem of freedom. The oboe d'amore plays the slightly varied melody of the slave theme accompanied by guitar *arpeggios*. The simple exposition of this theme for a solo woodwind instrument in slower tempo and without a dotted rhythm completely changes its emotional impact.

In the following music cue, entitled "Love Sequence" (#36, 13E), the slave theme grows into a love theme which accompanies the poetic scene between Spartacus and Varinia. The entire cue is arranged for strings. The main melody is played by violins *tutti* with occasional alternations to violin solo. This theme is heard while Spartacus speaks of freedom and his "hunger" for knowledge. When the couple becomes more intimate the violins bring Varinia's theme in counterpoint to a melodic line for violin solo.

The Defeat of Glabrus

A powerful and complex music cue, entitled "Glabrus' Defeat" (#37, 14B/15A-B), underscores the first victory of the gladiators' army. The rebels' patrol informs Spartacus that the Romans are setting up a camp in the valley. Spartacus decides to attack. The imperial encampment soon burns in flames, and the Roman standards blaze as they fall to earth. The music ends as the rebels surround the lone survivor. It is Glabrus, the commander of the Roman garrison. The music cue opens with an *ostinato* marching beat similar to the beginning of the cue "Vesuvius Montage." The trumpets announce the Spartacus theme with its opening motif of ascending fourths, and the exposition of the theme itself is interwoven within the dense orchestral texture, in the parts of horns and trombones. The character of the next musical section reminds one of a Khachaturian type of scherzo. It introduces a new theme played by the trumpets, piano, and piccolo:

Ex. 16

After several repetitions, the beginning part of this theme is exposed in augmented values in the parts of the violoncellos and trombones, and then imitated in a similar manner in the parts of muted horns and violas. There follows a recapitulation of the first section with the Spartacus theme, which provides this piece with contours of a ternary form. The burning of the Roman camp is underscored with the coda of this music cue, based on intense repetitive brass figures. "Glabrus' Defeat" is an exciting, virtuoso symphonic composition whose true musical value is even more evident when heard separately from the noisy action of the film.

The first act of the film is concluded with the music cue entitled "Glabrus Disgraced" (#38, 15C/D). The music starts as Spartacus breaks Glabrus' baton which symbolizes Roman power, and thrusts it into his tunic. The rebels place Glabrus on a horse and send him back to Rome to break the news of his defeat to the senate. In the final editing of the film the section between measures 9 and 27 was cut from the original music cue. The opening phrase is followed by the triumphant musical conclusion based on Spartacus' theme.

The Journey of the Slaves Toward the Sea

After the scene in the senate where Glabrus is being questioned and punished for disgracing the armies of Rome, there follows another series of four continuous musical sequences. The first one, entitled "On to the Sea" (#39, 16A), underscores the long journey of the rebels across the country, toward the sea. The music cue is the same one that was heard at the beginning of the "Overture." It is a compilation of several main thematic ideas: the Spartacus theme and the two Gladiator Army motifs (Exs. 1a–c). After the brief, partial exposition of the Spartacus' theme in the first section, the middle part of the piece is used for development of the two gladiator army motifs. At the end of the cue, the complete Spartacus theme is played by the entire orchestra. The music continues with a shot of life in the rebels' camp where Spartacus is consulting with his assistants, women milk goats, soldiers learn how to fight, etc. Whereas the previous cue "On to the Sea" was composed mainly for brass, the new sequence, entitled "Luceria Camp" (#40, 16B), is a delightful, gay piece for woodwinds, strings, and light percussions. In fact, it is a variation of the thematic idea from "Vesuvius Camp," played by oboes, clarinets, and ondioline:

Ex. 17

With the change of rhythm and orchestration the melody develops connotations of a frolicking folk tune. A wonderful rhythmic effect is achieved when the melody is played against the steady beat of the strings.

The ensuing romantic scene between Spartacus and Varinia serves as an emotional and musical interlude. Varinia is bathing in the pool when Spartacus comes and surprises her. She reveals to him that she is pregnant. The music cue is called "Beside the Pool" (#41/42), and it is entirely based on Varinia's theme. The soaring violins play the theme first in minor, and after the revelation of her pregnancy the theme is exposed in major.

This long musical block is concluded with a brief, martial musical sequence entitled "Dusty March" (#43, 17A). It is basically a concise reminiscence of the two gladiator army motifs from the cue "On to the Sea," and accompanies the enduring journey of the slaves toward the sea and their freedom.

While the Roman senate plans a new offensive against the rebels, Spartacus and his army enter the city of Metapontum where people welcome them. Their victorious march is underscored with the music cue "Metapontum Triumph" (#44, 17B), based on the two triumph motifs from the "Overture" of the film (Exs. 1 d-e). The entire cue was included in the "Overture" after the music from the cue "On to the Sea." In general, "Metapontum Triumph" belongs to the group of cues that celebrate the achievements and the victories of Spartacus' army, such as "Forest Meeting" (the first section), "Vesuvius Camp," "Vesuvius Montage," "Glabrus Defeat," "Glabrus Disgrace," "On to the Sea," "Dusty March," and others.

North's research of ancient Roman music is most evident in the cues that simulate ancient source music. These cues indicate the type of musical entertainment that presumably existed in the noble Roman homes. North usually uses this type of source music in the background of intimate conversations and debates of the Roman protagonists. Such is the case with the cue entitled "Roman Baths" (#45/46, 17C/18AA) which accompanies the meeting of Crassus, Gracchus, and Caesar in the steamy bath where they discuss Spartacus' rebellion. This time the instruments, replicas of the ancient sarrousophone (a wind instrument) and kithara (a plucked string instrument similar to lyre), are actually seen on the screen.

The army of slaves finally reaches its destination — the sea. This is accompanied by another victorious music cue entitled "Arrival at the Beach" (#47, 18A). This piece uses the thematic material from two previous music cues, "Glabrus' Defeat" and "On to the Sea." The first section brings the powerful, steady bass movement from the opening of the cue "Glabrus' Defeat" over which Spartacus' theme is heard. The second section concludes the cue with the first gladiator army motif (Ex. 1b) presented in similar manner as in the center part of the cue "On to the Sea." In the initial print of the film the Intermission was planned after the arrival of Spartacus' army at the sea. However, that would have made the Act One much longer than the Act Two. Therefore the intermission was set after the defeat of Glabrus' army. As in the case of the "Overture," North thought of several possible endings of Act One. There are also a couple of versions planned to be used as "Intermission Music." The cue sheet, however, indicates that the cue "Glabrus' Defeat" was to serve as entr'acte music. Similar to the "Overture," it ran over the drawn curtains in the theater and introduced the second half of the film.

After the arrival at the beach, the rebels gather together and celebrate to the sounds of dance tunes. North simulates the secular source music of the era quite differently than the "elite" source music heard previously in the film. The music of the Roman nobles mainly has continuous rhythmic and melodic flow, longer note values, light, not rhythmically determined percussion fillings, "plucking" string quality, and melodic lines for solo instruments. On the other hand, the music cue "Festival" (#51, 18B) is a lively tarantella in 6/8, organized in symmetric four measure phrases, with distinctive rhythmic movement and accents. It is composed for a big instrumental ensemble with the melody played by woodwinds *tutti*, mandolins, fixed piano, and ondioline. The rhythm and pulse of the music is supported by hecklephone, guitars, bass guitar, boo bams, clapper, and tambourine:

Ex. 18

The festive music continues in the background as the action transfers into Spartacus' tent where the leader meets with the pirate Tigranes who brings bad news: Crassus has paid the Semitic pirates to deprive the slaves of the ships. Thus, Spartacus' army is forced to turn back and march on Rome. The cue "Sound the Trumpets" (#52/53, 19X) starts as Spartacus asks Tigranes to leave. Spartacus' theme is heard, followed by the trumpets' repeated signal as the leader stands before the enormous group of slaves. He informs his people of the situation and tells them that they do not have any other choice but to fight the Roman army.

The Preparations for the Battle

The following three musical sequences accompany the preparations of both armies for the final battle. Crassus' army is shown marching out of Rome, while Spartacus' army marches toward them. Then, there is a cut back to Crassus' army, setting camp for the night. The three cues are entitled "Crassus' Legions" (#54, 19C), "Back from the Sea" (#55, 19D), and "Crassus' Camp" (#56, 19E). They musically illustrate the situation and the position of the rebels. The cues form a ternary form with the polyphonic version of Spartacus' theme being in the center, surrounded by the fanfare-like theme of the Roman army.

The night before the battle is underscored by two subsequent music cues. The first cue, entitled "Camp at Night" (#57, 20A), accompanies Spartacus as he walks around his camp, quietly watching his people rest. The musical piece is a lyrical variation of the theme from the "Vesuvius Montage" (Ex. 13):

Ex. 19

The beginning motif from Varinia's theme is interwoven within the transparent texture of the strings' tremolo chords from the middle section of the cue. Spartacus thoughtfully walks into his tent. His conversation with Varinia is supported by a music cue entitled "Expectant Parents" (#58, 21A). Spartacus shares his concerns with Varinia, and asks her to take good care of their son. After an eight measure introduction, there follows an extended variation of Varinia's theme for strings. The theme is developed in 9/8, accompanied by a somber violin counterpoint throughout the piece. The minor melody is brought out by the first two violins. The music cue is concluded with the exposition of the entire theme in its regular, 3/4 meter.

The Final Battle

The long scene of the final battle is underscored by three consecutive music cues. There is no speech, only martial music and sounds of weapons, horses, and fighting. The first music cue, entitled "Maneuvers" (#59, 21B), is a march for timpani, drums, and brass. There is a shot of the large battlefield with Spartacus' army standing on one side, and Crassus' legions on the other. Timpani soli establish the macabre beat. Each brass accent brings a visual close-up portraying a soldier from Spartacus' army. Then, the camera cuts to the marching of enormous Roman legions, always accompanied with brass fanfares and snare drums on the top of the constant timpani beat. This scene is a remarkable study of the power of compatible editing and music accompaniment. Spartacus' army is always shown closeup, with individual shots accompanied by timpani solo, as opposed to the distant shots of the Roman army accompanied with brass and other percussions. The music underlines the contrast between the individual strength and determination of Spartacus' men and the collective power of the Romans. It is clear that the Roman legions outnumber the rebels' army. The timpani beat and the fanfare figures become more and more intense and louder as the Romans approach Spartacus' army. As they get closer, the ominous, dark orchestral chords, dominated by brass, introduce the *ostinato* figure from the cue "Formations" (#60, 21C/22AA):

Ex. 20

The trumpets' signal is heard at the moment when Spartacus gives a command to his men to light the logs. The battle starts as the burning logs roll down the hill toward the Romans. The rebels attack. The music continues by segue with the cue entitled "The Battle" (#61/62, 22A). This is a long music sequence that enormously enhances the horror of the bloody combat and the defeat of Spartacus. The entire orchestra is involved throughout this exceptional symphonic composition. There are four of each of the woodwind instruments, six of each of the brass instruments plus contrabass trombone and two tubas, extended sets of percussions, organ, piano, sixteen violas, eight violoncellos, six basses, and no violins. The dense orchestral texture is characterized by a harsh clash between the high woodwinds and the low brass. The harmonies are dissonant filled with intervals of minor seconds and major sevenths, and the melodic nucleus of the virtuoso woodwinds derives from the scherzo theme used in the cue "Glabrus' Defeat" (Ex. 15). Now, the chromatic figure from that theme is developed into intense melodic passages for the woodwinds, thus indicating Spartacus' own defeat. The fanfare theme of the Roman army, used in the cues "Crassus' Legions" and "Crassus' Camp," is also interwoven within the compositional structure of this striking, war music. The immense intensity of the entire scene is astonishing. No wonder it has been many times compared to the battle scenes from Eisenstein's *Alexander Nevsky*. North's music for *Spartacus* can easily stand the comparison with Prokofiev's score for *Alexander Nevsky*.

The Conclusion and Final Farewell

The aftermath of the battle brings a horrifying picture of thousands of dead bodies. Crassus and a guard walk among the mutilated bodies. This scene initially included Varinia searching for Spartacus' body and giving birth to her child in the field. North composed a haunting music piece for this scene, entitled "Desolation/Elegy," but it was cut together with the scene. The final print of the film kept only the part of this scene in which Crassus walks among the dead slaves. The music cue that accompanies this scene is entitled "Fear of Death" (#63, 24C/25A), and it is a reminiscence of the slave theme, played by the violoncellos and bass clarinet.

The next music cue, "I Am Spartacus" (#64, 22C/23A), accompanies several subsequent scenes. Spartacus is seen among the survivors. Crassus offers freedom from crucifixion to any slave who identifies Spartacus. Each man stands up and claims that he is Spartacus. This emotionally charged scene is underscored with Spartacus' theme, this time exposed smoothly in augmented note values. The music cue is extended with a section for strings as Batiatus and Crassus find Varinia and her newborn child in the field.

The slave theme is heard again in the cue entitled "Recognition & Crucifixion March" (#65, 23B/24A) which accompanies the slaves' procession to Rome along the road lined with crosses on which the slaves are being crucified. The same theme appears in the later cue "Night Crucifixion" (#66, 23C) as the slaves' crucifixions continue during the night.

Crassus brings Varinia and her baby into his home. He treats her as a queen and wants her love. But Varinia can only love Spartacus. She speaks of him, not knowing yet that he is still alive. The ambience of the scene is set with the reprise of the cue "Snails and Oysters" (Ex. 12). The music cue "Varinia and Crassus" (#68, 24 B) follows in continuous movement. This beautiful lyric composition is actually a varied recapitulation of the piece entitled "Source Music #1" (Ex. 8), used earlier in the film when Crassus meets Varinia for the first time. The theme is developed for a chamber string ensemble in the same manner as in the earlier cue, but this time the repetitions of the theme are interspersed with orchestral dissonant clusters. The beginning phrase from Varinia's theme, played by ondioline, is interwoven within the dense orchestral texture. When Varinia speaks of Spartacus, the reminiscence of the slave theme, treated occasionally as their love theme as well, is played in the violoncellos and bass clarinet.

The next scene shows Spartacus and Antoninus seated beside the road, waiting to be crucified. In their final conversation Spartacus speaks of the slaves and their rebellion, He assumes Varinia and the baby are dead. He himself is not afraid to die, but Antoninus is. The mood of their conversation is supported by the polyphonic, canon-like treatment of the Spartacus theme in the cue entitled "Fear of Death/Alternate" (#69, 24C/25A). The compositional treatment is similar to that in the "Main Title" and the cue "New Recruits." However, in this cue the theme is exposed smoothly and in slower tempo which transforms its initial heroic mood into a lament.

The conversation between Spartacus and Antoninus is interrupted by Crassus' arrival. Crassus talks to Spartacus asking him to confirm his identity, but Spartacus refuses to answer. Crassus loses control, screams in anger, and slaps Spartacus. All he gets in return is spit in his face. He gives an order to have Spartacus and Antoninus fight to the death. The winner is going to be crucified. The music flows continuously from the previous cue. The new sequence is entitled "Spartacus Defies Crassus" (#70/71, 25 B). The arrival of Crassus is emphasized with the fanfare theme from the cue "Crassus' Legions." The rest of the cue basically intensifies the tension with the macabre rhythm of the timpani and ominous orchestral accents. The cue is concluded with an exposition of the melodic phrase linked to the death motif (Ex. 10) in the parts of the low strings.

The fight between Spartacus and Antoninus is underscored with the cue "The Last Fight" (#72, 25C/26A). Each of them tries hard to kill the other because they want to save each other from the horrible death on the cross. The music comprises the most important thematic ideas in the score. The Slave theme is exposed by the low strings in combination with the beginning motif from Varinia's theme. Spartacus asks Antoninus to forgive him as he delivers the final thrust with his sword.

When Crassus approaches Spartacus, he turns toward him and says: "He'll come back and he'll be millions." At that moment Spartacus' theme enters, played by a bass clarinet solo. Varinia's theme follows in continuity as Crassus reveals that Varinia and the baby are slaves in his house. The theme is exposed in the same manner as in the earlier cue "Varinia and Crassus." It is played by the ondioline over a dissonant cluster, and it is opposed by threatening horns and a funereal bass drum beat. Crassus gives an order to the guards to crucify Spartacus.

In his final effort to hurt Crassus, the senator Gracchus orders Batiatus to steal Varinia and her baby from Crassus' villa. Gracchus provides them with the papers that establish their freedom. The next morning Batiatus and Varinia with her child leave the city riding in Batiatus' cart along the road lined with crosses. The guards stop them and check their papers. At that moment Varinia sees Spartacus on the cross and walks toward him. She shows him his son and tells him that he is no longer a slave. Then she bids her final goodbye and leaves with Batiatus toward her freedom. The music for the "Final Farewell and End Title" (#73, 26B) is, in fact, a recapitulation of the complete version of Varinia's theme as it was heard in the music cue "Forest Meeting." The cue is concluded with the beginning motif from Spartacus' theme and the victorious motif (Ex. 1e) from the cue "Metapontum Triumph."

The "Exit Music" repeats Varinia's theme, the principal love theme of the score, in a romantic arrangement for strings. This music replaced the originally planned "Exit Music" which was similar to the "Overture" and consisted of the cues "Forest Meeting" and "Metapontum Triumph."

Comments

Some critics and film theoreticians consider *Spartacus* "the best epic about the ancient world ever produced for the screen."[16] However, after the release of *Spartacus* in October 1960, the critics found some aspects of the film less satisfactory than others. Many reviewers pointed out that the first third of the film is the strongest, and that the intensity of the story flattens after the gladiators' breakout. Nonetheless, *Variety* wrote that "Kubrick has out DeMilled the old master in spectacle,"[17] and the *Los Angeles Examiner* considered *Spartacus* "an Academy Award contender in all departments: acting, direction, production, camerawork, music, sound and costumes."[18] Interestingly, Kubrick, Douglas, Olivier, Simmons, Trumbo, and the film itself were not even nominated for Academy Awards. *The Apartment* was voted the best picture of that year, and Billy Wilder the best director. North's score for *Spartacus* rightfully earned an Oscar nomination. It was said that his music was worthy of the highest praise.[19] North's score lost, however, to Ernest Gold's music for *Exodus*.

The benefits of writing the music for *Spartacus* were numerous for North. He broke new personal ground in terms of composing for an extended symphonic orchestra, researching sources of ancient music prior to composing, and exploring new forms of musical expression that would be suitable for a historic epic. In this regard, *Spartacus* was a significant personal experience for North. Furthermore, the music for *Spartacus* continued the line of big epic scores, such as Rózsa's *Quo Vadis?* (1951),

JOHNNY GREEN
903 NORTH BEDFORD DRIVE
BEVERLY HILLS, CALIFORNIA

October 26th, 1960

Mr. Alex North,
498 St. Pierre Road,
Los Angeles 24, California.

Dear Alex:

Bonnie and I attended the "SPARTACUS" premiere and both of us were completely thrilled and delighted by your score. It's truly brilliant and a very real achievement, both as music and as drama.

Being a fan of yours is nothing new in my life; hearing wonderfully made music from you is no newer; but your score for "SPARTACUS" is a new thrill which does top the many thrills you have given me before.

Congratulations and all my warmest greetings to you and your family.

Most cordially,

JOHNNY GREEN

jg:jh

---

steven spielberg

December 12, 1984

Alex North
630 Resolano Drive
Pacific Palisades CA 90272

Dear Alex,

Your gift to me of the two Spartacus tapes is a treasure-trove of rare musical history.

As I've told you before, Spartacus is one of the best five pieces of music ever written for a motion picture.

I will listen to them again and again until I can hum back to you every single note.

I hope to see you very soon, but I will be listening to you in my car on the way home from work, and on my Walkman en route to London.

Warmest regards,

Steven

Top: Letter from Johnny Green to Alex Noth, October 26, 1960. Bottom: Letter from Steven Spielberg to Alex North, December 12, 1984.

Julius Caesar (1952), and *Ben-Hur* (1959). North went even a step further in providing *Spartacus* with a strong musical-thematic unity and highly contemporary musical commentary. But, above all, *Spartacus* stands apart from the previous three epics, as well as from North's next epic, *Cleopatra*, by the severity of its subject matter — slaves' rebellion in pre-Christian imperial Rome — which necessitates the "barbaric" quality of the music.

After this significant achievement, North was recognized as one of the leading and most versatile of film composers. He composed music for fifteen films during the Sixties, among them four epics.

9

The Misfits (1961)

> Human nature's a funny thing — man'll drop a bomb, kill
> a hundred thousand people, he's a hero. Same man kills a
> horse — all hell breaks loose.
> — *Gay Langland in* The Misfits *(Arthur Miller)*

General Perspective of Huston's and North's Relationship

The relationship of Alex North and John Huston developed during twenty-six years of professional collaboration. This resulted in five released projects and great mutual appreciation for one another's work. For this author, the analysis of these films was an exciting, inspiring experience and a rich source for understanding the function of music in film dramaturgy.

Alex North was, according to Huston's words, his favorite composer. Such a claim should not be taken lightly, considering the number of composers with whom Huston collaborated. The list includes Max Steiner (three films), Maurice Jarre (three films), Adolph Deutsch (two films), Jerry Goldsmith (two films), George Auric (two films), Dimitri Tiomkin, Georges Delerue, Miklós Rózsa, George Antheil, Hugo Friedhofer and many others. In a letter from April 16, 1986, regarding North's life achievement Academy Award, Huston wrote, "He is the first composer of my choice in motion pictures. I venture to say this openly so that he may better appreciate the extent and depth of my gratitude. Many scenes in pictures I have made would seem listless, lifeless even, without his musical comment..."[1]

North loved to work with Huston. He had great respect and appreciation for Huston's way of directing. In many of his interviews North pointed out that one of the best things about working with Huston was that, despite the imposing intellectuality of many of the works he attempted to translate to film, Huston himself never indulged in theorizing. In an interview with John Richardson for the *Daily News* North said that Huston "had a way of not getting terribly involved, as a lot of young directors or other directors who know everything about everything do. He just trusted me."[2] Later, in another interview with David Kraft for the *Hollywood Reporter*, North said that, "working with John was like two old pros collaborating together — that's how he treated the relationship. In a sense he would say, 'Alex, I know you know what you're doing. I trust your judgment,' and then he'd leave me alone.... John wouldn't even come to the recording sessions as he had infinite faith in my contribution."[3]

One would expect that this great professional collaboration was followed by close friendship or an intimate personal relationship. But, in fact, Alex North, as Annemarie North related, "has never been one of Huston's buddies."[4] The producer of *Wise Blood* and *Under the Volcano*, Michael Fitzgerald, who was personally very close to both of them, explained that Huston and North had very little in common as human beings, and that their lives were completely different. Therefore, there was very little socializing between them. According to Fitzgerald, "North was a modest, quiet man with a sort of quiet sense of humor. Obviously, a man who had an extremely interesting life. On the other hand, Huston was a man of incredible extravagance. He was known as a reckless man, a gambler, a man who loved horses, drink-

ing, women, hunting elephants, all that kind of rather macho type of thing. They really didn't have the same interests, except those as craftsmen. Each one of them knew a *lot* about their craft. That was so hard to explain, but they hardly even spoke to each other. Alex would come in for the spotting, and then he would go off and write the music. Then he would see the picture with John and myself, and John would say, 'Well, we'll make a little music here, then we'll cut a piece there.' Then we would discuss the orchestration, cutting in the music, we would work on the timing, and that would be it. They wouldn't see each other anymore until the next picture."[5]

The beginning of the collaboration between North and Huston goes back to 1961, when both masters were in the zenith of their careers. As previously mentioned, the spot where they found each other was the screenplay entitled *The Misfits*, written by a third master — the playwright Arthur Miller. In fact, Miller was the one who recommended North as a composer for this project. Huston agreed and, at the end, he

John Huston (left, seated) and Alex North.   was very satisfied with North's musical score. However, it happened that Huston and North did not have a chance to work together again until 1979 on *Wise Blood*. According to Tony Thomas, two years after *The Misfits* had been finished, Huston asked North to score *The Night of the Iguana*, but North refused because he did not feel any empathy for that film.[6] Nevertheless, from 1979 on, when this little incident was no longer of any concern, Huston was the one who gave Alex North more work than any other director in the last decade of the composer's career.

In the analysis of the musical scores that Alex North wrote for John Huston's films,

JOHN HUSTON

ALEX NORTH'S CHICKENS ARE FINALLY COMING HOME TO ROOST. CHICKENS DID I SAY? RATHER THEY ARE QUETZAL BIRDS -- SILVER PEACOCKS, BIRDS OF PARADISE.

HIS CONTRIBUTIONS HAVE BEEN MANY AND VARIED, BUT ALWAYS OF THE VERY HIGHEST QUALITY. HE IS THE FIRST COMPOSER OF MY CHOICE IN MOTION PICTURES. I VENTURE TO SAY THIS OPENLY SO THAT HE MAY BETTER APPRECIATE THE EXTENT AND DEPTH OF MY GRATITUDE. MANY SCENES IN PICTURES I HAVE MADE WOULD SEEM LISTLESS, LIFELESS EVEN, WITHOUT HIS MUSICAL COMMENT; BUT WITH IT SPRING TO LIFE AND TAKE THEIR PLACE AMONG THE BEST REMEMBERED OF MY WORK.

ALEX IS PAST MASTER AT SPEAKING TO THE UNCONSCIOUS. IT IS HIS GENIUS TO CONVEY AN EMOTION TO THE AUDIENCE WITH ITS HARDLY BEING AWARE OF THE EXISTENCE OF A SCORE. IN MANY INSTANCES IT IS ONLY AFTER A NUMBER OF EXPOSURES TO A FILM DOES IT ACTUALLY HEAR THE INSTRUMENTATION IN THE SO-CALLED BACKGROUND. ON THE OTHER HAND, WHEN THE OCCASION REQUIRES, IT CAN TAKE OVER TRIUMPHANTLY AND CAUSE THE IMAGES ON THE SCREEN TO SERVE AS ILLUSTRATIONS OF MANKIND'S GREATEST EXPRESSION.

MANY THANKS TO YOU, DEAR MAESTRO.

16 APRIL 1986

Letter from John Huston regarding North's Academy Award for lifetime achievement, April 16, 1986.

one can discover five different, innovative and witty ways of approaching film composition. Two of the scores, *The Misfits* and *Under the Volcano*, could be included in the category of original film music scores, while the other three scores, *Wise Blood*, *Prizzi's Honor*, and *The Dead*, are considered adaptations of already existing music. However, the compositional treatment in these adaptations is so particular, that they could be freely included in some of the most original music ever written for film.

Misfits in The Misfits

The Misfits has a special place in film history. It was the last completed film of Clark Gable and Marilyn Monroe, and one of the last projects for Montgomery Clift, as well.[7] When the film was released, expectations were really high, but the response of the reviewers was disappointing. Despite being a critical failure at the time, *The Misfits* has survived as a challenge to critical curiosity, and its final record is not complete. In the introduction of the printed script of *The Misfits*, the editors noted that the film was "much simpler in designs than the critics could comprehend. Perhaps it was, in the sense of timing, premature."[8]

The first screenplay by Arthur Miller is a true story about three modern-day cowboys. After the Second World War, in order to survive, they were obliged to round up wild mustangs and to sell them, as dog meat. "They were misfits in our modern jet age," said Miller, "as were the mustangs they still pursued..."[9]

In expanding his original short story for the screen, Miller added the character of Roslyn for Marilyn Monroe, to balance his lead cowboy, Gay Langland, played by Clark Gable. Eli Wallach and Montgomery Clift played the two other cowboys, Guido and Perce, with Thelma Ritter added in a role of the divorcee Isabelle.[10]

The wonder of *The Misfits* is that most of those who worked on this project were misfits in real life. John Huston also considered himself a misfit in the industry. "I hate the system," he said. "I'm free to make a damn fool of myself or to do something wonderful. The choice is mine and that's what counts."[11] Huston always disclaimed that he had a particular style. He was proud that his pictures were as diverse as they were, and often chose a film because it was unlike any other he had done.[12]

The Use and Development of the Musical Material

Alex North thoroughly explained the role of the music and its function in *The Misfits* in the book *The Story of The Misfits* by James Goode. "I was very much taken by the subject, the characterization, the quality of nonstorytelling," North said. "*The Misfits* has a dreamlike quality, made up of electronic motions, design, patterns; momentarily, spasmodically touching on human frailties and running the gamut from tenderness and frustration to cruelty... The music has to compensate for this pointillism, Miller's pattern of dots. The music has to have the function of tying together, joining these little strokes, enabling the picture to have a kind of flow in a rhythmic sense, that it apparently doesn't have. Because of this nervous quality in the picture, because of its unorthodox quality, I have to provide a structure that will sustain and frame..."[13]

In general, the film is divided into three sections. The first two sections stand apart from the third one — the legendary mustangs' roundup. This third section brings the film to a climax, "when everything is confronted head-on."[14] The music in the first two sections serves as personal characterization of the main female role, Roslyn, interacting with some source music.[15] North was convinced that he could afford to play against the changes of mood in certain scenes and still continue a musical thought.[16]

North always wanted to think of appropriate musical ways to provide the films with a sense of unity. In the case of *The Misfits* he thought that the music should have an internal quality. Therefore, he decided to use an overall theme rather than approach the film reel by reel. "I established a kind of nostalgic, poignant theme for Roslyn —

as a point of departure for scenes where she was involved with other characters—so the theme would take on variations in accordance with the moment," North commented.[17] And so it does; the main theme appears in different versions according to the different moods, behaviors and situations in which Roslyn is involved. It is interesting that the contrast between the variations is not achieved through changes in the melody of the theme, but more through changes of the key, rhythmical flow, tempo, musical form, harmonic connotations, and orchestral arrangements which vary from chamber ensemble to big-band and sixty-seven-piece symphonic orchestra. Also, the instrumentation of the exposed theme changes, and depends mostly on the mood and atmosphere of certain film situations.

As the third section becomes the dramatic culmination of the film, the music for it reflects that climax. It grows into a powerful dramatic comment on the action with ballet-like connotations. In this section North tried to do something in a more universal sense — "man's triumph over nature, man's attempt to prove virility — the music had to take on the form of greater abstraction and detachment."[18]

The Main Title Theme and Its Variations

The "Main Title" theme with its symphonic realization in the opening credits is a musical source which provides a continuous musical thought throughout the entire score. It is a nostalgic, and in some sense, a pathetic theme, carried by the strings in a grand melodic sweep. This opening music is built on the formal basis of incipient ternary song form *a a b a₁*, which is followed by short piano cadence and then repeated in shortened form *a a b + Coda*. The first part of the theme (*a a*) is a repeated phrase of eight measures characterized by a descending chromatic movement within the interval of a fifth. Through the score, this musical phrase is related to the main female protagonist, Roslyn. The chromatic instability of this principal thematic idea indicates, in a way, the psychological instability of Roslyn — a lonely woman in her search for love, freedom and trust.

Ex. 1

The second part *b* is also a phrase of eight measures, and contains a contrasting musical idea which is a diatonic melody developed, in general, in an ascending direction. It is often used throughout the musical score as a continuous phrase of part *a* (Ex. 1), but also to confront, complement or counterpoint it.

Ex. 2

The theme from the "Main Title" is followed by eight variations throughout the first two film sections. In the first film section the four characters are introduced: Roslyn, Isabelle, Gay Langland, and Guido. Roslyn and Gay begin their relationship and move in together.

The chromatic musical idea from the first part of the "Main Title" theme (Ex. 1) is exposed in the first variation entitled *New Life* (R2 P1), as Roslyn, standing on the bridge with Isabelle, for good luck throws her wedding ring into the water. Thus, from the very beginning of the film, part *a* is given the role of a principal musical idea related to the character of Roslyn and it becomes her musical symbol. It is a main clue which connects the numerous parts of this complex musical score. The main melody appears in the part of violoncellos, supported by a light, chamber orchestration of the strings, two alto flutes and two bassoons. In this brief exposition of the musical material, the second part of the main theme *b* is not included as a structural element, although it appears later as an inevitable part of the variations. In general, this musical sequence is rather a short character indication than a developed variation of the main theme.

The music sequence entitled "Roslyn's Theme" (R3 P2), is actually the second variation. It is treated very originally, as source music heard on the radio while Roslyn and Guido are dancing. The dance-band arrangement gives the theme an entirely different image, that of a jazz tune with sharp and syncopated rhythm. The formal scheme of the variation is *a a b a₁* ‖ *a a b a₁*, which is a repeated incipient ternary form (related to the form of the "Main Title"). It is exposed first in C minor, and then repeated in F minor. The varied musical ideas from part *a* (Ex. 3a) and part *b* (Ex.3b) look as follows:

Ex. 3a

Ex. 3b

The third variation, entitled "Roslyn" (R3 P3 / R4 P1) follows immediately after this scene. Alex North said that this scene depicts "a little princess dancing a dream ballet."[19] The chromatic theme from part *a* (Ex. 1) appears three times subsequently in the violoncellos and English horns, while the strings provide a harmonic background in a movement of triads, which provokes an impression of tonal instability. The time signature is changed to 6/8, and the key is G minor. This variation is closed with the exposition of the varied part *b* (Ex. 2) in the oboes. Thus, the final formal scheme of the variation is *a a a* ‖ *b*.

The theme appears in its regular incipient ternary form in the fourth variation, entitled "Loves Reverie" (R4 P3 and P4). But, this time the theme is encircled with new lyrical melodic material (*c*) which in the context of this variation has a role of an introduction and coda:

Ex. 4

In part *a*, the two phrases of the principal musical idea (Ex. 1) alternate between tenor saxophone and violoncellos. The flutes are the leading orchestral instruments in part *b* (Ex. 2). Afterwards, part *a* reappears in the violins in thirds. In the coda, the new melody is varied in its orchestral color and metric organization (the key signature is changed from 4/4 to 2/4). In its final musical structure the fourth variation could be presented with a scheme *c c* II *a a b* a_1 II c_1 c_1. The lyrical mood of this variation is indicated already with the title of this music cue, "Loves Reverie," and it matches the atmosphere of the romantic conversation between Roslyn and Gay, while they are driving toward his house.

The last music cue from the first section of the film is entitled "Love Idyll No. 2" (R4 P4). It accompanies the romantic idyll between Roslyn and Gay riding horses and spending time together on the beach. The music cue is based on new musical material, and regarding the construction of the entire musical score, acts as a music interlude between the first and the second section of the film. This musical material reappears at the end of the second section of the film as a part of the last, eighth variation.

Ex. 5

Regarding the melodic line of this new tune one could assume that its origin is in the part *b* of the "Main Title" (Ex. 2). This music cue is organized in two parts. In the first part the new music tune (*d*) is exposed in the form of a big period, and in the second it is varied and continued with a phrase from the previous, fourth variation (*c*, Ex. 4). The formal structure is *d d* || d_1 *c*.

In the second section of the film the four characters drive to Dayton, Nevada, to attend a rodeo. On their way, they meet Perce, the third cowboy, who joins them at the rodeo and, later, for the roundup of the wild mustangs. For this section of the film, following suggestions by Huston, North wrote mostly source music for the

The Misfits, still (United Artists, 1961). (left to right): Perce (Montgomery Clift), Roslyn (Marilyn Monroe) and Gay Langland (Clark Gable).

scenes which anticipate and follow the rodeo. However, the main thematic material reoccurs in the conversation scene between Perce and Roslyn in R8 P2, in a cue entitled "Compassion." Perce confesses to Roslyn his psychological problems which are rooted in his childhood, his feelings and his attitude toward his mother. This is the fifth variation, where part *a* appears as a nostalgic tune, exposed by the violins and then by tenor saxophone, while the flute again becomes the main instrument in part *b*. The form of this variation matches the regular scheme of the incipient ternary form *a a* || *b a₁*. In the sixth variation, "Compassion for Guido" (R8 P3), part *a* is exposed in the violins' part over agitated orchestral movement, which gives the impression that the theme appears in augmentation, although it keeps its original note values. Therefore, the first part of this variation contains only one phrase of eight measures instead of the usual two phrases. At the end of the variation, part *a* reoccurs shortened, in diminished note values. The formal structure of the sixth variation is *a b a₁*.

The seventh variation is entitled "Help" (R9 P1). It is developed stylistically as a boogi-woogie. In this intimate, melancholy scene between Gay and Roslyn, the first phrase of part *a* is played by the violins, and afterwards it is diminished and treated as a counterpoint to part *b*. On the other hand, part *b* is augmented which allows the diminished phrase from part *a* to appear three times as a contrapuntal movement for solo violoncello and solo oboe. The formal scheme of this variation is *a b* + codetta.

Ex. 6

The last music cue from the second film section is entitled "Disagreement" (R10 P1), and it is related to a different point of view between Roslyn and Gay regarding horse chasing. This music cue could be interpreted as an interlude between the second and the third section of the film, because it is mostly based on the thematic material from the earlier interlude which served as a bridge between the first and the second section of the film (Ex. 5). But also, it can be regarded as a final, eighth variation which unifies the musical ideas exposed throughout the two sections of the film. The lyrical theme *d* is repeated several times, first in its regular form of a big period, then it is rhythmically and melodically varied, thus forming the middle section of this music cue. At the end it reappears in combination with contrapuntal motifs from part *a*.

Ex. 7

Out of these contrapuntal motifs gradually appears the melody from part *a*, played by a soprano saxophone. It is followed by a short reminiscence of the tune *c* presented in the fourth variation (Ex. 4). The exposition of the principal thematic material at this particular point does not act only as the closing section of this variation, but also as a musical motto, encircling the entire set of variations. The formal structure of this music cue is *d d$_1$ d a c*.

The Roundup

The third film section begins with the mustangs' roundup. It is probably the most famous and the most exiting part of *The Misfits*. Many authors agree that for this dramatic climax in the film, the music possesses the aura of a ballet score. Even Alex North in an interview with Irwin Bazelon pointed out that he scored that scene in the form of a ballet.[20]

The author Joan Padrol also considers this section as music with ballet connotations, mentioning that the score was influenced by North's early work with Martha

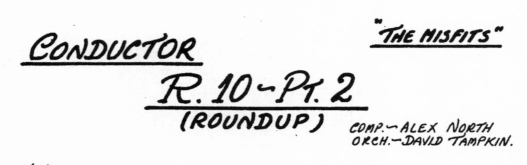

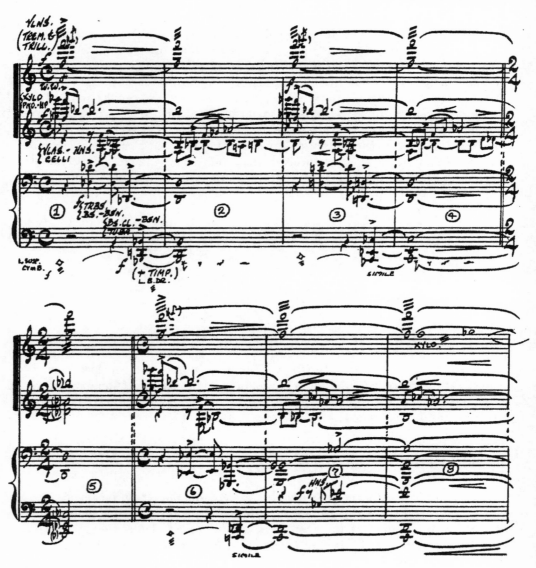

The Misfits (United Artists, 1961). Excerpt from the "Roundup." Conductor score.

Graham.[21] Irwin Bazelon observes it as a veritable four-part ballet. "The music builds from one episodic part to another with extraordinary vitality," he writes. "At the same time the ballet is not continuous: there are pauses between the sections, and the musical parts are sharply contrasted."[22]

If the function of music in this film is to tie together Arthur Miller's "pattern of dots," as North said, then this fully concentrated orchestral climax is significant as a point of release for the entire film. Actually, in this third film section there are five musical sequences which tie the chase of the mustangs into one unit. Four of these musical parts are so highly connected in terms of thematic work and motivic development that they could be considered a monothematic orchestral cycle. The fifth sequence is a remarkable finale based on the musical material of the "Main Title" theme.

The nucleus for the musical development can be found in the two main motifs from the introductory section of the first movement, entitled "Roundup" (R 10 P2). The first motif is the falling fifth (Ex. 8a), and immediately after it appears the second rising melodic motif (Ex. 8b).

Ex. 8a

Ex. 8b

The principal section of the movement starts in measure 10 with a repeated note motif in 5/8 meter:

Ex. 9

Starting in measure 28, the main theme is gradually built out of these three segments. This new theme connects all the movements of this orchestral cycle:

Ex. 10

Also, the connection with previous musical material is evident when Roslyn's theme reappears in a very low register at the end of this movement (measure 103). The scene of the "Roundup" begins when Guido's plane approaches the top of a mountain range and the horses are chased through the mountain pass.

The musical material of the second movement, "Chase" (R11 P1), derives completely from the previous movement, "Roundup." The different meter — alla breve — the domin-ation of the brass group of instruments, and the pointillistic "hiccup" treatment of the rhythmic component makes this scene quite intense. The two main motifs, the falling fifth and the rising stepwise motif, appear again in the introductory section. Both of them are gradually combined into a thematic figure derived from the "Roundup" theme shown in Ex. 10.

Ex. 11

The second movement is developed on the basis of the polyphonic treatment of this thematic figure (Ex. 11), which is imitated in various forms throughout different orchestral groups. This polyphonic approach gives the movement the characteristics of a fugato.

The third movement, entitled "Tension" (R12 P1), has the role of a slow movement in an orchestral cycle. There are two sections in this movement. The music of the first section reflects the disagreement between Roslyn and Guido in the van. The main theme from "Roundup" is varied and adjusted to the mood of a slow movement. It is exposed first in the trumpets, then in the strings and the oboes, and again in the trumpets, giving the impression of an instrumental ternary form.

Ex. 12

In the second section of this movement, the cowboys lasso and tie up the horses. The tension is raised by an agitated orchestral background, above which the varied main melodic phrase (Ex. 12) appears three times in continuous musical movement, thus forming the line of three short "variations." First, the theme is exposed in augmentation by clarinets and oboes, then it modulates chromatically in a lower key and appears in a more moving, dotted rhythm in the parts of oboes and trumpets. In its third appearance the theme returns to the previous key, varied in even more agitated rhythm and exposed by piccolo, flutes, violins and violas.

In the fourth movement, "Trying for Freedom" (R12 P2), the conspiracy between Roslyn and Perce is presented. They agree to free the mustangs, while Gay and Guido make a deal by the plane. The movement begins with an interesting appearance of the thematic material from part *b* of the "Main Title" (Ex. 2), and then it is developed into a waltz using the "Roundup" theme.

Ex. 13

The last sequence of the third film section, entitled "Resolved #1" (R13 P1), is a sublime ending of the big mustang roundup scene in both a musical and film sense. It shows Gay fighting to subdue the released horse, and ultimately being successful. The music for this final climax is built from thematic material taken from part *a* and part *b* of the "Main Title." Both melodic phrases (Ex. 1 and Ex. 2) are varied and used as the first and the second theme in the development of a double fugue. The thematic material of the fugue is announced by alternated short motifs from part *a* and part *b* at the beginning of the sequence. The first theme is based on the melody of the first part *a* which in this context appears in a strict, syncopated rhythmic movement which emphasizes its serious and quasi marching character. After the exposition of the first theme through different instruments and orchestral groups, the second theme is introduced in the development part of the fugue, playing the role of a new countersubject (Ex. 14). The double fugue is truly a remarkable musical ending for the film's third section and for the entire film, as well. In this manner all three sections of the film are united in their musical and dramatic essence.

Ex. 14

Comments

The score for *The Misfits* is highly organized in its development of the thematic material which follows and comments on the film's action. Here, the achievements from the musical past are used to serve the new film art by adjustments of traditional monothematic development to the exigencies of the film's dramaturgy. The orchestration of the score is also fascinating. The main orchestrator was Bernie Mayers, although some of the cues were orchestrated by Alex North himself. The orchestrator for the "Roundup" was David Tamkin.

Despite the critical failure of the film at the time, the score for *The Misfits* received deserved critical appreciation. The *Hollywood Reporter* critic James Powers wrote that "Alex North's score, a study in dissonance and lyricism, contrasting and moving, is an exceptionally fine one."[23] Justin Gilbert thought that Alex North's score was "impressive, frequently 'pointing up' the dramatic sequences."[24] The outstanding contribution of the music was also praised by the *Daily Variety* critic who found Alex North's score "melodically listenable, dramatically potent."[25]

The quality of the music greatly depended on the length of time North had to finish the score. He found that he would be rushed if he had to complete it in time for the nominations, and this would greatly impair its quality. Huston gave him several more weeks to write the score because of his infinite trust in North's judgment.[26] This understanding for each other's craft, as well as the versatility and the curiosity about the different subjects and parameters of the human condition, kept Huston and North together through all the years of their productive collaboration.

10

Under the Volcano (1984)

No se puede vivir sin amar. (One cannot live without love.)
— Under the Volcano *(Malcolm Lowry)*

Lowry's, Huston's and North's Mexico

The novel *Under the Volcano* by Malcolm Lowry was first published in 1947, eleven years after he wrote the short story of the same name, which served as a basis for the novel. The story takes place in the Mexican town of Quauhnahuac (Cuernavaca), which lies in the valley dominated by two volcanoes, Popocatepetl and Ixtaccihuatl. The action of the entire novel is limited to one day, the Day of the Dead on November 1, 1939 (in the film the year is 1938), which is celebrated in Mexico with a big fiesta, bullfighting, and singing and dancing on the streets. That is the tragic last day in the life of the former British consul in Mexico, Geoffrey Firmin, a desperate alcoholic trapped in the labyrinth of his own life situation. Lowry's work, beyond the personal tragedy of the Consul killed by Mexican fascist supporters called "pelados," integrates the fatalism of Mexico and the despair of Europe in the years between the Spanish Civil War and the Second World War. Thus the individual tragedy obtains universal dimensions, and the Consul becomes a modern hero, or rather anti-hero, who reflects the world extremity within his own tragic fatality. The novel contains autobiographical features, and seems to be Lowry's search for his own identity through the complexity of his experiences.

Considering John Huston's interest in anti-heroes and obsessed misfits in literature, the character of the Consul seemed to be an appropriate challenge for a film adaptation. Guy Gallo adapted the novel into a screenplay under Huston's supervision. It was not an easy task, because the novel was, as Vincent Canby pointed out,

173

"a difficult, maddening, sometimes spellbinding book in which absolutely nothing appears to have been left out: Peter Rabbit, the cabala, Dante, Aztec mythology, restaurant menus, Karl Freund's 1935 film adaptation of *The Hands of Orlac*, Cervantes, Mexican timetables, the degrees of sky clarity, Nazis, the Spanish Civil War, and on and on."[1] However, it seemed that Huston was ready to sacrifice large portions of Lowry's book to concentrate on what most interested him: the character of the Consul.[2] According to Huston, the Consul was the most complicated character he has ever had in a film. He was a victim, but also a giant, a kind of a hero, an adventurer.[3] In the Introduction of Lowry's novel, Stephen Spender pointed out that the Consul's failure to act becomes itself a kind of action. His refusal to be heroic makes him a hero.... His isolation seems to be his deepest truth. He rejects love to protect this isolation and he has to be killed because he rejects love.[4] A large portion of the Consul's life is happening in his confused mental world, and a very small portion is left visible to the outer world. The personal frustration and self-destruction of the Consul are mainly determined by two factors: the relationship with his wife Yvonne, who is the reason for his torn emotions, and the obsession with alcohol which distorts his mind. Yvonne, who had abandoned him for a while, is back on that special Day of the Dead, wishing to stay with him and help him, because she apparently loves her husband. But, there is still a trace of her brief involvement in an affair with the Consul's half-brother Hugh, a journalist with a recent experience from the Spanish Civil War. That fact poisons the emotional devotion of the Consul, who obviously has difficulty in dealing with his cuckoldry. He is pushed by the circumstances and by his own self-destructive temper closer and closer to the edge of the "abyss," where he finally falls to his own death and at the same time provokes accidentally the death of Yvonne, because "one cannot live without love."

When discussing his film adaptations of literary works, Huston always pointed out that he did nor seek to interpret or to put his own stamp on the material. "I try to be as faithful to the original material as I can," Huston stated.[5] The emotional plot of the novel *Under the Volcano* possessed enough material to inspire Huston's artistic vision as a filmmaker. "I'm a bold visionary with other people's work," he said. "It's the work of Malcolm Lowry given shape, so that it now has a dramatic form."[6] The result was a delightful, poetic film with excellent performances by Albert Finney in the role of the Consul, Jacqueline Bisset as Yvonne, and Anthony Andrews as Hugh.

Huston's attempt to translate Lowry's dark and difficult novel into film received mixed reviews. The main reason for that was the "unfilmablity" of the subject matter and complexity of the novel. Those who praised the film called it "a model of literary adaptation,"[7] then "a proud accomplishment on every count,"[8] or the film "that captures the heart of the Malcolm Lowry novel,"[9] and "ranks with the best work Mr. Huston has ever done."[10]

The Main Features and Organization of the Musical Score

In the Introduction to Lowry's novel, Stephen Spender tried to make an interesting comparison between music and the Consul's fatal personality. He pointed out that "the life of the Consul resembles variations on a theme of music by some composer such as Beethoven where the greatest possible variety of moods and rhythms are gone through without the elements of the theme being fundamentally altered."[11] This kind of general statement, however, could be related to anyone's personality, because everybody' s life might be interpreted as variations on a "theme." What makes the people different and special is the "theme" itself in the means of one's particular psychological constitution and individual personality. Alex North had a hard task in *Under the Volcano*—to create a "theme" that would musically present the emotional obsession of the Consul with his wife Yvonne and his mental obsession with alcohol which created the Consul's imaginary world. On the other hand, there was a necessity to illustrate musically the real, or rather the surreal world of Mexico and the peculiar celebration of the Day of the Dead, because, as Sheila Benson has pointed out, "Lowry's great feat in the novel was his ability to create a double world: the real Mexico in which the Consul lives, and the hallucinatory one that the Consul ... sees around him, [as] a result of his epic drinking. The problem has always been how to let us see both those worlds..."[12] That was the problem with which Huston had to deal in the translation of the novel into a film, as did Alex North in the creation of his musical score.

About his musical approach North said, "That was a strange score in the sense that I tried to establish the locale and the period in the use of the source music and tried to enrich the imagery of what Huston had done there, in the Mexican landscapes. And also I tried to get in the melancholy of the protagonist, the Consul, a sort of musical universality, so that the music was not Mexican at all. Just to reflect in a quiet way this man's problems."[13] This explanation exactly determines the concept of the musical score of *Under the Volcano*. The traditional Mexican source music depicts the outer world and suggests local atmosphere which, like a floating aura, surrounds the inner, personal world of the Consul, presented through dramatic, specially composed music.

Huston loved Mexico. He even spent the last period of his life living in Puerto Vallarta in Mexico. As much as the Consul's individuality inspired Huston's imagination as a filmmaker, "the exotic Mexican locale," as Arthur Knight wrote, "and especially the young Mexicans' joyous celebration of their Death Day, also attracted him; he has always been happier on location than in the studios."[14] On the other hand, Alex North loved Mexican music. In the late thirties he spent a year in Mexico with Anna Sokolow, as he was at that time a student of the Mexican composer Silvestre Revueltas. North had already applied that experience in several film scores such as *Viva Zapata* and *The Wonderful Country*. In the creation and organization of the score for *Under the Volcano,* North had a chance to use again his experience and knowledge of Mexican music. The film structure itself imposed a necessity for using large amount of Mexican source music which presents the spirit of the collective scenes and involvement of the main characters in the real world. North had to choose the appropriate Mexican traditional folk and popular tunes for these scenes, but he also wrote several tunes himself for this purpose. There are four blocks of Mexican source music which accompany the intense collective celebration on the Day of the Dead and divide the film (and the musical score) into several parts. The dramatic music cues which appear between the source music blocks reflect the individual world and the personality of the Consul, as well as his relationship with Yvonne and Hugh. These music cues usually do not have nothing in common with the Mexican musical style, because North wanted to emphasize musically the difference between the real world and the Consul's imaginary world as sharply as possible.

Many times over the years North claimed that he preferred scoring the films with which he could feel emotionally involved. These were mostly psychological dramas which demanded musical portraits of the main characters, and musical comments on their psychological states or emotional relationships. Since the writing of "character" music was of primary interest for North, it seemed that the contradictory personality of the Consul could be an excellent model for musical characterization. As previously mentioned, North had to create a "theme" which would define musically the obsessive character of the Consul. The nature of the Consul's obsession is made up of two parts, mental and emotional. The first involves his chronic obsession with alcohol which opens the door to his inner imaginary world of subconsciousness, mysticism and symbolism, and the second involves his preoccupation with Yvonne, or, in broader sense, with love. Therefore, North came out with two themes which served as musical "keys" for the further development of the film score. The first musical idea, like a dark shadow, follows the Consul in the variety of his alcoholic moods. It is an old religious theme which is exposed already in the second part of the "Main Title" by the muted French horns. However, as Vincent Canby pointed out, "though full of doom, *Under the Volcano* is also hugely romantic. The tangled love lives of the Consul, Yvonne and Hugh seem to have a contemporary importance..."[15] If the first idea is considered a musical sign of the doom, then the second musical idea could be interpreted as a musical mark of the film's reiterated motto, *No se puede vivir sin amar*; that is, a sensual romantic theme of Yvonne exposed by oboe d'amore. Yvonne's musical theme reflects, like a mirror, the emotional aspect of the Consul's character. It also balances the contradictions of his alcoholic obsession. It was not the first time that North used a musical theme of a female character for musical characterization of a male protagonist. This compositional device has become a landmark of his film scoring.

The two main themes, first exposed as separate units, sometimes appear together in the further development of the score, within the same music cue. In a way, they inspire, influence and provoke each other, because, as different as they are, they represent the two faces of the same character, or the "two sides of the same coin." There are also certain similarities between the melodic movements of these two themes, a fact that shows North's ability for thematic transformation through the use of the monothematic principle. The two main themes are almost always the nucleus of the dramatic music in the film, and they act as a creative impulse or given musical code for composition of rather free-treated character variations.

The anti-Nazi feelings of the Consul and his half-brother Hugh are revealed in several occasions within the film, but they are not illustrated with particular music. Only the Mexican peasant, who possibly represents the political left-wing orientation in the growing neo-Nazism of Mexico, has a special plaintive tune. It is exposed first as source music, played by the peasant on a primitive flute. Later, North used this tune to compose a remarkable music cue which follows the death of the peasant, murdered apparently by the Mexican neo-Nazi police.

The Analyses of the Musical Score and Development of the "Character Music" into a Dramatic Factor of the Film

Cue sheet for U.S. and Canadian distribution only

Fil "Volcano"

UNIVERSAL PICTURES

a division of Universal City Studios, Inc.
100 Universal City Plaza
Universal City, California 91608

MUSIC CUE SHEET

TITLE: UNDER THE VOLCANO
PROD. NO: 05327
DATE: September 27, 1984
RECORDED BY: A John Huston Film, An
Ithaca - Conacine Production, A
Universal Release

TITLE	PUBLISHER OR RIGHTS SECURED FROM		USAGE
	COMPOSER	PUBLISHER	
REEL I			
1. UNDER THE VOLCANO - (Main Title - Pt. I) and	Alex North (ASCAP)	Dylanna Music Co. (ASCAP)	Ins.Bkg. 1:07
2. UNDER THE VOLCANO - (Main Title - Pt. II)/ VOLCANO CHORD — and	"		" 1:50
3. WOMEN CHANT and	Traditional	-----------------	Voc.Bkg. 1:47
4. FEST #4	-Alex North (ASCAP)	Dylanna Music Co. (ASCAP)	Ins.Bkg. 1:40
5. FEST #5	"	"	" 1:06
6. FEST #8	"	"	" 1:12
REEL II			
7. PARADE	Alex North (ASCAP)	Dylanna Music Co. (ASCAP)	Ins.Vis. :54
8. BALLROOM RHUMBA			" 2:00
9. BALLROOM BALLAD RENDEZVOUS			1:40

The first page from the cue sheet for *Under the Volcano*, 1984.

The concept of the musical score of *Under the Volcano* includes basically three types of musical approach which are imposed and defined by the requirements of the film's drama and its general atmosphere. The lucidity of the Consul and his imaginary world of alcoholic contemplations are presented by contemporary orchestral sound based mostly on the use of linear compositional technique, which often results in dissonant harmonies and cluster structures. Yvonne's presence and the "love" subject matter demands different musical qualities. They are realized through a romantic, rather chamber sound which implies the use of a melodic principle and traditional tonal harmonic approach. The wild fiesta of the Day of the Dead and the surreal world of the Mexican "underground" are musically illustrated by traditional Mexican songs as source background music.

The volcano (Popocatepetl), which appears several times as a distant symbol of "impending doom,"[16] has also its musical valuation. That is a single cluster orchestral chord, which North entitled "Volcano Chord." Its cluster structure combines the sounds of B flat, B, C and C sharp major chords exposed through all orchestral groups, including certain percussions like waterphone gong, wind chimes, log drums etc. This vibrating tremolo chord characterizes the hidden tension and danger of the volcano which is a symbolic caution of the unpredictable nature of human destiny. The chord is used several times as an ominous ending of certain music cues.

The "Main Title" of the film presents an entire musical microuniverse which anticipates the surreal atmosphere of the Day of the Dead and the Mexican landscape. It also contains the main thematic material used later for characterization of the film's hero, and reveals the contemporary compositional approach of Alex North. The opening credits are combined with the dancing sequence of various skeleton dolls. Therefore, the music for the "Main Title" is called "The Dance of the Dead" or "Skeletal Dance," and it is "alone worth the price of admission," as Mike Snell pointed out.[17] The "Main Title" (R1 P1) is one of the most complex music cues in the entire musical score for *Under the Volcano*. It consists of two parts, "Main Title I" and "Main Title II."

The "Main Title I" is characterized by a pointillistic orchestral approach and a fragmentary thematic structure. The thematic material is based on Mexican motifs. The complete exposition of a dance-like tune (starting from measure 33) is prepared and anticipated by "hidden" and fragmentary structured thematic material of Mexican origin, exposed throughout two formal sections. The "main body" of the first section is a big period divided into two measure fragments by the strings' and xylophone's *glissandi*. This means that after each thematic fragment of two measures, played by bassoons I and II, there follows one measure *glissando* which "interrupts" the musical flow of the thematic material. The bassoons' *staccato* sounds organized in "hiccup" rhythmic figures provide this section with pointillistic features. The thematic fragments are accompanied by the strings' *flageolet* clusters which determine the dissonant sound quality. The Mexican origin of the thematic material is more evident in the section which follows. The second section contains a tune which is a big phrase of eight measures with fragmentary structure. This type of structure is conditioned by the melodic and rhythmic organization of the tune within one-measure figures which alternate between harp, synthesizer DX 7 and strings *pizzicato* on the one hand, and wind instruments on the other. The musical flow of both sections is enriched with particular metric organization. The meter changes every single measure from 4/4 to 3/4 and 2/4 in the first section, and from 3/4 to 4/4 in the second section. It seems that the fragmentary structure of the first and the second section imposes this metric variety, because as soon as the main tune begins with its exposition in the third section (measure 33) the meter is established as 3/4. The music of the second section leads directly into the exposition of the third section which contains the main music material of "Main Title I." This is a tune in a dance-like movement, full of life, which symbolically celebrates the value of Life on the Day of the Dead. The first two sections of "Main Title I" melodically and rhythmically prepare gradually for the exposition of this tune whose formal structure is an extended big period. It is played by flutes and piccolo and accompanied by a contrapuntal phrase in the trumpet's part.

Ex. 1

The other wind instruments unbalance the metric organization with unexpected accents and in that way complete the pointillistic image of this music cue. This image is enriched with string *pizzicato* offbeat accents in the second phrase of the tune.

The extraordinary rhythmic variety and complexity of "Main Title I" are achieved mostly by the use of an enormous number of percussions. According to Alex North's comment in Fred Karlin's book, he used the following percussion instruments in this music cue: sleigh bells, tambourine, xylophone (struck with large nails), booze bottle (struck with triangle beater), four castanets, guiro, Chinese blocks, log drum, cabasa/ maraca (one in each hand), marimba, vibes, cowbells, gong/water gong, and a chromatic series of boo-bams (one octave, from F below middle C to F above middle C).[18] The sharp impact between the instrumental colors, the variable rhythm, the pointillistic treatment, and the dissonant orchestral surrounding, all of these elements create quite a sarcastic musical image in "Main Title I."

While the "Main Title I" is concentrated on pure dancing and playful movement, "Main Title II" has a more "sophisticated" musical texture. North used an old religious theme as a basis for scoring the second part of the "Main Title."[19] According to Joan Padrol, the theme is a sequence from a musical motet, and it illustrates the celebration of the Day of the Dead.[20] More than that, this theme plays an essential role in the further development of the musical score. It is the first of the two basic themes which creates the "skeleton" of the entire score. Later on it would be used as a basis for the composition of deeply dramatic music cues related to the Consul's alcoholic desperation and illusions. Actually, the ways of the development of this theme and the situations in which it is used within the film classify it as a character theme of the Consul. In the "Main Title II" the theme is exposed by muted French horns in *legato* movement (Ex. 2a), while the cellos have a *pizzicato* countersubject (Ex. 2b) developed into a fugato by the string instruments.

Ex. 2a

Ex. 2b

After the exposition of the theme by the French horns, the polyphonic development continues with the strings' *pizzicato*. The linear movement is enriched with the vibraphone, xylophone and harp parts. The cellos' countersubject is divided into motifs which are used in intense rhythmic movement. The intensity grows and achieves its culmination with the entrance of the wind instruments and most of the previously mentioned percussions. The woodwinds take over the wild rhythmic

movement and parts of the strings' motifs, and multiply them into intervals of seconds, with added brass accents. For a while, within twenty-four measures, the wind
and the stringed instruments alternate their parts with approximately three measures each. The orchestral movement disappears into the cluster sound of the Volcano chord which opens the film's action.

The music of the "Main Title" displays two different profiles of the celebration
of the Day of the Dead. Appropriate to the character of the used thematic material,
"Main Title I" shows generally the profane side of the celebration, whereas "Main
Title II" points out its sacred meaning. The components which most connect both
parts are the brisk rhythmic movement, the pointillistic treatment and the modern
sound of this opening music.

The beginning of the film introduces the main character, Consul Geoffrey
Firmin, at the fiesta. His behavior and attitude expose him as a person addicted to
alcohol. This part of the film is mostly filled with fiesta source music. After the scene
in a chapel, where the Consul and his pal Dr. Vigil pray for the return of the Consul's wife, Yvonne, from whom he has been separated and divorced, the miracle happens. The next morning Yvonne really arrives in Cuernavaca. Her arrival is
accompanied by a beautiful, simple lyric theme played by oboe d'amore (Ex. 3).
Yvonne's theme is a small phrase of four measures starting in E major and modu-
lating to G major. As such it gives the impression of an unfinished compositional
unit. However, this theme is, together with the Consul's theme (Ex. 2a), the main
music clue for the development of the musical score, and it is used in its extended
or shortened form many times throughout the film. Jacqueline Bisset, who played
the role of Yvonne, wrote later a message to North to thank him for the music he
composed for her role, which she defined as "unpredictable."[21]

Ex. 3

In a detailed observation of the structure of this tune one could notice a similar-
ity in the beginning melodic movement of Yvonne's theme and the Consul's theme from
"Main Title II." Considering Alex North's talent for transformation of musical ideas, it
is very possible that Yvonne's theme actually originated from the Consul's theme. This
procedure of creating a new theme through the rhythmic (and melodic) changes of the
principal theme is a characteristic feature of the monothematic cyclic principle.

The exposition of the thematic material continues with the next music cue,
"Peon on Horse" (R3 P1). On their way home the Consul and Yvonne see the peasant riding a horse and playing a plaintive tune on a primitive flute. This tune, which
seems to be the accompanying source music of a short and not very important film
episode, was in reality composed by North and turns out to be the basis for a very
dramatic music cue, "Death of a Peasant" (R7 P2).

Ex. 4

The block of four continuous music cues accompanies the following film's scenes in the Consul's house. The polite conversation between Yvonne and the Consul on the terrace keeps hidden their stormy emotions. The Consul tries desperately to stay away from the alcohol during their conversation. But, as soon as Yvonne leaves to prepare herself for the fiesta, the Consul begins to search madly for a bottle. This scene is musically brought out by a music cue entitled "Desperation" (R4 P1). As Yvonne leaves the terrace the first two measures of her theme are played by a violoncello solo. The theme is interrupted by an orchestral cluster whose vibrating sound goes throughout three measures, obviously indicating the Consul's craving for alcohol. Yvonne's theme returns as she unpacks her suitcases. This time the entire phrase of the theme is exposed by oboe d'amore, but the beginning of the phrase is no longer in a major key. It begins with D minor and only then modulates to F major. The orchestral cluster appears again after this phrase and leads toward the Consul's theme exposed by two French horns in contrapuntal movement.

Ex. 5

At that moment the Consul starts his long desperate search for any left or hidden bottle of alcohol. Finally, he satisfies his alcoholic craving from a bottle hidden in the bushes of the yard. North found this scene difficult to score, as he had to indicate musically an invisible, hidden subject which accounted for the Consul's mad behavior.[22] According to the demands of this scene, the Consul's theme is extended and the rhythm is much more moving. It is harmonically supported by dissonant string *flageolets* which provide the theme with tragic connotations.

The next music cue, entitled "Stay" (R4 P2), is based on the exposition of Yvonne's theme. This time the theme is extended into a big phrase whose structure is 2+2+4 measures. Within this proportion the theme sounds more complete than in its first exposition (Ex. 3). The solo sound of oboe d'amore, accompanied by a beautiful romantic arrangement for chamber orchestra, thoroughly captures the nature of human solitude. This is the feeling with which Yvonne and the Consul are confronted after the unrealized love scene filled with the hidden fear of failure. The originally written music cue contains one more part in which the Consul's theme is exposed in combination with motifs from Yvonne's theme, and at the end the Volcano

Under the Volcano, still (Ithaca Enterprises, 1984).
The Consul Geoffrey Firmin (Albert Finney).

chord is added. Unfortunately, this part was cut in the editing of the film, but the complete music cue is recorded on the compact disc under the title "The Bedroom."

It seems that the only music cue in the score bearing the characteristics of the Mexican musical style, besides the source music, is "Cockroach Tango" (R5 P1). This piece has the dance-like character and the form of a rondo with one theme. The principal theme and the first episode are small periods, while the second episode is an extended small phrase. The principal theme in its last appearance is shortened and slightly varied. The most interesting contrast in this music cue is achieved with the quasi baroque phrase for harpsichord in the second episode of the rondo which has nothing in common with the Mexican dance. Still, it sounds very natural incorporated into this style, and intensifies the comic effect of this cue. The music is used in a "bathroom scene," where the drunk Consul prepares himself for the fiesta. Terrified by a cockroach he screams for help which brings Yvonne and Hugh into the bathroom. They shave him, help him to bathe, and take care of him. The beginning of the principal theme of the rondo which accompanies this comical, and at the same time sad scene, looks as follows:

Ex. 6

The trio (Yvonne, the Consul and Hugh) leave the house to join the fiesta. They make plans for the day. Yvonne stays behind the men and observes the volcano Popocatepetl, "the sleeping beauty," as she says in her impression of the view. Yvonne's theme is again the clue for a musical realization of this scene, entitled "One Cannot

Under the Volcano (Ithaca Enterprises, 1984). Excerpt from the cue "Desperation." Sketch.

Live Without Love" (R6 P1). The exposition of the entire Yvonne's theme by a solo violoncello in F# minor serves as an introduction to a rather romantic music cue. The widely developed melody in a major key (E major), carried by the strings, has obviously derived from Yvonne's theme (Ex. 7). The cue is formally organized within the big phrase with an added piano cadence as an inner extension of four measures. The ending piano phrase is based on the recognizable motif from Yvonne's theme in E minor, which encircles the music cue in a coherent unit.

Ex. 7

The bus ride to the fiesta is interrupted by an encounter with the wounded Mexican peasant — the flute player that Yvonne and the Consul previously saw on the street. He dies as the passengers kneel around his body. The peasant was probably a victim of an attack by the Nazi orientated bandits. The "police" arrive and scatter the crowd, while one of the passengers (obviously a "pelado") takes the peasant's money. The disturbed passengers continue their trip with feelings of tension and helplessness.

This scene ends with a shot of the volcano which appears as an ominous sign. The music which supports the dramaturgy of this scene is entitled "Death of a Peasant" (R7 P2). It is based on the combination of the plaintive peasant's tune played on the flute in the music cue "Peon on Horse" (Ex. 4), and the Consul's theme (Ex. 2a). The Peasant's theme is first exposed by a primitive flute in an out-of tune manner, within proportions of a big phrase. It is counterpointed by a clarinet tune and a short melodic figure played by french horns, which intensifies the dramatic value of this musical section. In the next four measures the strings anticipate the appearance of the Consul's theme, which is further exposed by the oboe, and accompanied by a syncopated flute counterpoint. The melodic movement of the Consul's theme is set against a vibrating orchestral background created by strings and bass marimba. The thematic material is rhythmically diminished and developed through eight measures (big phrase) in a steady rhythm of quarter notes:

Ex. 8

The Peasant's theme reappears in a changed orchestration and thus determines the simple ternary form of this music cue — *a b a_1*. The theme is shortened (only the

Under the Volcano, still (Ithaca Enterprises, 1984). (left to right) Consul (Albert Finney),
Yvonne (Jacqueline Bisset) and Hugh (Anthony Andrews).

first four measures are exposed), and brought out by the strings and French horns.
The dramatic horn figure from the first section appears this time in the violas and
violoncellos. Similar to "Main Title II," this music cue is based on the linear development of the music material. Fred Karlin has pointed out that "the melodic material and instrumental colors combine in making this cue so effective," which is a very
accurate comment.[23]

After the scenes of bullfighting and lunch in the out-of-doors restaurant, where
the Consul bitterly brings out Yvonne's adultery with Hugh, the last part of the film
begins. The Consul leaves Yvonne and Hugh, and in desperate anger, with a bottle
of alcohol in his hand, follows the path to his final destination — the brothel "El
Farolito." The music cue which accompanies the Consul's "run away" from Yvonne
and Hugh is entitled "Despair" (R9 P1). This music cue is developed on the basis of
the musical material from the Consul's theme, with a short introduction which uses
the material from Yvonne's theme, and the cluster Volcano chord at the end of the
cue as its conclusion. The introduction contains the first two measures of Yvonne's
theme which are extended by augmentation into a four-measure phrase. The Consul's theme follows, entirely exposed by muted horns and strings, but in a different,
6/8 movement:

Ex. 9

The Consul experiences total personal degradation and a "nightmare" in the bar-brothel El Farolito. According to Gay Gallo, Huston was most interested in getting to the Farolito, "where we have this nightmare vision of this man on the edge of his personal boundaries, which is what interested him in the book itself—that edge."[24] In the final scene the Consul is murdered by the bandits who represent the Mexican fascist supporters. Hearing the shooting, Yvonne runs back and accidentally gets hit by a running, escaped horse. The music cue "Denouement—Part I" (R11 P3) emphasizes musically the dramatic, tragic tension of this scene. The sharp contrast in the sound is achieved through a confrontation of the low strings, trombones and bassoons with the high woodwind instruments. The alternation of short rhythmic and melodic figures in these extreme sound ranges intensifies the entire orchestral volume. After fourteen measures, the theme in violins *tutti* enters with intense strength. It is based on movements of the interval of fourth in both directions, upwards and downwards, and balances the entire orchestral sound. At the end, the first phrase of Yvonne's theme is added. Played by horns, with extended note values and in *rubato* movement, it sounds like an epilog which matches the film's motto *No se puede vivir sin amar,* while Hugh holds in his hands Yvonne's dead body.

Ex. 10

The epilog continues in the cue "Denouement—Part II" with the exposition of the Consul's theme by the French horns, violas and violoncellos (Ex. 11). The theme is slightly rhythmically varied and syncopated, and harmonically supported by cluster sounds of violins' *flageolets*. In this last appearance the Consul's theme sounds almost religious while the camera moves slowly from the volcano to the face of the dead Consul. As one would expect, the cue is finished with the volcano chord which in a specific way combines all the sounds in one compact cluster structure.

Ex. 11

Fred Karlin pointed out that "sometimes a single instrument playing the melody is all that the scene requires, and can in fact be a welcome break from more complex orchestration."[25] This statement is very appropriate for the music of the "End Credits" for *Under the Volcano*. Alex North began a score for *Death of a Salesman* (1951) with a solo-flute theme, which was a very unusual beginning for a film score at that time. In the "End Credits" for *Under the Volcano*, he decided to finish the score with Yvonne's theme played by oboe solo, which served as a final emotional and tragic statement of the Consul's murder. After the complete exposition of Yvonne's theme, the orchestra joins in and repeats the short version of "Main Title II."

After the analyses of the music composed for *Under the Volcano* it can be easily concluded that this musical score represents a very serious orchestral work. It is carefully tailored to the film's requirements, and essentially fulfills the emotional and psychological image of the main protagonists. Thus, the score obtains, in general, qualities of "character music," which becomes an indispensable device in the dramatic interpretation of the Consul's personal tragedy. Each cue presents a specific musical piece based on separately exposed or combined musical themes. The themes themselves are regularly adjusted to the characters' demands. The formal organization of the score for *Under the Volcano* could be generally interpreted as a combination of very freely treated character variations, on the one hand, and symphonic pieces united through the use of the monothematic principle on the other hand.

Comments

North's compositional approach toward the scoring of *Under the Volcano* is based on the use of various compositional techniques. Many of the music cues are very contemporary and contain dissonant harmonies which derive from the linear development of the instrumental parts, or from the use of compact harmonic clusters. On the other hand, the traditional approach is mostly evident in the music cues which have a romantic melody as a leading part, thus requiring homophonic harmonic accompaniment. This variety of compositional techniques results in different musical styles, which range from neoromantic and neobaroque to pointillistic and polytonal musical realizations. However, this stylistic compilation should be interpreted rather as a proper intention of the composer to follow the emotional oscillations of the film's dramaturgy, than a consequence of musical eclecticism. The brilliant orchestration is due to the collaboration of Alex North with several excellent orchestrators: Al Woodbury ("Main Title," "Cockroach Tango," "Denouement I," "End Credits"), Lennie Niehaus ("Yvonne's Arrival," "One Cannot Live Without Love," "Despair," "Denouement II"), and Henry Brandt ("Stay," "Death of a Peasant").

It is an interesting fact that North wanted to include some of his old music in the score for *Under the Volcano*. For instance, "Main Title I" is a revised version of the second movement from the *Africa Suite*. Another sequence, "Ballroom Ballad Rendezvous," which appears as source music accompanying the hotel party in *Under the Volcano*, was previously used in a similar manner as bar source music in *The Misfits*. The musical material from *Wise Blood* is used for the creation of a new music cue entitled "Adventure," which was meant to be included in the score for *Under the*

Volcano instead of the cue "One Cannot Live Without Love" (R6 P1). Even though this music cue did not find its part in the film, it was recorded under the title "Pastorale" on the compact disc for the soundtrack of *Under the Volcano*.

Alex North's score for *Under the Volcano* was widely appreciated by the audience, his peers and the critics, as well. The score was nominated for an Academy Award (North's fifteenth nomination since 1951), but it did not win the Oscar. The critics were very affirmative about the music for *Under the Volcano*. Sheila Benson defined Alex North's work as a "superb musical score"[26]; Arthur Knight wrote that "Alex North's spare score, with its strange, ghostlike whispers in the strings, beautifully complements Huston's atmospherics"[27]; while David Sterritt thought that the music was "too strong."[28] Charles Champlin devoted an entire article in the *Los Angeles Times* to the work of Alex North, in which he wrote, "I suspect that North's film music reflects as much as anything his thorough grounding in jazz and folk as well as classical music, his taste and his reticence itself. His score for *Under the Volcano* is nothing so simple as 'The Mexican Hat Dance Revisited.' It has an ethnic flavor used as the most subtle of seasoning, and with it a sort of melancholy universalism, a quiet reminder that this is, after all, an expatriate Englishman dying in a cosmopolitan city in a foreign land."[29] Huston certainly knew how to inspire and how to direct his collaborators in the expression of their individual creativity. With his pictures he was able to create a challenge for all of those who worked with him. In return, his collaborators would always give him the best of their creations. Alex North was one of them. The score for *Under the Volcano* is one more proof of his genuine musical talent and enormous knowledge of film scoring.

11

Prizzi's Honor (1985)

Do I ice her, or do I marry her?
— *Charley Partanna in* Prizzi's Honor *(Richard Condon)*

The Aspects of Parody in Prizzi's Honor

Richard Condon, the author of many best-sellers, wrote a series of novels about the organized Mafia family known as Prizzi, but only the first, *Prizzi's Honor*, was filmed. Condon, with Janet Roach, adapted his novel written in 1982 into a screenplay for the 1985 film starring Jack Nicholson, Kathleen Turner and Anjelica Huston. The screenplay was nominated for an Academy Award, and Huston won the Oscar for best supporting actress.

Prizzi's Honor is a black comedy about the family loyalty and honor, love, hate and money. It contains the elements of comedy, satire, parody, allegory and melodrama. Even the title of the film seems to be satiric, after showing what the Prizzis are able to do in the name of honor. It is a kind of perverted honor, especially when it comes to the matter of money. Some reviewers considered *Prizzi's Honor* similar to *The Godfather*,[1] "with passionate, lyrical arias from Italian operas pointing up their low-grade sentimentality."[2] But, almost all the critics agreed on one point— *Prizzi's Honor* was one of the most entertaining comedies and one of the funniest movies made in 1985.

However, beneath the humorous and sometimes grotesque interpretation of the film's story, one discovers the tragic idea of how the family business of organized crime can corrupt one's sense of values, and become more important and more powerful than the personal feelings. It seems that in *Prizzi's Honor*, as Sheila Benson said, "every emotion is larger than life, but death is simply business."[3]

The story of *Prizzi's Honor* evolves from the love affair between Charley Partanna

(Jack Nicholson) and Irene Walker (Kathleen Turner). The plot itself apparently did not occupy John Huston as much as the working out of characters and milieu. Thus, the film turned out to be more "character comedy" than "action comedy." The characters are presented as extreme individuals. Charley Partanna is the efficient enforcer and the most confident "right hand" of Don Corrado (William Hickey), the head of the Prizzis. His way to the top of the Prizzi's hierarchy interferes with his love toward Irene Walker, the California "tax accountant," who turns out to be a first-class hit-woman. Charley's main conflict lies in the question of to whom he should be loyal — to the family or to his wife. His search for the right decision brings the story to its fatal and absurd ending. There is also another character who makes the relationships even more complicated. That is Maerose (Anjelica Huston), Don Corrado's grand-daughter and Charley's ex-girlfriend who was rejected by the family, because of an affair she had while she was in the relationship with Charley. She wants to revenge and regain her place and position in the family. All the characters are united through the subject of family "honor" and family "money," which seems to be more impor-tant than everything together, or, as Irene said, "Sicilian would rather eat his chil-dren than part with his money, and they are very fond of their children."

Prizzi's Honor brings out the aspects of parody while dealing with serious sub-jects and moral values. This defines the film as a black comedy. The reviewer Robert Osborne wrote: "Although *Prizzi's Honor* covers a rather bloody subject, there's vir-tually no blood ever shown on the screen. Maybe it just takes the old pros like John Huston and Alex North and Don Feld to show everyone how it can be done and how it should be done."[4]

The Concept of Musical Organization

Alex North was seventy-five when he started work on *Prizzi's Honor*. One should not forget that this was the fourth project on which North worked with Huston. Both masters were recognized craftsmen and old pros in their fields, they had known each other for almost twenty-five years, and they did not have any communication prob-lems regarding this project. On the contrary, in the whole history of film scoring it was probably the fastest agreement between the director and the composer. Their dis-cussion of the musical concept took no more than ten seconds. When they screened the film, North said, "John, before you say anything, I'd like to tell you what I think. My feeling is to do this opera-wise." Huston tapped him on his knee and said, "Okay, Alex, you can go home." And then he yelled, "Puccini! Puccini!" Which North really used with some Rossini, Verdi and Donizetti.[5] This was one of the favorite stories of Alex North, which he used to recall and tell many times at different occasions.

Regarding the work on *Prizzi's Honor*, one thing was common for both, Huston and North: they approached the film as a comedy. That was probably the reason they agreed so quickly about the concept of the musical score. The comical point of view both masters had toward this work did not come, however, merely from the subject of the novel upon which the film was based, but it came from their own wit and wis-dom regarding life. Obviously they had a great deal of fun working on this film. Needless to say, beneath the comical surface of the film lies pure craftsmanship based on witty ideas and solutions.

AMERICAN BROADCASTING COMPANY
A Division of American Broadcasting Companies, Inc. ("ABC")

MUSIC CUE SHEET   REVISED JANUARY 1986

PRODUCTION: "PRIZZI'S HONOR #04099

MUSIC
DIRECTOR: ALEX NORTH   RECORDING
                                         DATE: APRIL 9, 10, 11, 1985

COMPOSITION: ABC MOTION PICTURES LOGO   TIME: :14
COMPOSER: MICHAEL BODDICKER & TOM SCOTT   INSTRUMENTAL   X
PUBLISHER: ABC CIRCLE MUSIC, INC.   INSTRUMENTAL VISUAL
CLEARANCE: BMI   VOCAL
RECORDED: ABROAD___ LA COUNTY_X   VOCAL VISUAL

R1P2 COMPOSITION: ADOPTION AND TITLES   TIME: 1:20/85
COMPOSER: ALEX NORTH (based on Verdi's Alizira)   INSTRUMENTAL   X
PUBLISHER: AMERICAN BROADCASTING MUSIC, INC.   INSTRUMENTAL VISUAL
CLEARANCE: ASCAP   VOCAL
RECORDED: ABROAD___ LA COUNTY _X_   VOCAL VISUAL

R1P2 COMPOSITION: TUES PETRUS (Master Recording Used) TIME: :56-2/3
COMPOSER: TRADITIONAL GREGORIAN CHANT   INSTRUMENTAL
PUBLISHER: P.D.   INSTRUMENTAL VISUAL
CLEARANCE: P.D.   VOCAL   X
RECORDED: ABROAD___ LA COUNTY_X   VOCAL VISUAL

R1P2A COMPOSITION: MAIN TITLES (cont'd)   TIME: 1:21/45
COMPOSER: ALEX NORTH(based on Puccini's Gianni Schicchi) INSTRUMENTAL   X
PUBLISHER: G. RICORDI & CO., MILAN, ASSOCIATED MUSIC INSTRUMENTAL VISUAL
CLEARANCE: BMI   PUBLISHING, INC.   VOCAL
RECORDED: ABROAD___ LA COUNTY_X   SOLE SELLING AGENT VOCAL VISUAL

R1P4 COMPOSITION: AVA MARIA   TIME: 3:39/25
COMPOSER: FRANZ SCHUBERT (Arranged by Fred Steiner) INSTRUMENTAL   X
PUBLISHER: AMERICAN BROADCASTING MUSIC, INC.   INSTRUMENTAL VISUAL
CLEARANCE: ASCAP   VOCAL
RECORDED: ABROAD___ LA COUNTY_X   VOCAL VISUAL

R2P1 COMPOSITION: WEDDING MARCH   TIME: 1:55
COMPOSER: FELIX MENDELSSOHN (Arranged by Fred Steiner) INSTRUMENTAL   X
PUBLISHER: AMERICAN BROADCASTING MUSIC, INC.   INSTRUMENTAL VISUAL
CLEARANCE: ASCAP   VOCAL
RECORDED: ABROAD___ LA COUNTY_X   VOCAL VISUAL

R2P2 COMPOSITION: (I LOVE YOU) FOR SENTIMENTAL REASONS TIME: :18
COMPOSER: WILLIAM BEST-DEEK WATSON   INSTRUMENTAL
PUBLISHER: DUCHESS MUSIC CORPORATION   INSTRUMENTAL VISUAL   X
CLEARANCE: BMI   VOCAL
RECORDED: ABROAD___ LA COUNTY_X   VOCAL VISUAL

R2P3 COMPOSITION: TARANTELLA   TIME: 2:42
COMPOSER: TRADITIONAL (Arranged by Kenneth Wannberg) INSTRUMENTAL
PUBLISHER: ABC CIRCLE MUSIC, INC.   INSTRUMENTAL VISUAL   X
CLEARANCE: BMI   VOCAL
RECORDED: ABROAD___ LA COUNTY_X   VOCAL VISUAL

The first page from the cue sheet for *Prizzi's Honor*, 1985.

To use Italian opera sources as a basis for the musical score of a film which deals with the Italian Mafia from Brooklyn could be an expected and a logical choice in many ways. As Fred Steiner, the orchestrator of *Prizzi's* score, related, "it was kind of strange and yet not strange, because within many films, even TV shows, Italian gangsters love opera. It is such a stereotype, as, for instance, the belief that the Nazis always love Wagner."[6] Yet, if North's primary musical idea came as a first impulse and reaction to the film subject, the further development of the musical score shows serious research and analysis of the original opera sources, and great ingenuity in their treatment.

The final choice was preceded by a long process of study of nineteenth century Italian opera scores. According to Fred Steiner, Alex North had many difficulties in finding the appropriate music for each scene.[7] He obtained many scores of Rossini, Verdi and Puccini, then he played the records and analyzed the scores. It seems that North "liked Puccini, but did not care too much for Verdi."[8] The black humor of *Prizzi's Honor* called for the general use of the genre of comic opera as a main source for adaptation. The further specific choice of the scores was left to North's personal affinities and his sense for appropriate adaptation.

What were the reasons which led Alex North to choose certain operas as the main key to his musical score? It is hard to say precisely, but analyzing the music of *Prizzi's Honor*, one can assume that there were more reasons involved than pure personal attraction to certain operas. The genre of comic opera prevails because of the film's subject and mood, but besides that, there are sometimes amazing symbolic associations and connections between the original opera plots and the film story. Also, the chosen musical themes, some of them very popular and famous, possess certain qualities which enable them to be isolated from the original opera score and considered and recognized as musical essence *per se*. They were thus appropriate for further independent development and adjustment. Usually these themes contain very specific and recognizable motifs. This means that they, the themes, can be divided into separate units and as such used further in by themselves or in combination with other motifs to create new musical substance. From this point of view there is hardly any chance that the opera sources were chosen accidentally.

The score of *Prizzi's Honor* is a wonderful mixture of source, background music, and music of dramatic value. The source and background music very successfully provide the local color, the mood of the celebrations and parties, and the emotional background of certain scenes. But in several cases the source music is treated as a musical symbol with dramatic connotations, sometimes used as a subtle ironic counterpoint to the film's action. However, the key for understanding the musical score of *Prizzi's Honor* and its supportive dramatic role within the film dramaturgy is the music adapted from the opera sources. This part of the musical score is generally based on the themes from Puccini's *Gianni Schicchi* and Rossini's *La Gazza Ladra* (The Thieving Magpie) and *Il Barbiere di Siviglia* (The Barber of Seville). The lyrical antithesis of these three operas which represent the comical aspects of the film, is Puccini's string quartet *Crisantemi* . It is interesting that, despite the use of musical ideas from Italian operas, the dramatic part of the score is developed, treated and completed as a typical orchestral score. There are various types of compositional "interventions" within the original musical material, which emphasize the dramatic values and satyric connotations of the film's score. Whether the musical ideas are used in their original form or transformed in various ways, their purpose is always the same — to support and follow or anticipate the film's action. In this manner, they become an inevitable part of the film's drama. Therefore, the adapted musical material loses its primary connection with the original source and obtains independent dramatic value functioning within another media. Michael Walsh pointed out that "in opera, the orchestra acts as an unseen protagonist, commenting on the action and sometimes dictating it. It does the same thing in Huston's stylish film..."[9] The musical themes and motifs in this film are only partially used as personal leitmotifs. They function more as groups of "subjective" leitmotifs which comment, support and define the emotional and psychological background of the situations in which a certain *personage* is involved.

Musical Sources

The score of *Prizzi's Honor* is a musical adaptation of already existing music. The musical sources which have been adapted or used in their original form are numerous. For a further analysis and understanding of the scoring process in *Prizzi's Honor* there is an indispensable need to organize and group these sources into several categories, as follows:

1. Adapted opera music — musical ideas that originate from different operas, used to create a musical score for dramatic purpose.
2. Source music — music coming from the source which is visible or evident on the screen (such as radios, record players, stage music, etc.).
3. Music originally composed by Alex North — several short interludes usually used as background music.

The adapted opera sources include works of several opera composers:

1. Gioachino Rossini (1792–1868)
   –*Il Barbiere di Siviglia* (The Barber of Seville), a comic opera written in 1816 (R9 P1, R9 P5, R15 P4)
   –*La Gazza Ladra* (The Thieving Magpie), a comic opera written in 1817 (R5 P2, R5 P3, R9 P1)
   –*Semiramide* (Semiramis), a serious opera written in 1823 (R12 P7)

2. Giuseppe Verdi (1813–1901)
   –*Alzira*, an early serious opera written in 1845 (R1 P1)

3. Giacomo Puccini (1858–1924)
   –*Le Villi*, Puccini's first opera written in 1884 (R4 P4)
   –*Crisantemi*, a string quartet written in 1890. The fact that its two principal themes have been used later as thematic material in the third and the fourth act of *Manon Lescaut* allows one to include this work in the category of opera sources (R6 P1, R6 P2, R11 P2, R14 P1, R14 P2, R15 P3, R15 P4)

—*Manon Lescaut*, a romantic lyric opera written in 1893 (R14 P12)
—*Gianni Schicchi*, a comic opera in one act, written in 1918 as the third opera of *Il Tritico* (R1 P2A, R3/4 P2/1, R5 P2, R5 P3, R7/8 P5/1, R9 P1, R9 P1A, R10 P1, R13 P1, R14 P2, R15 P3)

The source music comprises musical excerpts by different composers and it occurs in its original form or has been arranged by the demands of particular scenes. In this film the source music functions usually as simple background music, but sometimes it achieves the qualities of music with more dramatic and symbolic meaning. The musical material applied as source music is various in its genre. There are classical musical excerpts, popular songs, and traditional folk tunes.

1. Classical musical excerpts:
   —"Ave Maria" by Franz Schubert, arranged by Fred Steiner (R1 P4)
   —"The Wedding March" by Felix Mendelssohn, arranged by Fred Steiner (R2 P1)
   —"O mio babbino caro," aria from *Gianni Schicchi* by Giacomo Puccini (R8 P2)
   —The March from *Aida* by Giuseppe Verdi, adapted by Alex North (R12 P4)
   —"Una Furtiva Lagrima," aria from *L'elisir d'amore* (The Elixir of Love) by Gaetano Donizetti, adapted by Alex North (R12 P6)
   —"Questo o quella," aria from *Rigoletto* by Giuseppe Verdi (R12 P8)

2. Popular songs:
   —"I Love You for Sentimental Reasons" by William Best and Deek Watson (R2 P2)
   —"Strangers in the Night" by B. Kaempfert, C. Singleton and R. Snyder (R3 P1)
   —"Dolce Irena" by Kenneth Wannberg (R4 P2)
   —"Noche di Ronda" by Maria Teresa Lara and Sunny Skylar (R4 P3, R7 P2, R15 P1)
   —"Cielito Lindo" by Carlos Fernandez, adapted by Fred Steiner (R7 P1)
   —"Band Climax" by Kenneth Wannberg (R12 P2)

3. Traditional folk dance:
   —"Tarantella" (R2 P3)

The original music by Alex North provides several scenes with background atmosphere. For instance, the music cues "Wild Source" (R7 P3) and "Apple Sauce" (R7 P4) add Mexican local color to the wedding scene of Charley Partanna and Irene Walke. Thus, one knows that the small town where they are married is across the border, in Mexico.

It should be mentioned also that the single use of a traditional Gregorian chant "Tu Es Petrus" cannot be included in any of the previously listed categories, because it does not appear as source music or as adapted opera music. It was applied in its original form in only one scene — the solemn ceremony when the young Charley Partanna becomes the "blood" member of the Prizzi family.

Compositional Treatment and Organization of the Adapted Opera Sources

The score of *Prizzi's Honor* is, in general, an orchestral work. Despite the idea to create the score on musical material borrowed from Italian operas, Alex North chose mostly the themes and the motifs from the overtures and the orchestral parts of the opera scores, which were apparently more convenient for orchestral development. Therefore, the qualities of the orchestral film score remind one of the role of the orchestra in the opera. It means that the orchestral music in the film was applied to support the actors and their actions, to define or confirm their psychological or emotional states, to prepare and anticipate or comment on the action etc. Michael Walsh was quite right when he entitled his article in *Film Comment* "Prizzi's Opera,"[10] for the actors in the film replace the vocalists in the opera.

Some of the opera excerpts and themes which are used in the *Prizzi's* score are almost identical with their originals, but as such they usually occur only once throughout the picture. More often, these chosen themes become the subject of various transformations and changes. The music by Puccini and Rossini ("borrowing prostitutes" as Darby and Du Bois call them),[11] has been used many times for film purposes. But, usually this music was applied in its original form, as music excerpt. For instance, Puccini's music is used in such films as *A Room with a View*, *Hannah and Her Sisters*, *Moonstruck*, *Fatal Attraction*, and *The Witches of Eastwick*, and there are famous examples of the use of music by Rossini in *A Clockwork Orange*, *Dark Eyes* etc. Nevertheless, Alex North's adaptation is unique in many ways, because the original opera music serves just as an idea, a base and beginning for development of an exceptionally creative musical score. Alex North himself described his approach as "a combination of adaptation, with changes in musical texture [orchestral], extending certain thematic material, and digesting some of it."[12]

The Adaptation of Puccini's Works

The main musical thread of the score derives from the thematic material of Puccini's *Gianni Schicchi*. The motifs from the opera are present throughout the entire score, and they are symbolically connected with the actions and personality of the main character Charley Partanna, the enforcer and the principal hit man of the Prizzi brotherhood. He is loyal and dedicated to the Prizzi family, he is involved in all the intrigues of the gangsters, public and private, he is an executor of Prizzi's will, and he is *like* a member of the family, but still he *is not*....

Prizzi's Honor is a black comedy about an Italian Mafia family. *Gianni Schicchi* is also a comedy about a rogue Italian family—the family of Buozo Donati. The opera plot was inspired by and based on the thirtieth canto from Dante's *Inferno*. Gianni Schicchi is a family "friend" who is asked to help solve the problem of the family's inheritance after the death of wealthy Buoso Donati. In his last testament, Donati left everything to the monks and the Church. Even though Donati's relatives despise and hate the "peasant" Schicchi, they are aware of his intelligence and power. Gianni Schicchi decides to disguise himself by dressing in the clothing of the freshly deceased Buoso Donati, in order to change the testament. At the end of the opera he has all the power to decide what each family member deserves to inherit, and ascribes the biggest portion of the inheritance to himself. The opera evidently contains elements derived from *commedia dell'arte* and *opera buffa*. According to Mosco Carner, Schicchi recalls Harlequin, his daughter Lauretta clearly echoes Columbine, and Simone, Donati's cousin, is reminiscent of Pantaloon.[13] In the film story, isn't Charley Partanna a kind of Harlequin figure, the one who is despised by the sons of Don Corrado Prizzi, but who is the closest and most trusted friend of Don Corrado, the one who will probably become the head of the Prizzi family after Don Corrado's death? The symbolic relationship between the opera and the film's main characters is obvious.

The "Main Title" of the film contains two parts. The first part shows Charley briefly as a baby in a hospital and Charley as a little boy playing with malicious toys. These scenes are separated by the main opening credits of Huston, Foreman, Nicholson and Turner. The first part (R1 P1) is accompanied by an excerpt from Verdi's light and delicate overture for *Alzira*, one of his early operas. The first theme of the overture is used in its original form, and musically announces the comical atmosphere of the film. It has the role of opening music or overture, and its material is not used anymore within the film score. This part is followed by an "intermezzo" which shows the ceremony of Charley's entering the Prizzi's brotherhood, accompanied by the already mentioned Gregorian chant "Tu Es Petrus" (R1 P2).

The second part of the "Main Title" (R1 P2A) introduces the rest of the opening credits, and musically is based on the motifs from *Gianni Schicchi*. This part is a compilation of the main musical ideas, briefly exposed one after another. The first two ideas are taken from the short orchestral prelude of the opera, and indicate the dramatic nucleus of the film score:

Ex. 1a

Ex. 1b

The first phrase (Ex. 1a) is based on the mourning motif, marked by Puccini and North *tumultuoso* (tumultuous). According to Carner, this example possesses an element of self-parody and shows features characteristic of the music used in Puccini's tragic death scenes: an *ostinato* figure with a drooping melody and an amusing placement of the *appoggiatura* which contrary to the normal practice, falls on the "weak beat" of the bar.[14] In the "Main Title," North applied the same *appoggiatura*, but later he changed the beginning of this figure to fall on the normal, strong beat. Carner finds equally comic the alternation of this figure between major and minor.[15] This is probably the most important musical idea, dominating the scenes within the entire film and undergoing some striking transformations. The second musical idea (Ex. 1b) is no more than a fragment which Puccini treats in the course of the work as a theme associated with the influence of Gianni Schicchi on the general action.[16] Since North compiled the motifs into continuous units, the second motif is immediately followed by one of Puccini's relatives motifs, concerning the inheritance of Buoso Donati:

Ex. 2

The *Main Title* is closed with a phrase which appears in *Gianni Schicchi* as an orchestral anticipation of the love duet between Rinuccio, Donati's nephew, and Lauretta, Schicchi's daughter:

Ex. 3

Thus, Alex North early on uses the "Main Title" for a brief exposition of the main motifs, connected and presented in continuous musical flow within a short musical unit. This type of compilation of the motifs from the same or different operas became one of North's favorite compositional devices in the musical adaptation of opera sources.

The next cue which continues to use the material from *Gianni Schicchi* is the one entitled "Exposition" (R3/4 P2/1). It introduces the main character, Charley Partanna. The music accompanies several continuous scenes: Partanna at his home trying to find information about Irene Walker, Partanna interrogated by the police about the murder of one gangster, Partanna returning home and talking on the phone with Maerose (Dominic Prizzi's daughter and his former lover). Therefore, the action demands mosaic musical structure to follow the mosaic of scenes. The obscure introduction contains parts of the mourning motif (Ex. 1a) in slow tempo and changed rhythm. Because of the importance of Charley Partanna as a main character, his first appearance is introduced with the music from the march-like tune of Gianni Schicchi, which appears in the opera when Schicchi explains how he will impersonate the deceased Buoso Donati in order to change his will. With this tune the character of

Charley Partanna is linked to the rogue Gianni Schicchi himself. The used musical material is very close to the original in its comic character and phrasing:

Ex. 4

The following encounter with the police detectives is portrayed musically by the recognizable use of the mourning motif, different in only one detail — the motif starts on the strong beat of the bar. When Charley comes back home and dials the number of Maerose, another relatives motif from *Gianni Schicchi* is heard (in the opera it is introduced by the character Zita):

Ex. 5

This motif turns immediately to Schicchi's tune (Ex. 4), but this time it appears in chords and in a *legato* movement, in slow tempo and augmented rhythm. Thus it provides his conversation with Maerose with a much more lyrical and intimate atmosphere. Ex. 4 and Ex. 5 were originally vocal tunes which were adjusted to function as orchestral motifs in Alex North's score. This is one of the rare moments that North uses vocal material for orchestral development.

The Schicchi's tune is used once more, as a musical anticipation of the family business meeting in Don Corrado's house. This cue, "Don's House" (R7/8 P5/1), is a variation of the previously exposed theme in Ex. 4. The change in the orchestration — a dialog for solo tenor sax and solo trombone — replaces the comic sting of the theme with a melody of melancholic character. Also the phrasing is smooth and *rubato*, rather than clipped and *staccato*. The main tune is exposed in light orchestration which contains the varied mourning motif (Ex. 1a) in the parts of the violins and the oboe:

Ex. 6

All the scenes which are connected with the Prizzi family's "business" are accompanied with at least one motif from *Gianni Schicchi*. For instance, the arrival of Maerose in Las Vegas is prepared with the mourning motif (Ex. 1a), exposed three times in different woodwind instruments. Thus, it is expected that she is there for "business" reasons (to get information about the involvement of Irene in the Las Vegas scam).

Only in one scene in the entire film is the music of *Gianni Schicchi* used in an emotional context, though it still involves Charley Partanna ("Gianni Schicchi" himself). This scene shows the emotional side of the main character and the relationship with his wife Irene Walker (it is a phone conversation while they are in two different cities).

Therefore, the music for this scene, entitled "Bedroom Chitchat" (R10 P1), is exposed in transparent orchestration for high strings, the tempo is slow, the rhythmical flow is calm, mostly in a movement of quarter notes, and the recognizable motifs are augmented. The Schicchi motif (Ex. 1b) looks as follows:

Ex. 7

In the structure of this cue is also interwoven a new simple and mock-serious theme from *Gianni Schicchi*, which Spike Hughes called a "will theme."[17] In its original form it is introduced by the orchestra the moment when Donati's relatives find out that Buozo has left everything to the Church (Ex. 8a). In the film music cue the theme is presented in augmentation (Ex. 8b).

Ex. 8a

Ex. 8b

This theme continues in a very natural way as an augmented and varied mourning motif (Ex. 1a) and finishes with the main motif from *Crisantemi*.

The last scene, which is completely based on the musical material from *Gianni Schicchi*, again introduces into the first plan the subjects of "business" and "money." Irene and Charley drive the van to the city to deliver Falagri to the police. Irene asks Charley to tell Prizzi that she wants her nine hundred thousand dollars back. This demand is accompanied by the mourning motif and Schicchi motifs in major (Ex. 1a and 1b), while Charley's answer that it will be hard to get the money back from Prizzi is accompanied by the same motifs in minor. This cue is completed with the relatives motif from Ex. 5.

Almost all the scenes in the film which concern the emotional content of the relationships in which Charley Partanna is involved, are based on the main theme from *Crisantemi* (Chrysanthemums). In general, it is Charley's "love theme" which portrays the emotional side of his character, and acts opposite to Schicchi's themes.

Ex. 9

As Carner pointed out, *Crisantemi*, composed originally for string quartet, is characteristic of Puccini's melancholy lyricism. Written on the death of Duke Amadeo of Savoy, it is a threnody in one continuous movement, rhapsodic in structure and clinging to the minor mode.[18] Its principal theme appears in the last, fourth act of *Manon Lescaut*—"In America"— when Manon and Des Grieux try to make their way to an English settlement across a vast desert. In the cue sheet of *Prizzi's Honor* the same theme is indicated as a source for *Crisantemi* and sometimes *Manon Lescaut*. But what is important is that within the film it is used as contrast thematic material, which on an emotional scale achieves romantic, lyric, melancholic, pathetic, and, at the end, tragic connotations.

This theme appears for the first time in the cue entitled "Dat's What Love Is" (R6 P1), when Charley tells Irene that he cannot change the way he feels about her, even though she is lying to him about her marriage and the money from the Las Vegas scam. Thus, this theme becomes a form of "fate" love theme, and in this case it occurs in its original form and arrangement for string quartet with added bass part. In the next music cue, "Revelation" (R6 P2), according to the score, Alex North intended to use both principal themes from *Crisantemi*. But in a final editing of the film only the last four measures of the second theme were left, and the rest was cut. These last measures from the second theme serve as a short introduction to the principle theme. This time the main theme is completely exposed (in three phrases) in a version for string orchestra. The music in this scene emphasizes Charley's anxiety after he has discovered that Irene works as a hit-woman.

The opening phrase from the principal theme of *Crisantemi* is used also for the short romantic love scene between Charley and Irene, entitled "Missed You" (R11 P2). The light mood of the scene is confirmed by an exposition of the theme in a major key, supported by jazzy harmonies. At the same time, in parallel movement with the theme from *Crisantemi*, Alex North added special counterpoint — a part of the "love theme" from the duet between Rinuccio and Lauretta from *Gianni Schicchi* (Ex. 3). A brilliant use of *quodlibet*.

Ex. 10

After all the conflicts between Irene and the Prizzi family, Charley is put under pressure to make a choice — the Prizzi family or his wife. The decision is very hard for Charley, but his choice is the family — the only place where he can be. This decision is followed by the principal theme from *Crisantemi*, which, although it appears in its original form without any changes, in this context sounds pathetic and supports the tragic mood of the scene. The cue is entitled "Decision" (R14 P1).

The last cue of the film, "Reconciliation" (R15 P3), is based on the combination of the principal theme from *Crisantemi* and motifs from *Gianni Schicchi*. The last look that Charley gives to Irene's car (where her dead body is hidden) is accompanied by the opening chromatic motif from the *Crisantemi* theme in augmentation

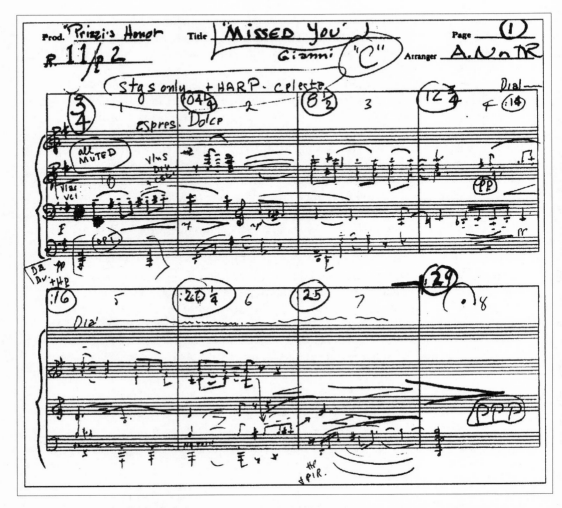

Prizzi's Honor (ABC Motion Picture, 1985). **Excerpt from the cue "Missed You." Sketch.**

and slow tempo, which is an appropriate ending for their unhappy love story. The music cue continues with the motifs from *Gianni Schicchi*, showing Charley taking a shower in his apartment. As expected, the Schicchi motif has the leading role in this part (Ex. 1b). First, it is played in slower tempo, reflecting Charley's mood after killing Irene, then the motif is divided and the beginning figure is transferred through different groups of woodwind instruments in *accelerando*. Within this motif, as contrapuntal movement in the low strings, appears the *ostinato* figure from the mourning motif (Ex. 1a). The phrase from *Crisantemi* again follows in continuous movement, as Charley dials the number of Maerose, tells her that Irene will not be back, and asks her for a date. The end of the *Crisantemi* theme is in major, matching Maerose's positive answer. Thus, the *Crisantemi* theme still keeps the qualities of a "love theme," but it changes its emotional direction toward Maerose. It is in these nuances that North shows his brilliance for adaptation.

One of the most complex music cues in the score is the one entitled *Pursuit* (R14 P2). It is based on the thematic material borrowed from *Manon Lescaut* and *Gianni Schicchi*. The compilation and fast changes of different motifs is required by the speed of the film's action. After the telephone conversation with Charley, when he tells Irene that "everything's O. K.," she realizes that she is going to be eliminated. The short chromatic opening of the *Crisantemi* motif is heard at this time. The scene in which Irene packs and leaves the note in which she says that she must go to California is accompanied by the music from the final act of *Manon Lescaut* — the act in which Manon, exhausted, dies in the desert. The following thematic material is used:

Ex. 11a

Ex. 11b

In continuous movement, as Charley leaves the meeting with Don Corrado, the motifs from *Gianni Schicchi* appear: first the mourning motif (Ex. 1a) in low strings in *pizzicato*, then the varied Schicchi motif (Ex. 1b) in the woodwinds' part, and again the Mourning motif, this time melodically exposed by the violins. Next, Irene is seen at the airport, buying the ticket for Hong Kong, which is accompanied by one of the will motifs from *Gianni Schicchi*. Charley's arriving in their apartment in New York is followed by a melodically and rhythmically varied mourning motif. As he enters their apartment, the tune of Gianni Schicchi is heard (Ex. 4). Introduced by brass instruments and further accepted by the whole orchestra, it sounds pompous, pathetic and ominous. After finding the note, Charley catches the plane and comes to Irene's apartment in California. Here is the end of this cue, encircled with the short *Crisantemi* motif. Despite the use of various motifs, the cue still possesses the qualities of a logical and coherent musical unit. It has a supportive role in the continuity and the speed of the film's action, but also a very powerful symbolic meaning. North uses the death scene music of *Manon Lescaut* to portray the end of Irene, while Schicchi's rogue theme portrays Charley's betrayal.

The Adaptation of Rossini's Music

In several scenes of the picture North uses with great ingenuity thematic material from the overtures of Rossini's *The Barber of Seville*, *The Thieving Magpie* and

Semiramis. For instance, when Dominic, Don Corrado's older son, offers Irene a contract to kill Charley Partanna (without knowing that she is his wife), the first theme from the overture of *The Barber of Seville* is used as a basis for a tango (R9 P5). With the simple change in the rhythmic movement and the orchestration of the original excerpt (without changing the melody of the theme at all), this scene achieves a hilarious comical effect. This was one of the favorite musical cues of the orchestrator Fred Steiner, who recalls that he had a lot of fun orchestrating it, and putting it in some real tango clarifications.[19] The same music is used for the "End Credits" (R 15 P4), in combination with the principal theme from *Crisantemi*.

An interesting adaptation of the original thematic material appears in the musical cues which use the themes from *The Thieving Magpie*. This musical material is heard for the first time when Charley comes to the house of Marxie Heller (Irene's husband) to kill him, because of his involvement in the Las Vegas scam, from which the Prizzis lossed seven hundred and twenty thousand dollars (is the matching with the opera title a coincidence?!). In this case Alex North combined the both themes from the overture, which in its original form is a *sonata allegro* without development. The cue, entitled *Marxie* (R5 P2), starts with four-measure introduction based on the mourning motif (Ex. 1a) from *Gianni Schicchi* (Charley arrives at Marxie's house). This short introduction is followed by the second theme from the overture of *The Thieving Magpie*. It is a period built by two phrases of eight measures. Unlike the original theme (G major), the first phrase is in A minor (ominous anticipation of the action), with the motif of the first theme of the overture as a counterpoint! The second phrase of the second theme has a fake designation of a major key, but it is still in minor, and it is followed in the most natural way by the second phrase of the first theme. Thus, both themes are used for the construction of one new continuous theme:

Ex. 12

The first theme of *The Thieving Magpie* also appears as an accompaniment for the next scene, "Marxie Iced" (R5 P3), when Charley takes Marxie to the garage to shoot him. This time the theme is used in its original form and orchestration. After the gunshot, Charley comes out of the garage and the music cue continues with Gianni Schicchi's tune (Ex. 4), which indicates that our hero successfully finished his job! Darby and Du Bois pointed out that these were good examples of using music in opposition to the action.[20] Moreover, the music twisted the meaning of a killing act into an act of cynic parody, which gives this film its attributes of a black comedy.

According to Alex North's statement in the book *On the Track* by Fred Karlin and Rayburn Wright, he used the principal theme from the overture to *The Thieving Magpie* as a "corrupt-bank-official kidnapping theme."[21] The culmination of its witty use is evident in its combination with the thematic material from *The Barber of Seville* and *Gianni Schicchi* in the music cue entitled "Filargi Hit" (R9 P1). This is the scene in which Prizzi, alias Charley and Irene, kidnap the bank president Rosario Filargi, and kill his bodyguard and an unexpected witness, who happens to be the wife of a police inspector. As in the case of the music cue "Exposition" (R3/4 P2/1), the specter of the following actions demands mosaic musical background. But this time the musical structure is even more complex, and derives from parallel contrapuntal movements, *quodlibets* and alternate use of motifs and themes from different works. For instance, the shooting of the bodyguard and the witness is accompanied by the alternation of motifs from the principal themes of the overtures to *The Barber of Seville* and *The Thieving Magpie*.

Ex. 13

In continuity, the principal theme from *The Barber* follows in *quodlibet* with the augmented Schicchi's tune (Ex. 4).

Ex. 14

Ex. 14 *cont.*

The romantic intermezzo follows afterwards, while Charley and Irene leave with Filargi in the elevator, and make plans for their honeymoon. It brings into the first plan the augmented second theme from *The Barber* enriched with a contrapuntal motif from the principal theme of *The Thieving Magpie*. Back to work — Filargi is put in the van, and Charley and Irene kiss each other goodbye: the musical material is borrowed from the bridge (!) between the first and the second theme of *The Barber*, and it appears in *quodlibet* with the principal theme from *The Thieving Magpie*.

Ex. 15

This complex music cue finishes with the principal theme from *The Barber*, finally presented in its original form, while one sees the van departing from the place of the crime. This is certainly one of the best examples showing the possibilities of a witty adaptation. Darby and Du Bois pointed out that, for example, in Kubrick's *A Clockwork Orange* (1971) the music by Rossini was used with far greater impact as extremely cynical accompaniment to violence.[22] Still, in the case of *Prizzi's Honor*, the music does not act only as a direct opponent to the action, but it also has the value of a special musical creation which symbolically connects the film characters in many ways.

There are only a few music cues which are based on a single use of original opera music.

1. The opening credits are introduced with the music from the already mentioned overture to *Alzira* by Verdi.

2. *Roll Over* (R4 P4) uses the frenetic "Witches Dance" from Puccini's opera *Le Villi*. It is a gay tarantella from the second part of the symphonic intermezzo of the opera, entitled "La Tragenda" ("The Spectre"). The music accompanies the scene of Charley and Irene making love.

3. "Dominic Iced" (R12 P7) is a music cue based on the principal theme from Rossini's overture to *Semiramis*. The music acts again as ironic counterpoint to the murder of Don Corrado Prizzi's son, Dominic.

Even though these musical excerpts possess valuable motif-like material for musical development, they have not been incorporated further in the main musical "body" of the adaptation. The basic idea of Alex North was to achieve various symbolic parallels between the film story and characters, and the main opera sources. Certainly, one cannot search for absolute consistency in transferring the opera plot and its music into the film, because that was not the primary intention of the director and the composer. Therefore, the critical comment of Darby and Du Bois that North's idea to imply a dramatic connection between events in *Prizzi's Honor* and Puccini's opera "was not borne out by subsequent musical dramatic juxtapositions,"[23] cannot be considered a valuable critical note. North was extremely consistent in implying the symbolic relationships between the musical themes and the film characters, and despite the variety of the musical motifs he achieved continuity and coherency in the organization and adaptation of the musical score.

The Use of Source Music

The source music is used in many scenes of *Prizzi's Honor*, and takes a big portion of the musical score. Besides locating the action and the atmosphere or the mood of certain scenes, it acts sometimes as an ironic musical background or a musical symbol.

The film begins with the wedding ceremony of Don Corrado Prizzi's granddaughter in the church. One can see the singer and the organist performing Schubert's "Ave Maria" which seems to be absolutely appropriate music for this solemn occasion. But, then the invited guest are shown. On one side is the complete police department, and on the other, the complete mafia family. The camera moves and produces close-ups of the main characters: Don Corrado who seems to be asleep, but suddenly opens his eyes and gives one cunning look, then the characters of Maerose, Charley Partanna and Irene Walker follow. In these circumstances Schubert's "Ave Maria" enhances the comic and parodic aspects of the film's opening. As the groom and the bride exit the church, "The Wedding March" by Mendelssohn is heard. The church ceremony is followed by a wedding party. The pop tune "I Love You for Sentimental Reasons" is played by the band on the stage, and afterwards, as Charley approaches Irene and asks her for a dance, a traditional Italian tarantella is heard. Irene receives a message that she has a phone call and she leaves Charley. Waiting for Irene, Charley encounters his former lover Maerose. Their conversation is accompanied by a tune "Strangers in the Night," which may indicate their dispute and separation in the past as a reason for the present reserved behavior.

One of the songs which appears as source music has a particular role within the film. That is "Noche di Ronda" ("Be Mine Tonight"), a popular song of Latin origin, which becomes Charley's and Irene's special song.

Ex. 16

This song is used in three scenes of the film. First, it is played by a band in a restaurant during the first meeting of Charley and Irene. Charley expresses his love to Irene and declares: "This is gonna be our song." Next, one can hear the same song in the same California restaurant when, despite all the circumstances, Charley and Irene decide to get married. But, this song also announces the end of their love, and the murder of Irene, when she consciously plays the song on the phonograph, knowing that the final moment in their relationship is coming. Thus, this unpretentious song becomes a musical symbol which appears in the most crucial stages of Charley's and Irene's relationship: its beginning, its realization and its tragic end.

There are several opera excerpts used as source music. At the party, arranged as a farewell for Dominic in his move to Las Vegas, the head of the Prizzi family, Don Corrado, steps on the stage accompanied by the famous "Triumphal March" from *Aida* by Verdi. Everything would seem in perfect context, if the march was not played in a peculiar band arrangement for tenor sax, guitar and bass. Adapted in this way by Alex North it sounds like a comical parody of Prizzi's glory. At the same party, a second-rate Italian tenor performs Nemorino's romance "Una furtiva lagrima" ("The Furtive Tear") from *The Elixir of Love* by Donizetti. It anticipates the sudden interruption of the party due to a fire caused by the gangsters who are fighting with the Prizzis.

Don Corrado is found listening to the Duke's aria "Questa o Quella" from Verdi's *Rigoletto* when Eduard Prizzi and Angelo Partanna bring the news about Dominic's murder. Darby and Du Bois logically assume that this aria, whose title means "This one or that one," may have been intended to "underpin the casualness with which people are rubbed out in *Prizzi's Honor*."[24]

The most remarkable example of the use of source music as ironic counterpoint to the film's action appears in the scene between Maerose and her father Dominic. In order to hurt him and avenge herself for her excommunication from the family, Maerose gives a detailed description of how Charley made love to her ("Three times, Papa, right on the floor. You had to see the size of him"). The culmination of the cynicism in this scene is achieved by applying the most famous aria from *Gianni Schicchi*, sung by Schicchi's daughter Lauretta — "Oh! Mio babbino caro" ("O dear daddy, he is so handsome") — as source music coming from the radio in the background. Michael Walsh correctly pointed out that "the counterpoint of references neatly summarizes not only the ethos of the film, but the function of music in opera as well."[25] Such a choice and use of a musical comment ultimately emphasized the role of music in *Prizzi's Honor* as an artistic representation of irony, allegory and parody.

After the analysis of the score it is obvious that the music in *Prizzi's Honor* serves as a perfect "shell" for the film's content, and helps to define the genre of the film as a black comedy. In this context the music, no matter in which form it has been applied, is not anymore an added or supplementary element of the film. It becomes the film itself.

Comments

Although Alex North was not feeling well at the time he prepared the score of *Prizzi's Honor*, he was working very hard, and the sketches he wrote, from a musical standpoint, were very complete. However, for the final realization of the score and especially for its orchestration, the contribution of the orchestrator Fred Steiner was very important. According to Steiner, Alex and he would check everything carefully, including the timing, and then they would discuss all the changes and suggestions for orchestral colors. In certain cases they followed exactly the original orchestration of the opera excerpts, because it simply was not necessary to change anything to underpin the satirical meaning (as in the use of Verdi's *Alzira*, Puccini's *Witches Dance* or Rossini's *Semiramis*). But, usually the orchestration needed to be changed in order to achieve the effect of musical irony. Fred Steiner admitted that sometimes he had trouble dealing with these masterpieces as material for musical jokes.[26] Besides helping Alex in the orchestration of the score, Fred Steiner also conducted the score in the recording sessions, because North was not physically able. Thirty minutes of music were recorded in two days or in twelve hours, with an average recording of three minutes of music per hour. Steiner recalled that "working with Alex was the most pleasant experience. He was such a great man with such a great sense of humor."[27]

After the realization, *Prizzi's Honor* received enormous publicity and very positive reviews. Most of the critics praised the excellent musical score and its special contribution to the picture. Sheila Benson in the *Los Angeles Times* wrote that "Huston guides them all in immaculate style, helped by a dangerously witty musical score by Alex North."[28] David Ansen in *Newsweek* mentioned Alex North's "clever Puccini-Rossini score with unhurried and supremely confident aplomb...."[29] Arthur Knight in the *Hollywood Reporter* considered that "Alex North's transparent, decidedly Italianate score... has skillfully contrived to keep the huge cast, and the many plot complications always in focus."[30] The *New Yorker's* critic Pauline Kael highly respected Alex North's score which "with its lush parodistic use of Puccini, and some Rossini, a little Verdi, and a dash of Donizetti, too, actively contributes to the whirling texture of the scenes. Even the musical jokes that you're not quite conscious of work on you."[31] Michael Walsh was also aware that "Huston's joke is telegraphed the minute Alex North's pastiche score begins..."[32] Vincent Canby in the *New York Times* praised the superior photography, production design, and Alex North's score "which makes liberal use of Puccini, though never to tease out a teardrop."[33] Besides these and all the other flattering reviews, Alex North received many personal letters of appreciation, among which was a letter from the composer William Schuman who thought that the score was "a masterpiece of its genre, and in fact a textbook on the way music should be written for film."[34]

After all these comments, one would expect, without doubt, that Alex North's score would find its deserved place on the list of Oscar nominations for the best music score Adaptation in 1985. However, the academy had annulled that category in 1983, and North's score was not considered eligible for the best original score, because it was based on various Italian opera themes. This provoked a great deal of protest among North's colleagues. Fred Steiner thought that either the category should be restored or many fine scores, such as *Prizzi's Honor*, were going to be neglected in

WILLIAM SCHUMAN

June 28, 1985

Mr. Alex North
630 Resolane Drive
Pacific Palisades, CA 90272

Dear Alex:

A few days ago Frankie and I took Ruth with us to see Prizzi's Honor. I couldn't get over your score. It is a masterpiece of its genre and in fact a textbook on the way music should be written for film. If only those idiot critics had ears as well as eyes, they would have some inkling of the enormous contribution you have made to this delightful film. For example, the music that you composed for the protagonist's first hilarious sexual romp is what gave the scene 50% of its humor and titillation. What a man you are to keep getting better and better at what you have done so well so long!

Norman once told me that you and he had taken a vow never to write in anything but the short forms. You do write in the short forms, but you string them together in the most ingenious way to create in actuality a cohesive force for the entire drama that you are illuminating in sound.

With admiration and affection I am

Faithfully,

Bill

Letter from William Schuman to Alex North, June 26, 1985.

the future.[35] The director Lamont Johnson wrote to the academy, "the fact that Alex's sophisticated use of operatic sources creates a whole new genre of film musical comment shouldn't disqualify it in the current categories—his adaptation and arrangement of the work of earlier masters is so masterful in its own right it becomes a genuine original before our eyes and ears."[36] Robert Osborne commented on this problem in *The Hollywood Reporter*, as follows: "The great irony, of course, is the fact that North's score is exactly the kind of film accomplishment for which the Oscars were created, and which justify the whole Academy Award game. What a waste that it may be scratched/ vetoed/ ignored simply because the current Academy rules don't seem to have a slot in which it easily slides."[37] Even Alex North himself expressed his opinion in a letter addressed to the academy, saying that "the music was so dramatically altered and integrated into various conflicts and situations in the *Prizzi's Honor* story as to constitute an intensely personal expression."[38]

Even though Alex North's score for *Prizzi's Honor* did not find its way to the list of Oscar nominations, it is considered to be one of the best and the most original achievements in the history of musical adaptation for film.

Epilogue

Considering Alex North's enormous musical opus and his extensive artistic contributions to the fields of film, theater, and modern dance, it is apparent that this work could not research *all* the aspects of his prolific music legacy. Therefore, this book is not an all-inclusive study on Alex North. It is rather the first attempt to gather and expose in a chronological continuity the available facts and information on North's life, career, and work, thus forming a wide basis for a further research of his musical achievements. An effort was also made toward a collection of the majority of studies and articles on North's music in order to found an extensive bibliographical database.

Despite the classical training and academic education, North basically formed his compositional style through writing functional music for modern dance, theater, and film. The experience that he gained as a stage composer for modern dance and theater greatly influenced his compositional approach toward film scoring. Many attributes that characterize the craft of North's film scoring derive from his previous experience as a stage composer, attributes that include: a special feeling for movement, a sense for musical timing and "tailoring" the music to the dynamic of the movement, a respect for dialogue and its careful underscoring, sparse orchestration, and individualization of the instruments and their solo treatment. Furthermore, for certain films he provided music with balletic qualities, such as the ballets for *Daddy Long Legs*, and the gladiators' training sequences in *Spartacus*, or "Roundup" sequences in *The Misfits*. The scoring of *The Rainmaker* was approached as a musical or operetta without singing, while *A Streetcar Named Desire* could be easily imagined in a revised form as a jazz-opera (the jazz-ballet version was already staged in 1952). It is interesting that North's stage experience did not develop in the direction of composing ballets, operas, or musicals, but it evolved into music for the cinema screen.

North belongs to the generation of film composers who confronted the middle-European traditions of Korngold and Steiner with popular Americana sounds. The roots of North's musical style are deeply linked to the immediate past of America.

Jazz, popular rhythm and dance idioms are naturally incorporated into his integral musical expression. North is remembered as a composer who composed the first jazz film score, employing jazz idioms in a dramatic manner (*A Streetcar Named Desire*).

North's jazz expression is close to the style of New Orleans jazz and Dixieland, with noticeable influence of the style of Duke Ellington. North considered jazz as the most authentic, indigenous ingredient of American music. Therefore, to use jazz in films which explored specific American and especially Southern subjects, was for North a very natural and appropriate decision. His "Southern scores," such as *Streetcar*, *Death of a Salesman*, *The Member of the Wedding*, *The Long Hot Summer*, *The Sound and the Fury*, *Sanctuary*, *The Misfits*, and others, brought him fame in the Fifties and the early Sixties. North's jazz scores are characterized by sparse orchestration with dissonant accents in intense jazz passages, on one hand, and sensible melodic lyricism, on the other hand. North used jazz as thematic, and, very often, as a rhythmic device to express Southern atmosphere, passionate emotions, sexual undercurrents, self-destructive tendencies, dark ambiences, and melodramatic or melancholic dispositions.

Many times in his career North approached the process of film scoring as a scholar. Such an approach was indispensable when dealing with historical, period films or with films whose action was located in foreign countries. For instance, he seriously researched ancient Roman music (*Spartacus*, *Cleopatra*), Renaissance Italian music (*The Agony and the Ecstasy*), and nineteenth century Italian opera (*Prizzi's Honor*) before he started to work on these particular projects. Further, he explored the folk and ethnic music of various regions in the world, such as Mexican music (*Viva Zapata*, *Under the Volcano*, and others), Italian music (*The Rose Tattoo*), Irish music (*The Dead*), Greek music (*A Dream of Kings*), African music (*Africa*), Indian music (*Cheyenne Autumn*), as well as popular American music (*Wise Blood*). The ability to adapt various musical idioms to the requirements of films is an imperative for a versatile film composer. North developed this essential feature of film composition into masterful art. He did not only skillfully apply various musical idioms into the texture of the film score, but he absorbed them to the level that he was able to create an original musical expression that would fit the requirements of the film dramaturgy. Therefore, the line that divides North's original film scores from his film music adaptations is very thin and delicate. The problem of the originality of film scores based on adapted musical material deserves special attention and discussion. The creativity and originality of the film composer *cannot* and *should not* be measured only upon the musical material that he uses for the creation of a film score, because this decision is often imposed by the necessities and requirements of the film subject, and not by the free musical choice of the film composer. The question that should be taken into consideration regarding this problem is not primarily *what* kind of musical material was used, but *how* it was applied and transformed in order to fit into the film dramaturgy.

The style and the compositional features of North's film music were often influenced by the genres of the films. During the forty years of his career as a film composer he had an opportunity to compose music for a variety of film genres ranging from mystery, adventure, horror, and western, to history, fantasy, musical, travelogue, and comedy.

But, the two main polarities in this variety of film genres were the genre of intimate dramas (mostly dramatic adaptations of literary works) and the genre of epic films. They defined North's two basic approaches toward film scoring which he described as subjective and objective writing. North personally always preferred to score smaller, intimate films. He felt that he could best express himself when he was able to empathize deeply with the intimate world and the feelings of the characters. In such cases he applied a subjective type of composition which implied use of smaller instrumental ensembles, chamber orchestration and individualized instrumental treatment in order to create a more personal musical statement. The function of these musical statements was to characterize the personalities of the protagonists, to underline their feelings, to emphasize the dramatic interaction of their relationships, and to capture the essence of their beings "hidden" beneath the surface of the visual action (*A Streetcar Named Desire, Death of a Salesman, The Bad Seed, The Member of the Wedding, The Rose Tattoo, The Children's Hour, Who's Afraid of Virginia Woolf?, Under the Volcano, The Dead*, and others). Many of these films were adaptations of literary works by such renowned authors as Tennessee Williams, Arthur Miller, Carson McCullers, Lillian Hellman, William March, Edward Albee, William Faulkner, Flannery O'Connor, Malcolm Lowry, and James Joyce, to mention a few. While the subjective musical approach was suitable for the individual aspects of intimate dramas, the scoring of the epic spectacles called for a more objective approach. For North, it was more difficult to identify with the subjects of the spectacles, although he felt closer to those pictures which dealt with social themes of universal significance, such as *Viva Zapata, Spartacus*, and *Cheyenne Autumn*. The vast, collective scenes of the spectacles implied use of an extended symphonic orchestra, and, frequently, various authentic and exotic instruments of the period. The objective writing could generally be described as the composing of programmatic, visual or descriptive music for the action, whereas the subjective writing leant toward the musical identification of the individual characters on a more personal level. However, it would be absurd to assert that a certain film score is based on purely one type of musical approach. In fact, North always tried to personalize the spectacles as much as possible, and to emphasize musically the dramatic interaction between the individual characters. Nevertheless, there is no doubt that North favored the subjective over the objective type of writing, or, from an aesthetic point of view, he always tried to emphasize the internal, emotional aspects of the film rather then the external aspects of the visual action.

North's orchestral textures are mostly transparent and clear with the prevalence of a linear concept and dominance of a melodic principle. He was famous for his ability to create touching themes with a very economical use of simple musical motifs (for instance, the themes of *Unchained, The Long Hot Summer, Who's Afraid of Virginia Woolf?*, the love theme from *Spartacus*, etc.). His invention in melodic transformation and variation of the principal themes is remarkable. One of North's most specific melodic treatments is the development of the melodic line through different instruments or instrumental groups. Some of the most lyrical themes in his oeuvre, besides the love themes, are those composed for characterization of the female heroines (for instance, the themes for Blanche, Roslyn, Yvonne, etc.). These themes or their musical motifs usually create dramatic values within the score and they are often used to underline certain emotional aspects of the male characters. North paid special attention to the details and subtle nuances in the musical characterization and psychological definition of the main protagonists.

While North's lyricism is characterized by gentle, mostly tonal and diatonic musical expression, his most dramatic statements feature wild orchestral passages with strong rhythmic punctuation, dynamic contrasts and accents, and violent dissonances. His symphonic style reveals his admiration for Prokofiev, but the percussive treatment of the orchestra and the barbaric, primal impact of certain orchestral passages show the influence of Bartók and Stravinsky. North as a lyricist best expresses himself through romantic, jazzy and bluesy, or Broadway-style mellow themes, while North as a dramatist is characterized by forceful, very contemporary musical expression. The dissonances are often incorporated into the orchestral texture, and the dissonant harmonies are usually an outcome of the linear, contrapuntal orchestral movement.

During his film career North collaborated with many distinguished orchestrators, such as Maurice de Packh, Henry Brant, and Edward Powell. However, the orchestrators followed very closely North's instrumental indications, which were always very detailed and precise. In general, North used smaller, chamber orchestras and instrumental ensembles for more intimate films and scenes which dealt with individual matters, and on the other hand, extended symphonic orchestras for spectacular, vast epic films. The chamber scores are usually sparse, with transparent and thin textures, and individualized instrumental treatment (*Who's Afraid of Virginia Woolf?*, *The Dead*). The symphonic scores are, on the contrary, very dense, with the dominance of low brass, shrill trumpets, harsh dynamic and rhythmic contrasts, and an extended use of percussions (*Viva Zapata*, *Spartacus*, *Cleopatra*). When composing for big orchestras, North loved to experiment with unusual, exotic and ethnic instruments (sistrum, sarusophone, kithara, lute, ondioline, bagpipes, recorder, Novachord, marimba, bongos, etc.). North's film scores show much more fondness for wind than for string instruments, and they are very often treated as separate instrumental groups. Some of his most distinguished introspective, lyric themes are composed for solo instruments, such as Willy's theme for alto flute from *Death of a Salesman*, or Yvonne's theme for oboe d'amore from *Under the Volcano*.

North used various compositional techniques to achieve the dramatic unity in his film scores. Among these techniques, the most characteristic are: motif-like development through the use of variants of leitmotif technique (*A Streetcar Named Desire*, *Spartacus*, *Prizzi's Honor*), applying a principal theme in the role of *idée fixe* (*Streetcar*, *Wise Blood*), use of the monothematic principle (*Under the Volcano*), and variation technique (*The Bad Seed*, *Who's Afraid of Virginia Woolf?*, *The Misfits*). Writing variation after variation on the same theme is not typical for North, although he left some brilliant examples of the use of variation technique as a dramatic musical device. He loved to incorporate independent pieces in his film scores that could be listened to as autonomous musical entities. The beauty of his musical mastery lies, however, in his witty combinations of various compositional approaches and musical idioms. For instance, he mixed jazz and folk idioms (*The Rose Tattoo*), Mexican and abstract music (*Under the Volcano*), jazz and the symphonic approach (*The Misfits*), and he combined the previously mentioned compositional techniques depending on the dramatic requirements.

North's film scores prove that the music can add another dimension to the visual aspects of the film. It has an ability to enrich and intensify the perception and reception of the film on a subconscious level, to heighten the emotional experience and make us empathize deeply with the characters. And whether it functions as a natural part of the action or as its emotional counterpoint, North's music is always in balance with all the other artistic components that make the film an integral work of art.

Appendix I: Filmography

The following abbreviations appear in the filmography: **AAN**— Academy Award nomination; **GG**— Golden Globe Award; **EAN**— Emmy Award nomination. These appear only when an award or nomination was for music or score.

1. ***A Streetcar Named Desire*** (drama). 1951, Warners. Directed by Elia Kazan, produced by Charles K. Feldman. Script: Tennessee Williams, adapted by Oscar Saul. Marlon Brando *(Stanley)*, Vivien Leigh *(Blanche)*, Kim Hunter *(Stella)*. AAN for Best Music Score of a Dramatic or Comedy Picture.

2. ***The 13th Letter*** (drama). 1951, 20th Century–Fox. Directed and produced by Otto Preminger. Script: Howard Koch, based on the story and screenplay *Le Corbeau* by Louis Chavance. Linda Darnell *(Denise)*, Charles Boyer *(Dr. Laurent)*, Michael Rennie *(Dr. Pearson)*, Constance Smith *(Cora Laurent)*.

3. ***Death of a Salesman*** (drama). 1951, Columbia. Directed by Laslo Benedek, produced by Stanley Kramer. Script: Arthur Miller. Fredric March *(Willy Loman)*, Mildred Dunnock *(Linda Loman)*, Kevin McCarthy *(Biff)*, Cameron Mitchell *(Happy)*. AAN for Best Music Score of a Dramatic or Comedy Picture.

4. ***Viva Zapata!*** (drama). 1952, 20th Century–Fox. Directed by Elia Kazan, produced by Darryl F. Zanuck. Script: John Steinbeck. Marlon Brando *(Emiliano Zapata)*, Jean Peters *(Josefa Espejo)*, Anthony Quinn *(Eufemio Zapata)*. AAN for Best Music Score of a Dramatic or Comedy Picture.

5. ***Les Misérables*** (drama). 1952, 20th Century–Fox. Directed by Lewis Milestone, produced by Fred Kohlmar. Script: Richard Murphy, based on the novel by Victor Hugo. Michael Rennie *(Jean Valjean)*, Debra Paget *(Cosette)*, Robert Newton *(Javert)*.

6. ***Pony Soldier*** (western). 1952, 20th Century–Fox. Directed by Joseph M. Newman, produced by Samuel G. Enge. Script: John C. Higgins, based on a story in *Saturday Evening Post* by Garnett Weston. Tyrone Power *(Duncan McDonald)*, Cameron Mitchell *(Konah)*.

7. *The Member of the Wedding* (drama). 1952, Columbia. Directed by Fred Zinnemann, produced by Stanley Kramer. Script: Edna and Edward Anhalt — based on the novel and play by Carson McCullers. Ethel Waters *(Bearnice Sadie Brown)*, Julie Harris *(Frankie Adams)*, Brandon De Wilde *(John Henry)*.

8. *Go, Man, Go!* (drama). 1954, United Artists. Directed by James Wong Howe, produced by Anton M. Leader. Script: Arnold Becker. Dane Clark *(Abe Saperstein)*, Pat Bresun *(Sylvia Saperstein)*, Sidney Poitier *(Inman Jackson)*.

9. *Desirée* (historical romance). 1954, 20th Century–Fox. Directed by Henry Koster, produced by Julian Blaustein. Script: Daniel Taradash, based on the novel by Annemarie Selinko. Marlon Brando *(Napoleon Bonaparte)*, Jean Simmons *(Desirée Clary)*, Merle Oberon *(Josephine)*.

10. *The Racers* (sports/drama). 1955, 20th Century–Fox. Directed by Henry Hathaway, produced by Julian Blaustein. Script: Charles Kaufman, based on the novel by Hans Ruesch. Kirk Douglas *(Gino)*, Bella Darvi *(Nicole)*, Gilbert Roland *(Dell 'Oro)*, Cesar Romero *(Carlos)*.

11. *Unchained* (prison drama). 1955, Warners. Directed and produced by Hall Bartlett. Script: Hall Bartlett, suggested by the life and work of Kenyon J. Scudder. Elroy Hirsch *(Steve Davitt)*, Barbara Hale *(Mary Davitt)*, Chester Morris *(Kenyon J. Scudder)*, Todd Duncan *(Bill Howard)*. AAN for Best Song for "Unchained Melody."

12. *Man with the Gun* (western). 1955, United Artists. Directed by Richard Wilson, produced by Samuel Goldwyn, Jr. Script: N. B. Stone, Jr., Richard Wilson. Robert Mitchum *(Clint Tollinger)*, Jan Sterling *(Nelly Bain)*, Karen Sharpe *(Stella Atkins)*, Henry Hull *(Marshal Sims)*.

13. *The Rose Tattoo* (drama). 1955, Paramount. Directed by Daniel Mann, produced by Hal B. Wallis. Script: Tennessee Williams, Hal Kanter, based on the play by Williams. Anna Magnani *(Serafina Delle Rose)*, Burt Lancaster *(Alvaro Magniacavallo)*, Marisa Pavan *(Rosa Delle Rose)*. AAN for Best Music Score of a Dramatic or Comedy Picture.

14. *I'll Cry Tomorrow* (drama/musical). 1955, M. G. M. Directed by Daniel Mann, produced by Lawrence Weingarten. Script: Helen Deutsch, Jay Richard Kennedy, based on the book by Lillian Roth. Susan Hayward *(Lillian Roth)*, Richard Conte *(Jony Bardeman)*, Eddie Albert *(Burt McGuire)*.

15. *The Bad Seed* (horror/drama). 1956, Warners. Directed and produced by Mervyn LeRoy. Script: John Lee Mahin, based on the play by Maxwell Anderson and the novel by William March. Nancy Kelly *(Christine)*, Patty McCormack *(Rhoda)*, Henry Jones *(LeRoy)*.

16. *The Rainmaker* (comedy). 1956, Paramount. Directed by Joseph Anthony, produced by Hal B. Wallis. Script: N. Richard Nash, based on his play. Burt Lancaster *(Starbuck)*, Katharine Hepburn *(Lizzie Curry)*, Wendell Corey *(File)*, Lloyd Bridges *(Noah Curry)*. AAN for Best Music Score of a Dramatic or Comedy Picture

17. **Four Girls in Town** (drama). 1956, Universal. Directed by Jack Sher, produced by Aaron Rosenberg. Script: Jack Sher. George Nader *(Mike Snowden)*, Julie Adams *(Kathy Convay)*, Marianne Cook *(Ina Schiller)*, Elsa Martinelli *(Maria Antonelli)*.

18. *The King and Four Queens* (comedy/drama/western). 1956, United Artists. Directed by Raoul Walsh, produced by David Hempstead. Script: Margaret Fitts, Richard Alan Simmon, based on a story by M. Fitts. Clark Gable *(Dan Kehoe)*, Eleanor Parker *(Sabina)*, Jo Van Fleet *(Ma McDade)*.

19. *The Bachelor Party* (drama). 1957, United Artists. Directed by Delbert Mann, produced by Harod Hecht. Script: Paddy Chayefsky, based on his story. Don Murray *(Charlie Samson)*, E. G. Marshall *(Walter)*, Jack Warden *(Eddie)*, Philip Abbott *(Arnold)*.

20. *The Long Hot Summer* (drama). 1958, 20th Century–Fox. Directed by Martin Ritt, produced by Jerry Wald. Script: Irving Ravetch, Harriet Frank, Jr., based on the novel *Hamlet* by William Faulkner. Paul Newman *(Ben Quick)*, Joanne Woodward *(Clara Varner)*, Anthony Franciosa *(Jody Varner)*, Orson Welles *(Will Varner)*.

21. *Stage Struck* (drama). 1958, RKO. Directed by Sidney Lumet, produced by Stuart Millar. Script: Ruth and Augustus Goetz, based on the play *Morning Glory* by Zoe Akins. Henry Fonda *(Lewis Easton)*, Susan Strasberg *(Eva Lovelace)*, Joan Greenwood *(Rita Vernon)*, Herbert Marshall *(Robert Hedges)*.

22. *Hot Spell* (drama). 1958, Paramount. Directed by Daniel Mann, produced by Hal B. Wallis. Script: James Poe, based on Lonnie Coleman's unproduced play *Next of Kin*. Shirlie Booth *(Alma Duval)*, Anthony Quinn *(Jack Duval)*, Shirley McLaine *(Virginia Duval)*, Earl Holliman *(Buddy Duval)*.

23. *South Seas Adventure* (travelogue). 1958, Cinerama. Directed and produced by Francis D. Lyon, Carl Dudley, Richard Goldstone, Walter Thompson, and Basil Wrangell. Script: Charles Kaufman, Joseph Ansen, Harold Medford. Tommy Zahn *(Ted)*, Diane Beardmore *(Kay)*.

24. *The Sound and the Fury* (drama). 1959, 20th Century–Fox. Directed by Martin Ritt, produced by Jerry Wald. Script: Irving Ravetch, Harriet Frank, based on the novel by William Faulkner. Yul Brynner *(Jason)*, Joanne Woodward *(Quentin)*, Margaret Leighton *(Caddy)*, Stuart Whitman *(Charls Busch)*.

25. *The Wonderful Country* (western). 1959, United Artists. Directed by Robert Parrish, produced by Chester Erskine. Script: Robert Ardrey, based on the novel by Tom Lea. Robert Mitchum *(Martin Brady)*, Julie London *(Ellen Colton)*, Gary Merrill *(Maj. Colton)*, Pedro Armendariz *(Gov. Castro)*.

26. *Spartacus* (historical epic). 1960, Universal. Directed by Stanley Kubrick, produced by Edward Lewis. Script: Dalton Trumbo, based on the novel by Howard Fast. Kirk Douglas *(Spartacus)*, Laurence Olivier *(Marcus Licinius Crassus)*, Tony Curtis *(Antoninus)*, Jean Simmons *(Varinia)*. AAN for Best Music Score of a Dramatic or Comedy Picture.

27. *The Children's Hour* (drama). 1961, United Artists. Directed and produced by William Wyler. Script: John Michael Hayes, adaptation by Lillian Hellman from her play. Audrey Hepburn *(Karen Wright)*, Shirley McLaine *(Martha Dobie)*, James Garner *(Dr. Joe Cardin)*, Miriam Hopkins *(Mrs. Lily Mortar)*.

28. *Sanctuary* (drama). 1961, 20th Century–Fox. Directed by Tony Richardson, produced by Richard D. Zanuck. Script: James Poe, based on the novels *Sanctuary* and *Requiem for a Nun* by William Faulkner. Lee Remick *(Temple Drake)*, Yves Montand *(Candy man)*, Bradford Dillman *(Gowan Stevens)*, Harry Townes *(Ira Bobbitt)*.

29. The Misfits (western). 1961, United Artists. Directed by John Huston, produced by Frank E. Taylor. Script: Arthur Miller. Clark Gable *(Gay Langland)*, Marilyn Monroe *(Roslyn Taber)*, Montgomery Clift *(Perce Howland)*, Thelma Ritter *(Isabelle Steers)*.

30. All Fall Down (drama). 1962, M.G.M. Directed by John Frankenheimer, produced by John Houseman. Script: William Inge, based on the novel by James Leo Herlihy. Eva Marie Saint *(Echo OBrien)*, Warren Beatty *(Berry-Berry Willart)*, Karl Malden *(Ralph Willart)*, Angela Lansbury *(Annabel Willart)*.

31. Cleopatra (historical epic). 1963, 20th Century–Fox. Directed by Joseph L. Mankievicz, produced by Walter Wanger. Script: J. Mankiewicz, Ronald MacDougall, Sidney Buchman, based on works by Plutarch, Appian, Suetonius and *The Life and Times of Cleopatra*, a novel by Carlo M. Franzero. Elizabeth Taylor *(Cleopatra)*, Richard Burton *(Mark Antony)*, Rex Harrison *(Julius Ceasar)*, Pamela Brown *(High Priestess)*. AAN for Best Music Score — Substantially Original.

32. The Outrage (western). 1964, M.G.M. Directed by Martin Ritt, produced by A. Ronald Lubin. Script: Michael Kanin, based on stories by Ryunosuke Akutagawa, film *Rashomon* by A. Kurosawa, and the play *Rashomon* by Fay and Michael Kanin. Paul Newman *(Juan Carrasco)*, Laurence Harvey *(Husband)*, Claire Bloom *(Wife)*, Edward G. Robinson *(Con Man)*.

33. Cheyenne Autumn (western). 1964, Warners. Directed by John Ford, produced by Bernard Smith. Script: James R. Webb, based on the novel by Mari Sandoz. Richard Widmark *(Cap. T. Archer)*, Carroll Baker *(Deborah Wright)*, Karl Malden *(Cap. O. Wessels)*, James Stewart *(Wyatt Earp)*.

34. The Agony and the Ecstasy (drama/biography). 1965, 20th Century–Fox. Directed and produced by Carol Reed. Script: Philip Dunne, based on the novel by Irving Stone. Charlton Heston *(Michelangelo)*, Rex Harrison *(Pope Julius II)*, Diane Cilento *(Contessina de Medici)*. AAN for Best Music Score — Substantially Original.

35. Who's Afraid of Virginia Woolf? (drama). 1966, Warners. Directed by Mike Nichols, produced by Ernest Lehman. Script: Ernest Lehman, based on the play by Edward Albee. Elizabeth Taylor *(Martha)*, Richard Burton *(George)*, George Segal *(Nick)*, Sandy Dennis *(Honey)*. AAN for Best Music, Original Score.

36. Africa (documentary). 1967, ABC TV Production. Produced by James Fleming and Blaine Littell. Gregory Peck (Narrator).

37. The Devil's Brigade (war adventure). 1968, United Artists. Directed by Andrew V. McLaglen, produced by David L. Wolper. Script: William Roberts, based on the book by Robert H. Adleman. William Holden *(Lt. R.Frederick)*, Cliff Robertson *(Maj. Alan Crown)*, Vince Edwards *(Maj. Cliff Brecker)*, Michael Rennie *(Lt. Mark Clark)*.

38. The Shoes of the Fisherman (religious drama). 1968, M.G.M. Directed by Michael Anderson, produced by George Englund. Script: John Patrick, James Kennaway, Morris L. West (uncredited), based on the novel by West. Anthony Quinn *(Kiril Lakota)*, Laurence Olivier *(Piotr I. Kamenev)*, Oskar Werner *(Father David Telemond)*, David Janssen *(George Faber)*. AAN for Best Original Score for a Motion Picture; GG for Best Original Score.

39. A Dream of Kings (drama). 1969, Nation General. Directed by Daniel Mann, produced by Jules Schermer. Script: Harry Mark Petrakis, Ian Hunter, based on the novel by Petrakis. Anthony Quinn *(Matsoukas)*, Irene Papas *(Caliope)*, Inger Stevens *(Anna)*, Sam Levene *(Cicero)*.

40. ***Hard Contract*** (crime/drama). 1969, 20th Century–Fox. Directed by S. Lee Pogostin, produced by Marvin Schwartz. Script: S. Lee Pogostin. James Coburn *(J. Cunningham)*, Lee Remick *(Sheila)*, Lilli Palmer *(Adrianne)*, Burgess Meredith *(Ramsey)*.

41. ***Willard*** (horror). 1971, Crosby/Cinerama. Directed by Daniel Mann, produced by Mort Briskin. Script: Gilbert A. Ralston, based on the novel *Ratman's Notebooks* by Stephen Gilbert. Bruce Davison *(Willard Stiles)*, Elsa Lanchester *(Henrietta Stiles)*, Ernest Borgnine *(Al Martin)*, Sondra Locke *(Joan)*.

42. ***Pocket Money*** (western). 1972, Coleytown–First Artists (Newman-Foreman). Directed by Stuart Rosenberg, produced by John Foreman. Script: Terry Malick, John Gay, based on the novel *Jim Kane* by J. P. S. Brown. Paul Newman *(Jim Kane)*, Lee Marvin *(Leonard)*, Strother Martin *(Garrett)*, Christine Belford *(Adelita)*.

43. ***Rebel Jesus.*** 1972, Independent. Produced by Lary Buchanan.

44. ***Once Upon a Scoundrel*** (comedy). 1973, Independent/Carlyle. Directed by George Schaefer, produced by James S. Elliot. Script: Rip Van Ronkel. Zero Mostel *(Carlos del Refugio)*, Katy Jurado *(Aunt Delfina)*, Titos Vandis *(Dr. Fernandez)*, Priscilla Garcia *(Alicia)*.

45. ***Lost in the Stars*** (musical film, adaptation of Kurt Weill's work). 1973, Ely Landay/American Film Theater. Directed by Daniel Mann, produced by Ely Landau. Script: Maxwell Anderson. Brock Peters, Melba Moore, Raymond St. Jacques, Clifton Davis, Paula Kelly.

46. ***Shanks*** (fantasy/drama). 1974, William Castle Prod. Directed by William Castle, produced by Steven North. Script: Ranald Graham. Marcel Marceau *(Malcolm Shanks/ Old Walker)*, Tsilla Chelton *(Mrs. Barton)*, Philippe Clay *(Mr. Barton)*, Cindy Eilbacher *(Celia)*. AAN for Best Original Dramatic Score.

47. ***Journey into Fear*** (spy drama). 1974, New World/Sterling Gold. Directed by Daniel Mann, produced by Trevor Wallace. Script: Trevor Wallace, based on the novel by Eric Ambler. Sam Waterston *(Graham)*, Zero Mostel, *(Kopeikin)*, Yvette Mimieux *(Josette)*, Scott Marlowe *(Jose)*.

48. ***Bite the Bullet*** (adventure). 1975, Columbia. Directed and produced by Richard Brooks. Script: Richard Brooks. Gene Hackman *(Sam Clayton)*, Candice Bergen *(Miss Jones)*, James Coburn *(Luke Matthews)*, Ben Johnson *(Mister)*. AAN for Best Original Score.

49. ***The Passover Plot*** (drama). 1976, Atlas Film. Directed by Michael Campus, produced by Wolf Schmidt. Script: Millard Cohan, Patricia Knop, based on the book by Hugh J. Schonfield. Harry Andrews *(Yohanan the Baptist)*, Hugh Griffith *(Caiaphas)*, Zalman King *(Jeshua)*, Donald Pleasence *(Pontius Pilate)*.

50. ***Somebody Killed Her Husband*** (comedy/crime). 1978, Columbia. Directed by Lamont Johnson, produced by Martin Poll. Script: Reginald Rose. Farrah Fawcett *(Jenny Moore)*, Jeff Bridges *(Jerry Green)*, John Wood *(Ernest V. Santen)*.

51. ***Wise Blood*** (drama). 1979, Ithaca-Anthea. Directed by John Huston, produced by Michael and Kathy Fitzgerald. Script: Benedict Fitzgerald, based on the novel by

Flannery O'Connor. Brad Dourif *(Hazel Motes)*, Ned Beatty *(Hoover Shoates)*, Harry Dean Stanton *(Asa Hawks)*, Daniel Shor *(Enoch Emery)*.

52. *Carny* (drama). 1980, Lorimar. Directed by Robert Kaylor, produced by Robbie Robertson. Script: Thomas Baum, based on a story by Phoebe Taylor, Robert Kaylor, Robbie Robertson. Gary Busey *(Frankie)*, Jodie Foster *(Donna)*, Robbie Robertson *(Patch)*, Meg Foster *(Gerta)*.

53. *Dragonslayer* (fantasy). 1981, Paramount/Disney. Directed by Matthew Robbins, produced by Hal Barwood. Script: Hal Barwood, Matthew Robbins. Peter MacNicol *(Galen)*, Caitlin Clarke *(Valerian)*, Ralph Richardson *(Ulrich)*, John Hallam *(Tyrian)*. AAN for Best Original Score.

54. *Under the Volcano* (drama). 1984, Ithaca. Directed by John Huston, produced by Michael and Kathy Fitzgerald. Script: Guy Gallo, based on the novel by Malcolm Lowry. Albert Finney *(Geofrey Firmin)*, Jacqueline Bisset *(Yvonne Firmin)*, Anthony Andrews *(Hugh Firmin)*. AAN for Best Original Score.

55. *Prizzi's Honor* (comedy/crime). 1985, ABC Motion Picture. Directed by John Huston, produced by John Foreman. Script: Richard Condon, Janet Roach, based on the novel by Richard Condon. Jack Nicholson *(Charley Partanna)*, Kathleen Turner *(Irene Walker)*, John Randolph *(Angelo Partanna)*, Anjelica Huston *(Maerose Prizzi)*, William Hickey *(Don Corrado)*.

56. *Death of a Salesman* (drama, TV version). 1985, Roxbury & Punch Prod. Directed by Volker Schlondorff, produced by Robert E. Colesberry. Script: Arthur Miller. Dustin Hoffman *(Willy)*, Kate Reid *(Linda)*, John Malkovich *(Biff)*, Stephen Lang *(Happy)*.

57. *The Dead* (drama). 1987, Liffey/Veston-Zenith. Directed by John Huston, produced by Wieland Schulz-Keil. Script: Tony Huston, based on the short story from *Dubliners* by James Joyce. Anjelica Huston *(Gretta Conroy)*, Donal McCann *(Gabriel Conroy)*, Rachael Dowling *(Lily)*, Cathleen Delany *(Aunt Julia Morkan)*.

58. *Good Morning, Vietnam* (comedy/drama). 1987, Disney/Touchstone-Silver. Directed by Barry Levinson, produced by Mark Johnson, Larry Brezner, Ben Moses, Harry Benn, produced by Mitch Markovitz. Robin Williams *(Adrian Cronauer)*, Forest Whitaker *(Edward Garlick)*, Tung Thanh Tran *(Tuan)*, Chinatra Sukapatana *(Trinh)*.

59. *The Penitent* (drama). 1988, Ithaca. Directed by Cliff Osmond, produced by Michael Fitzgerald. Script: Cliff Osmond. Raul Julia *(Ramon Guerola)*, Armand Assante *(Juan Marco)*, Rona Freed *(Celia Guerola)*, Julie Carmen *(Corina)*.

60. *The Last Butterfly* (drama). 1990, Co. Prod. HTV, CTE Film Export. Directed by Karel Kachyna, produced by Steven North. Script: Ota Hofman, based on the novel by Michael Jacot. Tom Courteney, Brigitte Fossey, Freddie Jones, Ingrid Held.

Appendix II:
List of Compositions

CONCERT MUSIC

Choral Music

Negro Mother, cantata (1940, with Langston Hughes)
Ballad of Valley Forge for soloist, chorus and orchestra (1942, with Alfred Kreymborg, published by Marks)
There's a Nation, chorus (1942, with Alfred Kreymborg)
Rhapsody, U. S. A., chorus (1942)
Morning Star, cantata (1946, with Millard Lampell)

Orchestral Music

Symphony No. 1 (1947)
Symphony No. 2 "To a New Continent"; originally composed for the documentary film *Africa* (1967)
Quest, symphonic suite (1937)
Holiday Set for chamber orchestra (1945)
Three Pieces for chamber orchestra (1950)
Streetcar Named Desire, symphonic suite
Death of a Salesman, symphonic suite

Music for Solo Instrument and Orchestra

Rhapsody for Piano and Orchestra (1941)
Revue for Clarinet and Orchestra (1946, published by Mills)

Chamber Music

Woodwind Trio for flute, clarinet and bassoon (1936)
String Quartet (1939)
Woodwind Quintet (1942)
Pastime Suite for clarinet and piano

Vocal Music (Songs)

"To My Son" (1936, with George Sklar)
"Down in the Clover" (1941)
"Elegy" (1946)
"I Belong to You" (1955, with Jack Brooks, from the film The Racers)
"Vino, Vino" (1955, with Hal David, from the film The Rose Tattoo)
"Unchained Melody" (1955, with Hy Zaret, from the film Unchained)
"I'll Cry Tomorrow" (1956)

"Handful of Dreams" (1958, with Paul Francis Webster)
"Long Hot Summer" (1958, with Sammy Cahn)
"Hey Eula" (1959, with Sammy Cahn)
"The One Love" (1960, with Sammy Cahn)
"Out of Time, Out of Space" (1960, with Johnny Mercer)
"Restless Love" (1961, with Harold Adamson)
"World of Love" (1963)
"The Nile" (1963, with Johnny Mercer)
"Who's Afraid of Love?"

Piano Music

Twelve Dance Preludes for solo piano (1947, or earlier)

MUSIC FOR CHILDREN

Musical

The Hither and Thither of Danny Dither (1941, lyrics by Jeremy Gury, published by Marks)

Works for Narrator and Orchestra

Waltzing Elephant (1945)
Little Indian Drum (1946)
Yank and Christopher Columbus (1943)
The City Sings for Michael

STAGE MUSIC

Ballets and Dances

Anti-War Trilogy (1933, later retitled Anti-War Cycle, Anna Sokolow)
Pre-Classic Suite (1933, Anna Sokolow)
Salutation to the Morning (1933, Anna Sokolow)
Into the Streets (1934, Anna Sokolow)
Song of Affirmation (1934)
Speaker (1935, Anna Sokolow)

Ballad in a Popular Style (1936, Anna Sokolow)
Inquisition '36 (1936, Anna Sokolow)
War is Beautiful (1937, Anna Sokolow)
War-Monger (1937, Anna Sokolow)
Façade — Exposizione Italiana (1937, Anna Sokolow)
Opening Dance (1937, Anna Sokolow)
Slaughter of the Innocents (1937, Anna Sokolow; retitled Madrid, 1937, revised 1943)
American Lyric (1937, Martha Graham)
The Last Waltz (1937, number from the revue Sing for Your Supper)
Exile (1939, Anna Sokolow)
Lupe (1940)
Nocturne (1940, Dorothy Bird)
Mooch Motif (1940, Dorothy Bird and William Bales)
Design for Five (1941)
Golden Fleece (1941, Hanya Holm)
Mama Beautiful (1941, Anna Sokolow)
Clay Ritual (1942, Truda Kaschmann)
Intersection (1947)
Ballad in a Popular Style No. 2 (1948, Anna Sokolow)
A Streetcar Named Desire (1952, Valerie Bettis; published by Widmark)
Wall Street Ballet (1953, Show of Shows, TV)
Daddy Long Legs Dream Ballet (1955, Fred Astair and Leslie Caron)
Mal de Siècle (1958, Rosella Hightower and James Starbuck)
Prelude (Marthe Krueger)
Trineke (Marthe Krueger)
Case History
Primitive Ritual
Overture to Dance
Black Panther
Little Dance Preludes
Humpty Dumpty
Bar Room Ballads
Ballet
Go Down Death
Bourbon's Gor Blues

Musical Shows and Revues

Sing for Your Supper (1938/39, Federal
  Theater Project)
'Tis of Thee (ILGWU, 1940)
You Can't Sleep Here (American Youth
  Theatre, 1941)
Of V We Sing (American Youth Theatre,
  1941)
Song of Our City (1946)
Queen of Sheba, musical (1950)

Incidental Music for Theater

Dog Beneath the Skin (1936)
Life and Death of an American (1939,
  directed by George Sklar)
The Great Campaign (1947, Experimental
  Theatre)
O'Daniel (1947, Experimental Theatre)
Death of a Salesman (1949)
The Innocents (1950)
Richard III (1953)
Coriolanus (1954)
The American Clock
A Time for Heroes

MUSIC FOR DOCUMENTARIES

China Strikes Back (1936)
Heart of Spain (1937, Frontier Films)

The People of the Cumberland (1938,
  Frontier Films)
*Venezuela: (a) Election, (b) Sports,
  (c) Recreation* (1939)
Rural Nurse (1940, Willard Pictures)
Mount Vernon (1940)
City Pastorale (1942 [6], State Depart-
  ment)
A Better Tomorrow (1945, Office of War
  Information)
Library of Congress (1945, Office of War
  Information)
Coney Island, U.S.A. (1950)
Decision for Chemistry (1953)
The American Road (1953 [?], Monsanto)

MUSIC FOR TELEVISION

Billy Rose Show (1950)
Playhouse 90 (1960, CBS)
Nero Wolfe (1966)
I'm A Lawyer
F. D. Roosvelt Series (1961, ABC)
Silent Night (1970, ABC Christmas Special)
The Man and the City (1972, Anthony
  Quinn series, Universal)
Rich Man Poor Man (1976)
The Word (1978)
Sister-Sister (1982)
77 Sunset Strip

Appendix III: Discography

FILM MUSIC ARRANGED IN CHRONOLOGICAL ORDER BY FILM RELEASE DATE

Title	Discography	Comments
A Streetacar Named Desire (1951)	Capitol P 387 (1 side)	Conducted by Ray Heindorf
	Capitol L 289	
	Capitol KDF 289	
	Columbia 2092/612	
	Angel S 36068	Reissue
	Dot DLP 3107 (1 cut)	Conducted by Elmer Bernstein
	Hamilton 108/12108	
	RCA LPM 1445 (1 cut)	
	3XX 2737 (1 cut)	
	Citadel CT 6023 (1 cut)	Musical director: Lionel Newman
	London 1513	
	Cloud Nine Records 5003	
	Nonesuch 79446-2	
	Varèse Sarabande VSD 5500 (1995)	Conducted by Jerry Goldsmith
The Thirteenth Letter (1951)	Citadel CT 6023 (1 cut)	
Death of a Salesman (1951)	Film Music Collection FMC 9 (1 side)	Conducted by Elmer Bernstein
	Decca DX 102	The integral theater play
	Brunswick LAT 8008	Dialogs with music excerpts
Viva Zapata! (1952)	Film Music Collection FMC 9 (1 side)	
	Dot DLP 3107	
	Hamilton 108/12108	
	Citadel CT 6023 (1 cut)	
	Nonesuch 79446-2	
	Nonesuch PRCD 8054 (1 cut)	

Title	*Discography*	*Comments*
(Viva Zapata! cont.)	Soundstage Records 620 (18 numbers)	Conducted by Alfred Newman
	Varèse Sarabande VSD 5900 (1998)	Conducted by Jerry Goldsmith
	Tsunami TSU 0118 (1 track)	
Les Misérables (1952)	Citadel CT 6023 (1 cut) Tsunami TSU 0118 (1 track)	
The Member of the Wedding (1952)	RCA LPM 1445 (1 cut)	
Desirée (1954)	Decca 8123 (2 cuts) Columbia 569 Dot DLP 3107 Citadel CT 6023 (1 cut) Tsunami TSU 0118 (1 track)	Musical director: Lionel Newman
Unchained (1955)	RCA LPM 1445 (1 cut) Citadel CT 6023 (1 cut) Camden (s) 795 Columbia 1371/8172 Dunhill (S) 50008 Harmony 7351/11151 London 1700/124 MGM 3127 Richmond 20060/30060 Decca Single 29441 (1955) Decca 8757 (1958) Varèse Sarabande, VSD 5930 Tsunami TSU 0118	Performed by Al Hibbler
The Racers (1955)	RCA LPM 1445 (1 cut) Citadel CT 6023 (1 cut)	
The Man with the Gun (1955)	Columbia 440624	Main Title / Single
The Rose Tattoo (1955)	Columbia CL 727 Decca (7) 4083 MGM 3294 RCA LPM 1445 (1 cut) Citadel CT 6023 (1 cut) Varèse Sarabande VCL 9001.5	
I'll Cry Tomorrow (1955)	Citadel CT 6023 (1 cut) Mercury 20123	
The Bad Seed (1956)	RCA LPM 1395 Citadel CT 6023 (1 cut) RCA Victor NL 45953 Tsunami TSU 0124 Nonesuch 79446-2	Conducted by Ray Heindorf
The Rainmaker (1956)	RCA LPM 1434 RCA Victor NL 45980 Tsunami TSU 0120	
Four Girls in Town	Decca DL 8424 (1 side) Varèse Sarabande VC 81074 Fonit DL 8424 (IT 33)	Rhapsody, conducted by Joseph Gershenson

ALEX NORTH   DISCOGRAPHIE

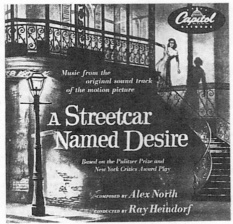

1951 A STREEETCAR NAMED DESIRE

1958 SOUTH SEAS ADVENTURE
1974 JOURNEY INTO FEAR

1963 CLEOPATRA (Vol. 1)

1959 THE SOUND AND
THE FURY

1963 CLEOPATRA (Vol. 2)
(erschienen 1984)

1951 DEATH OF A SALESMAN
1952 VIVA ZAPATA!

1956 THE RAINMAKER

1959 THE WONDERFUL COUNTRY

1963 CHEYENNE AUTUMN

1955 THE ROSE TATTOO

1956 FOUR GIRLS IN TOWN

1960 SPARTACUS

1965 THE AGONY
AND THE ECSTASY

1956 THE BAD SEED

1958 THE LONG, HOT SUMMER

1961 THE MISFITS

1966 WHO'S AFRAID
OF VIRGINIA WOOLF?

Alex North discography ...

1967 AFRICA

1979 SOMEBODY KILLED HER
HUSBAND (CHARADE 79')

1981 DRAGONSLAYER

1968 THE DEVILS BRIGADE

1980 CARNY

DEATH OF A SALESMAN
B way Cast. Reissue 1984

1968 THE SHOES OF
THE FISHERMAN

1969 A DREAM OF KINGS

1975 BITE THE BULLIT

... reprinted from *Spellbound: Das Deutsche Filmmusikmagazin*, no. 5 (May 1985).

232 APPENDIX III. DISCOGRAPHY

Title	Discography	Comments
The Bachelor Party (1957)	Citadel CT 6023 (1 cut) RCA 47 6806 (45)	
The Long Hot Summer (1958)	Roulette/Sonet R 25026 Roulette GES 3669 (JA 33) Sumiya SU 1002 Kapp (S) 3005 Varèse Sarabande— VCL 0202 1005	Conducted by Lionel Newman Reissue Reissue Reissue
Stage Struck (1958)	Citadel CT 6023 (1 cut)	
Hot Spell (1958)	RCA LPM 1445 (1 cut)	
South Seas Adventure (1958)	Audio Fidelity AFLP 1899 Citadel CT 7014 (1 side) Label X ATM CD 2004 Label X LXCD 2.24 tracks	Reissue without source music
The Sound and the Fury (1959)	Decca DL 8885/DL 78885 MCA VIM 7209 (JA 33) Varèse Sarabande VSD 5297	Conducted by Lionel Newman Reissue Reissue
The Wonderful Country (1959)	United Artists UAL 4050/UAS 5050 (1 side) United Artists DF 7/DFS 57 (1 side) Sonopresse UASF 5050 Ascot ALS 16501 (5 cuts) United Artists UAS 5087 (2 cuts) Tsunami TSU 0118	Original issue Reissue Reissue
Spartacus (1960)	Decca DL 9092/DL 79092 MCA 7139 (JA 33) Brunswick Lat 8363 (GB 33) Brunswick 009001 (FR 33) Festival FL 7244 (NZ 33) Arabella Eur. 204663 (FR 33) MCA 2068 Capitol 2627 MGM (S) 3894 Mercury 20640/60640 TRAX, modem 1012 (AAD) MCA MCAD 1025 C MCA 10256 (1991) Silva Screen FILMXCD 187 (2 tracks) Nonesuch 79446-2 SVC Records 5994 (1-2) Conducted by Alex North	Conducted by Alex North Reissue Reissue Two CDs with complete music.
The Chidren's Hour (1961)	Soundstage Records 620	Conducted by Alex North
The Sanctuary (1961)	Varèse Sarabande VCL 0202 1005	Conducted by Alex North
The Misfits (1961)	United Artists UAL 4087/UAS 5087 (1 side)	

Title	Discography	Comments
(The Misfits, cont.)	United Artists UA-LA 273 G	Reissue
	Columbia 1627/8427	
	Nonesuch 79446-2	
	Nonesuch PRCD 8054	
All Fall Down (1962)	Columbia 1880/8680	
Cleopatra (1963)	20th Century–Fox SXG 5008	Fold-out album, con. by North
	20th Century–Fox GHX 6050 (JA 33)	Reissue
	Fox TC 31122 (NZ 33)	
	Stateside SSL 10044 (GB 33)	
	Capitol 2075	
	Command 854	
	London 3327/44031	
	MGM 4144	
	Somerset 20200	
	Mercury 20887/60887	
	Time 304	
	United Artists 3290/6290 and 3303/6303	
	Columbia CS 8913/CL 2113	
	Columbia CS 8850	"Impressions of 'Cleopatra,'" Paul Horne—flute
	Impulse M:A 41/s:AS 41 (2 cuts)	"Feeling Jazzy," Paul Golsalves—tenor saxophone
	Tsunami TSU 1111	
	Varèse SarabandeVSD 5207 (1 track)	"The Prince and the Pauper," conducted by Charles Gerhardt
	Varèse SarabandeVSD 5561 (3 tracks)	"Blood & Thunder," conducted by Cliff Eidelman
	Varèse Sarabande 3020662242	Two CDs with complete music Reissue, conducted by North
Cheyenne Autmn (1964)	Label X LXSE 1-1003	
	Label X ATM CD 2004	
	Condor CDR 831106	
The Agony and the Ecstasy (1965)	Capitol MAS 2427/SMAS	Fold-out album
	Capitol YL 3030	Reissue
	Varèse Sarabande VSD 5901 (1997)	Conducted by Jerry Goldsmith
Who's Afraid of Virginia Woolf? (1966)	Warner Bros. B 1656/BS 1656	
	Warner Bros. 2 B 1657/2 BS 1657 (2 LPs)	
	Varèse SarabandeVSD 5207	Main Title
	Command 5005	
	Dunhill 5001	
	Fox 3192	
	London 44092	
	Tsunami TSU 0112	
	Varèse SarabandeVSD 5800	Conducted by Jerry Goldsmith
Africa (1967)	MGM E 4462/MGM SE 4462	*Africa Suite* and *Symphony to a New Continent*
Devil's Brigade (1968)	United Artists UAL 3654/UAS 6654	Arranged and conducted by Leroy Holmes
	Project 3 5027	

Title	Discography	Comments
The Shoes of the Fisherman (1968)	MGM S 1E 15 ST Command 941 Philips 600301 Gadfly GAD 94009	Fold-out album
2001: A Space Odyssey (1968)	Varèse Sarabande VSD 5400	Conducted by Jerry Goldsmith
A Dream of Kings (1969)	National General NG 1000	
Journey into Fear (1974)	Citadel 7014 (1 side) STV 81341 (1 side) Varèse SarabandeVSD 47341	
Bite the Bullet (1975)	RFO 102 Prometheus Records— PCR 504 (Belgium)	Conducted by Alex North
Somebody Killed Her Husband "Charade '79" (1978)	Seven Seas FML 108	
Carny (1980)	Warner Bros. HS 3455 (1 side)	
Dragonslayer (1981)	Label X LXSE 2-001 (2 LPs) Label X ATM CD 2004 MCAD 6210 SCSE CD-3	
Under the Volcano (1984)	Masters Film Music SRS 2011	
The Dead (1987)	STV 81341 (1 side) Varèse Sarabande VCD 47341	
Good Morning, Vietnam (1987)	A & M SP-3913/CD-3913	
The Last Butterfly (1990)	Varèse Sarabande VSD 5287	

TELEVISION MUSIC

Your Show of Shows TV variety series (1950/54)	RCA LPM 1445 (1 cut) *Wall Street Ballet*	North used this music in the
Playhouse 90 TV dramatic anthology series (1956/60)	Warner Bros. W 1290	North composed the title theme
77 Sunset Strip TV series (1959)	Warner Bros. W 1289	Only two themes
Rich Man, Poor Man TV series (1976)	Varèse Sarabande VSD 5423 MCA 2095	

ALBUMS

North of Hollywood	RCA LPM 1445/LSP 1445	Selection from *A Streetcar Named Desire*, *Wall Street*

Title	Discography	Comments
(North of Hollywood, cont.)		*Ballet, Hot Spell, American Road, Unchained, The Racers, The Rose Tattoo, A Member of a Wedding*
Film Music by Alex North	Citadel CT 6023	Selection from *Unchained, Viva Zapata!, The Bad Seed, A Streetcar Named Desire, The Bachelor Party, The Thirteenth Letter, Stage Struck, I'll Cry Tomorrow, Les Misérables, The Rose Tattoo, Desirée*
Alex North at the Movies	Label X ATM CD 2004	Music from *Cheyenne Autumn, Dragonslayer,* and *South Seas Adventure*
Unchained Melody	Bay Cities BCD 3010	Selection from *Unchained, The Racers, Viva Zapata!, The Bad Seed, A Streetcar Named Desire, The Bachelor Party, The Thirteenth Letter, Stage Struck, I'll Cry Tomorrow, Les Misérables, The Rose Tattoo, Desirée*

THEATER MUSIC

Coriolanus; Richard III Broadway plays	Varèse Sarabande VSD 5752	"Processional" and "Fanfare" from *Coriolanus*, "Three Fanfares" from *Richard III*

INSTRUMENTAL COMPOSITIONS

Holiday Set, Chamber Suite	Society of Participating Arts SPA 47	Recorded on the album "American Life"
Rhapsody for Piano and Orchestra	Koch/International Classics 3-7225-2H1	Soloist: David Beuchner; Conducted by James Sedares
A Streetcar Named Desire, Piano Suite	Premier Recordings PRCO 1013	Nine piano pieces recorded on the album "American Piano," vol. 1

Appendix IV: List of Awards Presented to Alex North

1947 Guggenheim Fellowship for Musical Composition

1951 Academy Award nomination for Best Music, Scoring of a Dramatic or Comedy Picture for *A Streetcar Named Desire*

1951 Academy Award nomination for Best Music, Scoring of a Dramatic or Comedy Picture for *Death of a Salesman*

1952 Academy Award nomination for Best Music, Scoring of a Dramatic or Comedy Picture for *Viva Zapata!*

1955 Academy Award nomination for Best Music, Song for *Unchained Melody* (lyrics by Hy Zaret)

1955 Academy Award nomination for Best Music, Scoring of a Dramatic or Comedy Picture for *The Rose Tattoo*

1955 Downbeat Magazine Music Award for *Daddy Long Legs Dream Ballet*

1956 Academy Award nomination for Best Music, Scoring of a Dramatic or Comedy Picture for *The Rainmaker*

1956 Exhibitor Laurel Award as the top film composer

1957 Exhibitor Laurel Award as the top film composer

1960 Academy Award nomination for Best Music, Scoring of a Dramatic or Comedy Picture for *Spartacus*

1963 Academy Award nomination for Best Music, Scoring of a Dramatic or Comedy Picture for *Cleopatra*

1963 First Annual Composers and Lyricists Guild Award for *Cleopatra*

1965 Academy Award nomination for Best Music, Score — Substantially Original for *The Agony and the Ecstasy*

1966   Academy Award nomination for Best Music, Original Music Score for *Who's Afraid of Virginia Woolf?*

1966   Grammy Award for Best Instrumental Theme for "Who's Afraid" from *Who's Afraid of Virginia Woolf?*

1966   Exhibitor Laurel Award as the top film composer

1967   Exhibitor Laurel Award as the top film composer

1968   Academy Award nomination for Best Music, Original Score for a Motion Picture for *The Shoes of the Fisherman*

1968   Golden Globe Award for Best Original Score for *The Shoes of the Fisherman*

1969   Exhibitor Laurel Award as the top film composer

1971   Exhibitor Laurel Award as the top film composer

1974   Academy Award nomination for Best Music, Original Dramatic Score for *Shanks*

1975   Academy Award nomination for Best Music, Original Score for *Bite the Bullet*

1976   Emmy Award for Outstanding Achievement in Music Composition for a Series for the television series *Rich Man, Poor Man*

1979   Emmy Award nomination for Outstanding Music Composition for a Limited Series or a Special for *The Word* (miniseries)

1981   Academy Award nomination for Best Music, Original Score for *Dragonslayer*

1984   Academy Award nomination for Best Music, Original Score for *Under the Volcano*

1986   Honorary Academy Award by the Academy of Motion Picture Arts and Sciences for lifetime achievement in film music

1986   Golden Soundtrack Award by the American Society of Composers, Authors and Publishers (ASCAP) for lifetime achievement in film and television music

1986   The Career Achievement Award by the Society for the Preservation of Film Music

1986   Golden Score Award by the American Society of Music Arrangers and Composers

1986   Los Angeles City Council Award for creative contributions as a composer who gives listening pleasure to a world-wide audience

1986   Emmy Award nomination for *Death of a Salesman* (television version)

1989   Crystal Phoenix Award by the Metro Phoenix Film Board

Chapter Notes

Preface

1. The term "James Dean sound" is borrowed from Christopher Palmer. See *The Composer in Hollywood*, London/New York: Marion Boyars, 1990, p. 294.
2. As quoted by Tony Thomas, *Film Score: The Art & Craft of Movie Music*, Burbank, California: Riverwood Press, 1991, p. 182.

1. From West to East

1. See Brooks Atkinson, "First Night at the Theatre," *New York Times* (February 2, 1950), p. 30.
2. See David Kraft, "A Conversation with Alex North," *Soundtrack! The Collector's Quarterly*, vol. 4, no. 13 (March, 1985), p. 5.
3. Most of the information about the origins of the Soifer family and the early period of the life of Alex North are provided from an interview of the author with Alex's youngest brother, Harry, and his wife, Esther North, Philadelphia, November 21, 1995.
4. See Patti Mengers, "Ex-Delco Man a Winner," *Delaware County Daily Times* (March 25, 1986), p. 35.
5. From Alex North's handwritten autobiographical notes, held at the "Margaret Herrick" library of the Academy of Motion Picture Arts and Sciences, Los Angeles (Special Collections).
6. From the speech that Dan North, Bessie's grandson and Alex's nephew, gave at her memorial.
7. David Raksin, an interview with Alex North for a radio program "The Subject is Film Music."

8. From Alex North's handwritten autobiographical notes.
9. David Raksin, an interview with Alex North.
10. *Ibid.*
11. See Michael Segel, "Movie Composer Is 'Home' For Reunion With Family," *Jewish Exponent* (September 10, 1965).
12. See Ernie Schier, "Ex-Philadelphian Sets 'Spartacus' to Music," *Evening Bulletin*— Philadelphia (September 29, 1960), p. F4.
13. *Ibid.*
14. See Howard Lucraft, "The Hollywood Film Composers: I Like to relate to a story, says Alex North," *Crescendo International*, 24 (November, 1987), p. 10.
15. See Ernie Schier.
16. *Ibid.*
17. From the personal interview with Harry and Esther North.
18. See Michael Segel.
19. See Mildred Norton, "Oscar Playing Footsie with Another Alex North Score," *Sunday News*— Los Angeles (February 22, 1953).
20. From an interview of the author with Anna Sokolow, New York, November 23, 1995.
21. As quoted by Larry Warren, *Anna Sokolow: The Rebellious Spirit*, Princeton, New Jersey: Princeton Book Company Pub., 1991, p. 36.
22. From the personal interview of the author with Anna Sokolow.
23. *Ibid.*
24. As quoted by Larry Warren, p. 37.
25. The information about the *Anti-War Trilogy* is obtained from the book by Larry Warren, p. 47.

26. As quoted by Larry Warren, p. 39. See more about the relationship, pp. 36–39.

27. See Michael Segel.

28. David Raksin, an interview with Alex North.

29. As quoted by Tony Thomas, *Film Score: The Art & Craft of Movie Music*, p.184.

30. See Tony Thomas, pp. 183–184; Christopher Palmer, "Film Music Profile: Alex North," *Crescendo International* (April, 1975), p. 28; David Ewen, *American Composer Today: A Biographical and Critical Guide*, New York: H. W. Wilson Company, 1949, p. 179.

31. As quoted by Larry Warren, p.51.

32. See Alex Soifer, "A Music Student in Soviet Russia," *Dynamics* (April 5, 1935), p. 6.

33. *Ibid.*

34. See Alex North, "Dance in the Soviet Union," *Dance Observer*, no. 4 (May, 1934), p. 37.

35. From the letter that Anna Sokolow wrote to her friend Ronya Chernin, as quoted in Larry Warren, p. 53.

36. Anna wrote about *Prince Igor* in the letter to her sister Rose, as quoted by Larry Warren, p. 54, and Alex mentioned, in the radio interview with David Raksin, how thrilled he was by *Katerina Izmailova*.

37. From the personal interview with Anna Sokolow.

38. See David Ewen, *American Composer Today: A Biographical and Critical Guide*, New York: H. W. Wilson Company, 1949, p. 179.

39. David Raksin, an interview with Alex North.

40. *Ibid.*

2. Music and Movement

1. See Alex North, "Music Should Be Communicative," *Mills Music Commentator* (1947), p. 1.

2. From the personal interview with Annemarie North, Pacific Palisades, May 20, 1995.

3. As quoted by Stephen Farber, "Alex North and His Oscar Make Musical Movie History," *New York Times* (1986), p. 17.

4. As quoted in Aaron Copland/Vivian Perlis, *Copland since 1943*, vol. 2, New York: St. Martin's Press, 1989, p. 7.

5. *Ibid.*

6. David Raksin, an interview with Alex North.

7. As quoted by Tony Thomas, *Film Score: The Art & Craft of Movie Music*, p. 184.

8. Joel Reisner and Bruce Kane, "An Interview with Alex North," *Cinema* (December, 1969), p. 43.

9. See Larry Warren, p. 68.

10. *Ibid.*

11. *Ibid.*, pp. 68–69.

12. See Elie Siegmeister, *The Music Lover's Handbook*, New York: William Morrow and Company, 1943, p. 770.

13. See Martin McCall, "Music," *Daily Worker* (October 16, 1937).

14. *Ibid.*

15. See Elizabeth Noble, "Heart of Spain," *New Masses for Spain* (1938), *op. cit.*, p. 18.

16. See Larry Warren, p. 76.

17. See Rudy Behlemer, "Alex North on 'A Streetcar Named Desire,'" *Cue Sheet* (September, 1986), p. 36.

18. See Elie Siegmeister, p. 770.

19. From the interview with Leonard Bernstein, as quoted in Aaron Copland/Vivian Perlis, *Copland: 1900 through 1942*, vol. 1, New York: St. Martin's/Marek, 1984, p. 336.

20. See John Martin, "The Dance: New Blood," *New York Times* (August 29, 1937), p. 8.

21. See Elie Siegmeister, p. 770.

22. As quoted by Larry Warren, p. 72.

23. From the personal interview with Harry and Esther North.

24. See more in Lou Cooper's article "Alex North Evaluates Modern Theatre Music Technique," *Show of the Month News* (Summer, 1949).

25. For more details about Anna Sokolow performances in Mexico refer to Larry Warren, chapter "Mexico," pp. 81–96.

26. David Raksin, an interview with Alex North.

27. From the personal interview with Anna Sokolow.

28. See more, Larry Warren, p. 86.

29. See Martin McCall, "American Ballad Singers and Young Composer Heard in Excellent Programs," *Daily Worker* (February 22, 1940), p. 7.

30. See Larry Warren, *ibid.*, p. 105.

31. *Ibid.*, p. 77.

3. New York, New York

1. As quoted by Christopher Palmer, "Film Music Profile: Alex North," *Crescendo International* (April, 1975), pp. 28–29.

2. From an interview of the author with Sherle North, Bel Air (Los Angeles), December 11, 1995.

3. *Ibid.*

4. See John Martin, "Hanya Holm Group Offers a Ballet," *New York Times* (March 18, 1941).

5. See Louis Biancolli, "Holm Group Portrays Variety," *World Telegram* (March 18, 1941).

6. See the article "Marthe Krueger To Open School Here on Monday," *Ridgefield Press* (May 14, 1942).

7. See Marian Murray, "'Elements of Magic' Has Its Premiere At Avery Memorial," *Hartford Times* (May 23, 1942).

8. See Elie Siegmeister, *The Music Lover's Handbook*, p. 770.

9. *Ibid.*, p. 771.

10. From the personal interview with Sherle North.

11. From the article "Composer Sends Blessings from Camp," *Hartford Times* (April 12, 1943).

12. From David Raksin's interview with Alex North.

13. See Mildred Norton, "Stage and Screen," *Sunday News— Los Angeles* (February 22, 1953).

14. See A. V. B. [*sic*], "CIO Chorus Presents New Cantata By Lampell and North at Town Hall," *New York Herald Tribune* (May 26, 1947), p. 17.

15. See Howard Lucraft, "I Like to Relate to a Story, Says Alex North," *Crescendo International* (November, 1987), p. 10.

16. See H. T. [*sic*], "Bernstein Leads Three Premieres," *New York Times* (November 19, 1946), p. 40.

17. See Robert Hague, "Goodman Is Soloist with Bernstein Band," *PM* (November 20, 1946).

18. From the personal interview with Sherle North.

19. See John Briggs, "Records: Works by Scriabin and Ives," *New York Times* (May 23, 1954), p. 6.

20. See H. C. S. [*sic*], "Joan Slessinger Heard in Town Hall," *New York Sun* (September 22, 1947).

21. See J. S. H. [*sic*], "Philharmonic Performs For Children Under Nine," *New York Herald Tribune* (October 19, 1947).

22. From an interview of the author with Steven North, Los Angeles, November 29, 1995.

23. See Brooks Atkinson, "The New Play: Arnold Sundgaard's 'The Great Campaign,'" *New York Times* (April 1, 1947), p. 33.

24. See Louis Kronenberger, "A Folk Play with Music and Political Meaning," *PM Daily* (April 1, 1947), p. 16.

25. See Otis Guernsey Jr., "Sundgaard Play: 'The Great Campaign' Presented at the Princess Theater," *New York Herald Tribune* (March 31, 1947), p. 15.

26. As quoted by Rudy Behlemer, "Alex North on 'A Streetcar Named Desire,'" *Cue Sheet* (September 1986), p. 36.

27. From the personal interview with Sherle North.

28. From an interview of the author with Arthur Miller, New York, November 28, 1995.

29. *Ibid.*

30. As quoted by Lou Cooper, "Alex North Evaluates…," *Show of the Month News* (Summer, 1949).

31. See Barbara Strong, "Theatre: Not So Incidental," *Concerto* (February, 1950), p. 5.

32. *Ibid.*

33. From the personal interview with Arthur Miller.

34. *Ibid.*

35. See Barbara Strong, p. 6.

4. Welcome to Hollywood

1. As quoted by Irwin Bazelon, *Knowing the Score: Notes on Film Music* (an interview with Alex North), New York: Van Nostrand Reinhold Company, 1975, p. 223.

2. See the Preface for the names of the composers Kazan introduced to Hollywood.

3. Fred Steiner, an oral interview with Alex North, Pacific Palisades, April 27, 1976.

4. From the personal interview with Steven North, Los Angeles, November 29, 1995, and the personal interview with Sherle North, Bel Air, December 11, 1995.

5. David Raksin, an interview with Alex North for a radio program "The Subject Is Film Music."

6. *Ibid.*

7. See David Kraft, "A Conversation with Alex North," *Soundtrack! The Collector's Quarterly*, vol. 4, no. 13 (March, 1985), p. 5.

8. *Ibid.*

9. David Raksin, an interview with Alex North.

10. See Steven Smith, "The Tenacious Alex North," *Los AngelesTimes/Calendar* (March 23, 1986), p. 82.

11. See David Kraft, p. 5.

12. Fred Steiner, an interview with Alex North; see also Rudy Behlemer, "Alex North on 'A Streetcar Named Desire,'" *The Cue Sheet* (September, 1986), p. 37.

13. As quoted by Tony Thomas, *Film Score: The Art & Craft of Movie Music*, p. 185.

14. See Joan Padrol, "Alex North: La Aventura del Gran Norte," *Encuentro International de Musica de Cine* (1991), pp. 73, 75.

15. Fred Steiner, an interview with Alex North.

16. *Ibid.*

17. From the personal interview with Sherle North; see also Rudy Behlemer, p. 37.

18. As quoted by Tony Thomas, *Music for the Movies*, South Brunswick, New Jersey: A. S. Barnes and Company, 1973, pp. 182–183.

19. See John Steinbeck, *Viva Zapata!*, New York: The Viking Press, 1975, p. 140.

20. See Lan Adomian, "Viva Zapata," *Film Music*, vol. 11, no. 4 (March/April, 1952), p. 4.

21. David Raksin, an interview with Alex North; see also Lan Adomian, p. 7, and Tony Thomas, *Film Score: The Art & Craft of Movie Music*, p. 186.

22. See Alex North's comments on the differences in theater and film scoring in: Raymond

Kendall, "Saga of Hollywood Music: North Composes for Stage, Screen," *Mirror News*— Los Angeles (October 12, 1959), part 2, p. 5; David Cloud and Leslie Zador, "Alex North Interview: The Missing Score for '2001,'" *Los Angeles Free Press*, vol. 7, no. 48 (Friday, November 27, 1970), p. 39.

23. David Raksin, an interview with Alex North.

24. From the personal interview with Arthur Miller.

25. See more, Arthur Miller, '*Salesman*' *in Beijing*, pp. 52–53.

26. See more, Joan Padrol, "Alex North: La Aventura del Gran Norte," p. 66.

27. Fred Steiner, an interview with Alex North.

28. David Raksin, an interview with Alex North.

29. See Irwin Bazelon, *Knowing the Score: Notes on Film Music* (an interview with Alex North), p. 222.

30. See Brog [*sic*], "Film Reviews: 'Go, Man, Go,'" *Variety*, vol. 193, no. 7 (Wednesday, January 20, 1954), p. 18.

31. As quoted by Jack Gaver, "Conductor Finds Background Music for TV Exacting Job," *Argus*— Rock Island, Ill. (October 26, 1953).

32. As quoted by Daniël Mangodt, "An Interview with Steven and Anne-Marie North," *Soundtrack*, vol. 10, no. 40 (December, 1991), p. 7.

33. From the personal interview with Steven North.

34. From the personal interview with Arthur Miller.

35. As quoted by Steven Smith, "The Tenacious Alex North," *Los Angeles Times/Calendar* (Sunday, March 23, 1986), p. 82.

36. From the personal interview with Sherle North.

37. From an interview of the author with Harry and Esther North, Philadelphia, November 21, 1995.

38. From the personal interview with Sherle North.

39. *Ibid.*

40. As quoted by Steven Smith, "The Tenacious Alex North," p. 82.

41. From an interview of the author with Farley Granger, New York, November 25, 1995.

42. From an interview of the author with David Amram, Brewster, November 24, 1995.

43. As quoted by John P. Shanley, "Alex North — Composer Turns to Television," *New York Times* (March 4, 1962).

44. Fred Steiner, an interview with Alex North.

45. From North's statement in Tony Thomas, *Music for the Movies*, p. 184.

46. See Alex North, "Notes on the Score of 'The Rose Tattoo,'" *Film Music*, vol. 15, no. 2 (Winter, 1955), p. 3.

47. *Ibid.*

48. *Ibid.*

49. See John Gruen's review of the original soundtrack recording in the same issue of *Film Music* (Winter, 1955), p. 3.

50. See Alex North, "Notes on 'The Rainmaker,'" *Film and TV Music*, 16, no. 3 (Spring, 1957), p. 3.

51. *Ibid.*

52. See Mark Evans, *Soundtrack: The Music of the Movies*. New York: Hopkinson and Blake, 1975, p. 149.

53. See Jay Robert Nash and Stanley Ralph Ross, *The Motion Picture Guide*, Chicago: Cinebooks, 1985, p. 919.

54. *Ibid.*, p. 119.

55. See Ross Care, "Hot Spells: Alex North's Southern Gothic Film Scores," *Performing Arts at the Library of Congress* (1992), p. 21.

56. As quoted by Arnold Zeitlin, "The Frustrated Alex North," *Sunday Bulletin Magazine* (July 15, 1962), p. 4.

57. See Jay Robert Nash and Stanley Ralph Ross, p. 1282.

58. See Ross Care, "New from Label 'X': The Cinema Maestro Series— Cinerama 'South Seas Adventure,'" *Film Score Monthly*, no. 38 (October, 1993), p. 13.

59. As quoted by Gene Phillips, *Fiction, Film, and Faulkner: The Art of Adaptation*, Knoxville: University of Tennessee Press, 1988, pp. 150, 162.

60. *Ibid.*, p. 163.

61. See William Darby and Jack DuBois, *American Film Music: Major Composers, Techniques, Trends, 1915–1990*, Jefferson, North Carolina: McFarland & Company, Inc., 1990, p. 422.

5. The Decade of the Big Epics

1. As quoted by Ernie Schier, "Ex-Philadelphian Sets 'Spartacus' to Music." *Evening Bulletin*— Philadelphia (September 29, 1960), F4.

2. From the personal interview with Steven North.

3. See Daniël Mangodt, "An Interview with Steven and Anne-Marie North," *Soundtrack*, vol. 10, no. 40 (December, 1991), p. 7.

4. For detailed analyses of two musical sequences from *The Children's Hour*, refer to George Burt, *The Art of Film Music: Special Emphasis on Hugo Friedhofer, Alex North, David Raksin, Leonard Rosenman*, Boston: Northeastern University Press, 1994, pp. 59–63.

5. As quoted by Tony Thomas, *Film Score: The Art & Craft of Movie Music*, p. 190.

6. David Raksin, an interview with Alex North.

7. See more in William Darby and Jack Du Bois, *American Film Music: Major Composers, Techniques, Trends, 1915–1990*, p. 414.

8. See Greg Rose, "Alex North," *Cue Sheet*, vol. 7, no. 1 (January, 1990), p. 32.

9. See Page Cook, "The Sound Track," *Films in Review*, vol. 15, no. 6 (June/July, 1964), p. 364.

10. As quoted by Stephen Farber, "Alex North and His Oscar Make Musical Movie History," *New York Times* (March 1986), p. 17.

11. See Tony Thomas, p. 189.

12. As quoted by Tony Thomas, *Film Score: The Art & Craft of Movie Music*, pp.189–190.

13. *Ibid.*, p. 190.

14. *Ibid.*, p. 191.

15. See more in William Darby and Jack Du Bois, pp. 414–415.

16. As quoted by Tony Thomas, *Film Score: The Art & Craft of Movie Music*, p. 190.

17. For more information on North's use of the Renaissance musical sources in *The Agony and the Ecstasy* refer to the article by Florella Orowan, "A Look at Alex North's Use of Historical Source music," *Film Music Notebook*, vol. 3, no. 1 (1977), pp. 9–14.

18. David Raksin, an interview with Alex North.

19. See North's comments in David Cloud and Leslie Zador, "Alex North Interview: The Missing Score for '2001,'" *Los Angeles Free Press*, vol. 7, no. 48 (November 27, 1970), p. 39.

20. *Ibid.*, p. 39.

21. See Joan Padrol, "Alex North: La Aventura del Gran Norte," p. 76.

22. See Rudy Behlemer, "Alex North on 'A Streetcar Named Desire,'" *Cue Sheet*, vol. 3, no. 3 (September, 1986), p. 37.

23. As quoted by Tony Thomas, *Film Score: The Art & Craft of Movie Music*, p. 191; see also David Cloud and Leslie Zador, "Alex North Interview…"; Donald Chase, *Film Making: The Collaborative Art*, Boston/Toronto: Little, Brown and Company, 1975, p. 275.

24. Different authors interpreted the idea of this theme in different ways. For more information see Robert Emmett Dolan, *Music in Modern Media…*, p. 96; Donald Chase, p. 287; George Burt, *The Art of Film Music*, pp. 33–34; William Darby and Jack Du Bois, p. 423; Page Cook, "The Sound Track," *Films in Review*, vol. 17, no. 7 (August/September, 1966), p. 441.

25. For more detailed comments on certain music cues from *Who's Afraid of Virginia Woolf?* refer to George Burt, *The Art of Film Music*, pp. 11–13, 33–35, 100–111 ("Moon," "Prelude," "Bergin" with musical examples), Mark Evans, *Soundtrack: The Music of the Movies*, pp. 214–215 ("Martha," "The Party's Over," "Colloquy").

26. See Mark Evans, *Soundtrack: The Music of the Movies*, p. 215.

27. From the personal interview with Steven North.

28. From the personal interview with Farley Granger.

29. From the personal interview with Sherle North.

30. As quoted by Christopher Palmer, "Film Music Profile: Alex North," *Crescendo International* (April, 1975), pp. 29, 32.

31. *Ibid.*, p. 32.

32. As published in Jerome Agel (ed.), *The Making of Kubrick's 2001*, pp. 198–199.

33. As quoted by David Cloud and Leslie Zador, "The Missing Score for '2001,'" *Los Angeles Free Press* (November 27, 1970), p. 42.

34. See Jerry Goldsmith, Matthew Peak and Robert Townson, "2001: Alex North's Odyssey," *Movie Collector*, vol. 1, no. 2 (November/December, 1993), p. 64.

35. See Pauline Finch-Durichen, "Celestial Symphony," *Kitchner-Waterloo Record* (February 24, 1994), D8.

36. See Page Cook, "The Sound Track," *Films in Review*, vol. 20, no. 1 (January, 1969), p. 48.

37. As quoted by Tony Thomas, *Film Score: The Art & Craft of Movie Music*, p. 190.

38. See Joan Padrol, "Alex North: La Aventura Del Gran Norte," p. 71.

39. See more in Florella Orowan, "A Look at Alex North's Use of Historical Source Music," pp. 12–13.

6. The Final Stage

1. As quoted by Steven Smith, "The Tenacious Alex North," *Los Angeles Times/Calendar* (March 23, 1986), p. 82.

2. As quoted by Fred Karlin, *Listening to Movies: The Film Lover's Guide to Film Music*, New York: Schirmer Books, p. 244.

3. See Irwin Bazelon, *Knowing the Score: Notes on Film Music* (an interview with Alex North), p. 218.

4. From the personal interview with Farley Granger.

5. From the personal interview with Arthur Miller.

6. As quoted by Donald Chase, *Film Making: The Collaborative Art*, p. 288.

7. See Joan Padrol, "Alex North: La Aventura del Gran Norte," p. 78.

8. From the personal interview with Farley Granger.

9. As published on the cover of the LP record (Citadel 7014), and the compact disc (Varèse Sarabande, 47341).

10. From the personal interview with Steven North.

11. See for more information the detailed review of the score by Page Cook, "The Sound

Track," *Films in Review*, vol. 25, no. 10 (December, 1974), p. 613.

12. See George Burt, *The Art of Film Music*, p. 242.

13. See David Kraft, "A Conversation with Alex North," *Soundtrack! The Collector's Quarterly*, vol. 4, no. 13 (March, 1985), p. 8.

14. As quoted by Steven Smith, "The Tenacious Alex North," *Los Angeles Times/Calendar* (March 23, 1986), p. 82.

15. As published in the notes for the compact disc release of the soundtrack of *Rich Man, Poor Man* (Varèse Sarabande, VSD-5423).

16. As quoted by Page Cook, "The Sound Track," *Films in Review*, vol. 31, no. 8 (October, 1980), p. 483.

17. *Ibid.*

18. *Ibid.*, p. 484.

19. *Ibid.*, p. 483.

20. As quoted by Page Cook, p. 484.

21. As quoted by Kevin Jackson, "Whistling Dixie," *Independent* (September 28, 1991), p. 31.

22. See Ken Sutak, "A 'Dragonslayer' Inquiry: From Two Heady Notes Toward Some Hard Questions About the Score," *Pro Musica Sana*, vol. 9, no. 4 — PMS 36 (Summer, 1982), p. 14.

23. As told by Annemarie North, Pacific Palisades, May 20, 1995; see also David Kraft, "A Conversation with Alex North," p. 6.

24. See John Fitzpatrick and William Finn, "'Dragonslayer': Two Views on Alex North's Most Ambitious Score in Years," *Pro Musica Sana*, vol. 9, no. 2 — PMS 34 (Summer, 1982), p. 3.

25. As quoted in the notes for the compact disc release of the soundtrack of *Dragonslayer* (SCSE CD-3).

26. See David Kraft, "A Conversation with Alex North," *Soundtrack! …*, p. 7.

27. As quoted in the notes for the compact disc release of the soundtrack of *Dragonslayer* (SCSE CD-3).

28. See Page Cook, "The Sound Track," *Films in Review* (April, 1988), p. 250.

29. See Jack Mathews, "Alex North's Troubles with Oscar," *Los Angeles Times — Calendar* (Sunday, April 10, 1988), p. 9.

30. From the personal interview with Arthur Miller.

31. From an interview of the author with Michael Fitzgerald, Los Angeles, August 19, 1995.

32. See Robert Townson's notes for the compact disc release of the soundtrack of *The Last Butterfly* (Varèse Sarabande, VSD-5287).

33. As quoted by Page Cook, "The Sound Track," *Films in Review*, vol. 37, no. 6/7 (June/July, 1986), p. 378.

34. From Huston's letter honoring Alex North's Academy Award for lifetime achievement, 1986.

7. *A Streetcar Named Desire*

1. See Elia Kazan, *A Life*, New York: Anchor Books, Doubleday, 1988, p. 383.

2. As quoted in Gene D. Phillips, *The Films of Tennessee Williams*, Philadelphia: Art Alliance Press, 1980, p. 75.

3. As quoted by Elia Kazan, *A Life*, p. 329.

4. From the letter Williams wrote to his agent Audrey Wood in August, 1947. As quoted by Brenda Murphy, *Tennessee Williams and Elia Kazan*, Cambridge University Press, 1992, p. 19.

5. As quoted by Elia Kazan, *A Life*, p. 330.

6. Compare Brenda Murphy, p. 20, and Gene D. Phillips, p. 75. Murphy quotes Williams from a 1981 interview in which he describes his sister's love affair with a young man, while Phillips quotes Williams from a *New York Times* article where he explains that the personality of his aunt is similar in many aspects to Blanche's character.

7. See Jeff Young, *Kazan, The Master Director Discusses His Films: Interviews with Elia Kazan*, New York: Newmarket Press, 1999, pp. 83–84.

8. See Elia Kazan, *A Life*, pp. 353, 733.

9. Most of the Broadway cast was hired to do the film, including Marlon Brando, Kim Hunter, and Karl Malden. Only Jessica Tandy was replaced with Vivien Leigh because the producers felt that the film should have at least one film star who would draw the audience into the theater, and Leigh already knew the part from the London production of the play.

10. Some authors credit North with the music of the stage version of *Streetcar*. Ken Sutak mentioned in his article "The Return of 'A Streetcar Named Desire'" that North had done some very beautiful "things" with music for Kazan in the *Streetcar* and *Salesman* stage productions (*Pro Musica Sana*, vol. 3, no. 4 , Winter, 1974/75, p. 13). Also, Brenda Murphy stated in her book *Tennessee Williams and Elia Kazan* that North had been involved with the project from the beginning of the stage production, pp. 18, 23. But North did not compose the incidental score. Engel Lehman was the musical advisor in the stage production. Only in one book, *Tennessee Williams and Friends: An Informal Biography* by Gilbert Maxwell, is there a reference that Paul Bowles provided the backstage music for the play (Cleveland/New York: The World Publishing Company, 1965, p. 120).

11. From the transcript of Bill Tusher's radio interview with Alex North for KFWB.

12. See Tennessee Williams, *A Streetcar Named Desire*, A Signet Book, New American Library, 1947, p. 18.

13. From the Tusher interview for KFWB.

14. As quoted by David Ewen, *American Composer Today: A Biographical and Critical Guide*, p. 180.

15. See Rudy Behlemer, p. 36.

16. As quoted by Tony Thomas, *Music for the Movies*, South Brunswick, New Jersey: A.S. Barnes and Company, 1973, p. 182.

17. Christopher Palmer uses the terms "realistic and commentative jazz" to describe the difference between source music and North's original music in jazz style used in dramatic context. In *The Composer in Hollywood*, London/New York: Marion Boyars, 1990, p. 295–296.

18. As quoted by Frank Lewin, "A Streetcar Named Desire," *Film Music*, XI/3 (January/February, 1952), p. 13.

19. See more about the objective and subjective music in *Streetcar* in the essay "Realism and Theatricalism" by Mary Ann Corrigan, published in *Modern Critical Interpretations: Tennessee Williams's A Streetcar Named Desire* (ed. Harold Bloom), New York/Philadelphia: Chelsea House Publishers, 1988, pp. 52–53; also see Christopher Palmer's comments on realistic and commentative music, pp. 295–296.

20. See detailed description of Kazan's treatment of the music in the play in Brenda Murphy's book, *ibid.*, pp. 28–31.

21. See Rudy Behlemer, p. 36.

22. *Ibid.*, p. 37.

23. See David Kraft, p. 5.

24. See Rudy Behlemer, p. 37.

25. See William Darby and Jack Du Bois, *American Film Music: Major Composers, Techniques, Trends, 1915–1990*, Jefferson, North Carolina: McFarland & Company, Inc., 1990, p. 406.

26. See Ken Sutak, "The Return of 'A Streetcar Named Desire,'" pp. 13–14.

27. This is probably one of the most popular quotes by Alex North. It is cited in many books and articles. North's quote is used here as it is given in the article written by Frank Lewin, p. 13.

28. See more in Maurice Yacowar, *Tennessee Williams and Film*, New York: Frederick Ungar Publishing, 1977, pp. 17–20.

29. See more in Gene Phillips, pp. 67–68.

30. See more in Maurice Yacowar, p. 17; also Gene Phillips, pp. 69–70.

31. As quoted by Les Wedman, "Brando Is a Sexy Sax," *Vancouver Sun* (Friday, May 4, 1973), p. 10.

32. See Tennessee Williams, *A Streetcar Named Desire*, p. 55.

33. *Ibid.*, p. 56.

34. See Ross Care, "Hot Spell: Alex North's Film Score for 'A Streetcar Named Desire,'" in *Performing Arts Annual — 1989*, Washington, D.C.: Library of Congress, 1990, p. 12.

35. See Brenda Murphy, p. 41.

36. See David Cloud and Leslie Zador, "Alex North Interview: The Missing Score for '2001,'" *Los Angeles Press*, vol. 7, no. 48 (November 27, 1970), p. 39.

37. See more in Maurice Yacowar, p. 20.

38. As quoted by Gene Phillips, p. 84.

39. For more information and analyses of the score for *A Streetcar Named Desire* refer to the following selected sources:

Books: Christopher Palmer, *The Composer in Hollywood*, London/New York: Marion Boyars, 1990, pp. 295–300.

Tony Thomas, *Film Score: The Art & Craft of Movie Music*, Burbank, California: Riverwood Press, 1991, p. 185.

William Darby and Jack Du Bois, *American Film Music: Major Composers, Techniques, Trends, 1915–1990*, Jefferson, North Carolina: McFarland & Company, Inc., 1990, pp. 402–406.

Mark Evans, *Soundtrack: The Music of the Movies*, New York: Hopkinson and Blake, 1975, pp. 121–122, 225, 254.

Roy M. Prendergast, *Film Music, A Neglected Art: A Critical Study of Music in Films*, New York/London: W. W. Norton & Co., 1977, pp. 104–107.

Periodicals: Ross Care, "Alex North's Film Score For 'A Streetcar Named Desire,'" *Performing Arts Annual* (1989), pp. 4–23.

Ken Sutak, "The Return of 'A Streetcar named Desire,'" *Pro Musica Sana*, vol. 3, no. 1 (Spring, 1974), pp. 4–10; vol. 3, no. 4 (Winter, 1974/75), pp. 9–15; vol. 4, no. 3 (1976), pp. 13–18.

Frank Lewin, "A Street Car Named Desire," *Film Music*, vol. 11, no. 3 (January/February, 1952), pp. 13–20.

Interview: Rudy Behlemer, "Alex North on 'A Streetcar Named Desire,'" *Cue Sheet*, vol. 3, no. 3 (September, 1986), pp. 36–38.

40. See Ken Sutak, p. 13.

41. See Tony Thomas, *Music for the Movies*, p. 181.

42. From the personal interview with Arthur Miller.

8. *Spartacus*

1. See more in *Stanley Kubrick: Biography* by John Baxter, New York: Carroll & Graf Publishers, Inc., 1997, pp. 124–126.

2. As quoted by Norman Kagan, *The Cinema*

of Stanley Kubrick, New York: Holt, Rinehart and Winston, 1972, p. 69.

3. See Norman Kagan, p. 80.

4. As quoted in the booklet of the soundtrack release, SVC Records (SVC 5994 [1–2]).

5. As quoted by David Cloud and Leslie Zador, "Alex North Interview: The Missing Score for '2001,'" *Los Angeles Free Press,* vol. 7, no. 48 (November 27, 1970), p. 39.

6. As quoted by Christopher Palmer, "Film Music Profile: Alex North," *Crescendo International* (April, 1975), p. 29.

7. As quoted in the article "Film Scoring a Joy for North" (signed by S.L.S. [*sic*]), *Philadelphia Inquirer* (October 2, 1960), p. 2.

8. As quoted by Christopher Palmer, *ibid.*, p. 29.

9. As quoted by Joel Reisner and Bruce Kane, "An Interview with Alex North," *Cinema,* vol. 5, no. 4 (December, 1969), p. 43.

10. As quoted by J. D. Callaghan, "Music for the Movies—the Unsung Artists," *Detroit Free Press* (September 25, 1960).

11. As quoted by Donald Chase, *Film Making: The Collaborative Art,* Boston/Toronto: Little, Brown and Company, 1975, p. 286.

12. As suggested by Kubrick's biographer John Baxter, p. 147.

13. As quoted in the booklet of the soundtrack release, SVC Records (SVC 5994 [1–2]).

14. As quoted by Ernie Schier, "Ex-Philadelphian Sets 'Spartacus' to Music," *Evening Bulletin,* Philadelphia (September 29, 1960), F4.

15. As quoted in the article "Film Scoring a Joy for North," p. 2.

16. See Jay Robert Nash and Stanley Ralph Ross, *The Motion Picture Guide,* Chicago: Cinebooks, 1985, p. 3058.

17. As quoted by John Baxter, p. 151.

18. See Sara Hamilton, "'Spartacus' Big; Called Great Film," *Los Angeles Examiner* (October 20, 1960), Sec. 2.

19. *Ibid.*

9. *The Misfits*

1. From Huston's letter honoring Alex North's Academy Award for lifetime achievement, 1986.

2. See John H. Richardson, " Huston's Legacy is One of Respect," *Daily News* (December 15, 1987), p. 15.

3. See David Kraft, "Alex North: The Master Speaks," *Hollywood Reporter,* vol. 300, no. 41 (January 22, 1988), S-57.

4. From an interview of the author with Annemarie North, Pacific Palisades, May 20, 1995.

5. From the an interview of the author with Michael Fitzgerald, Los Angeles, August 18–19, 1995.

6. See Tony Thomas, *Film Score: The Art & Craft of Movie Music,* p. 192.

7. By the time of the film's release, Clark Gable was dead of a heart attack. A year and a half later, Marilyn Monroe committed suicide, and five years later Montgomery Clift was dead.

8. See *Film Scripts Three,* edited by G. P. Garrett, O. B. Hardison, Jr., J. R. Gelfman, New York: Irvington Publishers, Inc., 1972, p. 203.

9. As quoted by William Nolan, *John Huston: King Rebel,* Los Angeles: Sherbourne Press, Inc., 1965, p. 180.

10. For complete cast and credits refer to *Film Scripts Three,* edited by G. P. Garrett, O. B. Hardison Jr., J. R. Gelfman, p. 204.

11. As quoted by William Nolan, *John Huston: King Rebel,* pp. 183–184.

12. See Lawrence Grobel, *The Hustons,* New York: Avon Books, 1989. p. 709.

13. As quoted by James Goode, *The Story of "The Misfits,"* Indianapolis/New York: The Bobbs-Merrill Company, Inc., 1963, pp. 318–319.

14. See George Burt, *The Art of Film Music,* p. 131.

15. Source music is applied in many scenes of the film, as for instance, the tune in a bar entitled "Rendez Vous," the dance "Humpty Dumpty" in Guido's house, "Rockabilly Boogie" from the betting scene in a bar before the rodeo, the music from the "Galop di Rodeo," and others.

16. As quoted by George Burt, p. 130.

17. As quoted by James Goode, p. 319.

18. As quoted by George Burt, p. 131.

19. See James Goode, p. 320.

20. See Irwin Bazelon, *Knowing the Score: Notes on Film Music* (an interview with Alex North), p. 222.

21. See Joan Padrol, "Alex North: La Aventura del Gran Norte," *Encuentro International de Musica de Cine* (1991), p. 63.

22. See Irwin Bazelon, p. 80.

23. See James Powers, "'The Misfits': Provocative, Stimulating Production," *Hollywood Reporter* (Wednesday, February 1, 1961), p. 3.

24. See Justin Gilbert, "Gable, MM Spark 'Misfits,'" *New York Mirror* (Thursday, February 2, 1961).

25. See Tube [*sic*], "The Misfits," *Daily Variety* (Wednesday, February 1, 1961), pp. 3, 16.

26. See Lawrence Grobel, *The Hustons,* p. 500; see also Daniël Mangodt, "An Interview with Steven and Anne-Marie North," *Soundtrack,* vol. 10, no. 40 (December, 1991), p. 31.

10. *Under the Volcano*

1. See Vincent Canby, "Huston's 'Volcano' Pays Homage to the Novel," *The New York Times* (Sunday, June 24, 1984), sec. 2, p. 1.

2. Compare Lawrence Grobel, *The Hustons*, p. 744.

3. See *ibid.*, p. 745.

4. Compare Stephen Spender, Introduction to Malcolm Lowry's *Under the Volcano*, pp. XX–XXI.

5. As quoted by Louis Gianetti, *Understanding Movies*, Englewood Cliffs, New Jersey: Prentice-Hall, 1990, p. 364.

6. As quoted by Lawrence Grobel, *The Hustons*, p. 746.

7. See David Sterritt, "'Under the Volcano': A Model of How to Film a Book," *Christian Science Monitor* (July 5, 1984), p. 25.

8. See Arthur Knight, "Smoldering 'Volcano': Huston Landmark of Great Filmmaking," *Hollywood Reporter* (June 18, 1984), p. 9.

9. See Sheila Benson, "Under the Volcano," *Los Angeles Times* (July 6, 1984), part 6, p. 1.

10. See Vincent Canby, "Huston's 'Volcano' Pays Homage to The Novel," p. 19.

11. See Stephen Spender, Introduction to Lowry's *Under the Volcano*, p. XXX.

12. See Sheila Benson, "Under the Volcano," p. 1.

13. As quoted by Fred Karlin and Rayburn Wright, *On the Track: A Guide to Contemporary Film Scoring*, New York: Schirmer Books, 1990, p. 273.

14. See Arthur Knight, "Smoldering 'Volcano': Huston Landmark of Great Filmmaking," p. 9.

15. See Vincent Canby, "Huston's 'Volcano' Pays Homage to The Novel," p. 19.

16. See Arthur Knight, "Smoldering 'Volcano': Huston Landmark of Great Filmmaking," p. 9.

17. See Mike Snell, "Under the Volcano," *Quirk's Reviews* (June, 1984), p. 16.

18. As quoted in Fred Karlin and Rayburn Wright, *On the Track…*, pp. 273, 275.

19. *Ibid.*, p. 273.

20. Compare Joan Padrol, "Alex North: La Aventura del Gran Norte," *Encuentro International de Musica de Cine* (1991), p. 72.

21. *Ibid.*

22. See Joan Padrol, "Alex North: Un clásico de la banda sonora" [an interview with Alex North], *Dirigido por…* (June, 1989), p. 53.

23. See Fred Karlin and Rayburn Wright, *On the Track…*, p. 273.

24. As quoted by Lawrence Grobel, *The Hustons*, p. 746.

25. See Fred Karlin and Rayburn Wright, *ibid.*, p. 182.

26. See Sheila Benson, "Under the Volcano," *Los Angeles Times* (Friday, July 6, 1984), part 6, p. 13.

27. See Arthur Knight, " Smoldering 'Volcano': Huston Landmark of Great Filmmaking," *Hollywood Reporter* (Monday, June 18, 1984), p. 9.

28. See David Sterritt, "'Under the Volcano': A Model of How to Film a Book," *Christian Science Monitor* (Thursday, July 5, 1984), p. 25.

29. See Charles Champlin, "Alex North: A Score for Reticence," *Los Angeles Times* (Thursday, August 23, 1984), sec. 6, p. 8.

11. *Prizzi's Honor*

1. See Stephanie von Buchau, "Film," *Pacific Sun — San Francisco* (June, 1985).

2. See Pauline Kael, "The Current Cinema: Ripeness," *The New Yorker* (July 1, 1985), p. 84.

3. See Sheila Benson, "To Love, Honor and Va Voom," *Los Angeles Times* (June 14, 1985), p. 1.

4. Robert Osborne, an interview with Marcia Brandwynne (regarding *Prizzi's Honor*) for KTTV, Channel 11, News (December 6, 1985, at 10:40 p.m.).

5. See Lawrence Grobel, *The Hustons*, p. 762; see also J. H. Richardson, "Huston's Legacy is One of Respect," *Daily News* (December 15, 1987), p. 15.

6. From an interview of the author with the composer and musicologist Fred Steiner, Los Angeles, September 16, 1995.

7. *Ibid.*

8. *Ibid.*

9. See Michael Walsh, "Prizzi's Opera," *Film Comment* (October, 1985), p. 6.

10. *Ibid.*

11. See William Darby and Jack Du Bois, *American Film Music: Major Composers, Techniques, Trends, 1915–1990*, p. 421.

12. As quoted by Fred Karlin and Rayburn Wright, *On the Track: A Guide to Contemporary Film Scoring*, p. 513.

13. See Mosco Carner, *Puccini: A Critical Biography*, New York: Holmes & Meier Publishers, 1977, p. 445.

14. *Ibid.*, p.453.

15. *Ibid.*

16. See Spike Hughes, *Famous Puccini Operas*, New York: Dover Publications, Inc., 1972, p. 198.

17. *Ibid.*, p. 200.

18. See Mosco Carner, *Puccini: A Critical Biography*, p. 305.

19. From the personal interview with Fred Steiner.

20. See William Darby and Jack Du Bois, p. 418.

21. See Fred Karlin and Rayburn Wright, p. 513.

22. See William Darby and Jack Du Bois, p. 420.

23. *Ibid.*, p. 418.

24. *Ibid.*, p. 420.

25. See Michael Walsh, "Prizzi's Opera," *Film Comment*, p. 6.

26. From the personal interview with Fred Steiner.

27. *Ibid.*

28. See Sheila Benson, "To Love, Honor and Va Voom," *Los Angeles Times* (June 14, 1985), p.10.

29. See David Ansen, "Hit Man Meets Hit Woman," *Newsweek* (June 17,1985), p. 89.

30. See Arthur Knight, "Prizzi's Honor," *Hollywood Reporter* (June 5, 1985), p. 12.

31. See Pauline Kael, "The Current Cinema: Ripeness," *New Yorker* (July 1, 1985), p. 85.

32. See Michael Walsh, "Prizzi's Opera, *Film Comment*, p. 5.

33. See Vincent Canby, "Prizzi's Honor," *New York Times* (June 14, 1985), C8.

34. From the letter that William Schuman wrote to Alex North, June 28, 1985.

35. From the personal interview with Fred Steiner.

36. From the letter that Lamont Johnson wrote to the Academy of Motion Picture Arts and Sciences, October 27, 1985.

37. See Robert Osborne, "Rambling Reporter," *Hollywood Reporter* (January 16, 1986), p. 7.

38. As quoted by Robert Osborne.

Bibliography

Monographs

Agel, Jerome (ed). *The Making of Kubrick's 2001.* New York: A Signet Book, New American Library, 1970, pp. 198–199.

Bazelon, Irwin. *Knowing the Score: Notes on Film Music.* New York: Van Nostrand Reinhold Company, 1975, pp. 80, 95, 100, 106, 111, 122, 142–144; 214–223 (an interview); 308–311, 330–332, 342–344 (music excerpts).

Beguiristain, Mario Eugenio. "Theatrical Realism: An American Film Style of the Fifties." Ph.D. Dissertation, University of Southern California, 1978.

Bloom, Julius (ed). *The Year in American Music, 1946–47.* New York: Allen, Towne & Heath, Inc., 1947, pp. 27, 78, 106, 193, 261.

Burt, George. *The Art of Film Music: Special Emphasis on Hugo Friedhofer, Alex North, David Raksin, Leonard Rosenman.* Boston: Northeastern University Press, 1994, pp. 3, 11–12, 29, 33–34, 59–60, 62–63, 67–68, 71, 100–07, 126, 130–132, 211, 233–235, 239, 240, 242; 13, 29, 34, 60–62, 63, 71–73, 107–111, 133–142 (music excerpts).

Campbell, Russell. *Cinema Strikes Back: Radical Filmmaking in the United States, 1930–42.* Ann Arbor, Michigan: UMI Research Press, 1982, pp. 168, 194, 220.

Chase, Donald. *Film Making: The Collaborative Art.* Boston/Toronto: Little, Brown and Company, 1975, pp. 275–291.

Copland, Aaron, and Vivian Perlis. *Copland: 1900 through 1942.* New York: St. Martin's/Marek, 1984, p. 336.

_____. *Copland since 1943.* New York: St. Martin's Press, 1989, p. 7.

Darby, William, and Jack Du Bois. *American Film Music: Major Composers, Techniques, Trends, 1915–1990.* Jefferson, North Carolina: McFarland & Company, Inc., 1990, pp. 398–424.

Dick, Bernard F. *Hellman in Hollywood.* London/Toronto: Associated University Presses, 1982, p. 45.

Dolan, Robert Emmett. *Music in Modern Media: Techniques in Tape, Disc and Film Recording, Motion Picture and Television Scoring and Electronic Music.* New York: G. Schirmer, 1967, pp. 96–97.

Evans, Mark. *Soundtrack: The Music of the Movies.* New York: Hopkinson and Blake, 1975, pp. 121–123, 136–137, 146, 148–150, 214–215, 225, 243–244, 254.

Gertner, Richard. *Motion Picture Almanac.* New York/London: Quigley Publ. Co., 1982, p. 194.

Goode, James. *The Story of The Misfits.* Indianapolis/New York: The Bobbs-Merrill–Company, Inc., 1963, pp. 315–323.

Gordon, Eric A. *Mark the Music: The Life and Work of Marc Blitzstein.* New York: St. Martin's Press, 1989, pp. 99, 169, 185, 212, 297, 553.

Grobel, Lawrence. *The Hustons.* New York: Avon Books, 1989, pp. 500, 714, 758, 762, 777.

Karlin, Fred. *Listening to Movies: The Film Lover's Guide to Film Music.* New York: Schirmer Books, 1994, pp. 293–294.

_____, and Rayburn Wright. *On the Track: A Guide to Contemporary Film Scoring.* New York: Schirmer Books, 1990, pp. 14, 44, 77, 132, 162, 171, 182, 183–184, 186, 238–239, 273–275, 313, 494, 503, 513.

Limbacher, James L. (ed.). *Film Music: From*

Violins to Video. Metuchen, New Jersey: The Scarecrow Press, Inc., 1974.

McCarty, John. *The Films of John Huston.* Secaucus, New Jersey: Citadel Press, 1987, p. 232.

Miller, Arthur. *'Salesman' in Beijing.* New York: Viking Press, 1983, pp. 53–55.

Murphy, Brenda. *Tennessee Williams and Elia Kazan.* Cambridge: Cambridge University Press, 1992, pp. 18, 23, 24, 30.

Padrol, Joan. *Encuentro International de Música de Cine.* Sevilla: Luis Cernuda Fundation, 1991, pp. 55–81.

Palmer, Christopher. *The Composer in Hollywood.* London/New York: Marion Boyars, 1990, pp. 294–300.

Prendergast, Roy M. *Film Music, A Neglected Art: A Critical Study of Music in Films.* New York/London: W. W. Norton & Co., 1977, pp. 104–107.

Reis, Claire R. *Composers in America: Biographical Sketches of Contemporary Composers with a Record of Their Works.* New York: Macmillan Company, 1947, pp. 270–271.

Scharf, Walter. *The History of Film Scoring.* Studio City: Cinema Songs, Inc., 1988, pp. 62, 78.

Siegmeister, Elie. *The Music Lover's Handbook.* New York: William Morrow and Company, 1943, pp. 769–771.

Skiles, Marlin. *Music Scoring for TV and Motion Picture.* Blue Ridge Summit, PA.: Tab Books, 1976, pp. 248–253 (an interview).

"Speaker at N. Y. Herald Tribune 1930–1945: Alex North." In: *New York Herald Tribune. Annual Forum, 1946.* New York: N. Y. Tribune, 1946, pp. 7, 263.

Steinbeck, John. *Viva Zapata!* New York: Viking Press, 1975, pp. 140–141.

Sutak, Ken. *The Great Motion Picture Soundtrack Robbery: An Analysis of Copyright Protection.* Hamden, Conn.: Archon Books, 1976, pp. 57, 62, 66, 82.

Thomas, Tony. *Film Score: The Art & Craft of Movie Music.* Burbank, California: Riverwood Press, 1991, pp. 182–194.

_____. *Music for the Movies.* South Brunswick, New Jersey: A. S. Barnes and Company, 1973, pp. 179–185.

Warren, Larry. *Anna Sokolow: The Rebellious Spirit.* Princeton, New Jersey: Princeton Book Company Pub., 1991, pp. 36–39, 50–60, 69–70, 72, 74, 76–77, 82, 83, 86–87; music by, 47–48, 67–68, 73–74, 102, 104–105, 109.

Wayland, Drew. *Dragonslayer.* New York: Del Ray, 1981.

Reference Works

ASCAP Biographical Dictionary. 4th ed. New York: R. R. Bowker Company, 1980, p. 373.

Ewen, David. *American Composer Today: A Biographical and Critical Guide.* New York: H. W. Wilson Company, 1949, pp. 179–180.

Kay, Ernest (ed.). *International Who's Who in Music and Musicians' Directory.* 11th ed. Cambridge, England: Melrose Press, 1988, p. 676.

Limbacher, James L. *Keeping Score: Film Music 1972–1979.* Metuchen, New Jersey: Scarecrow Press, Inc., 1981.

_____, and Stephen H. Wright. *Keeping Score: Film and Television Music, 1980–1988.* Metuchen, New Jersey: Scarecrow Press, Inc., 1991.

Manvell, Roger, and Jacobs Lewis. *The International Encyclopedia of Film.* New York: Crown Publ., 1972, p. 374.

McCarty, Clifford. *Film Composers in America : A Checklist of Their Work.* New York: Da Capo Press, 1972.

McGill, Raymond (ed.). *Notable Names in the American Theatre.* Clifton, New Jersey: James T. White & Company, 1976, pp. 1019–1020.

Nash, Jay Robert, and Stanley Ralph Ross. *The Motion Picture Guide.* Chicago: Cinebooks, 1985.

Palmer, Christopher. "North, Alex." In: *The New Grove Dictionary of Music and Musicians* (edited by Stanley Sadie). London: Macmillan Publishers, Ltd., 1980, p. 286.

Press, Jaques Cattell (ed.). *Who's Who in American Music: Classical First Edition.* New York: R. R. Bowker Company, 1983, p. 319.

Sigoloff, Marc. *The Films of the Seventies: A Filmography of American, British and Canadian Films, 1970–1979.* Jefferson, North Carolina: McFarland & Company, Inc., Publishers, 1984.

Smith, Steven C. (ed.). "North Alex." (Filmography). In: *Film Composers Guide.* Beverly Hills: Lone Eagle Publishing Co., 1992, p. 116.

Vinton, John (ed.). *Dictionary of Contemporary Music.* New York: E. P. Dutton & Co., Inc., 1974, pp. 517, 544.

Wescott, Steven D. *A Comprehensive Bibliography of Music for Film and Television.* Detroit: Information Coordinators, 1985.

Who's Who in America. Chicago: Marquis, 1982/83, p. 2486.

Newspaper Articles

A. V. B. "C. I. O. Chorus: Alex North's 'Morning Star' Featured in Concert." *New York Herald Tribune,* vol. 107 (Monday, May 26, 1947), p. 17.

_____. "Modern Music Recital by Metropolitan School." *New York Herald Tribune,* vol. 108 (Monday, January 10, 1949), p. 13.

A. W. P. "Prokofiev Choruses Sung in Town Hall." *New York Sun* (Monday, March 17, 1947).

Aaronson, Charles S. "Spartacus." *Product Digest Section* (Saturday, October 15, 1960).

"Alex North." *Limelight* (Thursday, May 4, 1961).

"Alex North a Busy Man." *New York Times* (August 13, 1949).

"Alex North, Composer, Dies at 80; Had 40-Year Hollywood Career." *New York Times*, vol. 140 (Wednesday, September 11, 1991), A 17 (N), B 12 (L).

"Alex North Teaches at Krueger School." *Ridgefield Press* — Ridgefield, Conn. (Thursday, June 18, 1942).

"Anna Sokolow, Alex North." *TAC* (March 1, 1940), pp. 9, 12.

Atkinson, Brooks. "First Night at the Theatre." *New York Times*, vol. 99 (Thursday, February 2, 1950), p. 30 (L+).

_____. "The New Play: Arnold Sundgaard's 'The Great Campaign.'" *The New York Times*, vol. 96 (Tuesday, April 1, 1947), p. 33 (L++).

Benson, Sheila. "Huston's Graceful Farewell Stirs Emotions in 'The Dead.'" *Los Angeles Times* (Thursday, December 17, 1987), part 6, pp. 1, 14.

_____. "Nicholson Triumphant in 'Prizzi's.'" *Atlantic City Press* (Sunday, June 16, 1985).

_____. "To Love, Honor and Va Voom." *Los Angeles Times/Calendar* (Friday, June 14, 1985), part 6, pp. 1, 10.

_____. "'Under the Volcano.'" *Los Angeles Times* (Friday, July 6, 1984), part 6, pp. 1, 13.

Biancolli, Louis. "Holm Group Portrays Variety." *World Telegram* (Tuesday, March 18, 1941).

_____. "'Streetcar' Lives Again in Dance." *New York World/Telegram and Sun* (Tuesday, December 9, 1952).

Bradley, Jeff. "Epic '2001' Sound Track Bumped an Original Score." *The Sunday Denver Post* (Sunday, October 31, 1993), 1 E, 8 E.

Briggs, John. "Records: Works Scriabin and Ives." *The New York Times*, vol. 103 (Sunday, May 23, 1954) sec. 2, p. 6 (X).

Brookhouser, Frank. "Chester Man Writes Movie Sound Tracks." *Evening Bulletin* — Philadelphia (Thursday, September 2, 1965), p. 23.

_____. "Man About Town." *Evening Bulletin* — Philadelphia (Wednesday, January 3, 1962), p. 20.

C. H. "Joan Slessinger heard." *New York Times*, vol. 97 (Monday, September 22, 1947), p. 29 (L).

Callaghan, J. D. "Music for the Movies — the Unsung Artists." *Detroit Free Press* (Sunday, September 25, 1960).

Canby, Vincent. "Film: 'Prizzi's Honor' Starring Jack Nicholson." *The New York Times*, vol. 134 (Friday, June 14, 1985), C 8.

Carmack, Michael. "'Shanks' — His 12th Oscar Nomination: North Battling the Big Guys." *Los Angeles Hearld Examiner* (Sunday, March 16, 1975), E-5, E-6.

Carroll, Harrison. "'Streetcar' is Oscar-Bait." *Los Angeles Evening Herald & Express*, vol. 81, no. 152 (Wednesday, September 19, 1951), B 4.

Carroll, Kathleen. "The Dead." *Daily News* — New York (Thursday, December 17, 1987).

_____. "'Spartacus': Glory, Gore of Ancient Rome." *Los Angeles Herald & Express*, vol. 90, no. 178 (Thursday, October 20, 1960), B 4.

Champlin, Charles. "Alex North: A Score for Reticence." *Los Angeles Times*, vol. 103 (Thursday, August 23, 1984), sec. 6, pp. 1, 8.

_____. "Fundamentalist Fever in 'Blood.'" *Los Angeles Times* (Wednesday, December 12, 1979), part 4, pp. 1, 30.

"CIO Chorus Gives Its First Major Concert at Town Hall Next Saturday Night." *New York Times*, vol. 96 (Sunday, May 18, 1947), sec. 2, p. 7 (X).

Clark, Mike. "Prizzi's Is Mobbed with Prize Talent." *USA Today/Life* (Friday, June 14, 1985), D1.

Cloud, David, and Leslie Zador. "Alex North Interview: The Missing Score for '2001.'" *Los Angeles Free Press*, vol. 7, no. 48 (Friday, November 27, 1970), pp. 39, 42.

Coe, Richard L. "One on the Aisle: A Composer of His Time." *Washington Post*, 83rd year, no. 297 (Tuesday, September 27, 1960), B 6.

_____. "One on the Aisle: 'Salesman' Arrives on Ontario Screen." *Washington Post* (Thursday, March 6, 1952), p. 19 (A).

Cohn, Lawrence. "'2001': A Space CD." *New York Post* (Wednesday, September 1, 1993), p. 21.

"Composer Sends Blessings From Camp." *Hartford Times* (April 12, 1943).

Crowther, Bosley. "North to Compose for 'Cleopatra.'" *New York Times*, vol. 111 (Wednesday, May 2, 1962), p. 30 (C).

_____. "Screen: John Huston's 'The Misfits.'" *New York Times*, vol. 110 (Thursday, February 2, 1961), p. 24 (L).

_____. "Screen: 'Spartacus' Enters the Arena." *New York Times*, vol. 110 (Friday, October 7, 1960), p. 28 (L).

Di Nardo, Tom. "Film Giant North, 81, Knew the Score." *Philadelphia Daily News* (Wednesday, September 11, 1991), p. 39.

_____. "2001: The Original Score." *Philadelphia Daily News* (Tuesday, October 19, 1993), p. 38.

Dreyer, Benjamin. "'The Dead.'" *Windi City Times/Entertainment* (Thursday, December 17, 1987), pp. 15, 16.

Durgin, Cyrus. "Music for 'Spartacus,' North's Hollywood Peak." *Boston Globe* (October, 1960).

E. L. H. "The Dance." [Anna Sokolow.] *Boston Herald* (Thursday, May 7, 1942).

"Famous Composer Stationed In Camp." *Camp Robinson News* (Friday, February 19, 1943).

Farber, Stephen. "Alex North and His Oscar Make Musical Movie History." *New York Times* (March, 1986), pp. 17–18.

Finch-Durichen, Pauline. "Celestial Symphony."

Kitchener-Waterloo Record (Thursday, February 24, 1994), D 8.

Flynn, Hazel. "Top Cast Is 'Spartacus' Magnet." *Beverly Hills Citizen* (Thursday, October 20, 1960).

Folkart, Burt A. "Alex North, 81, Prolific Composer of Film Scores, Dies." *Los Angeles TImes,* vol. 110 (Tuesday, September 10, 1991), B 1.

Freedley, George. "The Stage Today." *The Morning Telegraph* (Tuesday, April 1, 1947).

Gaghan, Jerry. "Score Takes Spartian Effort." *Philadelphia Daily News* (Thursday, October 6, 1960).

Gale, Joseph. "The Spotlight." *The Arkansas Gazette*— Little Rock (Friday, February 26, 1943).

Gaver, Jack. "Along the Great White Way." *Daily News*— Los Angeles (Friday, December 12, 1952), p. 37.

_____. "Conductor Finds Background Music for TV Exacting Job." *Argus*— Rock Island, Ill (October 26, 1953).

Gilbert, Justin. "Alex North: Daring Composer." *New York Mirror* (Sunday, October 9, 1960), p. 68.

_____. "Gable, MM Spark 'Misfits.'" *New York Mirror* (Thursday, February 2, 1961).

_____. "'Spartacus,' Gory Spectacle." *New York Mirror* (Friday, October 7, 1960).

Gill, Frank P. "Little Glory for Man Who Make Movie Music." *Detroit Sunday Times* (Sunday, October 2, 1960), B 7.

Guernsey, Otis L. Jr. "Sundgaard Play: 'The Great Campaign' Presented at the Princess Theater." *New York Herald Tribune,* vol. 106 (Monday, March 31, 1947), p. 15.

H. C. S. "Joan Slessinger Heard in Town Hall." *New York Sun* (Monday, September 22, 1947).

H. T. "Bernstein Leads Three Premieres." *New York Times,* vol.96 (Tuesday, November 19, 1946), p. 40 (L++).

Hague, Robert A. "Goodman Is Soloist with Bernstein Band." *PM* (November 20, 1946).

Hamilton, Sara. "'Spartacus' Big; Called Great Film." *Los Angeles Examiner* (Thursday, October 20, 1960), sec. 2, p. 6.

Harmetz, Aljean. "Oscars Go to 'Out of Africa' and Its Director, Sydney Pollack." [1986 Academy Awards.] *New York Times,* vol. 135 (Tuesday, March 25, 1986), pp. 20 (N), C 15.

Harrison, Jay S. "Writing Film Scores Is a Bed of Thorns." *New York Herald Tribune,* vol. 120 (Sunday, October 30, 1960), sec. 4, p. 6.

Hilliard, William. "In the Groove." *Sunday Oregonian* (Sunday, October 30, 1960).

Holmberg, Michael. "Alex North Swings West to Hit the Real Jackpot." *Pittsburgh Press* (Thursday, September 29, 1960).

Hughes, Elinor. "'Spartacus' a Challenge: Film Composers Fail to Get Due Recognition, North

Says." *The Boston Herald* (Friday, November 11, 1960).

J. S. H. "Philharmonic Performs for Children Under Nine." *New York Herald Tribune* (October 19, 1947).

Jackson, Kevin. "Whistling Dixie." *Independent* (Saturday, September 28, 1991), p. 31.

Kendall, Raymond. "Saga of Hollywood Music: North Composes for Stage, Screen." *Mirror News*— Los Angeles (Monday, October 12, 1959), part 2, p. 5.

Kisselgoff, Anna. "Dance: Harlem Troupe Performs 'Streetcar.'" *New York Times,* vol. 131 (Saturday, January 16, 1982), pp. 14 (N), 11 (LC).

Krauss, David. "'Prizzi's Honor': A Miasma of Blood, Love and Money." *Gazette*— Greenwich, Connecticut (Thursday, June 20, 1985), pp. 9, 17.

Kronenberger, Louis. "A Folk Play with Music and Political Meaning." *PM Daily*— New York, vol. 7, no. 246 (Tuesday, April 1, 1947), p. 16.

Lawson, Kyle. "Events." *Phoenix Gazette* (Saturday, March 18, 1989), p. 8.

Lees, Gene. "Movies: Hugo Friedhofer Scores as Dean of Movie Composers." *Los Angeles Times/ Calendar,* vol. 94 (Sunday, March 30, 1975), p. 24.

Levy, Dick. "Sharps and Flats." *The Gateway and the Trading Post* (Wednesday, November 2, 1960).

Lyons, Leonard. "The Lyons Den." [*Misfits.*] *New York Post* (Tuesday, November 29, 1960), p. 29.

M. O. C. "Anna Sokolow Gives Recital of Dance at Avery." *Hartford Courant* (March 26, 1942).

MacArthur, Harry. "The Passing Show: Then He Wrote a Song That Bought a House." *The Evening Star*— Washington D. C. (Tuesday, September 27, 1960).

Martin, John. "Ballet Company Stages 'Streetcar.'" *New York Times* (Tuesday, December 9, 1952).

_____. "The Dance: New Blood." *New York Times,* vol. 86 (Sunday, August 29, 1937), sec. 10, p. 8 (X).

_____. "Hanya Holm Group Offers a Ballet." *New York Times* (March 18, 1941).

_____. "The Week's Premieres." *New York Times,* vol. 102 (Sunday, December 7, 1952), sec. 2, part 2, p. 12 (X).

Mathews, Jack. "Alex North's Troubles with Oscar." *Los Angeles Times/Calendar* (Sunday, April 10, 1988), p. 9.

M[cCall], M[artin]. "Music." *Daily Worker* (May 8, 1936).

McCall, Martin. "American Ballad Singers and Young Composer Heard in Excellent Programs." *Daily Worker,* vol. 17, no. 46 (Thursday, February 22, 1940), p. 7.

_____. "Music." [Heart of Spain, China Strikes Back.] *Daily Worker* (October 16, 1937).

McQueen, Max. "Composer Score with Music, Awards." *Mesa Tribune* (Friday, March 24, 1989), D 1, D 4.

Mengers, Patti. "Ex-Delco Man a Winner." *Delaware County Daily Times* (Tuesday, March 25, 1986), p. 35.

_____. "'Oscar' Takes Note of Ex-Delco Man." *Delaware County Daily Times* (Monday, March 24, 1986), p. 5.

Moffitt, Jack. "Sanctuary." *Limelight* (February 23, 1961).

Monahan, Kaspar. "Music Composer for 'Spartacus' to Visit Here." *Pittsburgh Press* (Friday, September 16, 1960).

"'Morning Star' Offers Hope That a New Day of Justice Will Dawn for Mankind." *New York Herald Tribune*, vol. 106 (Sunday, November 3, 1946), sec. 10, p. 3.

Murray, Marian. "'Elements of Magic' Has Its Premiere at Avery Memorial." *Hartford Times* (Saturday, May 23, 1942).

"The Music Man." *Sunday Star*—Washington, D. C. (Sunday, October 9, 1960), pp. 8, 9.

"Musical 'Streetcar.'" *Valley Times* (Monday, December 31, 1951).

"New York Composer of Functional Music at 30 Has Long List." *Hartford Times* (Thursday, May 21, 1942).

"North Comes East, Doesn't Like West." [Philadelphia] *Daily News* (September 22, 1965).

"North to Compose for 'Cleopatra.'" *New York Times* (Wednesday, May 2, 1962), p. 30 (C).

Norton, Mildred. "Stage and Screen: Oscar's Playing Footsie with Another Alex North Score." *Sunday News*—Los Angeles (Sunday, February 22, 1953).

_____. "'Streetcar' Is Torrid Ballet." *Daily News*—Los Angeles (Tuesday, March 31, 1953), p. 16.

Pacher, Maurus. "Der Grosvater des Jazz." *TZ*—München (Tuesday, July 15, 1969).

Pam, Jerry. "Olivier Magnificent in 'Spartacus' Production." *Valley Times Today* (Thursday, October 20, 1960).

Perkins, Francis D. "N. Y. City Symphony." *New York Herald Tribune*, vol. 106 (Wednesday, November 20, 1946), p. 22.

"'Prizzi': A Prize for Grownups." *New York Post* (June 14, 1985).

Richardson, John H. "Huston's Legacy Is One of Respect." *Daily News* (Tuesday, December 15, 1987), pp. 15, 16.

"Ridgefield Personal and Social Items: Marthe Krueger to Open School Here on Monday." *Ridgefield Press*—Ridgefield, Conn. (Thursday, May 14, 1942).

R[oss], P[armenter]. "CIO Chorus Offers Town Hall Recital." *The New York Times*, vol. 96 (Sunday, May 25, 1947), sec. 1, p. 55 (L+).

Ryan, Desmond. "Film: Everyone's Out to Make a Killing." *Philadelphia Inquirer* (Friday, June 14, 1985), p. 22.

S. L. S. "Film Scoring a Joy for North." *Philadelphia Inquirer* (Monday, October 2, 1960), p. 2.

S. R. "Anna Sokolow, Alex North in Joint Recital." *Daily Worker*, vol. 17, no. 44 (February 20, 1940), p. 7.

Saunders, Sandra. "'Wonderful Country' at Viking." *Philadelphia Daily News* (October 26, 1959).

Schallert, Edwin. "Brando, Simmons with Interest in 'Desire.'" *Los Angeles Times*, vol. 73 (Friday, November 19, 1954), part 3, p. 8.

_____. "'Cannery Row' in Work as Stage Musical." *Los Angeles Times* (Tuesday, December 11, 1951), part 2, p. 7.

_____. "'Streetcar Named Desire' Powerful Drama on Screen." *Los Angeles Times*, vol. 70 (Wednesday, September 19, 1951), part 3, p. 8.

Schauensee, Max de. "'The Wonderful Country' a Mexican 'Western.'" *Philadelphia Bulletin* (October 26, 1959).

Schier, Ernie. "Ex-Philadelphian Sets 'Spartacus' to Music." *Evening Bulletin*—Philadelphia (Thursday, September 29, 1960), F4.

Schumach, Murray. "Play's Tunes Piped from Padded Cell." *New York Times* (Wednesday, March 16, 1949).

Segel, Michael. "Movie Composer Is 'Home' for Reunion With Family." *Jewish Exponent* (September 10, 1965).

"Settlement School to Cite Composer." *Jewish Exponent* (November 12, 1965).

Shanley, John P. "Alex North—Composer Turns to Television." *New York Times* (March 4, 1962).

"Short Take on Alex North." *Daily News*—Los Angeles (Monday, January 21, 1953).

Skolsky, Sidney. "Hollywood Is My Beat." *New York Post* (Tuesday, November 1, 1960), p. 58.

Smith, Steven. "The Tenacious Alex North." *Los Angeles Times/Calendar* (Sunday, March 23, 1986), p. 82.

"Stars in Musical." *New York Journal and American* (Saturday, October 21, 1940).

Sterritt, David. "'Under the Volcano': A Model of How to Film a Book." *Christian Science Monitor*, vol. 76 (Thursday, July 5, 1984), p. 25.

Terry, Walter. "The Dance World: 'Streetcar' and 'Mlle. Fifi,' New Hits for New Dance Troupe." *New York Herald Tribune*, vol. 112 (Sunday, December 14, 1952), sec. 4, p. 4.

W. A. "'Streetcar' Highlight of Ballet Event." *Los Angeles Times*, vol. 72 (Tuesday, March 31, 1953), part 2, p. 7.

Webster, Daniel. "An Interview With Alex North." *Philadelphia Inquirer* (Wednesday, September 8, 1965).

Wedman, Les. "Brando Is a Sexy Sax." *Vancouver Sun* (Friday, May 4, 1973), p. 10 (A).

Williams, Dick. "'Streetcar' Superb in Ballet Form." *New York Mirror/Entertainment* (December 17, 1952).

Williams, Stephen. "A Film Score's Odyssey from Death to Rebirth." *New York Newsday Fanfare* (Sunday, November 14, 1993).

_____. "New Cult Chases Rare Soundtracks." [An interview with Jerry Goldsmith.] *Boston Sunday Globe* (Sunday, August 20, 1972), B 35, B 39.

Zeitlin, Arnold. "The Frustrated Alex North." *The Sunday Bulletin Magazine* (July 15, 1962), p. 4.

Periodical Articles

Adomian, Lan. "Viva Zapata." *Film Music*, vol. 11, no. 4 (March/April, 1952), pp. 4–14.

"Alex North Receives S. P. F. M. Career Achievement Award." *Cue Sheet*, vol. 3, no. 3 (September, 1986), pp. 32–35, 41.

"The American Ballet Theatre: 'A Streetcar Named Desire.'" *Musical Opinion*, 80 (October, 1956), p. 7.

Ansen, David. "Hit Man Meets Hit Woman." *Newsweek* (June 17, 1985), p. 89.

Behlemer, Rudy. "Alex North on 'A Streetcar Named Desire.'" *Cue Sheet*, vol. 3, no. 3 (September, 1986), pp. 36–38.

Bennett, Diane. "Soundtrack." *Hollywood Reporter* (March 19, 1975).

Bernstein, Elmer. "Music in Films Has Changed Dramatically, Not in All Ways for the Better, During Last 20 Years; It's Big Biz — and Hot Antitrust Issue." *Daily Variety*, 39th Anniversary Edition, vol. 153, no. 39 (Tuesday, October 31, 1972), p. 20.

Bettis, Valerie. "Streetcar Named Desire." *Ballet News*, 7 (February, 1986), p. 25.

Bohn, Ronald L., Jean Pierre Pecqueriaux, and Daniël Mangodt. "Filmography / Discography: Alex North." *Soundtrack Collector's Newsletter*, 1 (December, 1982), pp. 14–16.

Brog [sic]. "Daddy Long Legs." *Variety* (Wednesday, May 4, 1955).

_____. "Film Review: 'The Rose Tattoo.'" *Variety* (Wednesday, November 2, 1955).

_____. "Film Review: 'Unchained.'" *Variety* (Wednesday, January 26, 1955).

_____. "Film Reviews: 'Go, Man, Go.'" *Variety*, vol. 193, no. 7 (Wednesday, January 20, 1954), p. 18.

_____. "The Member of the Wedding." *Variety*, vol. 189, no. 2 (Wednesday, December 17, 1952), p. 6.

_____. "Pony Soldier." *Variety*, vol. 188, no. 9 (Wednesday, November 5, 1952), p. 6.

Brown, Royal S. "Soundtrack Albums: Why?" *High Fidelity/Musical America,* 25 (July, 1975), pp. 49–55.

Buchanan, Loren G. "The Art of Composing

Music Scores for Films: Alex North, an Expert, Comments on His Craft." *Motion Picture Herald*, vol. 234, no. 8 (October 13, 1965), pp. 12, 36. Reprinted in James Limbacher, *Film Music: From Violins to Video* (Metuchen, N.J.: Scarecrow, 1974), pp. 29–31.

Buchau, Stephanie. "Film." *Pacific Sun* — San Francisco (June, 1985).

Burr, Ty. "Original '2001' Music Resurfaces: An Old Score Settled." *Entertainment Weekly* (January 14, 1994), p. 54.

[Califano, Albert]. "'The Member of the Wedding': Short on Popular Appeal." *The Hollywood Reporter*, vol. 122, no. 14 (Monday, December 15, 1952), p. 3.

Care, Ross. "Hot Spell: Alex North's Film Score for 'A Streetcar Named Desire.'" In: *Performing Arts Annual — 1989*. Washington, D.C.: Library of Congress, 1990, pp. 4–23.

_____. "Hot Spells: Alex North's Southern Gothic Film Scores." In: *Performing Arts at the Library of Congress*. Washington, D.C.: Library of Congress, 1992, pp. 21–25.

_____. "Memoirs of a Movie Chilhood in Harrisburg's Film Palaces." In: *Performing Arts Annual — 1986*. Washington, D.C.: Library of Congress, 1986, pp. 78–97 (pp. 95–97 on Alex North).

_____. "New from Label 'X': The Cinema Maestro Series — Cinerama 'South Seas Adventure.'" [Record review.] *Film Score Monthly*, no. 38 (October, 1993), p. 13.

"Cleopatra." [Soundtrack Review.] *High Fidelity/Musical America* (October, 1963), p. 163.

Colón, Carlos. "Jerry Goldsmith." In: *VII Encuentro International de Música Cinemátografica y Escénica* — Sevilla (October, 1993), pp. 11–28.

"Competition and Awards." *International Musician* (September, 1986), p. 13.

Cook, Page. "The Sound Track." [Academy Award for Life Achievement.] *Films in Review*, vol. 37, no. 6/7 (June/July, 1986), pp. 377–378.

_____. "The Sound Track." [*The Agony and the Ecstasy.*] *Films in Review*, vol. 16, no. 9 (November, 1965), pp. 573–575.

_____. "The Sound Track." [*The Agony and the Ecstasy.*] *Films in Review*, vol. 25, no. 3 (March, 1974), pp. 171–174.

_____. "The Sound Track." [*Carny.*] *Films in Review*, vol. 31, no. 8 (October, 1980), pp. 483–485.

_____. "The Sound Track." [*Carny.*] *Films in Review*, vol. 32, no. 2 (February, 1981), pp. 108–110, 115.

_____. "The Sound Track." [*Cleopatra.*] *Films in Review*, vol. 14, no. 10 (December, 1963), pp. 622–623.

_____. "The Sound Track." [*Cleopatra.*] *Films in Review*, vol. 15, no. 6 (June/July, 1964), pp. 363–364.

_____. "The Sound Track." [*Cheyenne Autumn.*] *Films in Review*, vol. 16, no. 2 (February, 1965), pp. 105–106.

_____. "The Sound Track." [*The Dead.*] *Films in Review*, vol. 39, no. 4 (April, 1988), p. 250.

_____. "The Sound Track." [*Dragonslayer.*] *Films in Review*, vol. 33, no. 2 (February, 1982), pp. 115–119.

_____. "The Sound Track." [North of Hollywood.] *Films in Review*, vol. 28, no. 9 (November, 1977), pp. 550–553.

_____. "The Sound Track." [*Shanks.*] *Films in Review*, vol. 25, no. 10 (December, 1974), pp. 611–613, 619.

_____. "The Sound Track." [*Shanks.*] *Films in Review*, vol. 26, no. 2 (February, 1975), pp. 113–115.

_____. "The Sound Track." [*The Shoes of a Fisherman.*] *Films in Review*, vol. 20, no. 1 (January, 1969), pp. 46–48.

_____. "The Sound Track." [*Who's Afraid of Virginia Woolf?*] *Films in Review*, vol. 17, no. 7 (August/September, 1966), pp. 440–442.

Cooper, Lou. "Alex North Evaluates Modern Theatre Music Technique." *Show of the Month News*, vol. 11, no. 8 (Summer, 1949).

_____. "Sight and Sounds: Anna Sokolow Recital." *New Masses*, vol. 39 (April 1, 1941), p. 28.

DeMary, Tom. "Alex North's 2001." [Record review.] *Cue Sheet*, vol. 10, nos. 3 and 4 (1993/1994), pp. 47–50.

Dugan, James. "Sight and Sounds: Documentary of Tennessee Life." *New Masses*, vol. 27 (May 31, 1938), p. 28.

Edba [*sic*]. "O'Daniel." *Variety* (Wednesday, February 26, 1947).

Embler, Jefrey. "The Structure of Film Music." *Films in Review*, vol. 4, no. 7 (August/September, 1953), pp. 332–335. Reprinted in James Limbacher, *Film Music: From Violins to Video*, pp. 61–66.

"An Exclusive In-Depth Interview with Alex North." *RTS Music Gazette*, I part (September, 1976), II part (October, 1976), III part (November, 1976), IV part (December, 1976), V part (January, 1977).

Fagen, Laurie. "1989 Academy Awards, Phoenix Style." *AFT & T — Arizona Film, Theatre & Television* (March, 1989), pp. 1–2.

Fiedel, Robert. "Film Music by Alex North." *High Fidelity/Musical America*, 28 (February, 1978), p. 102.

Fitzpatrick, John, and William Finn. "'Dragonslayer': Two Views on Alex North's Most Ambitious Score in Years." *Pro Musica Sana*, vol. 9, no. 2 — PMS 34 (Summer, 1982), p. 3.

"The Film Career of Alex North." *Max Steiner Music Society News Letter*, no. 47 (Summer, 1976), p. 10.

Gene [*sic*]. "Film Review: 'The Rose Tattoo.'"

Variety, vol. 200, no. 9 (Wednesday, November 2, 1955), p. 6.

Goldsmith, Jerry, Matthew Peak and Robert Townson. "'2001': Alex North's Odyssey." *Movie Collector*, vol. 1, issue 2 (November/December, 1993), pp. 63–67.

Gruen, John. "The Rose Tattoo." *Film Music*, vol. 15, no. 2 (Winter, 1955), p. 3.

Heimansberg, Udo (ed.). "Alex North im Interview." *Spellbound: Das Deutsche Filmmusikmagazin*, no. 5 (May, 1985), pp.12–17.

_____. "Alex North: Werkschau / Discographie." *Spellbound: Das Deutsche Filmmusikmagazin*, no. 5 (May, 1985), pp. 20–23.

_____. "Stationen seines Lebens." *Spellbound: Das Deutsche Filmmusikmagazin*, no. 5 (May, 1985), pp. 7–11.

_____. "Wer hat Angst vor Alex North: Frisher Wind in Hollywood." *Spellbound: Das Deutsche Filmmusikmagazin*, no. 5 (May, 1985), pp. 3, 5–6.

Hemming, Roy. "Vintage: 'A Streetcar Named Desire,' The Original Director's Version." *Entertainment Weekly* (June 18, 1994), p. 109.

Hickman, Sharpless C. "Movies and Music." *Music Journal*, vol. 11, no. 2 (February, 1953), pp. 28–29.

Hobe [*sic*]. "'Tis of Thee." *Variety* (October, 1940), pp. 56, 58.

Indcox, John F. "The Music for 'Cleopatra' [recordings]." *High Fidelity/Musical America*, 13 (September, 1963), pp. 112–113.

Kael, Pauline. "The Current Cinema: Irish Voices." *New Yorker* (December, 1987), pp. 144, 147–149.

_____. "The Current Cinema: Ripeness." *New Yorker* (July 1, 1985), pp. 84–86.

Kahle, Birgit (ed.) "Latest News: Die Wichtigsten 'Oscars' der Academy of Motion Picture Arts and Sciences 1985/86." *Filmharmonische Blätter* — Berlin, no. 002 (Winter/Spring, 1986), p. 32.

Klein, Andy. "Dead Men Get Their Due." *Cinema*.

Knight, Arthur. "Prizzi's Honor." *Hollywood Reporter*, vol. 287, no. 16 (Wednesday, June 5, 1985), pp. 3, 12.

_____. "Smoldering 'Volcano': Huston Landmark of Great Filmmaking." *Hollywood Reporter*, vol. 282, no. 22 (Monday, June 18, 1984), pp. 4, 9.

Korté, Steve. "Alex North's '2001.'" *CD Review* (April, 1994), p. 31.

Kowalski, Alfons. "Alex North: Personalstil eines Komponisten." *Spellbound: Das Deutsche Filmmusikmagazin*, no. 5 (May, 1985), pp. 4–5.

Kraft, David. "Alex North: The Master Speaks." *Hollywood Reporter*, vol. 300, no. 41 (Friday, January 22, 1988), S-56, 57.

_____. "A Conversation with Alex North." *Soundtrack! The Collector's Quarterly*, vol. 4, no. 13 (March, 1985), pp. 3–8.

Kyle, Kelli Marguerite. "Alex North." In the article: "AmerAllegro Premiers, Recent Performances, New Releases," *Pan Pipes of Sigma Alpha Iota*, vol. 44, no. 2 (January, 1952), p. 40.

Land [sic]. "South Seas Adventure." *Variety*, vol. 211, no. 7 (Wednesday, July 16, 1958), p. 6.

Lasher, John Steven. "Film Music in the Concert Hall." *Symphony News* (February/March, 1974), pp. 9–13.

Lewin, Frank. "A Streetcar Named Desire." *Film Music*, vol. 11, no. 3 (January/February, 1952), pp. 13–20.

Lichtman, Irv. "Indict 'Unchained Melody' Claimer." *Billboard*, 92 (May 10, 1980), p. 29.

_____. "Links in 'Unchained Melody': Lyricist Recalls Its Inception." *Billboard*, 103 (March 30, 1991), p. 44.

"Lifelines." [Obituary.] *Billboard*, 103 (September 21, 1991), p. 81.

"Lights... Camera... Music!" *Newsweek* (July 24, 1967), p. 77.

Loynd, Ray. "Film Reviews: 'Prizzi's Honor.'" *Daily Variety*, vol. 207, no. 63 (Monday, June 3, 1985), pp. 3, 12, 18.

Luban, Milton. "Daddy Long Legs." *Hollywood Reporter* (Wednesday, May 4, 1955), p. 3.

_____. "The Member of the Wedding." *Hollywood Reporter* (Monday, December 15, 1952), p. 3.

Lucraft, Howard. "The Hollywood Film Composers: I Like to Relate to a Story." *Crescendo International*, 24 (November, 1987), pp. 10–11.

_____. "North, Man of Music and Conscience." *Daily Variety*, 55th Anniversary Issue, vol. 221, no. 37 (Tuesday, October 25, 1988), p. 176.

Mangodt, Daniël. "An Interview with Steven and Anne-Marie North." *Soundtrack*, vol. 10, no. 40 (December, 1991), pp. 6–7, 31.

Maremaa, Thomas. "The Sound of Movie Music." *New York Times Magazine* (March 28, 1976), pp. 40, 45–50.

Maxford, Howard. "Also Sprach Alex." *Top* (December, 1993).

McBride, Joseph. "Composer Alex North Dead at 81." *Daily Variety*, vol. 233, no. 3 (September 10, 1991), pp. 3, 21.

McDonagh, Michael. "Alex North: Viva Zapata." [Review of Varèse Sarabande CD Release]. *In Tune*, no. 55 (1998), pp. 91–92 (p. 33 in the Japanese print of the magazine).

_____."Alex North's Music." [Review of *Nonesuch* CD Release.] *In Tune* (November, 1997), pp. 71–72.

_____. "Henry Brant on Alex North." *Cue Sheet*, vol. 15, no. 4 (October, 1999), pp. 14–26.

Moffitt, Jack. "'Racers' Timely Action Pic; 'Ten Men' Is Good Western." *Hollywood Reporter*, vol. 133, no. 11 (Wednesday, February 2, 1955), p. 3.

_____. "'Rose Tattoo' Highlighted by Memorable Acting." *Hollywood Reporter*, vol. 137, no. 2 (Tuesday, November 1, 1955), p. 3.

Morris, Chris, and Phyllis Stark. "Curb Single Sparks 'Melody' Battle." *Billboard*, 102 (October 6, 1990), pp. 6, 13.

Morse, Leon. "Experimental Theater: 'The Great Campaign.'" *The Billboard* (April, 1947).

"Music Should Be Communicative, Says Alex North." *Mills Music Commentator* (1947), pp. 1, 8.

Noble, Elizabeth. "Heart of Spain." *New Masses for Spain* (1938), p. 18.

North, Alex. "Dance in the Soviet Union." *Dance Observer*, vol. 1, no. 4 (May, 1934), pp. 37, 41.

_____. "Music Should Be Communicative." *Mills Music Commentator* (1947), pp. 1, 8.

_____. "New Film Directors Accenting Music as Potent Dramatic Angle: Alex North." *Variety*, vol. 220 (October 12, 1960), p. 59.

_____. "Notes on 'Rainmaker.'" *Film and TV Music*, vol. 16, no. 3 (Spring, 1957), pp. 3–15.

_____. "Notes on the Score of 'The Rose Tattoo.'" *Film Music*, vol. 15, no. 2 (Winter, 1955), pp. 3–15.

"North Writes Score for Nadar Picture." *The Philadelphia Inquirer* (November 4, 1956), C7.

"Obituary." *Cue Sheet*, vol. 8, no. 3 (September, 1991), cover & p. 96.

"Obituary." *Gramophone*, 69 (November, 1991), p. 32.

"Obituary." *Orchester*, vol. 39, no. 12 (1991), p. 1437.

"Obituary." *Variety*, 344 (September 16, 1991), p. 102.

Orowan, Florelle. "A Look at Alex North's Use of Historical Source Music." *Film Music Notebook*, vol. 3, no. 1 (1977), pp. 9–14.

Osborne, Robert. "Rambling Reporter." *Hollywood Reporter*, vol. 290, no. 19 (Thursday, January 16, 1986), p. 7.

Padrol, Joan. "Alex North: Un clásico de la banda sonora." *Dirigido por...* — Barcelona, no. 170 (June, 1989), pp. 50–53.

Palmer, Christopher. "Alex North." [Obituary.] *Independent Newspaper* — London (1991).

_____. "Film Music Profile: Alex North." *Crescendo International*, 13 (April, 1975), pp. 28–29. Reprinted in *Film Music Notebook*, 3, no. 1 (1977), pp. 2–8.

Perez, Michel. "'Wise Blood' de John Huston; les brasiers de la foi." *Le Matin* (May 25, 1979), p. 35.

Pool, Jeannie. "David Raksin Conducts Music of Alex North in Spain." *Cue Sheet*, vol. 8, no. 3 (September, 1991), pp. 87–96.

Powers, James. "'The Misfits': Provocative, Stimulating Production." *Hollywood Reporter*, vol. 163, no. 42 (Wednesday, February 1, 1961), p. 3.

_____. "'Spartacus' Magnificent Picture, Should Be a Smash Attraction." *Hollywood Reporter*, vol. 162, no. 12 (Friday, October 7, 1960), p. 3.

Pry[or], [Thomas]. "Film Review: 'Spartacus.'" *Daily Variety*, vol. 109, no. 24 (Friday, October 7, 1960), pp. 3, 4.

R. F. "Theater and Film." *High Fidelity/Musical America* (February, 1978), p. 102.

R. S. "'2001' (North)." *Gramophone* (March, 1994), p. 109.

Reisner, Joel, and Bruce Kane. "An Interview with Alex North." *Cinema* [Beverly Hills], vol. 5, no. 4 (December, 1969), pp. 42–45.

Robertson, Robbie. "Records: Carny." *Rolling Stone*, 338 (March 5, 1981), p. 62.

Robinson, Ruth A. "Film Composers: An Independent Breed." *Hollywood Reporter*, vol. 273, no. 7 (Friday, August 13, 1982), S-83, 84.

Rose, Greg. "Alex North." *Cue Sheet*, vol. 7, no. 1 (January, 1990), pp. 30–35.

Ruddy, Jonah M. "'The Misfits': Requiem to Clark Gable." *Hollywood Diary* (February 6, 1961).

_____. "'Sanctuary,' The Year's Most Daring Motion Picture.'"*Hollywood Diary* (March 6, 1961).

Scharper, Al. "Record Review." *Daily Variety*, vol. 73, no. 7 (Friday, September 14, 1951), p. 8.

Shoilevska, Sanya. "Alex North's Music for 'The Misfits.'"*Cue Sheet*, vol. 12, no. 2 (April, 1996), pp. 13–27.

Siegmeister, Elie. "Music for Films." *Direction* (April, 1940).

Simon, Robert A. "Musical Events: More Novelties." *New Yorker*, vol. 22 (November 30, 1946), pp. 128, 130.

Smith, Jack. "The Sound Track." [2001.] *Films in Review* (1993), p. 350.

Snell, Mike. "Under the Volcano." *Quirk's Reviews*, no. 55 (June, 1984), pp. 13, 16.

Soifer, Alex [Alex North]. "A Music Student in Soviet Russia." *Dynamics* (April 5, 1935), pp. 6, 7.

Spolar, Betsey, and Merrilyn Hammond. "How to Work in Hollywood and Still Be Happy!" *Theatre Arts*, 37 (August, 1953), p. 80.

Sragow, Michael. "Prizzi's Honor." *Boston Phoenix*, no. 1 (June 18, 1985), Part III — Arts, pp. 1–2.

"'Streetcar' Music Recorded." *Capitol Record*, vol. 2, no. 286 (October 1, 1951).

Strong, Barbara. "Not So Incidental." *Concerto* (February, 1950), pp. 5–6.

Sutak, Ken. "'A Dragonslayer' Inquiry: From Two Heady Notes Toward Some Hard Questions About the Score." *Pro Musica Sana*, vol. 9, no. 4 (Summer, 1982), pp. 7–15.

_____. "The Return of 'A Streetcar Named Desire.'" *Pro Musica Sana*, vol. 3, no. 1 (Spring, 1974), pp. 4–10.

_____. "The Return of 'A Streetcar Named Desire.'" *Pro Musica Sana*, vol. 3, no. 4 (Winter, 1974/75), pp. 9–15.

_____. "The Return of 'A Streetcar Named Desire.'" *Pro Musica Sana*, vol. 4, no. 2 (1975), pp. 18–24.

_____. "The Return of 'A Streetcar Named Desire.'" *Pro Musica Sana*, vol. 4, no. 3 (1976), pp. 13–18.

"The 13th Letter." *Hollywood Reporter* (Friday, January 19, 1951), p. 3.

"Three Pieces for Chamber Orchestra, First Performed by New York Chamber Orchestra." *Music News*, 42 (June, 1950), p. 21.

Tube [*sic*]. "Film Review: 'Sanctuary.'" *Variety*, vol. 221, no. 18 (Wednesday, February 22, 1961), p. 6.

_____. "The Misfits." *Daily Variety*, vol. 110, no. 40 (Wednesday, February 1, 1961), pp. 3, 16.

Tynan, J. "North on the Jazz Frontier." *Down Beat*, 28 (March 16, 1961), p. 14.

Walsh, Michael. "Prizzi's Opera." *Film Comment* (October, 1985), pp. 5–6.

Watt, Douglas. "He Couldn't Have a Pleasanter Name; Some Inside Stuff." *New Yorker* (July 21, 1949).

_____. "Musical Events: Back to New Orleans." *New Yorker*, vol. 28 (December 20, 1952), pp. 103–104.

Weiden, Marc. "Source Music and the Singles Life: 2001, Short Cuts, Woody Allen & Mick Jones." *Pulse,* Holiday Issue '93.

Willsmer, Trevor. "Soundtrack Reviews: Alex North's 2001." *Movie Collector*, vol. 1, issue 2 (November/December, 1993), p. 68.

Wright, Diane. "Composer's Creation Is Invisible Brilliance." _____ (August 2, 1981), p. 5.

Wolthuis, Julius J. C. "De Port Filmmuziek van Stanley Kubrick." *Skoop* — Amsterdam, 16 (October, 1980), p. 38.

Lecture

North, Alex. Seminar on Film Music. American Film Institute/CAPS, October 18, 1971 (3:15 p.m.). Transcript of the seminar is held at the AFI / Louis B. Mayer Library (Los Angeles).

Interviews

Osborne, Robert. An interview with Marcia Brandwynne (regarding *Prizzi's Honor*) for KTTV, Channel 11, News (December 6, 1985, at 10:40 p. m.). Transcript.

Raksin, David. "The Subject Is Film Music." An interview with Alex North as a part of the Yale University oral history program (American Music Series). A copy of the transcript is held at the "Margaret Herrick " Library — Academy of Motion Picture Arts and Sciences (Special Collections).

Steiner, Fred. An interview with Alex North, Pacific Palisades, April 27, 1976. Audio tape and transcript. Private possesion of Fred Steiner.

Index

Numbers in *italics* refer to pages with photographs.

259